Until Then

Until Then

CINDY WOODSMALL
& ERIN WOODSMALL

Tyndale House Publishers
Carol Stream, Illinois

Visit Tyndale online at tyndale.com.

Visit Cindy Woodsmall online at cindywoodsmall.com.

Tyndale and Tyndale's quill logo are registered trademarks of Tyndale House Ministries.

Until Then

Cover designed by Libby Dykstra

Edited by Sarah Mason Rische

The Author is represented by Ambassador Literary, Nashville, TN.

Until Then is a work of fiction. Where real people, events, establishments, organizations, or locales appear, they are used fictitiously. All other elements of the novel are drawn from the authors' imaginations.

For information about special discounts for bulk purchases, please contact Tyndale House Publishers at csresponse@tyndale.com, or call 1-855-277-9400.

Library of Congress Cataloging-in-Publication Data

A catalog record for this book is available from the Library of Congress.

ISBN 978-1-4964-8326-3 (HC)

ISBN 978-1-4964-5426-3 (SC)

Printed in the United States of America

29	28	27	26	25	24	23
7	6	5	4	3	2	1

*To the brave abolitionists of all faiths, making
special note of the Quakers and Amish.*

*And to all who, in the name of love and faith, dare to fight the good
fight, to stand for the Golden Rule and stand against greediness
and selfishness. May we all be willing to sacrifice in order to make
a constructive difference during our time on this planet.*

Chapter One

JULY 1985

A mix of excitement and anxiety warred in Celeste Lantz as she brought the rig to a halt under a shade tree in her driveway. The midmorning sun filled the lush green valley, dissolving last night's remaining fog that still clung to the rolling mountains. Their rental home with its white clapboard siding and black shutters was always a welcome sight, with a peek of Vin's woodshop from around the back. She loved this place, but none of it belonged to them. Maybe one day.

She grabbed the bags of groceries and the yard sale items and headed for the steps that led to the porch. After she got the little ones out from under their *dat's* feet so he could begin his workday, she'd tend to the horse and rig.

Time had an inconvenient way of slipping by.

She couldn't wait to show Vin the things she'd found . . . but guilt for holding him up from his workday also clung to her. At twenty-four years old, she should be better at balancing her time.

Laughter of little ones filled the air, sounding as if it was coming from the small, fenced backyard. She set the groceries on the porch, keeping the yard sale items with her.

A grin tugged at her lips and refused to let go. Late or not, Vin would be pleased. That man and books went together like a frosty glass of lemonade and a summer day.

"Dat, geh dabber." Four-year-old Steven giggled while telling his dad to go quickly.

What was Vin doing? She strode around the corner of the house. Vin wore a blue- and white-striped ball cap and sat inside a cardboard box that he'd apparently painted to look like a train while she was gone. Were the suspenders to his pants on his head instead of his shoulders?

"Choo-choo," Vin said over and over, making the appropriate noises. One-year-old Drew was in his lap, patting his dat's face and babbling excitedly beyond recognition in any language. Steven was behind his dat, his little arms clutched around his neck.

"Dear *Gott*, I love this man," Celeste whispered.

Drew wiggled out of his dat's arms, getting out of the box. Yep, suspenders on Vin's head and pants pulled up to his chest. He turned his head, grinning at her.

She burst into laughter. "Vin Lantz, what are you doing?"

Without missing a beat, he tugged on an imaginary cord. *"Woooo. Wooo.* You're home."

"I am. None too soon, I see."

"Too soon. I meant to return to looking all cool and suave before you saw me."

"You missed that particular train. What are you wearing?"

He shrugged, chuckling. "I'm a conductor of old and these are my bib overalls."

"I thought maybe you'd taken it on yourself to redesign the way Amish men wear their pants."

When he stood and she saw that the hem of his pants hit just below his knees while the waist was on his chest, she burst into laughter that wouldn't stop. Were those his father's pants? They were extra baggy, giving him enough room to pull them up high like that. He eased Steven's feet to the ground and both boys got in the box, making train noises.

"Are you laughing at me?" His grin warmed her heart, but she started backing away.

"You bet I am."

He picked up his pace, striding toward her. She turned and took off running. He caught her from behind and lifted her feet off the ground.

She squealed. "Put me down."

"Never." He mocked an evil laugh.

"If you put me down, I'll give you a gift." Her words were jumbled through her laughter.

"A gift, you say?" He set her down. "I'm being good now." He moved to stand in front of her. "Is it a kiss, despite how I look?" He lifted his brows in quick succession, teasing.

She studied him, looking deep into his dark-brown eyes. How had she thought he'd be displeased with her for running late?

He grew serious. "What thoughts are behind those beautiful blue eyes, Celeste?"

She shrugged. "I . . . I thought you might be frustrated with me for leaving you responsible for the children too long. I know that if I were better organized, I wouldn't need to run to the store like this anyway, and now you're getting to today's work later than you should."

"Nah." He removed the suspenders from his head and released them on his shoulders. Then he cupped her cheek. "That's not how I feel at all. Ever. We juggle a lot every week, and I think we do a good job of it." He took off the baseball cap. White strips of tape lined the dark-blue hat that Vin had found in a ditch near their home weeks ago—Vin's creativity turning it into a conductor's hat. "If I didn't need your help in the woodshop a few days each week, you'd have time to keep up with everything else. Plus, I figured you had a good reason for needing extra time, and it gave me a chance to do something with our boys that I'd been promising to do for nearly a month."

She looked at the boys sitting inside the cardboard box, playing happily, before she pulled one of the three books from the plastic bag, showing him the best one first. "The history of Ohio, and it begins a hundred years before a white man stepped foot onto its soil."

With a tenderness she knew well, he lifted the book from her hands. "Seriously?" His face looked like she'd just handed him a stack of money.

Always an avid reader, his interest over the past couple of months had been the early days of Ohio. His curiosity sparked after the bishop and his wife visited Ohio and toured a newly built information center about the Plain folk—mostly Amish, Quakers, Dunkards, and Mennonites. The bishop began weaving some of the religious history he'd learned into his sermons, but he didn't know much about the everyday life of the early settlers in that region. Vin had been on a quest to know more ever since. He ran his fingers across the tattered binding and the brown cloth hardback cover. There wasn't a single word or letter on the front or back, only gold lettering on the spine.

She tapped the book. "You may need to sit before you look at the copyright."

But he didn't budge as he opened the book. His eyes grew

large. "Seriously?" he repeated his earlier question. "The book-dealer I work with out of Philly couldn't find anything printed before 1880."

"Printed in 1860. It has chapters covering the history from the late 1500s until the French fur traders arrived. But here's your really good news. Starting with 1790, each decade has its own chapter."

He carefully flipped pages, landing on a dog-eared one that said *1820s*. He began reading, and she waited. He turned the page. "Celeste," he whispered. "This is incredible."

"*Jah*, I know. I found two other books that are excellent too, but this one is the best find. The author was a great-grandson of early settlers, and he used the ledgers, diaries, and maps his ances-tors had passed down from one generation to the next."

Without looking up from reading, Vin whispered, *"Denki."*

"You are most welcome, Husband."

He closed the book. "It already has my full interest, but the workday must come first."

She tapped the book. "Per usual for these old books, it only has two or three rough sketches in it. All of these 1800s authors needed your talent for drawing and sketching, and their books would be so much better, jah?"

He studied her. "Celeste . . ."

"Jah?"

His eyes seemed glued to hers for a moment. Then he looked at the book in his hand and smiled. "This will be my most trea-sured book, but it doesn't compare to the best find ever. You." He grinned. "I'd been surly with my dat for sending me to Indiana to *volunteer* to work an entire summer for a great-uncle I'd met once. Then, only days after arriving, I stepped into a sandwich shop and saw you behind the counter." He chuckled. "We bantered, and I was smitten, never before talking to anyone like you. You agreed to go on your lunch break and sit in a booth with me. We talked and laughed, and too soon we both had to get back to work. I knew then one summer would never be enough."

She'd been seventeen, a year younger than him, and that summer they went out together every chance they had. When fall arrived, and he had to return to Pennsylvania, he'd called her nearly every night and they wrote to each other endlessly. His long-distance phone bills had to have cost him a small fortune. Added to that expense, every chance he got, he traveled by train and bus to visit her. He kept that up until they married fifteen months after they met.

She leaned in. "If you're asking me," she whispered, "a lifetime won't be enough either." She brushed his lips with a kiss. "Now get to work. After lunch, I'll join you to help for a few hours."

"Sounds like a lot to your day."

"We're busy people." She took a step back and removed the book from his hands. "Now go. Do I need to draw a map for you of how to get there?"

He glanced at the woodshop a few hundred feet away. "I think I can remember." He winked at her. "Oh, and late this afternoon, after our teamwork project is done, I'll need to make some deliveries. It could be close to dark before I'm home."

"We'll be here when you get back."

Daylight waned through the open window of their bedroom, and Celeste's body ached from the long day of constant movement. Still, the pleasure of finding those antique books at the yard sale earlier today gave her a bit of energy. The scent of lilacs filled the air as she ran a dustcloth behind the headboard of the bed. She and Vin had worked side by side in the cabinet shop for a good portion of the afternoon, and once the boys were up from their naps, they'd played in their secure spot in the woodshop or in the fenced area, under the shade trees. Her summertime workdays in the shop while taking care of the children and the garden and meals were especially tiring, but Vin didn't need her help more than a couple of days a week, and she enjoyed being a part of the cabinetry business. Still, on those days, finishing up housework after she got her two little ones down for the night wasn't unusual.

Sweat dripped down her neck as she leaned in farther, trying to reach every strand of a cobweb behind Vin's and her bed. Something hard fell to the floor. Probably one of Vin's history books he often fell asleep reading or a book belonging to one of the children. She knelt and grabbed it from under the bed, touching pages—it was a book. She smiled, realizing it was one of Vin's sketch pads. Getting to her feet, she flipped open the cover.

Her own eyes stared back.

Celeste's breath caught. The dustcloth fell from her hands. She plunked onto the side of her bed. Thoughts raced, but a rational one wouldn't come to mind as her heart thudded like mad. She tried to take in a full breath but had to settle for a few tiny ones.

She looked again. In the drawing on the first page of the sketch pad, she was standing on a hill, the wind blowing strands of her hair forward from under her prayer *Kapp*.

She remembered that day. She and Vin had found a bounty of wild blueberries while taking a walk. She'd been pregnant with Steven but hadn't known it yet.

Perhaps this sketch was a leftover—an item from *before* that Vin had forgotten about. She longed to believe that, but it didn't add up. Studying the artwork with its intricate detail and umpteen thousand pencil strokes, she knew no artist could forget about something that took so many meticulous hours of work.

Maybe this wasn't a sign of open rebellion. Of betrayal. Maybe . . . Her thoughts circled, hoping to find solid ground for denying what this meant. The clock on the wall ticked, crickets outside chirped, and the truth seeped into her mind.

Her husband had been hiding this from her.

She flipped the page. Another drawing of her, but this time up close. She was laughing, hair loosened as she wore it when they were in bed together. He'd captured the fine details of her face, like her long nose, one asymmetrical dimple, and light eyes, though on the page they were shades of pencil instead of clear blue.

Shunned. The word thundered inside her, as if the bishop were standing next to her speaking it. He'd warned them.

Englischers thought they understood shunning. But no one outside the Plain folk knew the reality. It brought unbearable shame on the person, on their family, a shame that didn't dissipate for decades after it was over. To join the church, Vin and Celeste had stood before God and the church and taken a vow to uphold the Amish ways.

Not too long after that, Vin broke that vow.

She turned the page again and saw their Steven as a tiny newborn, eyes shut in the deep slumber of a brand-new person, swaddled in layers of blankets. A man's hand, Vin's, lay as a protective shield over Steven's chest, illustrating the full extent of their baby's smallness. It made her breath catch. She'd forgotten how tiny their two children were as newborns, even with Steven only four years old now and little Drew just one. Goodness, she longed to keep this picture. She kept flipping through the book, and memory after memory jumped out at her, as fresh as the times they'd made them. Mementos from their six years of marriage.

Faces. Why did Vin have to include their faces? For a decade now, most Amish had been allowed to draw animals. Their bishop was more open-minded than most, and he allowed Vin to draw his family to remember those precious times—their backs, their hands, their feet. Bishop Mark considered none of those things idolatry. But all Amish drew the line at drawing faces.

Was it idolatry, though? Something done in Vin's loving hand didn't seem the same as the Englischers and their photographs. But maybe it was. What did she know? At twenty-four years old, she'd barely figured anything out. Vin was only a year older than her. Didn't the people who made the rules know more of the answers than they did?

Not long after they married, the bishop had dropped by for a visit. While talking with them, he had picked up Vin's newspaper from the coffee table, saying something about a local horse show. The next thing Celeste knew, Bishop Mark lifted a sketch pad that had been under the newspaper. Vin drew in the pad almost every evening as they talked about their day, and she mended items. When the bishop opened the book, both he and Celeste saw that Vin had been drawing idolatrous things, the kind of stuff he'd drawn before they took their vows and joined the church. It should've been a pleasant evening of visiting, but the incident marred the early years of their marriage with dire warnings and invasive visits by the bishop. Vin could've faced shunning. Maybe Celeste too. But Vin had voiced sincere repentance, and the bishop didn't mention it to anyone, although he'd kept a sharp eye on Vin for a couple of years. Had Vin only become better at hiding the evidence?

"Celeste, the wheel on the rig isn't right, so don't—" Vin entered the bedroom carrying the history book she'd purchased at the yard sale earlier today. He stopped in his tracks, his dark-brown eyes wide.

She stood, holding out the sketchbook filled with forbidden images.

Vin drew a deep breath and eased it from her hand. "I'm sorry."

She shook her head. It was her duty to tell him she forgave him, but she couldn't get those words past her lips. "I don't know what to say. You said you were sorry to Bishop Mark, too. And yet you were still drawing faces, just hiding it."

"Portraits, Celeste." He set the book on top of a stack of history books next to the bed. "And when I say I'm sorry, I mean that I'm sorry for hiding it from you."

"Sorry for hiding it. But not for doing it?"

His eyes held sorrow when he turned back to her, but he gave a slight shrug. "Jah, I guess so."

"Vin! You made a promise. *We* made a promise! Our way says this is idolatry!" She needed to keep her voice down or else she'd wake the children. Then nothing would get resolved. But measuring her tone was outside of her ability right now.

"Oh, horse neck!" Vin shouted.

"Don't yell at me with your version of non–swear words!"

"I'm not yelling at you. It's all just so frustrating! The Old Ways call it idolatry, and I tried accepting that, but I can't! I just don't agree. Not anymore."

"How can you stand there and admit that you don't agree with the Old Ways, and yet you've not once talked to me about it?"

"I don't know. I started to tell you numerous times, but I didn't want to upset you."

"Well, you failed on that, didn't you?" Why was she screaming at him? She didn't recognize herself . . . or him.

"I'm not exalting these drawings to a place of worship. I have no faith in them as if they were a golden calf or had any power. I worship the one true God." He grabbed the sketchbook, opened it, and pointed to the second drawing she'd seen, the one of her with loose hair. "His creation—you, our children, *people*, are beautiful. He's the ultimate artist. Capturing a tiny piece of that beauty on paper makes me feel alive."

"But our vows! The promise we made to the church was to honor the Old Ways. It doesn't matter if we agree or not."

"The Old Ways change. Look at our propane-powered refrigerator. You think our ancestors had that? You think they'd have approved?"

"Refrigeration was never a matter of idolatry, so that's off topic!"

"It's not. The ministers, the *Ordnung*, they're all trying to translate God's Word, but they mess it up. I'm telling you, in my heart, I know that art isn't evil."

"And you're allowed to make art. You can draw any animal, any plant, any place with as much detail as your heart desires."

"The Ordnung didn't allow those things fifteen years ago. Doesn't that fact help you see my point?"

"But faces *are* forbidden now. Why must you draw faces, Vin?"

"Eyes and faces are the windows to people's souls, and faces change over time. One day, our faces will gain wrinkles and marks of time. How is it evil to want to remember our years together? Our children's little faces while they're babies? Look at Steven and how big he already is. Without drawings, would I be able to remember all the details?"

Some of her rolling anger seemed to disappear, like moving a boiling pot off a hot burner. She'd felt that magic when looking at the pictures. All the little things she wouldn't have thought of if not for the reminder: baby Steven's downy fluff of hair that was thicker at the sides of his head, his cute lips in the shape of a bow that folded inward at the center. But there were other ways to deal with the no-images rule of the Old Ways. "We hold those things in our hearts. We don't need something physical to remember them."

"Our minds are imperfect, though. It was only four years ago, but can you honestly tell me you remember every tiny detail of Steven's face as a newborn?"

He was right, but it didn't matter. "We took a vow that said we would always abide by the Old Ways. Convincing me your artwork is not idolatry will do you no good. You lied to me. You've been sitting in the room with me while drawing forbidden things, Vin."

He moved in closer to her. "I . . . I didn't think about it like that."

Celeste put her forehead on his muscular chest. He'd been well-built at eighteen when they'd first gone on a date, but the subsequent seven years of hard work crafting heavy tables and cabinets had put even more muscle on his frame.

He wrapped his arms around her. "I'm sorry I hurt you. I should've talked with you, but I'm not sure I care what the ministers think."

She pulled back. "That's not true. You *do* care or you wouldn't be hiding it. Your family—me, Steven, Drew, and any future children we have—are counting on you. If you're shunned, we're all punished. How can we guide our children to accept the Old Ways as young adults and remain Amish, keeping our precious family together, if you rebel against those ways?"

"Maybe this isn't the healthiest place to raise our family, then."

What? Was he considering leaving their way of life, their family, their friends, over art? "You mean Lancaster County or the Old Ways?"

"I don't know yet."

She stepped backward until she ran into the bed, sitting down hard. How long had he been harboring these thoughts? "You've been considering this for a while, haven't you?"

"Celeste, I was nineteen and you were eighteen when we married. We made all these vows to the church when we were still children ourselves. How were we supposed to know what we wanted?"

An unfamiliar pain clutched her, an all-consuming one. "What other vows are you now doubting, Vin?"

"What?" He tilted his head, confused.

"You heard me! Answer me!"

"I have never doubted the vows I made to you. You're my wife, now and forever. I only meant the promises we made to live like this, when it seemed the only way of living. Everyone wanted this life for us—our parents, siblings, aunts, uncles, cousins, former schoolteachers, the ministers—and we followed this path, but now I'm not so sure."

"Vin, we'd lose everything if we left. Our families, our livelihood, *everything*." And what would that mean for their souls? The Old Ways were the path to heaven, weren't they? Did he doubt that too? If they left, would they be setting their children on a path toward hell?

"Look . . ." Vin rubbed his thick beard. "I know it'd be a new and hard start. But we could do it as a team."

He couldn't be serious! Her insides trembled. "Vin, I can't. I just *can't*!"

His face turned red, and he moved to look out the window. "So I'm in the same place I've been for years—desperate to extinguish a piece of myself in order to uphold my vow. I . . . I was hoping you, of all people, would understand." He took a step toward the door.

"Vin? Where are you going?" This was their time together after the little ones went to sleep. He wanted to be away from her?

"I've got to clear my head. It's *stifling* here. And I don't mean the July heat."

That was reasonable, wasn't it? To want to get some space? But something in her was screaming. Her inner voice wanted to be unreasonable. *Stop! Don't go, please!* She wanted to yell it at the top of her lungs, not caring if the neighbors heard.

He touched the wooden doorframe, turning his head over his shoulder to look at her. "I'll be back before you fall asleep. Promise."

Was that true or something he was saying to keep the peace, to appease her? She'd believed in who they were since their earliest days of dating, but now . . . who was he? Who were they? Did she know him or just the version of himself he was willing to let her see? All she thought she knew of who they were seemed to have crumbled under her feet in less than ten minutes. A hundred questions haunted her. But this time, she knew she couldn't trust Vin to help her figure out the truth.

Chapter Two

Vin's mind spun as he made his way to the barn. The disappointment in Celeste's eyes twisted him into knots. She was right. He'd made a vow, and God's Word was clear about accepting the pain and suffering of making a promise, of swearing to your own hurt in order to keep your word. But when it came to his art, to expressing who he was, it felt as if he were being forced to live inside a half-used-up pickle jar . . . and he hated pickles. He'd failed to help her understand. He had two hobbies he loved: sketching portraits and reading history. The Ordnung, the rules the Amish lived by, allowed one. The other? Forbidden. But both were essential parts of who he was.

He sighed. He hadn't explained much of anything well. Even worse, the words he had said haunted him. He shouldn't have mentioned leaving the Amish, especially at the start of the conversation. Of course Celeste would find the very idea upsetting. He did too, and yet he'd rushed headlong into venting rather than discussing. How had this much time passed with this issue weighing on him, and yet he'd been unprepared to explain himself in a way that caused his wife to *see* him, to hear his heart beyond her hurt? What should he have said?

He picked up the shafts to the buggy and rolled the carriage out of its corner in the barn. Once it was in the aisle, he noticed for the second time this evening that the hub of the wheel wasn't sitting right. It was always something.

He grabbed a rubber mallet from the corner of the barn. The wheel needed a blacksmith to fix it, but Vin's efforts would have to do for tonight. He needed to go up on Kissin' Mountain and talk to God. Vin smacked the hub, trying to get the flange, bearings, and rivets to line up enough to keep the wheel on. The mallet flew from his hands, going in the opposite direction from the rig.

He looked at the wheel. It appeared quite secured to the hub now. "That'll do." He hitched Sugar Bear to the rig, got into the buggy, and drove toward the path to his beloved Kissin' Mountain. Why was it called that, anyway? No one drove up that narrow, overgrown path to make out. Too many more easily accessible places to steal a kiss or two. The start of the dead-end path was pretty well hidden by long grass and underbrush. But once at the top, he could sit on a granite boulder that jutted out and look over the Hanook Valley. Lancaster County had a lot prettier overlooks, many that included a beautiful view of the Susquehanna River. Still, he and Sugar Bear had been going to this spot since Vin was a kid, a place to think and pray and center himself. Celeste didn't know where this spot was, not really. She knew he went somewhere off the beaten path a few miles from their house when wanting time alone. Since she hadn't been raised in the area, she didn't think much about the various mountains or overlooks. Plus, it was a part of who she was to give freedom and privacy. Was it his way to take advantage of that?

Oddly enough, he'd brought Steven up here a handful of times, thinking he, too, might want a private spot to think and pray on his own in another five or so years.

As Sugar Bear plodded up the rutty path, Vin drew a deep breath. *"Gott, bin Ich aa draus in da Welt?"*

He'd asked God a hundred thousand times if he was too out in the world. But clarity never came. Was that because he was so very wrong or because he felt the weight of everyone's opinions about it? His parents and preachers had taught him about idolatry from the time he was a baby, and everyone he'd grown up with believed images of the face were idol worship. Many frowned on Vin drawing hands or backs, feeling that, too, crossed a line.

"Gott, *helfe* me, please. I need Your help. You know I do. I've cried out to You until I'm sick of hearing my own wailing. The need to draw faces, to look in someone's eyes and re-create the light I see, burns inside me like a hunger I can't ease. Why? It's too much." He tugged on the reins, reminding his old girl to watch out for the rock ahead, the one sometimes hidden by tall grass. She nodded. She understood him well and was a responsive horse.

A verse came to mind, one he'd quoted to God a few times. "Gott, Your Word says You are faithful and will not let a person be tempted beyond what he can bear. I need You to rescue me from this miserable temptation or let me know it's fine to do as I wish, even if Celeste and I need to leave the Amish." He finished his prayer, unsure what else to say. Hadn't he said it all before?

The sky was a deep purple as light drained from this side of the world. Cicadas buzzed. Crickets chirped. The mountain chorus of frogs sang. Creatures, from insects to workhorses, seemed to know what they were born for. No one expected a bird not to sing, a cricket not to chirp, a horse not to graze the fields.

When Sugar Bear slowed because of the steepness, Vin brought her to a full stop, got out, and led her the rest of the way up the incline until the path ended. Dusk was deepening. He realized he should've brought a lantern with him, but the quarter moon was rising and would be high soon. This open space for the path ran between a tall hill on one side and a cliff on the other. Per his usual, he eased the horse and rig into a semicircle until both were facing downhill. While he was in the middle of unhitching Sugar Bear from the rig, she took several steps back.

"Whoa, girl. None of that." He grabbed her rein, but she still took a few steps back, pushing the rig toward the cliff. "Sugar Bear," he scolded. She stopped, and then he saw what caused her to do that unusual move. Patches of sweetgrass were behind her, and she wanted to get to them. "Fine. We'll do it your way." He finished unhitching her. He'd be here awhile, suffering in miserable ways that he had no answers for. His faithful old girl might as well enjoy herself, especially since he had a halter in the rig. He took off her bridle and put the harness and lead rope on her. She went to the closest patch of grass, and he placed a small rock on top of the lead rope. "Better?" He rubbed her neck, withers, and back. She nickered, sounding satisfied. Vin had gotten her as a six-month-old filly for his twelfth birthday. He'd worked with her from the start, but he let her grow for four years before he started riding her or asking her to pull a rig. She was a bit spoiled, and like every horse, she had her own personality, with desires that didn't always match his goals. He had to both listen to her and hold his ground. Was that what God was doing with Vin?

He moved to his spot on the granite boulder and sat. Even though this spot was all brambles and underbrush except for a narrow path and a series of dirty boulders jutting out over nothing important, Vin saw it as gorgeous, created by the original artist. He breathed in the cool air as the sky continued to deepen into shades of dark orange and deep purple.

All of life held beauty, and Vin knew he had so much to be grateful for. He loved Celeste far more than she could see. Their sons filled their lives with new meaning. Words couldn't describe what all three of them meant to him. Love abounded in their home. He had a cabinetry and furniture business that, from time to time, allowed him to express his artistry through scrollwork and ornate patterns on panels for Englischers. Their community wasn't contentious or backbiting. The ministers had reacted with kindness and forgiveness when the bishop discovered Vin's idolatrous drawings.

Yet . . . he chafed on the inside, like a man stuffed inside clothes three times too small for him or inside a baby's bassinet or . . . a half-used-up pickle jar.

He sighed. "What's wrong with me that I can't just be satisfied?"

Then again, what was wrong with everyone else that they had to make a sinful case out of something that should be as freeing as drawing a whole person, face included?

An awful feeling bubbled up from somewhere deep inside him. Maybe he'd been born during the wrong time. Not long ago, Amish hadn't allowed any artistry of nature, not trees or birds or faceless people. If he'd been born twenty or thirty years from right now, would the Amish allow images of faces?

But then he'd only know Celeste as an elderly woman. Would she be better off without him?

Anger stirred as he realized he was lying to himself. His real question, the one lurking behind his self-serving one, was, would he be better off if he was free of her? Free to go where he wanted? Be who he wanted?

Was that why he was a restless soul . . . because he wanted to be free?

The rig creaked and gravel fell into the ravine. He stood, trying to see under the now-silvery night sky. What would've caused that? He got off the boulder, just in case the noise he'd heard was rocks falling from under the jutting. He studied his surroundings.

A glint caught his attention. Moonlight bounced against something on the flat ground six or so feet to the side of where he stood. He squinted. Was that two rappel rings bolted into the ground? A double rope ran across the ground, from the rings to over the side of the cliff.

Someone had been up here? He scanned the area again.

Sugar Bear was still grazing, content. But the rig was sitting oddly, wasn't it? He went to it and saw that the wheel he'd pounded onto the hub before leaving his house was sitting lopsided, not fully off, but not upright either, and now it was pushing over the edge. He grabbed the shafts on the rig and pulled. It wasn't hard to move the rig forward and away from the edge. Or it shouldn't be, but the broken, wonky wheel had snagged on the edge of the boulder and it wasn't budging.

He yanked hard, and the wheel came off. *No!*

The rig tilted toward the ravine. He pushed down hard on the far shaft. He could still save it! But its weight angled toward the now-missing wheel. No choice. He had to let go or be dragged with it. The rig went over the side. The sound of its crash reverberated through the canyon.

His heart going wild, he eased to the edge, seeing fairly well in the moonlight as the sound faded. Disbelief kept echoing inside him. How had he not realized the rig was too close to the edge?

The sight of it sort of matched what his insides felt like—something splintered across an overgrown, barren land no one cared about. Would anyone ever see the broken rig? Not likely.

He sighed. How embarrassing would this be to explain to Celeste? Rigs were expensive. He'd known it needed repair, so why hadn't he thought about what coming up this rutty, rocky path would do to that already-damaged wheel? At least he could ride Sugar Bear home rather than having to walk, so he wouldn't add being home late to the other items on the list—forbidden artwork, a desire to break free of the Amish, and a destroyed buggy. As it was, she had a lot of disappointments to contend with. She deserved better, and sometimes he seemed determined to remind her of that.

He peered over the ledge again, trying to see if any useful parts of the buggy might be retrievable. Something else caught his eye, near where the broken rig was now sprawled. Was that . . . clothing? Was someone lying on the ground down there?

He blinked and inched forward to see better. Loose gravel under his feet shifted. *Horse neck!* He tried to scramble back, but his foot slipped. He fell to the ground, but the edge of the rock seemed to disintegrate, and as gravel slid out from under him, gravity pulled him toward the ravine.

No! His heart pounded and catching a breath seemed impossible. He didn't want to die. He couldn't! Not after leaving Celeste like that! Scrambling with all he had, he flipped over to his belly, trying to crawl from the edge, but within seconds he was going over the side. He reached out in front of him and his fingers clawed onto some jutted-out rock he'd never seen when sitting above it. His breathing came in short spurts as his legs dangled, searching for footing. But he had too little of a hold on the rock, and he couldn't pull himself up. He closed his eyes, regret engulfing him like flames from a barn on fire. Dizziness spun him as he tried to hold on, and his awareness of this place seemed to fade, as if he was going to sleep.

Suddenly . . . he was nowhere and everywhere. Was he falling?

Everything faded and the one truth that mattered rose from deep within. He screamed their names as loud as he could with struggling lungs. "Celeste! Steven! Drew! I love you!"

* * *

Celeste startled awake. Was that a noise coming from the road? With Drew asleep in her arms, she got out of the rocking chair and moved to the open window, listening for hooves on the pavement. Her long white gown clung to her sweaty body. The cicadas chirped loudly and not a breeze stirred the sultry air. She neither saw nor heard anything that sounded like a horse and buggy coming her way. A car topped the hill, its headlights piercing the dark. She looked at the clock on the wall. Three.

"Vin, where are you?"

Just in case he'd slipped in while she was dozing in the rocker, she padded down the hall and peered into their bedroom. Still empty. She went back to the nursery and put Drew in his bed, asking God to give him some relief for his sore gums from teething, letting him rest easy tonight.

She lit a kerosene lamp and carried it with her. Maybe Vin had returned and was asleep in the barn. The screen door creaked as she left the house, and then it flopped against the frame. The gravel driveway pinched the bottoms of her feet a bit. "Vin?" She went into the barn and lifted the lantern, looking for signs of him. The dim, wavery light bounced off emptiness. No family buggy. No Sugar Bear. No husband.

The dirt floor of the barn felt cool and smooth against her bare feet. The aroma of old wood and fresh hay filled the humid air. "Vin?" Her voice cracked. Why was she calling for him when there were no signs he was there?

She left the barn and walked the short distance to the cabinetry shop. Since the rig wasn't in sight, it was silly to check the shop, but she opened the door and went inside anyway. The aroma of sawdust, paint, and the sweat of her husband's brow filled her senses. Echoes of yesterday surrounded her. She'd been so sure of who he was . . . who they were together . . .

The wall clock's ticks sounded loud in the quiet of the night. How often over the years had they relied on that old thing to keep track of time for them? All that time together that she treasured . . . how long had he wanted another life?

A wave of grief flooded her. She stood there, lost and overwhelmed in the most familiar of places—home. Biting back tears, she returned to the house. Should she call someone? Was it worth the upset it would cause others if Vin simply hadn't returned yet? On the other hand . . . No. He'd be home soon. She was sure of it.

Once inside, she got a bowl down from the cabinet. Baking always made her feel better. Busyness was a balm to a troubled mind. Her hand rested on the cabinet and she stroked the wood. Vin had made these. The house was old, but the cabinets were new, an anniversary gift to her. Emotions crashed against her. Anger. Hurt. Panic. Since he asked her to marry him at seventeen years old, she hadn't known how to get through a day without hearing his calm voice and quick laughter. But if he came home right now, she wouldn't know what to do—hug him with all her heart or scream at him until she lost her voice. Maybe both.

"Mamm?"

Celeste turned to see little Steven half-dressed, his suspenders over his nightshirt with his pants underneath.

"Wo's Dat?"

At four years old, Steven knew very little English. He often talked in a mix of Pennsylvania Dutch, their everyday language, and High German, the language from parts of the church meetings and from when they read the Bible out loud. She forced a smile and knelt in front of her son, hoping to avoid answering his question. *"Du sollen sein in Bett."* How was her response of *you should be in bed* any sort of helpful answer to this precious boy who wanted to know where his dad was?

"*Ich traum. Ich mussen mei dat.*"

"Ah." She brushed sweaty hair from his face. He'd had a dream and needed his dat. She needed Vin too, but it was even worse for Steven, as a daddy's boy. Whenever Steven had a bad dream, she could scarcely comfort him, but Vin knew just what to say. Then Vin would wrap Steven in his arms while in his and Celeste's big bed, and they'd both go back to sleep. She choked back tears as she told her son that his dat wasn't there.

"*Awwer Dat versprochen mich.*"

Celeste didn't know what Vin had promised Steven, but it didn't matter. He wasn't here to keep that promise. She kissed his cheek. "*Kumm.*" She told him she'd tuck him in bed and read him his favorite story.

The pout remained on Steven's face, like he might burst into tears at any moment, but he turned and headed for his bed. Steven was sure his dat had hung the sun and the moon. She was too old to believe that, but sometimes it felt as if Vin could do those things if he wanted to.

She took Steven's hand in hers as they walked down the hallway. The house echoed with silence in a way she'd never experienced before, and the home that always felt warm and inviting seemed to be filled with fear.

Dear God, please bring Vin home safe and sound. Please.

Chapter Three

Vin opened his eyes, darkness surrounding him. Crickets and tree frogs sang. He didn't remember hitting the ground, so why was he sprawled facedown on thick grass? He'd felt no thud—and had no pain or injuries that he could feel. The damp grass cooled his skin, and he took a few deep breaths. A fall from the top of the ravine would've meant hitting rocks on his way down, but he didn't feel bruised or broken. Had he passed out? He sat up, his head spinning, then stood. Spotting his straw hat, he grabbed it and put it on. His splintered, broken buggy should be close by.

He walked one direction for ten or so feet and then another. Where was he? Where were the cliff and boulders? A silver light covered everything, illuminating it well, but the land appeared flat and green. He'd never been at the bottom of the ravine, but he'd seen it from the top of Kissin' Mountain since he was a kid, and he knew what it should look like, didn't he? Where were the rocks and overgrown underbrush—or the broken and scattered rig?

Maybe he was looking a gift horse in the mouth. He was alive—a miracle—and it was time to head home. He was done regretting what he couldn't do. He was ready to be all in, and what he wanted to do most was love. Love his wife. His sons. His heavenly Father. After all, how many people on this earth couldn't use a skill they loved? His portrait art would be among that lot. He didn't have to agree with the curbing of art to surrender peacefully to the Old Ways and the ministers' edicts.

He studied the ground. Perhaps if he figured out which way he'd been lying when he woke up, he could figure out how to get back. Woke? That was right, he did wake. But had he passed out? It didn't matter. He found the indention in the grass where his body had pressed it down. He'd been facing the cliff when he fell, so if he turned in the opposite direction, that should put him heading east. It might take a few hours to reach one of the Englischer houses he often saw from the top of Kissin' Mountain. But he could do it.

Poor Sugar Bear. She had to be so confused. What a relief that he'd just set a rock on the rope rather than tie her to a tree or boulder. How long would she wait for him before she pulled the lead rope free and walked home? Or when she pulled free, would she only eat more sweetgrass, not moving any closer to home? She could stay a long time grazing on Kissin' Mountain, especially if she made her way to the spring water not far off the path.

He walked for hours by the light of the stars and quarter moon, studying the land as he went. It looked so different from how he'd thought it would, but then again, a new perspective changed everything. If you took one back road over another, it could look as if you were in another county.

He studied the land. "Or a different state . . . ," he mumbled.

As dawn peeped over the horizon, he saw several riders bareback on horses. Good. They could be Amish or from a nearby Englisch horse farm. Returning home on a horse would be preferable to a car—especially given the argument he'd had with Celeste.

The riders ambled along. Vin hurried in that direction. Then he stopped cold and blinked, trying to see clearer than the dawn was allowing. They were men, but their shirts and pants didn't look like anything he'd ever seen. No hats. Some had long hair. Some were near bald with tufts of hair . . . and were those feathers? He'd never seen men who looked like this. Their skin appeared to be darker than his and maybe a different shade. When one spoke in a loud voice, Vin paused at the strangeness of the language. He pressed himself against a nearby tree, watching.

Were they Indians? Was there a reservation or off-reservation trust land in Pennsylvania?

The men had their backs to Vin, riding away. One stopped his horse. Was he turning his animal around? Vin didn't wait to know for sure. He removed his hat and eased to the other side of the tree until he heard the horses' hooves fade into the distance.

Celeste's countertops held endless baked goods. And no husband to appreciate them. Hours ago, hints of daylight arrived. Breakfast at dawn for her early rising boys. Some hours dragged their feet like exhausted men coming home after a blazing hot day of baling hay, and other hours rushed past her like a swollen river during a spring thaw.

Now afternoon brightness shone across the land. Where was he? Maybe he'd ridden into Reading to her favorite tea shop and bought a gift to help make up for leaving as he had. Maybe after a long night of thinking, rather than coming home, he'd gone to a job site to adjust a set of cabinets he'd installed.

She rubbed her forehead, weary of jumbled thoughts that went round and round and landed nowhere helpful.

"Dear God, please bring him home safe and sound . . . and soon. Please, Father. He's got some serious stuff to work out with You, but I've always believed that You brought us together. I . . . I wouldn't even know how to breathe if he left me or if something were to happen to him."

She needed to pray longer and harder, but words failed her as she looked through the window for signs of him.

Although rays of light were illuminating the world, she couldn't quite see through the fogginess that surrounded her soul. Bright darkness, that's what today looked like. At least the black of night had held hope that he might be close or could be heading home. Day told a different story.

The boys were outside playing with the hose, Steven holding the nozzle and making shapes in the air while baby Drew sat and clapped his hands, both giggling like children do when lazy summer days get mixed with endless cool water. She glanced at the clock. How had time not stopped or at least paused to give her a chance to accept on some level what was going on? What *was* going on? Was her beloved in a ditch in need of help and she was here wasting time? Had Vin left the Old Ways behind? Left her and their sons? Before Vin revealed his true feelings last night, she would've bet her life he'd never leave his family. But right now she was so unsure it made her queasy.

She couldn't justify waiting any longer. She had to call someone. It was time—way past time. She wiped her hands on her grimy black apron, feeling the grains of hidden flour as she trudged to the phone shanty. What would she say?

The slow clip-clop of hooves on asphalt caught her attention and she turned, looking at the road.

Sugar Bear.

Alone.

Meandering as if nothing pressed her, Sugar Bear left the road and walked up the dirt driveway. Celeste's feet were glued to the ground. Where was the horse's rigging from pulling the buggy? She had on a halter with a lead rope that dragged across the dusty driveway.

Sugar Bear stopped.

Celeste's feet finally obeyed her, and she sprinted past the horse to the road. "Vin?" She ran one direction and then the other, eyes scanning the road and land. Nothing. She cupped her hands around her mouth. "Vin!"

Silence roared in her ears, and the stillness she observed, the utter emptiness of the country road, pierced her heart. She turned back to look at Sugar Bear. She was still waiting in the middle of the driveway, reminding Celeste of an abandoned car waiting along the side of a highway. Those always made her wonder if the owner would return for them or cut their losses and just go on with life.

Celeste strode to her. "Easy, girl." She ran her hands over Sugar Bear's barrel, shoulders, and legs, looking for signs of physical harm. There were none. Not a single hint of injury or trauma. The mare had hardly broken a sweat on this hot day. It was as if someone had fed her well and set her free to return home.

"Where's Vin, Sugar Bear? We need him . . . I need him." Her voice cracked. Vin's beloved horse shook her head as if shaking off Celeste's words. She drew a breath, weary of her strange, garbled thoughts. She picked up the lead rope and led Sugar Bear to a nearby hitching post. After looping the rope to the post, she went into the phone shanty.

She put her trembling fingers on the handset of the rotary phone, trying to decide whom to call. She should start with Bishop Mark. His decisions would keep the guesswork out of this for her.

Parents—Vin's or hers—would have strong opinions, but Bishop Mark's word was final. He was levelheaded, and whatever he said, his words were a message that God ordained.

God.

The thought of an all-powerful, loving being watching this mess without interference didn't bring her comfort. Vin had walked out and not returned. Had God left her too?

She wiped tears from her eyes and picked up the handset.

Chapter Four

Lush grass and tall trees surrounded Vin as he walked, hoping to hear the sound of trickling water. He kept a keen eye on his surroundings. It'd been three days . . . hadn't it? Did the fall addle his memory? He'd fallen from the crag at night and begun walking. Had he been going for two days or three since he'd seen those men on horseback . . . or any human? All he'd seen since were bears, bobcats, and snakes. He'd been basing his direction on the sun's path and walking east, but he still didn't know where he was.

Tall, thick grass and an abundance of trees hid things that could kill him, so he understood his need to be watchful. His mouth felt full of cotton balls stuffed inside sand. His body was desperate for water. His vision wavered as if everything was a mirage. He stumbled, landing on all fours. Was that the sound of water he heard?

Get up!

But his body didn't listen, seemed unable to listen. He had nothing to help him along the way—other than the sun, which let him know east and west. No pocketknife to kill or skin a fish . . . if he could even manage to catch one in his straw hat. No gun to shoot any of the rabbits, squirrels, or deer he'd seen—and he'd never seen as much wildlife as he had in the last few days. If he had matches, the heat and light from a fire would ward off critters at night, and he could use a fire to cook . . . not that he'd caught anything to eat. A blanket could add a bit of protection between himself and the ground, with its endless bugs and spiders and the occasional snake.

Stop grumbling and get up!

He tried to move from his knees to his feet. He fell flat. Wherever he was, he might die before he could find water. He fought to keep his eyes open, but he couldn't. Closing them, he felt consciousness drain from him.

Something cool touched his lips. He tried to open his eyes. Was someone near him?

"Come on, drink." A deep, soothing voice spoke and cool water poured into Vin's mouth.

Vin tried to swallow, but it hurt, and he coughed. Yet he wanted more of that kind of pain. He took several good swallows, then opened his eyes, seeing a dark night. No stars. No moon. Just blackness. His hands shook as he reached for whatever held the water.

"Easy now." The deep voice spoke as he poured a little more of the cool water into Vin's mouth. The world seemed to fade in and out, but whenever Vin woke, the same voice greeted him. The liquid entering his mouth now had a taste of meat to it, a broth of some sort. Was that smoke he smelled? Vin swallowed the broth, feeling bits of some type of meat go down with the liquid. Then he faded out again.

He opened his eyes, trying to stir. How could a body that had no food for days weigh so much he couldn't move it?

More liquid entered his mouth. Vin couldn't see a face, but someone was taking care of him.

"God." Vin's voice was raspy. "You showed up."

The being chuckled. "I'm just a man, wondering what you're doin' way off out here."

"I . . . I fell. Where are we?"

"We were hoping you could tell us that, mister."

"We?" Vin opened his eyes, only seeing a lone, shadowy figure. He tried to keep his eyes open, but he couldn't.

"Me and my son."

"You're lost too?"

"We are and we're not, I suppose. We lost the trail a long time ago, but we know we're heading north."

"I . . . I need to go east. My house, my wife and sons, they're east of where I was when I fell."

"Mister, we can't fix all that. We'll leave you some food and water, but after we sleep for a spell, we got to head north again."

"Thank you."

The man didn't answer.

Vin pried his eyes open. Where did the man go? "Hello?"

"I'm here, mister." A large figure seemed to amble toward Vin through the darkness.

Had Vin fallen asleep or passed out that time?

"We were looking for a walking stick for you."

They had to be hikers. If Vin had wandered into a national park, it made sense why there was so much land and so few people.

"We found one, mister." Another voice, slightly higher. Perhaps the man's son, like he'd said before.

"Please don't call me that."

"What? *Mister?*" the first man asked.

"Sorry." Why was Vin correcting these helpful strangers? He must be really out of it. "It's just that we Amish don't hold to anyone having a title. All people are equal. My name's Vin."

"I'm George. My son is Tandey, but in all my days I never heard tell of such a thing. All men are equal?" He paused. "Who are you to think like that?"

"I'm just a man who broke his wife's heart and is now lost in an unfamiliar, harsh land."

Celeste. Vin shut his eyes. Images of his beautiful blonde-haired blue-eyed wife danced in his mind's eye.

"Maybe you ain't lost. Maybe you just ain't figured out where you are yet."

How was that not being lost? Vin wanted to ask, but his lips wouldn't move and his eyes wouldn't open.

The sound of birds singing called Vin from his sleep, as if it were an alarm going off. Was he at home in his bed? He opened his eyes, hoping the odd memories had been dreams. But he wasn't in his bed. He was under a shade tree, and the sun was high. It was noon or after. He managed to push himself to a sitting position, his head spinning. A strange-looking balloon thing was beside him. He picked it up. A waterskin? Maybe. It sloshed with liquid. There was also a walking stick and a bowl woven out of grass and filled with blackberries.

Vague memories of a man helping him during the night tugged at him. "Hello?" he called out. But he knew no one would answer. They'd left him water, food, and a walking stick. He was on his own again.

He ate some of the blackberries. He'd never been so grateful for *food.*

The kindness of strangers had saved his life last night. But as thankful as he was, he wasn't anywhere near out of danger of dying in this vast, lush land. He was weak and had no tools to help him survive, save the waterskin, and no way of fending for himself. Using the walking stick, he got to his feet. His legs shook as he walked. He had to keep going, keep searching for answers, for help, for a way home.

He put one foot in front of the other, walking as slowly and unsurely as a young toddler. *Guess this is how little Drew feels. No wonder he throws fits sometimes.*

Hours passed. Despite that the sun was setting, the heat was stifling. Vin pulled the last of the berries from his pant pocket and ate them.

An odd sound, quick and gone, flashed in the air. The hair on the back of his neck prickled, and he studied the land. Nothing made sense, not the land or the strangers who took care of him last night. Was he going crazy from the lack of anything adding up?

A different smell rode on the air. He breathed deep. Smoke? He looked around, seeing a lot of trees and nothing else. It could be his imagination or maybe a hallucination. Was any of this real? If so, had he been going in circles? Maybe he really had gone crazy. Or he'd died in the fall from the cliff and this was all the heaven he deserved—a lonely, desolate place with food he couldn't catch, no way to keep the pests away, and no shelter. Worse, not an ounce of comfort, the kind only home gave to one's soul. His Christian faith didn't teach of that kind of heaven. Still, that's what he felt he deserved, and he was experiencing a lonely, desolate place . . . wasn't he?

The ground shook, and a loud boom ripped through the air. He made a full circle, looking for any sign of what caused the noise. Through the trees on the far side of a dry gully, he saw a bit of a clearing, and he thought he saw a plume of smoke. He couldn't be sure. He worked his way across the gully. As quickly as he could, he staggered to the clearing, using his walking stick to stay upright.

There was a knoll ahead of him, and it appeared as if a small stream of smoke moved skyward just beyond it. The smoke could be much farther away than just over the hill, but the top of the knoll was only a few hundred yards ahead. If there was a chance of finding people, he had to try. But fear held him in place. Darkness was falling fast, and he could step in a pothole from where an animal burrowed or where the rain created ruts before grass grew over it. Even the flattest of ground out here was anything but smooth walking. There were no easy paths compacted by heavy machinery, and at this time of day, he wouldn't be able to see where he stepped, making it easy to injure his leg or ankle. An injury would strand him.

But the idea of talking to someone, getting directions or, better yet, getting a lift home was thrilling. He started up the knoll, trying to hurry while also keeping an eye out for small holes in the ground that could lead to an injury or snakebite. Everything seemed worse by him having no one to talk to. Talking with George during the night had helped. But the previous days of utter loneliness . . . no voice of another human to help him get his bearings or deal with his emotions . . . Until Vin woke to George giving him water, God had seemed as quiet as death too. Still, Vin had talked to Him nonstop in his mind and heart since his fall.

Out of breath, he had to slow. He'd need another five minutes to get to the top of the knoll. What if whatever caused that sound was miles and miles away rather than just over the hill? If people were part of the noise and smoke, they could be gone before he got to them. But with how lost he was, his only way of figuring out how to get back home was to connect with other people.

"Celeste," he whispered for the umpteen-thousandth time. His poor wife. How was she coping without him? She had to be assuming the worst.

"*Nee!*" he panted to the heavens. "I don't want to be free of my wife and children, Gott."

His lungs hurt, and spots floated in his vision, but he'd almost reached the top of the knoll. Even the grassy hills around here had trees everywhere, and as he passed them, he pushed his palms against some to keep himself going. Horses whinnied and a man's voice bellowed. Excitement and fear ricocheted inside Vin, causing his core to shake as much as his legs were. Another loud voice followed, sounding angry. Standing on the pinnacle now, Vin took in all he could in the small dip of a valley below him.

A bonfire. A man several yards from the fire, swinging a flaming stick, yelling. Another man had a rifle leveled at . . . something, but not at the man with the burning stick.

A covered wagon?

Vin rubbed his eyes. Was he hallucinating? Another ground-shaking boom echoed, and Vin knew the man had shot his rifle, though he'd never heard a rifle make such a noise. Vin saw what appeared to be an enormous bear running from the men. One of the three horses reared and broke free. It ran hard, with reins flopping on the ground as it headed toward him.

He pressed his back against the nearest tree. The horse slowed as it topped the hill. Using his walking stick, Vin hurried after it and stomped on a rein. The horse jolted him, and Vin dropped the stick, his leg twisting out from under him. Pain shot through his knee, but as he fell to the ground, he grabbed the rein.

"Whoa. Easy." He spoke softly but firmly, and she responded like a well-trained horse. He pushed to his feet, limping as his right knee threatened to buckle, and clicked his tongue. "Kumm." He plucked a handful of grass and held it out. She eased toward him. Soon he had full control of her and was patting her neck. "Let's get you home, girl." His right knee throbbed, but he put his left foot in the stirrup and swung himself into the saddle. His head spun as weakness from hunger took its toll.

"Stop! Ye! Stop!" a woman yelled. She had a thick accent that he couldn't make out.

He turned the horse and saw the end of a hunting rifle. His eyes moved up the barrel of the gun. Was that a flintlock rifle? He studied the woman. Her long sage-green dress had more pleats than an Amish woman's, making it look as if it was neither Amish nor Englisch, but her hair was pinned up, similar to how Amish women wore theirs. Was she Amish? It didn't seem likely since she had the barrel of the gun pointed at him.

"Easy." He splayed his hands, keeping the reins between his fingers. "Tell me what you want."

She pointed the barrel toward the ground and back at him. Clearly she understood his words.

"Absolutely. I'm getting down right now." He slid off the horse. Dizziness hit hard, and he staggered a bit before using the horse to steady his body.

She had to be with the people in the wagon. There was nowhere else she could've come from. He patted the horse. "I was taking her back to the wagon. That's where she ran from."

She eyed him, scowling. She was a tiny woman, maybe thirty-five years old. It was hard to tell as night closed in. He'd never seen a rifle barrel that long, although he'd grown up with hunting rifles of all types.

"Go." She used the barrel of her rifle to let him know which direction, signaling him away from where the wagon sat.

She was warning him to go the opposite direction of the wagon. Most likely everything that mattered to her was there. At a previous time, he would've done as told and gone on his way, but desperation clawed at him.

"I need help. Please." Vin's voice wavered. "I . . . don't know where I am or how I got here. I own nothing to help me—"

"Go!" She growled and cocked the gun.

He nodded and started walking. Pain shot through his right knee and he limped. How much longer would his shaky legs hold him, especially with this fresh injury?

"Ohio," she said in her thick accent.

He stopped. "Ohio? How?" He'd fallen off a cliff in eastern Pennsylvania, hundreds of miles from the Ohio border.

Her eyes narrowed as she walked a few steps closer. "Are ye daft?" Her gruffness had a ring of sincerity to it. He wished he knew accents better than he did. Maybe if he hadn't lived such a secluded life or if he listened to the radio or watched television, he'd recognize it, but his best guess was that she was from England.

He shook his head. "Not daft."

Maybe crazy, dead, or in a never-ending nightmare, but not foolish or brain injured. At least he didn't think he was. Then again, he'd fallen from a cliff and been near starved for days.

His ears rang with a high-pitched buzz, and the world seemed to waver like a heat mirage on hot pavement. His legs buckled and everything went black.

Chapter Five

The night air was sticky, and thunder rumbled in the distance as Celeste stood on the porch, holding the baby and staring at the horizon. The bishop and his wife, Lovina, were near her, sipping lemonade and chatting quietly. They'd stayed close since she'd made the call four days ago, offering loving support while most of Vin's family looked at her as if she were lying. She didn't blame them. It all felt like a made-up story, and she would've never believed Vin wanted to leave the Amish without hearing it straight from him.

A horse in the barn whinnied, and two others answered, catching her attention for a moment. Her people had filled the barn to capacity with horses. Buggies lined her driveway and yard because Amish from far and wide had ridden here days ago, and even some by train. Four police cars were in the driveway. Through the open windows, she heard the constant buzz of a busy home—dishes clanking, voices of about sixty Amish talking softly, comparing notes of what they'd seen in their days of searching for Vin. More Amish, at least a hundred, maybe two hundred, were from other parts of the state and country and were staying in various homes throughout the community.

The porch door opened, and Vin's parents walked out of the house.

Eli approached her while his wife, Naomi, tugged on his arm. He pulled free, staring at Celeste. "I want to know what you did. Did you run my son off, or worse?"

"Eli," Naomi whispered. "Please, not now. Not with our grandson in her arms."

He scoffed. "You did something—or there's something you're not saying. I know it. My son would never abandon his vows or his family. And I don't believe for a second that he was entertaining the idea of leaving the Amish."

Drew started crying, and Celeste bounced and patted him, assuring him everything was fine. But Eli's words beat a dead horse inside her. Maybe his accusations should hurt or anger her, but she'd known for days that this moment was coming. He was exhausted, worn-out with grief and embarrassment that his son had disobeyed the Old Ways. He needed to blame someone, but she blamed herself far worse than he did. Her husband had needed her to see his pain and struggle, and all she'd seen was his breaking of the rules.

Eli clicked his tongue. "What else are you lying about? All these people here are giving up their time and money to support you in all your sadness and with tears in your eyes. Yet you didn't even tell anyone he was gone until he'd already been missing an entire night! Why?"

"That's enough, Eli." Bishop Mark put his hand on Eli's shoulder.

Eli pulled free of the bishop's hand and pointed at Celeste. "If you've done anything to hurt him . . ."

How could anyone think such a horrible thing? "I . . . I want him to return more than anyone. I want my sons to have their father, and I want my husband home."

"Some good Amish heard you screaming at my son and then he disappeared?"

"Eli." Bishop Mark squeezed his shoulder. "Temperance."

No one could've heard her screaming at Vin. Had she lost her temper that badly? She didn't remember doing so. Maybe someone had been out walking. They did keep the windows open in summer.

Eli shook his finger at her. "You better hope he does come home, because I give you my word: if he doesn't, me and mine will not support you. Not with time or money or anything in any way."

She'd often suspected that Eli didn't like her, but he trusted nothing about her? What had she ever done to make him think so poorly of her?

"Kumm now," Bishop Mark said. "You and your family are exhausted and upset, Eli, and rightly so, but unforgiveness and anger are not our way. The Lord commands us to forgive and to see that no root of bitterness springs up and causes trouble."

"Forgive?" Celeste asked. "What have I done that needs Eli's forgiveness?"

The bishop seemed dumbfounded, as if she should know her part. She wasn't able to hear more than half of what anyone was saying these days, but did all of them hold her accountable for Vin being missing?

"Mrs. Lantz?" a detective called to her as he strode from his car near the barn toward the porch.

She tried to see through her foggy thoughts and recall his name. It came to her. Jasper Powell. That was it: Detective Jasper Powell.

"Ma'am." He continued walking toward her. "I need a moment."

The middle-aged man had on a light-gray suit with a burgundy tie and black leather belt. He stuck out among the Amish as much as the uniformed policeman. On Friday afternoon, he'd asked her dozens of questions, and then he returned every so often with more questions or a brief update.

Her parents came out of the house, as did some of the other Amish, all ready to hear what this man had to say, including those who filled the open windows, watching and listening.

For four days, including Sunday, the police and a multitude of Amish volunteers had scoured the countryside on foot. Some had gone to local towns by a hired driver—all hoping to find Vin . . . or at least some clue about where he'd gone off to. Some women joined them in the search, but most stayed behind, keeping three meals a day on the table, tending to the children, praying with Celeste, and doing laundry as needed.

Once again, she stumbled over how odd time felt right now. Hours dripped by like molasses in winter, while also running like molasses in spring. Everything was jumbled and confusing. Would she ever hold a clear thought again? Would the pain ever ease to something bearable? She'd never known humiliation before, and now it clung closer than her next breath and heavier than her house filled with people.

"Mrs. Lantz." The detective came up the steps and nodded at her.

She pulled her attention from scattered thoughts to the detective. Did he have a wife who was missing him while he worked endless hours trying to find Celeste's husband?

"What is it?" the bishop asked when Celeste failed to speak.

"I'm sorry to say this." The detective took off his hat. "Truly sorry. But we're calling off the search, ma'am."

Lovina put her arm around Celeste. "It's just for the day, I'm sure."

"No." The detective shook his head. "I'm sorry. The search is being called off for good, ma'am."

"You can't!" Eli pointed at the detective. "My son's out there, probably injured. Or else he'd be back by now. I know he didn't leave his family or his faith."

Celeste longed to wake from this nightmare, but that wouldn't happen until Vin was home safe and sound. "For good?" There was nothing *good* about this.

"I'd like for you all to understand what we're looking at. Today was the fourth full day of searching for any signs of Ervin. Out of respect for your community and the fact that a married Amish person has never come up missing in this state without foul play involved, we've spent far more time and resources searching for him than would be usual for a case like this. His horse returned home last Friday with no injuries and no sign of trauma. Someone had unhitched her from the rig and had put a halter on her. There was no evidence that she'd broken free. We also know Ervin left home of his own free will, and according to you, Celeste, he was upset with the Amish restrictions and even spoke of leaving them, an idea you didn't support. So as much as we all hate the idea, it's highly likely that he chose to leave."

"You can't stop looking!" Vin's dat shouted. "He's out there— injured! That's the only possible reason that he's not back! We can't give up now!"

Was he out there, alive and injured? *Dear God, it hurts too much to imagine that.* Perhaps more than thinking he'd chosen to leave her and his sons behind in order to pursue artistry unrestrained. Was he dead? Should she continue hoping he'd come home or accept that he never would? She was in limbo, with nowhere to land her grief.

How was she to raise two boys without her husband? How could she stay sane not knowing what happened to him? "Please, you can't stop, not yet."

The detective scratched his forehead. "Of course we'll continue to keep our eyes and ears out for any information regarding his disappearance. However, we serve a large community, and we can't afford to keep diverting so many resources."

She choked back tears. "But—"

"Celeste." The bishop's tone held gentle correction. "It's time to accept that the police, and all the Amish, must return to their lives."

Her throat tightened and stung, but she would not cry in front of them. "Jah, I understand. I'm sorry. Denki for all your help."

"I wish we had better news, Mrs. Lantz, truly." The detective went down the steps.

Soon police, both in and out of uniform, gathered in the yard and driveway. They got into plain cars or police cars and drove away.

If only she could curl up in a ball, then wake to a day when Vin was here. The ache to feel his arms around her was so deep she could hardly breathe, let alone eat or sleep. How could things ever be normal again?

Eli squared his hat. "We'll keep looking for him, but we won't do it from this house. It's no longer the center of any gathering for us." He turned to his wife. "Naomi, tell the Lantz family. The whole lot of us are leaving *now*."

He walked off toward the barn. Naomi seemed sad but did as he said, and soon many others left the house, following him. Vin's brothers and sisters and their spouses. His aunts, uncles, nieces, and nephews all left, and not one turned to speak to Celeste. She struggled to catch her breath.

But their emotions and disbelief made sense. Even she hadn't believed Vin when he'd told her. How could anyone else believe her account of it? None of them knew the bishop had warned Vin about his artwork, even after he'd taken his vows to the church and to her. But she and Vin had two precious children that were family, too. If Vin didn't return home, would his family come around after a bit of time for their sake?

Had Vin really abandoned her? If he loved her, even just one tiny fraction as much as she loved him, it'd be impossible for him to just walk away. But maybe he'd hidden how he really felt about her, just like he'd hidden all those drawings. Hidden his thoughts of leaving the Amish. Hidden everything about who he was.

"Celeste." Bishop Mark's gentle voice called to her, and she tried to return from wherever it was she went these past few days. He placed his hand on her shoulder, and she came to herself a bit.

"Jah?" Her gravelly voice echoed with tears she'd spend a long time shedding in privacy.

"Our community doesn't have much, but we'll take care of you and your babies. You don't need to worry about that."

Her people were givers. She and Vin had also given when others' needs arose, and they'd done without seeing a doctor or buying a much-needed coat or shoes before cold weather hit. Amish knew how to give, and they often found it impossible to decline helping. All of them had large families, but none of them had health insurance or retirement plans, and that meant someone always needed more money than was available.

Her folks didn't live in the area, although they'd come to help search. She was the oldest of her siblings and cousins, and they had little money to help support another household. Her in-laws were fairly comfortable, but they apparently believed she was a liar . . . and worse. Much worse.

Something besides grief and fear stirred from deep within her. "No." Her raspy voice was a whisper. Had he heard her?

"No?" Mark tilted his head, looking confused.

"I want to work the shop myself, building tables and chairs. Please give me permission for that. I know I can't do cabinetry or designs like Vin can, but I can build some of the other things."

"Amish women don't work in a woodshop. The other elders didn't look at me favorably when I gave you and Vin permission to work together in the shop. Besides that, as much as you've been a good helper to Vin, he was—is a master carpenter. The business is based on his skill set."

"My sons will need a trade. They'll need a way to identify with the good parts of a man who may never return, and they need to know the three of us are strong enough to overcome this together."

He pursed his lips, pausing a long moment. "You have good points, although perhaps I'm completely mad with exhaustion and grief to agree to let a woman run a woodshop." He put a hand up. "Wait here."

He went into the house, leaving her by herself, and she could imagine how very lonely life was going to get by this time tomorrow. Vin's family wanted nothing to do with her. The police had given up, and all the Amish volunteers who lived close would return to their homes tonight. The others, including her parents and siblings, would leave sometime tomorrow, desperate to return to normal life so they could put food on the table after missing days of work. She couldn't blame them for it.

The bishop returned with two young people beside him. "Celeste, you may remember, but this is my nephew Josiah Engle and his fiancée, Lois Yoder."

Fiancée? Josiah looked to be about fifteen years old, and Lois looked like his slightly older sister.

"They live in the city of Lancaster, twenty-five miles north of here. The family hired a van driver to get here to help in the search. His dat is my brother Daniel, and he seems bent on at least one of his sons helping you as if you're a widow. Daniel owns one of the finest cabinetry shops in Lancaster, so Josiah knows his stuff. Josiah is the fourth of his five sons, so my brother said he could spare him one or two days a week until you get the hang of building some smaller pieces of furniture on your own."

A teenage stranger coming to help Celeste fill Vin's shoes on the orders of his father. It was a terrifying idea.

She choked back tears and held out her hand, hoping Josiah didn't notice how much she was trembling. "Denki."

Chapter Six

Loud noises pricked Vin's sleep, and he roused. Pots clanged, and moans of wood and metal came from around him in all directions. He opened his eyes. A white canvas was overhead, reminding him of a canopy bed he'd once built for a client. His body jiggled and jolted, the movement both familiar and not. Where was he? Or perhaps . . . *when* was he? The thought shocked him as if he'd been doused with cold water. Was he in a different time? Could it be true?

He paused. This was a moving rig of some sort. His head spun as he sat up and observed his surroundings. Canvas cover. Barrels. Large, bulging burlap sacks. Metal pots stacked. He was inside a covered wagon, most likely the one he'd seen when on the knoll.

A child cried out, and he spotted a red-faced boy, around ten years old, turning in jerky movements in his sleep, under a pile of blankets.

"God, where am I?" Vin muttered. Since waking after falling

from the cliff, he'd experienced endless land without homes or stores. He'd seen what must've been Indians and hadn't seen the man and son who gave him enough sustenance that he lived to make it this far. But now he was in a wagon? A short list of possibilities ran through his mind again. Since time travel was impossible, he must be unconscious and dreaming or dead, wandering through the wilderness in search of heaven. Despite what his faith had taught about heaven, his thoughts continually clung to what this felt like—him wandering in search of what he did not deserve.

Please, God, wherever I am, whatever I did to get here . . . wherever here is, please have mercy and let me return to my wife and children.

He needed to understand what was happening. Though the world seemed to wobble, he mustered his shaky legs and got to his feet. His right knee screamed at him. He put his weight on his other leg, hunkered low, and hobbled his way to the front of the wagon. The path was narrow and everything in the wagon—from barrels to sacks to pots to dishes to chests to stacks of blankets—shook or whined or clattered. He peered through the front opening of the wagon, and he glimpsed a man with suspenders over a grimy white shirt. *"Hallo?"*

The man glanced at Vin, then shifted his rifle, motioning for Vin to come out. "Slow." The man pulled his set of reins.

Vin blinked, looking twice at the two animals pulling the wagon. *Oxen?*

"Awake again, are ye?" The man's accent matched the woman's from earlier. "Come." He motioned again. "We aren't stopping for the night yet, but I've slowed for ye."

"Thank you." Vin's mind ran with confusion as he crawled over burlap sacks and over the seat to sit on the bench. "Have I been awake before now?"

"A few times. Do ye not remember?"

Vin shook his head.

"Well, ye weren't awake long, but ye drank water before ye fell back asleep." The man reached under his seat and pulled out a small burlap bag. He passed it to Vin. "Jerky. It's not much, but it'll hol' ye until we stop, and my wife can cook."

"Thank you." Vin took it, grateful for any food. Soon he'd need a moment alone in the woods to relieve himself. "Where are we?"

"Still Ohio."

Ohio? A faint recollection came to him of a woman telling him that before he passed out. He'd been in eastern Pennsylvania. How did he cross the state to its western border and enter Ohio? He'd walked east for days, not west.

Some of his last thoughts before he'd fallen from the cliff returned to him: *Maybe he'd been born during the wrong time. Would Celeste be better off without him? Did he want to be free to go where he wanted? Be who he wanted?*

Nausea rolled and his head throbbed. "What day is this?" *What century?* He feared the answer, but he had to know.

"Bridget?" the man shouted. "That's my wife. My name's Patrick McLaughlin."

A woman walked around from the side of the wagon and peered up, moving alongside it. "Aye?"

Vin recognized her—the same woman from the knoll.

"He's sitting upright, talking reasonable this time. He wants to know what day it is."

Bridget put a foot on a step, grabbed the side of the seat, and pulled herself up. "You've a name?"

"Vin Lantz."

"Why the odd beard, Vin?" Bridget asked. "No mustache to speak of."

He touched his face. He had a few whiskers across the top of his lip, but not much for the days that had passed since he'd shaved. "I'm Amish. It's how we do things."

"Amish, are ye?" Patrick asked. "I woulda thought so by the look of your beard, but I didn't know any Amish had ventured this far west. Seems—"

"I'm Bridget," the woman said. "That's our boy in the back, Brendan. He's sick. Since we brought ye along, I've been hoping ye were . . . able . . . Well, do ye know anything that can help our boy?"

Was that the reason they'd not left him where he'd passed out—they were hoping he could help their child? "Prayer and a doctor. That's everything I know about healing. What's wrong with him?"

"He's burning up and weak. Was heaving up his boots until he couldn't lift his head. I've been hoping all this time ye might be able to help." She leaned forward, peering around Vin to look at her husband. "Anke knows about healing, often more than a doctor does."

Patrick stared straight ahead. "She can heal folks. Few can pray and connect with God like she can."

Should Vin ask who Anke was? Probably best to mind his own business.

For now, he could play along with the impossible scenario his mind had put him in. He was a modern man trying to help a sick child in a covered wagon.

He focused, drawing to him all the wisdom he'd gleaned regarding sickness. The boy was under a bundle of quilts. That was an easy fix. "If he's got a fever, he needs to cool down. That means get those blankets off him and dip a rag in tepid water. Someone will need to rub it over him."

"That's daft," Patrick said. "The boy's cold. He's got chills and goose bumps."

How did this simple piece of information not make sense? How could he convince them?

"Where are ye from, Vin?" Bridget asked.

"Peach Bell, Pennsylvania."

"Peach Bell, Pennsylvania?" Patrick asked. "Never heard of it."

"It's a small town in Lancaster County."

"That's odd. We lived in Lancaster County for years 'cause of connections with my oldest brother's wife. Betwixt that, work, and gettin' ready for this journey, I've been all over Lancaster County more times than I care to think about. Never heard of Peach Bell. Almost everything we own was bought in that county, including this rifle and this wagon."

Patrick shifted the reins, freeing one hand. "Maybe ye know some of the same folks we do in Lancaster township. We stayed with William and Margaret Cooper for quite a while."

"Can't say I know them."

"But ye have heard of them," Patrick said. "Had to. They're prominent folks. Quakers. They built that redbrick mansion on Harvest about ten years ago. It sits on nearly two hundred acres. They helped build a hospital in Philadelphia. Good people. Few people would be willing to do all they do for others. That's for sure."

On Harvest? Vin knew Harvest Road well, and he knew of one outstanding redbrick mansion. His mouth and throat turned to sand. Patrick couldn't mean the estate where the preservation society was housed, could he? Half of it was a museum, and the other half held some sort of government offices. It was over a hundred and fifty years old, not a decade old. He and Celeste had toured the place the first year they were married, taken most of a Saturday to go through the museum. They'd walked the grounds and found several old outbuildings that hadn't been kept up or restored in any way.

The thought returned again—maybe he'd been born during the wrong time. Nausea rolled and his head throbbed.

He shouldn't have mentioned the town or county he was from. What were the odds of meeting up with folks like this and them being so familiar with Lancaster? "I'm sorry."

Patrick narrowed his eyes. "But you're from Lancaster?"

"Jah, from a small town in the southern part of the county."

That was true, and maybe that indirect answer would be acceptable to Patrick. This could still all be a dream, and he was arguing with a part of his own mind.

Patrick didn't respond.

Bridget raised a brow. "Tell us. What are ye doing way out here with nothing to survive on?"

"I don't know. I . . . I fell from a cliff."

"Ye fell?" She scowled. "Ye don't look as if ye could survive tripping over your own feet, let alone falling off a cliff."

He'd once felt powerful, but now he was so weak he could hardly walk, especially with an injured knee, so he couldn't argue her point. "I can't place your accent."

"We're from Ireland," she said. "Patrick's oldest brother, James, came to America first almost a decade ago now. After the war, he made his way to Ohio, and we're headed to his home."

War? Vin had so many questions, but if he asked them, they'd think he wasn't of sound mind. That might cause them to leave him behind.

Bridget shifted in her seat, rubbing her lower back. "James has a cabin and lots of land to work. He sent money for Patrick and his brother Liam to come to America two years back. They got here and moved in with the Coopers, James's wife's relatives. Well, they're sort-of relatives. Ester, that's James's wife, and her sister, Anke, lost their parents to illness about ten years ago, and the Coopers took them in and raised them, so they're not blood. They helped Patrick and Liam get jobs. When Patrick and Liam had enough money saved, they sent for us women and children. The Coopers let all of us move in with them for a while. Me and Liam's wife, Delia, and our children followed this year. Liam's family is in a wagon ahead of us."

Vin nodded. Her family information wouldn't help him—

though their story of immigration from Ireland painted a picture of olden times. Not good. "What day is it?"

She studied him, looking as if something was on her mind. Finally she opened her mouth to speak. "If I've been counting the days right, it's Wednesday, July 17. It could be Thursday, July 18."

That sounded close to what he expected the date to be. He and Celeste had argued the evening of July 11. But what year was it? He pondered Bridget's answer for several minutes, trying to make things add up. He had to be wrong. He *couldn't* be back in time, but what other explanation fit what he was experiencing? "And the year?"

Patrick shifted. "You've been in and outta consciousness for days. When Bridget told me and Liam that a man had passed out, I was tempted to leave ye in case ye were sick. Bridget said ye were addled, not sick. Ye been sick?"

"No. I don't remember the last time I was sick."

"That's not helping ye," Bridget said. "Ye don't seem to remember much of anything since I met ye, including where ye are or even what year."

He shrugged. "It was quite a fall." Apparently a fall from the eastern part of Pennsylvania into Ohio. "The year?"

"Tell me about yer fall," Bridget said.

"She thinks ye may have fallen from heaven." Patrick sighed. "Bridget, if God had given him any power to heal, he'd not have needed days of rest in our wagon."

"Maybe God's testing us, or maybe this is what happens when one falls from heaven."

Her reasoning had more emotion than practical thinking, making her sound as desperate to save her son as Vin felt for God to return him to his wife and sons.

Patrick shrugged. "Our boy will live or die by God's will without the likes of this Vin from Pennsylvania." He stretched his back. "It's 1822."

What? Vin couldn't breathe. He gripped his seat, trying to keep himself from falling over.

1822? How? Why? Was he crazy? *1822?*

He sucked air into his lungs and did the math. He was 163 years in the past?

His heart threatened to stop. If this was happening, if he wasn't in some dream or purgatory, was time moving forward at the same rate for Celeste and his boys?

Again some of his last thoughts came to him, the ones he had right before falling off the cliff: Would he be better off if he was free to go where he wanted? Be who he wanted?

Was he the reason he'd landed here? He'd been reading about Ohio in the 1820s, thinking how amazing it would be to experience this time. Wallowing in inconsiderate thoughts of nonsense and anger, had he somehow willed himself to a different time?

Could he repent and pray and will himself home again? He didn't want to be free of Celeste. He loved her. They were a team. They were best friends. Had he lost her because he was cranky and out of sorts with the restrictions of the Ordnung?

Bridget got off the moving wagon. He should follow. He stepped down and stumbled—with his mind on the situation he'd forgotten about his knee. Bridget caught him.

"Denki."

She sighed and shook her head. He bet he looked useless to her. He steadied himself and released her, limping. But his need was bigger than a minute in the woods for a call of nature—he needed to walk, chew on jerky to regain strength, and pray.

1822?

Back in his own time, had he been so selfish that God decided to put him in this one? If he learned what he needed to and repented, would God have mercy and return him to Celeste and his sons?

Chapter Seven

With the afternoon sun streaming through the overhead skylights, Josiah dipped his foam brush back into the paint tray filled with mahogany-colored wood stain, the sharp smell stinging his nose. But he didn't mind. The aromas and sounds within this shop flooded him with memories. He held the brush the way his father had taught him when he was but a little boy. How would Steven and Drew remember learning skills like this? Their dat should be teaching them.

The door to the shop opened. "Hi." Lois smiled and waved.

"Hey there." He grinned, his heart thumping louder. Focusing on painting would be more difficult now. "Kumm on in." He placed the foam brush on the unfinished table and ran it along the grain. After he finished staining this piece, he was done for the day. "Did we have plans for dinner?"

"Nee." She shrugged. "If we had, you'd be very late because it's almost six. By the time you showered and hitched a buggy, you wouldn't be to my house until seven . . . which is way past supper-time for us."

Without plans, it meant something was on her mind, or else she wouldn't be here. But he knew she liked to think before she spoke, and if he prodded her, she'd grow quieter.

"Well, I'm sure glad to see ya. I'll be done soon, and I know Mamm and Dat would love it if you stayed for supper."

She ambled toward him, looking at the pieces of furniture in their various stages of completion.

His three older brothers had gone to an Englischer home today to install cabinets, and when they were done, they'd go home to their wives and children. His older sisters were married with homes too. Just Josiah and his two younger siblings still lived with their parents, but he wouldn't be there too much longer. He looked forward to getting wed in seven months. His folks were great, but at twenty, he was ready to be married. Then one day soon, he and Lois would get to begin their legacy of children— a thrilling thought.

He dipped the brush again. "How's this year's crop of celery growing?" It was an Amish tradition to serve creamed celery at every wedding, but because Lois's parents wanted her to wait until she turned eighteen to marry, they couldn't marry until late February. So she'd planted a late crop, hoping it'd be ready to harvest before the first frost and could be canned for their winter wedding.

She drew a breath. "Josiah . . ."

He set the brush aside. "Jah, what's on your mind, sweet one?"

She wrapped her index finger around a string from her prayer Kapp. "I've been hearing things about Celeste Lantz."

"Jah, people are saying unkind things, but the gossip will die down."

"My cousin has a friend in Peach Bell, and his sister was walking past their house the night Celeste's husband disappeared, and she heard them arguing something fierce."

"Husbands and wives argue. We've had a couple of arguments ourselves." They might be on their way to another. "Celeste told the bishop about their argument. I'd be yelling, too, if my spouse was hiding forbidden things from me and had been secretly pondering leaving the Amish."

"But those things don't justify harming him."

"Of course not, but she didn't hurt him."

"Open your eyes, Josiah. They argued. He came up missing that same night, and her own father-in-law thinks she did something awful to Vin."

"Then Eli is blind with grief. You saw her. She's broken from the loss."

Lois pursed her lips. "Well, jah. She's upset about what she did."

"Nee. We don't listen to idle gossip nor add to it. I believe they argued, he left to cool off, and something or someone took his life, but it wasn't Celeste."

"Neither of us knew her before her husband went missing. Eli has known her since before she and Vin married. What makes you think you can read her better than he can?"

"Eli isn't seeing straight right now, and fear and anger flow from his mouth. Maybe I'd be committing the same wrongs if I'd lost a son, but he's a persuasive man, and he's using that to turn people against a widow with young children. He'll regret his words one day. So will everyone who is buying his snake oil."

She scrunched her brows. "What makes you so sure?"

He placed his hands on her shoulders, looking deep into her eyes. "Lois, sweetheart, if I'm wrong, then I'm a fool who gave too much in the name of mercy and grace. I'd rather be that fool than refuse to help a woman whose husband got caught breaking the

Ordnung, went out to cool off after the argument, and died before he could get home."

She studied him. "How are you so sure he's dead? Even she doesn't know if he died or if he left her."

His hands moved up the smooth skin of her neck and he rested his thumbs on her cheeks. "I'm not. I just have a strong feeling. It's a shame how it all played out. So much pain over artwork. Impressive artwork to be sure, but still . . ."

"Artwork?" She pulled from him. "It's an abomination!"

"It might be a sin. I don't know."

"Surely you agree that he was keeping secrets from everyone, including his wife. We don't keep secrets."

"Really?" He grinned. "You sure about that? Because I know of a beautiful Amish girl who has her driver's license and she kept it hidden from everyone."

Since she was the girl, he expected her to nod and realize she was being a bit judgmental, but she stiffened. "It's not the same at all."

He shrugged. "Okay." But he knew it was a tad similar. She'd gone through great efforts to earn her license in secret. She and Josiah would make their vows to join the Amish faith late next month—mandatory in order to get married this wedding season— yet she didn't intend to confess it or turn it over. She hadn't told Josiah about it until a few weeks after he asked her to marry him. That might have offended a lot of men, but he admired her courage to get the license *and* to tell him. She'd said she wanted to hold on to it just in case she needed to drive an Englischer car during an emergency someday. He suspected she wanted to keep it because it gave her a little sense of power in a world where submission to a higher authority ruled even the way she parted her hair.

He understood feeling that way. He'd had a few secrets of his own. She knew them, but no one else did. Like all the Amish men before him, he'd toss, give away, or sell his secret stash—a guitar and an old car in a shop downtown that he'd restored—before he made his vows to join the church. Vin's secret was different—the gift of drawing. It wasn't as if he could sell his gift and go on his way like Josiah would sell his guitar and car. Yes, Vin had gone too far using his gift, but why was Lois so harsh in her judgment of him?

She raised her brows at Josiah. "You think I'm wrong to put stock in what I'm being told."

"I do." He winked. "But I love ya just the same."

Maybe he'd find her willingness to believe the worst of Celeste annoying if she were older. But he'd been quick to believe gossip and had made unfair judgments of his own when he was seventeen.

She moved in closer. "She's stunning, and you're going over there every week for the foreseeable future."

"Is she? I give ya my word I hadn't taken notice. I see a broken woman with two little boys to raise on her own and a community who's treating her poorly. I imagined what it would be like if you, my own mamm, or any of my sisters were caught in such a painful situation, and when Dat insisted someone volunteer to help her, I didn't object when my brothers volunteered me."

She tilted her head. "You didn't notice her beauty?"

"I didn't, but I noticed yours the first time I saw you and every time since."

"And you say Eli has a way with words." She chuckled. "I see your points."

"Gut." He kissed her forehead. "Thomas and Bartholomew are going to Celeste's to help me get a handle on the current orders Vin had under contract. You're welcome to go then and more than welcome to go every time. Jah?"

She nodded. "Jah. That's what I'll do. I'll go with you until I can see for myself what kind of woman she is."

"I'm feeling rather good that you're a bit jealous. Maybe I mean more to ya than you let on."

"Maybe." She shrugged. "But I agreed to marry you. What else do you need to convince you?"

He touched his lips. "A kiss would help."

"Jah?" She moved in close.

Chapter Eight

Hours passed, and Vin continued walking beside the wagon. The pain in his knee had eased with the movement, and he'd been able to walk with a near-normal gait, but still, nothing about his being in 1822 made sense.

"We're here!" Patrick hollered.

Another wagon rested under a shade tree, and people seemed to be emptying out the entire thing.

Patrick brought his wagon to a stop. "Ye find fresh water, Liam?"

A thin middle-aged man waved. He was dressed very much like Patrick—brown pants, dirty white shirt, and suspenders. "Not yet. Fergus is out looking now. But according to the map, we should find a good-sized creek by this time tomorrow."

A map? If the map included Pennsylvania, maybe Vin could locate his hometown—or close to it.

Liam lifted a shovel. "There's a snake in the wagon, so we'll be late getting the fire started tonight."

"When ours is going well, I'll bring you some embers," Patrick said.

Liam gave a nod before returning to his task.

Bridget made her way to the other wagon.

Patrick got down, turning to Vin. "There's a lot to do tonight and in the morning. You'll need to either pull your weight or move on."

He needed food. Did he have the strength to prove useful enough to feed? "I'll do my best."

"Good. You know how to start a fire?"

Jah, with matches. Amish used fire all the time, and he'd made them his entire life. But were matches even invented yet?

"I . . . think so." Vin steadied his breathing, trying to calm his pounding heart. *Dear God, please send me back to my wife and children.*

"Ye think?" Patrick sighed, shaking his head. "Usually Bridget gathers kindling and small logs along the trail for the evening and morning fires, but her mind is preoccupied. Filled only with thoughts of our son. Go see her first—" Patrick gestured at Bridget, who was walking from the other wagon toward them with a blanket in hand—"but if she's not prepared to start a fire, go gather dried leaves, small sticks for kindling, and larger pieces for firewood. Get a fire started. While it builds heat for cooking, help Bridget unpack what she needs to get us fed. If you find a creek or spring in the woods while gathering firewood, let us know."

Vin nodded and followed Bridget to the back of the wagon.

She climbed in and knelt beside the boy, putting another blanket on him. "Brendan, we're stopped for the day." She shook him. "Come stretch yer legs."

If she wanted him to get up, why was she covering him with another blanket?

Brendan moaned. The boy's face was no longer red. It was pale as a sheet.

Vin reached in and tugged on a quilt. "He needs the blankets removed. A room temperature bath would help, but you need to force liquids. That's the most important."

Confusion etched across her face. His words . . . would they hold meaning in this time?

Still, she nodded and began peeling the blankets away, but Brendan grabbed them with pale knuckles.

"He's cold." Bridget motioned. "Can't ye see?"

Maybe her mothering heart didn't want to make him suffer if he might die either way. But Vin had to try. "My advice may not save him, but listening to me is your best chance."

"Ye sure?"

Vin nodded, though he didn't feel sure. He motioned for her to move forward and he climbed into the wagon. "Let's get him somewhere cooler than this tent in July." Vin pulled the blankets off the boy, ignoring Brendan's faint complaints. The boy had little fight or color left in him. "You got water?"

"Yeah. It's in barrels, and ye can have all of it if it'll save my boy, but if we use it all, then the animals won't have the strength to pull the wagon tomorrow."

"Good to know. Let's begin with a bowl or half pail of water." He picked up the boy, and pain shot through Vin's knee. Ignoring it, he climbed out of the wagon.

Bridget followed, bringing a blanket.

"Put it under the shade tree." Vin gestured at the area.

She did, and Vin laid Brendan on it. While Vin peeled Brendan out of his clothes, Bridget fetched a cloth and water.

Vin dipped the cloth into the half-filled pail. "Wring the cloth out a bit." He lifted the rag from the pail and demonstrated. "Squeeze the rag over the pail to save water but leave plenty of liquid on the cloth. Then gently brush the rag over his skin."

When the water touched Brendan's skin, he roused, moaning in displeasure and trying to push Vin's hand away. The boy seemed as strong as a newborn kitten. Could he make it through the night?

Vin continued wiping a cloth across Brendan's bare stomach. "You can talk or sing to him, but even if he complains, don't stop."

If the boy died while his mother ignored his moans to stop, would she blame Vin?

She nodded.

Vin left Brendan with his mamm and did as Patrick had told him. Everyone else stayed busy trying to get food ready and the animals tended to, but Vin met Patrick's family from the other wagon—Liam, Delia, and their four children, Fergus, Cormac, Nora, and Sibby. Liam said Brendan was Patrick and Bridget's last surviving child. Their youngest died on the way to America, and the oldest died a year ago while working to construct locks and dams on the Conestoga River from the Susquehanna.

His heart hurt . . . their third child was gravely ill after they lost two others. How did Patrick and Bridget manage to keep pushing forward every day?

All Vin could do was help out as best he could, while he begged God to send him back to his wife and children. Toting water from the barrels for the animals was tough with a hurt knee, and he longed for something as simple as Bayer aspirin or Tylenol. He was unsuccessful at starting a fire with flint. Liam had his fire going first, but he'd brought embers in an iron pot to Vin. These simple tasks—at home they'd be easy, but here they seemed impossible. Finding the faith to pray was even harder.

Were Celeste and his boys frozen in time, waiting on him to

return? That didn't make sense, not that anything else did either. When he was at work or asleep, life moved on normally for his family. He had to assume this worked the same way, and that meant for Celeste, Vin had been gone for about a week. *Dear God, I have to get back to them. Please show me how.*

Once the livestock was tended to and the fire was hot, Bridget cooked a meal and Vin continuously ran damp cloths over Brendan's motionless body. If he could just get Brendan to drink some water . . . A syringe would make it easier. He could fill it with water, put it at the back of Brendan's mouth, and slowly release it. That's what Celeste did when their boys needed fluid but were too sleepy or groggy to drink.

Nothing about this kind of living was easy. He'd thought the Old Order Amish way was hard, and it was, compared to how the Englisch lived, but the modern Amish had certain comforts—like matches and syringes. How had Vin landed here? He didn't know, but he missed Celeste, Steven, and Drew every moment. And goodness, he also missed his bed, having a shower, and opening a refrigerator to get whatever he wanted. If only he had a medicine cabinet with fever-reducing pills for this child—or a phone shanty to call the doctor's office. A medical professional could save him.

Each woman cooked supper on a metal grate over the open fires. Everyone sat on blankets or logs not too far from where Brendan was sleeping. They seemed grateful for a moment of rest and something to eat. Food had never tasted so good. Bacon, beans, rice, and a biscuit. After the meal, everyone had different chores to finish.

When the work was done for the day, Vin spread a blanket about twenty feet from Brendan and his parents. Dusk had settled over them, and he guessed it must've been around eight thirty. He stared into the sky. The clouds were shades of deep pink and purple. Neither stars nor the moon were visible. Still, their beauty and vastness awed him—things he'd never understand.

"Gott, You set the moon and stars. Just like my wife and sons, the sun, moon, and stars are there but I can't see them or get to them. Help me get home. Please. I just want to get to my Celeste and my young sons."

He prayed as his eyelids grew heavy, longing to find himself back with his beloved Celeste and their precious sons. If desire alone could make a thing happen, he'd wake at home.

❧

JULY 1985

Celeste stood barefoot inside her dark house, dressed in her nightgown, sweat dripping down her back. The clock on the wall ticked; crickets outside chirped. Tonight felt exactly like the night when Vin walked out. Only it felt eerie. The house seemed empty of joy and full of mockery. How had she not known her own husband?

"Dear Gott . . ." She tried to think clearly enough to pray, but her thoughts seemed lost inside all her emotions.

"Dat!" Steven screamed.

She heard his little feet pattering through the house, sounding as if he was running as fast as he could.

Dat! Wo bischt du?

Again. Her heart moved to her throat, but she hurried through the dark toward her son. He woke several times a night, screaming for his father, asking, *Where are you?*

She bit back tears and scooped him up. *"Ich bin do, Steven."*

I am here.

He slapped at her and pushed her away. "Nee! Dat!" He screamed down the hall, trying to run toward someone who was no longer there.

"Shh. Mei Bobbeli. Es iss allrecht."

He didn't relax even a little when she'd said, *My baby. It is all right.* When he woke like this, he was inconsolable.

"Nee!" He took her face into his hands, staring at her. *"Ich brauchen mei dat! Bitte, Mamm, bitte."*

He was begging her, repeating *please* again and again. She melted to the floor. "I need him too." She pulled him into her arms, never knowing what to tell him.

If she knew whether Vin was missing or dead, it would help her at least know which piece of information to try to form into something a four-year-old could understand. Should she say he was lost? That would sound terrifying to a child, to know an adult could leave and get so lost they couldn't find their way home. Would saying his dat was dead be of any comfort? What if Vin then showed up in a month or a year or a decade?

"Shh, mei Sohn." She held him firmly, trying to wrap him in enough love that he could feel safe and fall back to sleep. "Shh. Shh. Shh." She hummed a tune they often sang in church, hoping he'd find comfort in it.

Steven stopped fighting her. *"Ich brauchen mei dat, Mamm."*

"Ich verschteh." I understand.

"Ich du duh net verschteh." He rubbed his eyes, looking sleepy.

He didn't understand. That's what he'd said, and she felt that same torment.

"I know." She brushed his damp, sweaty hair from his forehead and kissed it.

She had to tell Steven something that helped him. "Steven," she whispered. *"Die dat iss tot."*

Your dat is dead.

As awful as that information was, it would be the only explanation that would make sense to him. Steven didn't respond. She shifted him, looking in his face. He was asleep. Many times, when he got like this, she wasn't sure he'd even been awake.

She held him tight, rocking back and forth from her spot on the floor. "Vin, where are you? How could you do this to your sons?"

She blew a stream of air from her lips like she did when in hard labor and got up, still holding Steven. She moved through the dark, quiet space she used to call home and put her son back in his bed, knowing his cries and running through the house looking for his father would all begin again before morning arrived.

Chapter Nine

JULY 1822

Vin startled awake, sitting upright like a bolt of lightning. Where was he? It was hard to tell in the dark, but there was a blanket spread on the ground under him. *Ach.* He must've fallen asleep while on Kissin' Mountain! Such strange dreams he'd had.

"Vin," a woman called, startling him anew.

Had Celeste found him on the mountain?

He jumped up, longing to apologize and hold her and start anew. "Celeste?"

He blinked, trying to understand. The starry night was dark, with no moonlight to help him see anything, but he made out oxen. A wagon. A low-burning campfire. Was he still dreaming?

"Vin," she called again.

He looked around and saw a woman who wasn't Celeste near the trunk of a tree. A wave of grief hit. He wasn't waking on Kissin'

Mountain mere miles from home. He wasn't in rural Lancaster County or in Pennsylvania, even. He was somewhere in Ohio in 1822.

The reality of it made his head swim and his stomach churn. Vin put his hands on his knees and his right one screamed at him. *Dear God, whatever I've done that You sent me here, have mercy, teach me my lesson, and please, send me home again.* He prayed silently while breathing deep for a moment. A fresh longing to get home hit hard. In this moment, he knew, despite the obstacles, *that's* where he needed to be—Lancaster County, Pennsylvania. Peach Bell might not exist yet, but he yearned to be where his wife and sons lived, even though more than one and a half centuries lay between them. How could he get there? He was physically weak. How would he traverse nearly five hundred miles across primitive America?

He didn't know, but evidently other people did it. Patrick and his family were proof. Vin stood, moving as slowly as an old man. His knee was stiff and painful again, despite almost feeling normal during part of yesterday. He hobbled to Bridget and Patrick. The night sky now had a hint of color to it—a dark purple—and Vin knew it meant the first rays of daylight were minutes away.

"I . . . I think Brendan is better." Bridget gazed up at Vin, and despite the darkness, he saw pleading in her eyes. "He woke for a moment."

"Aye." Patrick gestured at his son. "He spoke to us, asking for his clothes."

Vin had agreed to putting a lightweight blanket over Brendan last night. He knelt and put a hand on the boy's forehead. "He's a lot cooler. That's good." Vin pinched the skin on Brendan's knuckle. It didn't pop back quickly as it would on someone well hydrated, but it responded better than yesterday. It was muggy and hot, even for this time of day, but . . . "He can change the blanket for a shirt and pants. A bit of a fever can be useful, and there's no need to try to avoid it. But whenever he wakes, we must use that time to get water or broth in him."

"I have fish broth," Bridget said. "He doesn't like it heated, so it's ready whenever he is."

Wait. Something sounded wrong. "There's no body of water near us. How do you have fish broth?"

Patrick chuckled. "Brendan's a fisherman, and he caught fish a couple of days ago, before he got sick."

"How do you store it?"

"In the small kettle in the wagon," Bridget said. "I saved it for him, and I checked it earlier. It's not spoiled yet."

Vin weighed his thoughts. Didn't cholera hit Ohio hard in the mid-1800s? It was a food- and waterborne illness. Could that be what was happening here? What was the difference between cholera and food poisoning? A memory flitted to the surface—cholera was severe, and it went through entire towns like an epidemic. This had to be food poisoning. But it sounded like they didn't know enough about food safety and hand cleanliness. These parents didn't need guilt added to their boy's illness, but . . . "I wouldn't eat anything cooked with fresh meat after a few hours."

"That's daft." She tsked. "We have bacon. Ye ate it for supper."

"Jah, but it's salted, cured, and you cooked it for several minutes after it started sizzling. But if you make a broth with fish or even bacon, the liquid can spoil before it smells ruined." Was that saying too much? "I know a bit about such things, and I can write it down for you."

Patrick scoffed. "Write it with what? Did ye bring paper and pen with ye when ye fell from the sky? Besides that, we can't read."

Vin studied the ground, embarrassed at how naive he was. Patrick and Bridget had come from a poor country to America in the early 1800s. Why had he assumed they could read?

Dear God, I forgot all I had to be thankful for. I was so focused on what I wasn't allowed to do, I forgot what a gift my life was. Did his difficult, ungrateful attitude land him here? Or were the two things unrelated?

Brendan moaned. "Da."

Patrick moved in closer. "I'm here, Son."

"I'm thirsty."

"Thirsty, are ye?" Patrick grinned. "Aye." He dipped a cup into the pail—the same one they'd used to cool the boy's body.

"Nee!" Vin barely stopped himself from knocking the cup from Patrick's hands. He drew a breath. "Not that water. Bridget boiled water last night and set it a few feet from the fire to cool. He needs that and only that."

Patrick nodded and headed toward the campfire.

Vin removed his hat and scratched his head. "Bridget, throw the kettle of fish soup out. Like I said earlier, you have to either consume broth shortly after making it or toss it. I know you've done it your way without trouble many times, but unsafe food can kill people. I know this sounds odd, but can you trust me?"

Bridget touched Brendan's face and smiled. "I trust ye."

"Gut. We need to talk more, but I need to stoke the fire and gather more wood first."

Patrick returned with a cup of clean water.

"Just a few sips at a time," Vin said. "Too much can make him sick to his stomach again."

Patrick helped his son sit up. "Vin, ye take the rifle this morning. We're low on food. If ye see a rabbit or squirrel, kill it for supper."

They trusted him more today. Good. He needed this family, at least until he could get his feet under him and learn how to survive here. Once at the wagon, he grabbed the hatchet, the canvas pouch for kindling, and the rifle. He limped into the woods. At least his knee injury didn't render him useless. At its worst, it didn't bend well and it hurt, but he could walk.

Stepping over fallen trees, even small ones, was challenging. He wanted to return to a rotted log and use the hatchet on it and gather kindling for tonight's fire. He'd failed at starting a fire last night, but tonight would be different. Until he was capable of surviving on his own, he had to prove himself worthy of staying with Patrick. A few days or a week could give his mind and emotions time to accept this new reality and let him get his bearings.

But he'd also need money—a way to purchase his own gun, knife, and horse. With his knee the way it was, he couldn't travel far on hard trails, over mountains, or across creeks and rivers. He might need a month to heal, but he hoped not.

Focus on today.

Could he save the embers from this morning's fire in an iron pot in the wagon to start a fire tonight, or would it catch the wagon on fire?

Movement caught his eye. Then, out of nowhere, he stood face-to-face with a Black man. Vin choked on nothing and coughed. The man fell backward, scrambling away, his eyes on the barrel of Vin's gun. Vin realized the barrel was pointed at the man. He pointed it skyward. The man, maybe thirty-five, had mere rags for his shirt and short pants. His feet were bare, and his ankles appeared chewed up by a dog . . . or something.

Vin held up one hand. "I'm sorry. I mean ya no harm." His heart raced, but he lowered his hand, offering to help the man stand.

The man didn't take it. He moved to his feet, staring at Vin. "You happen to know what state we're in now?"

Wait. This man's voice . . . he knew it. "George?" From the time they met in thick darkness, Vin had an image of George in his mind's eye, a godlike being—strong, the best clothes and boots money could buy, a man so powerful he could do anything he set his will to. But this man in tattered clothes and torn skin around his ankles didn't fit that idea. What had caused that injury to the man's ankles? Vin's mind ran fast. Slavery was legal in 1822. What horrors had George and Tandey faced before landing here?

"That's me," George said.

Concern over the man's son weighed heavy. It was a brutal land to survive. "Where's Tandey? Is he all right?"

"He is." George looked behind Vin. "Come on out, Tandey. It ain't nobody but Vin. You remember him."

A rustling noise came from somewhere, and Vin hobbled to one side, catching a glimpse of an arm from behind a tree before it disappeared. "Hi, Tandey." Maybe Vin looked more intimidating standing up. Plus, he had a rifle this time. "You've nothing to be afraid of from me." But if they needed help like Vin had needed from them days ago, he had nothing to offer. Did he have the right to even invite them back to the wagon for a meal? It wasn't his wagon or his food.

Tandey looked about twelve years old. He took his time ambling toward them, looking as if he had something slung over one shoulder behind him.

Vin turned back to George. It dawned on Vin what was wrong with the man's ankles—he'd been in chains, and it'd cost him skin to get them off. He imagined the scabs got pulled off daily as they trekked toward freedom. George needed the wounds cleaned and bandaged before infection set in . . . if it hadn't already.

"I woke up in a wagon yesterday. Apparently I'd passed out and those good folks took me with them. They said this is Ohio."

"We made to Ohio, Son. We made it to freedom." George nodded, looking reflective. "I guess one of the rivers we crossed was the Ohio River. I was hoping so."

Tandey grinned. His clothes were in a little better shape than George's, and he didn't have scabs or scars or open wounds on his ankles like his dat did. "You for us or against us now that you with other white folks?"

The boy's words hit so hard Vin couldn't speak for a moment. "Am I against you? Never. Slavery is wrong. It's wicked. And . . . and if you'll have me, we're friends. Add to all of that, I owe you and your dat. You saved my life."

George's body relaxed, and the boy grinned. Vin could only assume slaves were used to being used—helping a white person when needed and then being tossed aside or set against.

"You one of them runaway indentured servants?" George asked.

Indentured servant? Wait, he'd read this once in a history book. An indentured servant wasn't much better off than a slave, except they could earn their freedom after five to seven years. "No. I recently lost everything." That was an understatement, and the heartache of it threatened to steal Vin's footing.

"Vin, we need to look at a map," George said. "We're tryin' to get to Medina. It's supposed to be a safe place for people like us. Rumors said there are people there who'll help us build a new life. We know it's north, but that's all we know. Do those folks in the wagon have maps?"

"Jah. I haven't seen them, but I heard them talking about their maps."

"Can you read the names of the towns for us?"

"Sure can."

Tandey pulled on what looked like handmade rope, lifting what was flung behind his shoulders: two squirrels. "We'll trade fresh squirrels for a good look at a map. Killed 'em this mornin'."

"How did you kill squirrels?" Vin asked.

"Snared them." Tandey held out a thin rope woven out of grass.

Vin needed to know what these two knew about survival, and they needed a few doors opened for them . . . and to learn to read. "Let's go see the McLaughlins."

Would Patrick and Bridget let these men have Vin's breakfast? They'd been kind, so perhaps they would. As they walked toward the camp, doubts nagged at Vin. He hadn't gotten kindling or wood. His guests had small game, but Vin had nothing to do with that success. He wasn't carrying his fair share of the work. The smell of food was strong now, and his mouth watered. "Hello?" he called out while approaching the camp, hoping to not catch anyone off guard by having strangers with him.

Patrick rounded the side of the wagon and halted. His eyes moved up and down, sizing up George.

"This is George—" Vin gestured—"and his boy Tandey. I ran into them a few days back, and they saved my life. They got two squirrels, hoping to barter those for a good look at your maps."

Patrick stared at the Black man. He shook his head. "Liam." He spoke calmly, looking toward his brother's campsite. "Could ye walk this way? Gonna need yer thoughts."

Bridget came from the far side of the wagon, and soon Liam joined them, his rifle resting easy in his hands.

Patrick repeated what Vin had said—their names and their current condition. "Ye think these men are part of what James wrote to us about?"

Vin wanted to know what James had written. But if they couldn't read, how did they know what James wrote? Now wasn't the time to ask.

"Maybe," Liam said. "What I know for sure is we have an epidemic of men crossing our paths who have need for food and shelter." His words were flat as if he was deciding what to do.

"We're not asking for food or shelter," George said. "We need to study your map of Ohio. And we brought two squirrels in exchange for it."

Liam shook his head. "If slave catchers are after ye, being in the free state of Ohio won't save ye."

"Slave catchers?" Vin couldn't believe his ears. He knew the history . . . sort of. His knowledge only equaled a drop in an ocean. But seeing this firsthand felt every bit as crazy as falling from a cliff and landing in a different time.

"Yes, sir. We know," George said.

"I don't know," Vin said.

Liam rested the barrel of his rifle against his shoulder. "It's against the law in this state for us to help runaways. If patrollers come while they're with us—"

Patrollers? "Wait." Vin held up his hand. Were they familiar with the stop hand signal? "Patrollers?"

"Aye." Patrick's eyes were wide. "Slave catchers and patrollers are the same. Armed men that hunt down slaves. They have the legal rights to hunt runaways, and if we do anything to help, we could go to jail . . . or be hung."

"Hold on." Vin looked from one McLaughlin brother to the other. "Just wait." Was he about to risk his fragile standing with this family? Fear blocked his throat, making it difficult to breathe and talk. Could the McLaughlins be mistaken about the law? Since they couldn't read, maybe someone had told them an inaccurate version. Those couldn't be the laws in his home state of Pennsylvania—not in any time in history. He'd read about it.

"Besides—" Liam shifted his gun and took a step back—"the Bible allows for slaves."

Vin had to speak. "Look, this father and son need thirty minutes of your help, maybe less."

"You got mud in your ears?" Liam asked. "If we help them in any way and it comes to light, those patrollers will hunt us down and burn our homes." He sighed. "Are you blind too? Look at them. George can't stop shifting from one foot to the other with his ankles all torn up. They're both exhausted. They may be asking to look at maps, but they need far more than that. Everyone standing here knows it except you, Vin."

Was that true about the patrollers hunting down the McLaughlins? Besides that, how would patrollers learn of such help? But people survived by listening to their fears, and fear had a grip on Liam right now.

Vin hoped to steer his fear in the right direction. "We're all God-fearing people here, and He commanded us to love others as ourselves. I've been guilty plenty of times of breaking the Golden Rule." Did they know that term in this era? Their eyes and body language said they understood it. "But I know that there's no slave owner who would want to be enslaved. Our Messiah, the very Lord we pray to, is a Savior to *all* of us, and He was clear on how we're to treat one another. That truth is abundant in Christ's life and teachings."

Liam looked at Patrick. "He sounds just like the Coopers and Anke. I expected it from the Coopers because they're Quakers, but then Anke and now Vin? Maybe it's the way those Lancaster folks think."

Patrick pursed his lips, studying Vin. "Aye."

Vin looked from one brother to another. "Maybe Anke was onto something."

"Onto something?" Patrick's face scrunched. "What does that mean?"

Vin had to do a better job avoiding modern slang. "Maybe she understood Christ's meaning. William Penn founded Pennsylvania so that men and women were free to follow their inner light. He welcomed those fleeing religious persecution, all of them: Quakers, Huguenots, Mennonites, Amish, Lutherans, Baptists, Methodists. He gave people safety from unjust laws that tried to limit what they could believe and how they were to worship. Was he wrong?"

Bridget drew a breath. "'If thou wouldst rule well, thou must rule for God, and to do that, thou must be ruled by Him . . . Those who will not be governed by God will be ruled by tyrants.' That's what William Penn said."

Vin blinked. "I didn't know that quote."

"We all do." Patrick nodded. "William Cooper repeated that before every meal."

Liam clicked his tongue and sighed. "We can't stand here all morning, discussing this. There's work to do, and I'm heading out. I intend to stay ahead of trouble." He walked toward his wagon.

What did that mean? Were George, Tandey, and Vin now on their own, no shelter or weapons or tools? These two runaways might fare a little better, be a bit safer, with an injured white man traveling with them. Vin wouldn't survive on his own, but they knew how to survive, and Vin could walk into a town without all eyes turning, without causing a whisper that might reach the ears of patrollers. But he'd slow them down, so there was that part of it to consider.

Patrick scowled. "I sent ye out to provide for our needs, and ye came back with danger. If this is how ye do yer work, ye might be more trouble than ye are worth."

Vin swallowed hard. "You're turning us away, then?"

Bridget moved in closer to her husband. "Our son was at death's door—we saw the signs of it." Her voice broke. "Vin's daft thinking wasn't daft. He dared to speak against me, dared to anger us, and because of that, our son lives. We owe him, and he's in no condition to take off with these runaways."

Was she right? Even with George and Tandey helping him, was Vin unable to survive without a horse or wagon carrying him?

Bridget held out her hand toward Tandey. He passed her the squirrels.

"I'll clean these and cook 'em to be eaten before heading out this morning." She gestured toward the campfire. "But to get you started, I got some beans, biscuits, and bacon ye can have."

It seemed she'd spoken her piece and was leaving the rest in Patrick's hands.

George and Tandey went to the campfire. Vin, Patrick, and Bridget stayed put. Vin imagined Brendan was fast asleep on the blanket under the tree, too weak to do anything but sleep and wake long enough to drink water.

Patrick removed his hat and scratched his head. "James wrote something about Black people."

Was now the time to ask? "How do you know what he wrote?"

"Ye just go to the nearest church. Preachers can read, and they're trustworthy to say what's in a letter no matter how bad the news. I just didn't quite understand what the preacher read about escaped slaves, and I didn't want to ask him to read it again."

"Do you still have the letter?" He regretted his question. What if the letter said to do nothing to help runaway slaves?

Patrick shook his head. "Nay. The preacher asked to hold on to the letters he read for us, something about record keeping. James will have to tell us what he wrote about when we see him."

"Until then?"

Patrick studied the trodden path behind them. "Liam is right. Those men are exhausted and need a few days of our help more than they need to read our maps. We shouldn't run across anybody else between here and where we're going, but ye put the small one in the back of the wagon to keep a sharp lookout on the woods and the path behind us for any signs of trackers. I think James will know where they can go for safety, and we'll be there in a few days."

Relief coursed through Vin. "I can't tell you how much I appreciate what you're doing."

He nodded. "We get the three of ye to James's, and that pays our debt to ye. Ye understand?"

"Jah." Although he didn't fully understand. Were they thinking once they were at James's place that Vin would be healed enough to head out with George and Tandey? Or was Patrick just clarifying that once at his brother's farm, James would do the deciding without aid or intervention by Patrick or Bridget? "But one more thing, please. The man's ankles need tending. I'll also need some clean cloth, water, and whiskey if ya got some."

"We have some. Bridget can help ye."

"And Liam?"

"I know my brother, and he will go on ahead, separating himself from us in case there's trouble. This is my wagon, and I get to have the last word on who we take or leave behind. James will have the final word once we're on his land. That's all I know for now."

The kindness made Vin's eyes water. This ensured he had a way to survive while he prayed ceaselessly for God to send him home.

"Go eat." Patrick gestured toward the campfire. "Do you know how to gut and skin squirrel?"

Vin did. His dat had taught him. "Jah."

"When that's done, help clean up and pack the wagon. We got a lot of land to cover and many mouths to feed before the day is through."

Vin limped toward George and Tandey. "Patrick and Bridget said that both of you can travel with them, with us, share their food and bedding until we get to his brother's place. Is that what you want to do?"

George's eyes grew wide before he glanced at his son. Tandey nodded and wiped the back of his hand across his watery eyes.

"Yes," George whispered, seeming unable to say more.

"Good." Vin pointed to George's ankles. "And we'll get you mending too."

What would become of them once James had his say? If James sent them all away before Vin's knee or George's ankles healed, could they make it to the nearest town? How far away was that? And if they made it to a town, what would that do for them? They had no money and as far as Vin knew, they had no way of making money. Still, all three of them needed to get to Pennsylvania—the two because Pennsylvania law didn't allow runaways to be caught and returned to their owners. Slave catchers could still drag them back, but not legally, and that made a huge difference. As for Vin, his instinct said his best chance of understanding why he was here and how to get home was to be in Peach Bell, or whatever name it currently went by.

Vin had never imagined encountering such vulnerabilities in life . . . or such kindness from strangers. He'd never considered sacrificing his own food to feed someone else. What kind of a man was he, really?

If it be Your will, God, I beg of You to have mercy on me and send me back to Celeste, Steven, and Drew. I'll put effort into being a better person. Until then, may I use my time as You desire.

Chapter Ten

Celeste tugged on the reins, bringing the rig to a halt in Vin's parents' driveway. She needed childcare today—someone the boys loved and trusted. She'd called Eli's phone shanty numerous times before he answered. When she asked, he said they'd keep the boys, but only because Naomi needed to see them so badly.

Sugar Bear stopped, and Celeste set the brake on the buggy that the bishop had loaned her. She recalled putting her sons in the rig, but she didn't remember driving here. Or fixing breakfast or getting dressed. She ran her hands down the front of her black dress and apron and over her head. Jah, she'd dressed herself. Life came in patchwork pieces strewn across the day like fallen leaves across a windy yard.

A reel mower sat in the grassy front yard. How many times had Vin used that mower as a child?

83

The front door of Vin's childhood home opened, and his parents came outside. She fought tears as she got out of the carriage. "Hallo."

Naomi offered a smile as she hurried toward the rig to get her grandsons. Eli's face seemed carved of stone. Celeste unbuckled Drew from his infant seat, and Naomi held out her hands, smiling at him. He climbed into her arms. Naomi held out a hand to Steven, but he shook his head.

Naomi carried Drew toward the house, stopping a few feet from the porch. Steven hopped from the buggy and grabbed on to his mamm's dress.

Eli said nothing to Celeste or his grandson. She didn't want to be here—she didn't want to be out of bed. It'd only been two weeks since she and Vin argued and he disappeared. Two weeks. Every part of her wanted to wait. Wait a month. Wait a year. Wait a decade before she had to muster the strength to keep moving. But the bishop had arranged for her to meet Josiah Engle and his brothers at the woodshop today. He'd apologized for the quickness of it but assured her it was necessary. What was the old saying, beggars can't be choosers?

She was a beggar.

She'd always thought Vin's family, which was most of their district, and the rest of the community would support her no matter what. How many things could one person be so very wrong about?

Drew's perfect giggle rang through the air, lifting Celeste's bruised heart a tiny amount, the way the late-summer breeze barely stirred the oppressive heat. Naomi held him high, making faces before wrapping him in her arms.

Eli crossed his arms, studying the baby in Naomi's arms. He missed his son. No doubt.

Celeste's suffocating heartbreak could be lighter if she knew what to grieve. Was Vin dead and therefore he couldn't return? Or had he purposefully abandoned her to this misery? She couldn't wrap her head around it. Was Vin the type of person who would choose to leave her and their sons to fend for themselves while he sketched whatever his heart desired? His absence was overwhelming, and each possible reason for it held its own set of agonies, but worse was not knowing. It might drive her mad.

"You should be on your way." Eli's tone was even.

He had dark circles under his eyes. She wasn't the only one not sleeping or the only one ripped to shreds by grief, confusion, embarrassment, guilt, and shame. She'd never be free of missing Vin—all she could do was accept it. She couldn't make him come back, and she'd never get any closure. The last time she went to the police station a few days ago, desperate for some nugget of hope, a detective had shared the grim stats of situations like Vin's.

"Celeste?" Eli called to her, almost sounding as if he cared.

She blinked, wondering how long she'd spaced out, lost inside herself. "I . . . I need to head out. I'll be back by seven tonight. And it's all right if Drew falls asleep for the night before then. Naomi knows what to do."

Eli scoffed. "Of course she does. She's been a mother for longer than you've been alive."

This man would find fault in anything she said. "Denki for having them over and feeding them."

Eli sighed. "*They* are always welcome. Since you seem concerned for their well-being, which I assume means their reputations, attached to yours, I have to ask: will there be proper chaperoning when this young man comes to your home?"

"Jah. Josiah's fiancée, Lois, will be there, as well as two of his older brothers. And going forward, at least one other person will come with him when he assists me."

"It makes no sense for Josiah to come from the city of Lancaster to here. Those twenty-five miles will cost him a lot of money to hire a driver each way, and he can't use a horse and buggy. There's no train or bus between here and there."

She held her tongue rather than suggesting that Eli could help her instead of Josiah. He wasn't nearly as skilled as Vin, but he'd taught his son woodworking. There were a few other woodworking families in the district, but no one had volunteered. Both Celeste and Eli knew why.

She swatted at a nearby gnat. "I agree the cost is high, going back and forth from Peach Bell to Lancaster. But I can't fill any of the orders without help or without someone teaching me, and the Engle family volunteered. No one is trying to be underhanded or lack propriety. I don't expect you to like me, but for your grandsons' sakes, I ask you to treat me with the same respect you would any other church member in good standing."

Eli gestured as if trying to shoo her away. "Here I am, doing you a favor of watching your children, and you'd accuse me of disrespect. I'm only looking out for my grandsons!"

Right. It was clear. This man had never liked her, but she'd avoided his wrath before this. Apparently she'd never stepped out of line. What must it have been like for Vin, growing up in this hard-hearted man's house?

"Again, denki for watching them. I'll return around seven."

Celeste knelt next to Steven and kissed him on the forehead. She murmured reassurances in Pennsylvania Dutch, confirming to him she'd be back soon, that his *grossmammi* had missed playing with him, and how he was going to have fun with her. Steven had been Celeste's little shadow since Vin left. She understood—but it made it all the harder. She had to stay strong. If she broke down in front of the little guy, it'd disrupt his world even more.

It was near impossible to give the boy any answers about where his dat was. If Vin were dead, the church could have a service and give his grieving son a bit of understanding and closure. As it was, she had to settle for stumbling over her words, telling Steven how much his dat loved him. She explained how his dat had gone for a ride and didn't come home. The community had come together and looked everywhere for him, but no one could find him. What a heartbreaking, unsettling answer for a small boy.

She led Steven to Naomi and Drew and bade them all goodbye.

Celeste got in the rig, grateful the bishop had loaned one to her. She'd have to buy one of her own as soon as she could, but the rent money on their home was due soon, and that was foremost in her mind. The minutes rushed by, and soon she was standing in the shop waiting for Josiah and his group. The 650-square-foot room smelled of sawdust and paint. Vin had lined two of the walls with shelves that mostly held raw wood. There were different stations throughout the room to accommodate making different types of furniture; each held a type of table saw and its stand. The saws ran off of air pressure, which was powered by a diesel engine that sat out back of the shop.

The shop . . . she used to love it. It'd brought her and Vin closer, or so she thought, and gave them time together to accomplish a common goal. How was she supposed to keep it going without him?

Do I have a choice? She didn't. This business was already profitable. If she searched for something else that could make money, it'd take months to build. Or longer. And any other business wouldn't allow her to give Steven and Drew something important from their father—Vin's trade. Her sons needed that much. Maybe he'd left her in the cold, not caring if she spent the rest of her life wondering who she was, who she'd been to him, and who they'd been together. But she wouldn't let their sons struggle under the weight of that kind of confusion and pain. If she could learn enough to hold on to the shop, and learn enough to pass it to her sons, they would feel whole. As much as they could without their father.

It was the Amish way for boys to learn their father's trade and to feel connected to themselves, their ancestral past, and their hopeful future through the work and the time spent next to their father. Other Amish boys throughout Lancaster County had that from their families, and she'd do the same for her boys . . . no matter how hard or embarrassing the journey would be.

Someone tapped on the shop door, and Celeste opened it.

"Good morning!" Josiah greeted her with a smile. His blond hair peeked out from under his straw hat. "You remember Lois."

"Hi." Lois waved from behind him.

He turned and motioned. "These guys are my two oldest brothers Thomas and Bartholomew."

Josiah's brothers appeared to be in their mid- to late twenties. Then again, Josiah looked fifteen to her. Whatever their age, she deeply appreciated their time and help.

"Hallo." Celeste took a step back. "*Kumm rei.* This is the shop."

All four of them entered, and Celeste took a few minutes to show them around. She pointed out all the tools, the plans, and the projects Vin had begun before he disappeared. As she looked at them all, she felt like a millstone on her heart was dragging her deeper and deeper underwater. How was she to complete any of these? She wasn't the artisan—Vin was! She was just the assistant. The helper. That was always the plan: she helped Vin in the shop, but her primary purpose was raising their precious children while waiting to be blessed with more. That's how it was *supposed* to be. And now she had to learn how to do everything on her own.

Thomas thumbed through the work orders on Vin's desk. "We were talking on the way over—" he gestured at his younger brothers—"and I think we can complete the kitchen cabinet projects at our shop. You can't do them on your own or put them up in the homes, and we can't spend that much time here."

"You'll take over those contracts?" What a relief. She'd been dreading calling those who were depending on Vin and explaining why she had to break their agreements.

"Jah, we can take those contracts, but we'll split the money in a fair way. Don't worry." Thomas nodded at Josiah.

"Oh, jah, I'll help one or two days a week, Friday or Saturday or both, for three months. During that time, we'll figure out projects that you can build without help. You can sell some of the other contracts to us or to another shop closer to the clients. Uncle Mark already told me you were insistent that you didn't want charity. We understand and respect that, but we're all glad to help you out."

He looked like a teen but talked like a businessman. Josiah was so smooth that he sounded as if he'd been told what to say and practiced it, but perhaps he hadn't. Most Amish boys graduated at thirteen or fourteen, and like them, Josiah had been working next to his dat and older brothers full-time since then.

Celeste hoped her words were as helpful and courteous as theirs. "You're doing plenty just coming here and helping me figure this stuff out. Please, regarding the contracts I keep, we'll split the money for those as well."

Josiah nodded. "We'll see. We can't let you lose money. Dat would kill us, and that's just so not Amish."

His humor caught her off guard, and she chuckled. Her laugh sounded strange to her and out of place since Vin left.

Lois laughed too, smiling at Josiah.

Thomas grinned. "Josiah is a bit of a mess. You'll either kick him out or enjoy him. There's no middle ground where he's concerned."

Thomas passed Josiah one of the work orders he'd gotten off the desk. Vin's handwriting.

"This still needs work, but according to the orders, it was due a week ago."

Bartholomew was looking at two half-completed items: a pie safe and a Hoosier cabinet. An Englisch family had ordered them for a mother-in-law suite they were building behind the main house. What if she couldn't do justice to the project? What if there was nothing she could build without Vin?

The moment of lightheartedness Josiah had stirred was long gone. Celeste sighed. She leaned, palms down, on the messy workbench—and the artist would never be back to help her make sense of it.

"Are you all right?" Josiah asked.

Lois nudged him with her elbow.

"*Ach*, that was a stupid question," Josiah said. "I'll just come out and say it—we want to be sensitive to what you're going through, but we're used to working with men and this is awkward. Subtlety isn't my best trait."

To the point. She appreciated that. Celeste turned and gave him her best half smile—all she could muster. "You can speak your mind. Always. But despite helping my husband as best I could for the past six years, I don't know what I'm doing in this shop, and somehow I have to pretend like I do."

"Woodworking? Nah, it's easy. I mean, for the stuff that most people want. Kitchen cabinets, phew, that's another story. But you don't have to offer that stuff. Or if you do, team up with my brothers and me. It wouldn't be charity for us because we'd be getting business too."

"All of this help feels like charity."

He shrugged. "Everyone needs help sometimes."

Lois took his hand. "On the day Josiah met my parents, both my dat and my three oldest brothers had to get his rig out of a mudhole."

"That's right. I was trying to make a good impression and instead got the whole family wet and covered in mud. You should've seen the look on her mamm's face when she saw how much she'd have to wash."

Celeste managed a smile. "Guess they decided to keep you."

"Jah. Guess so. Let's make a table," Josiah said.

"What? Right now?"

"It's next on Vin's to-do list, and you'll feel better if you make something. Something you can do with your hands and appreciate its beauty when you're done. It's why woodworking is so great. You see your results right there. Functional pieces created out of something that was formless."

That wasn't far-off from what Vin used to say about making art. That stone inside felt heavy again. "Okay. I'll try."

"Now, since we only have today to convince you that you're capable of doing this, you and I are going to make several pieces. Each will be something that you can complete before we leave. While we do that, Thomas and Bartholomew will work on the orders that take advanced skill and are past due."

His confidence gave Celeste a hint of courage. "I'll need to take notes."

Josiah looked to his girl. "Lois, would you take notes while we work?"

"Jah. Rather do that than nothing all day." Lois went to the desk, rummaging for paper and pen.

Josiah studied the shelves of raw wood, each one holding a different size, shape, and type.

"Denki, Lois," Celeste said. "There's a clipboard in the top drawer to your left."

"Ah, gut." Lois jerked the drawer open and grabbed it.

Josiah walked toward a shelf. "Let's start with an old-fashioned farmhouse coffee table." He gestured at the shelves. "Clearly you have enough wood for any project we do today. I brought a set of plans, but I imagine you have a very similar set here?"

"Jah, we have many plans for coffee tables." Celeste went to the file cabinet and pulled out a stack. She set it on the desk, put the strings to her prayer Kapp behind her, and tied a knot so they'd stay out of her way. After thumbing through the plans, she found a farmhouse table she thought could sell. "Let's get started." She made herself sound more at ease than she felt.

Minutes slipped into hours, and she realized this work wasn't as difficult as she thought. Once she began working with the wood, the muscle memory of helping Vin came back to her—the measuring, cutting, sanding, drilling holes to use pegs instead of nails. Josiah only touched the wood when showing her the next step. He never touched the tools, just instructed her using clear and simple phrases, while he answered her multitude of questions.

Miraculously, after four hours, she had a chunky-style farmhouse coffee table with the frame and lower shelves painted white and a dark mahogany top. Resting her hands on her hips, she marveled at it. Wow. Maybe Vin and Josiah were onto something after all. This was satisfying, and it didn't look half-bad. It was just a simple thing—knee-high tall, three feet wide, and four feet long—made of pine and mahogany. Incredible . . . something she'd made looked good enough to sell in a shop.

Josiah gestured to the table. "You look happy with it."

"I am. I . . . I didn't think I'd be able to do it."

"You're a natural."

Was she? Her mind ran with ideas of unique designs for coffee tables. Warmth washed over her, and she could see Vin smiling. Tears welled. This moment of feeling something other than misery was worth holding on to. Could she?

This business was as real and tangible as the table in front of her. She needed a positive, concrete focus so all the what-ifs couldn't drive her mad. Through this business, she could provide for her children and give them a real trade. As she looked at the coffee table, it all seemed possible.

She turned to Josiah and Lois. "Denki." She wiped a tear. "Truly. Deeply. Denki."

Josiah grinned. "Our dat will be pleased to know how well you did and how grateful you are."

Celeste could do this. She couldn't afford to let herself get dragged down in grief, and she couldn't be like Vin's dat, letting grief run roughshod over his relationships. She wouldn't let the hurt ruin her view on love and life.

Vin was gone.

But she was here for their sons. *Denki, Gott, for that.*

It was a gift, and she'd be the best parent she could for her boys. Whether Vin was alive or dead, whether he would return one day, sorrowful of his decision, or whether his life was over, she'd find the strength to be the mother her boys needed.

Josiah leaned in, catching her eye. His eyes held pleasure for her and kindness, and he smiled. "What do you wish to build next, Celeste?"

Something clanged against concrete, and Celeste turned to see the clipboard on the floor.

Lois seemed surprised, but also like she was holding back anger. Had she dropped it or thrown it? She'd seemed fine this morning, but as the hours went by, her mood seemed to change.

Celeste glanced at the clock. It was past noon. Maybe Lois needed a break from this shop and being an assistant for Celeste. Added to that, for the first time since Vin left, Celeste was hungry. She'd roasted a chicken yesterday so she could make sandwiches today. "Let's go to the house and eat some lunch before we do anything else."

"Sounds gut." Josiah picked up the clipboard from the floor, studying his fiancée before holding out his hand to her. Lois didn't seem to notice as she walked around him and toward the door of the shop.

Celeste held the door for her. "I really appreciate your help. I'm sure you had other things you'd rather be doing."

Lois shrugged. "It's a lot, but Josiah's dat insisted."

Celeste turned to look behind her. The three men were discussing a half-finished pie safe. The Old Ways kept clear lines between men and women. Even during church services, the men sat on one side and the women on the other. Was her need for help causing issues between Josiah and Lois?

If it was, Celeste couldn't change things for now. She was hanging on to a ledge, and she had bills to pay and little boys to feed. It was hard enough trying to take on her husband's trade. The last thing she needed was for anyone to feel she was using Vin's absence as a way to get close to another man.

How fast could she learn what she needed and release Josiah from this obligation?

Chapter Eleven

People filled every chair at the long table in the dining room of the McLaughlin home. Vin shifted, leaning in to see George as Tandey told an amusing incident that had happened earlier this week. George chuckled, shaking his head. The sounds of plates clinking together echoed as Ester and Bridget gathered them and moved about the table, removing supper dishes. The room rumbled with voices of people who had come to matter to Vin.

This home had similarities to the one he shared with Celeste— simple furnishings and no electricity. They used oil lamps instead of kerosene. He hadn't asked, but it sounded as if kerosene lamps had yet to be invented. They used lots of candles. The glass windows had so many waves and bubbles that you couldn't make out much of anything when trying to look through them, but they let in a lot of light. The walls inside and out were rough-hewn logs.

There were no interior doors in the cabin, only drapes that a person could pull for privacy. No indoor plumbing, and they had to draw all their water from a nearby well.

Good folks filled the chairs of the table—people who'd helped him and people he'd tried to help. All the McLaughlins except Liam were here. He fell into the *good people* category too, but he'd left four days ago, driving a loaded wagon from the fall harvest to the nearest town. Lots of hardworking, busy people on this growing farm. None tried to control him with a list of things *they* thought were right or wrong.

"Vin." Ester poured water into his empty glass. "Once thee is off the horse each day, elevate the injured leg as much as possible. Sleep with it elevated."

Well, no one except Ester. She was a gentle soul with an unmovable determination. Her use of *thee* and *thine* came from the Quaker side of her, but she didn't use those words consistently, which made sense. She and her sister, Anke, had been Amish until their parents died, so Ester spoke German. Vin's Pennsylvania Dutch, an Americanized slang of German, wasn't a language they could converse in, so he was now pretty good at High German.

James chuckled. "That's my wife's polite speak for don't undo her work or else."

Vin smiled. "I will take excellent care of this knee you've worked so faithfully to heal."

Although he'd only known Ester two months, she felt like a sister to him. She'd done her best to get his knee better. The limp had persisted—maybe it always would—but he was only in half the pain he was before, and his leg now had a reasonable amount of strength. Ester had ordered him to bed in her house. She'd used rest, ice, and poultices to get his knee as healed as possible, not batting one eye at using ice on his knee for weeks despite they'd used the last of it. The family couldn't replenish it until winter froze their pond and they could harvest ice again. She also didn't bat an eye over welcoming George and Tandey into her home. This was part of the Underground Railroad—the start of it, at least. Vin had studied it in his time. Right now people knew it as the abolition movement or antislavery movement.

James and Ester were die-hard abolitionists, and the only reason the brothers hadn't known that was the number of years they'd been separated by a continent. Also, since Patrick and Liam couldn't read and someone had to read the letters to them, Ester and James wrote almost nothing about the movement.

James and Ester aimed to earn enough money so their family had food, clothing, and shelter, but after that, they lived so that when they met God, He was pleased with them. That was their treasure. They were careful and savvy in order to do the most good they could, but they had no fear of dying and counted it a joy to meet God. Vin couldn't meet God yet . . . not without seeing Celeste and their boys again.

"My sister could've helped your knee so much better than me," Ester said. "Anke knows how to cross the Gott Brucke."

"Gott Brucke?" George asked.

"God bridge." Vin and Ester said it at the same time and then laughed.

Vin shook his head. "Ester has mentioned the Gott Brucke to me before, and I know what the words mean but can't say I understand it."

"It means Gott Brucke." Ester mockingly lifted her brows, as if he was being silly to not get it. "A bridge built by faith from where we are to God; then we can know things only God knows."

"It sounds like the work of the Holy Spirit to me," Patrick said.

Ester nodded. "His Spirit is at work in every good thing. But the Gott Brucke is a human seeking to build a connection with the God who knows the plans He has for us. Those who aim to cross the Gott Brucke are seeking a word of knowledge that is outside of what we know or perhaps outside of the time we live in. God knows all. When appropriate, we seek a piece of His knowledge."

Ester's words—*outside of the time we live in*—struck thunder inside Vin. He desperately needed a Gott Brucke, to know why he was here and how to get back. Anke was skilled at crossing the Gott Brucke? Could she help him learn how to get home? Hope circled inside him, gaining energy. His need was odd. Time travel. But he had to approach her about it at his first opportunity. Maybe he could avoid mentioning the time travel part. Accepting that topic was too much to ask of anyone, especially someone in early America.

Ester patted his shoulder and went to the kitchen.

Although Vin was deeply grateful for all God had done to save him and connect him to these good people, he chafed to still be here. It'd taken seven weeks to rehab his knee enough that Ester and James felt he could travel five hundred miles to Lancaster. They hadn't been wrong. As proof he was ready for this trip, he had to walk a few miles each day on the farm, without his knee locking up or buckling on him. He'd succeeded in that goal only a few days ago. Ester and James felt his knee needed more time to heal, but Vin knew if he didn't leave soon, snows would catch them along the way, stopping them from going farther for weeks at a time and making the trek more dangerous as they crossed the Alleghenies and other mountains.

He was heading east first thing tomorrow morning. He intended to ride the horse he'd purchased throughout as much of the five-hundred-mile trip as possible, but he needed to walk long distances at times, leading the horse through narrow, dangerous paths. Some mountains were too steep, and the traveling days were too long for a horse to always carry two hundred pounds on its back.

This might be his last night with these people, except George and Tandey. They were going with him. When George learned that it was illegal in Pennsylvania to capture runaway slaves and send them back to their owners, he decided that's where he and Tandey should build a life. Added to that, George wasn't fond of the idea of Vin traveling by himself.

But if God in His mercy returned Vin to his wife and children, he'd never see the McLaughlins again, nor would they be able to receive a letter from him. So tonight he took note of how precious time was with people he cared about.

Still, he'd gratefully part ways with them for the rest of his life if he could be reunited with Celeste and his children. George felt similarly about his wife, Maud. He'd talked openly with Vin about her one day. But the last George heard, she'd been sold to a plantation in the Deep South. That happened nearly five years ago, and George had long feared she was dead.

Brendan came to the table with a book Vin had created using paper and a quill pen. Vin had made the story up and drawn pictures to go with it, and Brendan loved it. "Teacher, ye forgot to pack this one." The boy brushed his hand across the front of it.

Vin smiled. "I made it for you, and you're to keep it."

Brendan grinned. "I can keep it?"

"Jah. Pass it to your own children one day and tell them about the strange man your folks saved from the wilds of Ohio in 1822 and how he created books and taught you how to begin to read."

If he could, he'd find a published children's book and get it shipped, but to get it here, he'd have to find a family or someone coming out this way. That's how Ester got letters to her sister and the McLaughlins, but it took time and was iffy at best. For now, Vin had created two books for each child to leave under their pillows as gifts before he headed out in the morning.

"Thank you." Brendan hugged him. "You're a good teacher."

"Well, I'm glad you think so, because I had to do something with my time since your aunt Ester demanded I rest all day."

James chuckled. "You did a lot more than teach reading and writing, and it'll help the abolitionist movement and the McLaughlin farms prosper."

"Gut. I hope so." He missed life with Celeste and the boys. The grief swallowed him whole some days, and he prayed endlessly that God would help him get back to them, but at least while he was here, he'd been useful. He'd been able to help the McLaughlins know which crops would be the most lucrative over the coming decades—for example, telling them that although growing hemp had been profitable for generations, it would bottom out. He couldn't tell how he knew, but they took his word for it. Who knew that knowing a little of such history would ever prove useful? He'd simply found it fascinating. Maybe he wouldn't have if he'd owned a radio or television, but the winter nights were long, and he loved reading history and drawing.

He'd also spent hours in the last weeks drawing copies of hard-to-come-by maps, some for people to understand the roads and towns and others to help abolitionists get information to escapees so they could navigate the land and find the homes of those who would help.

The conversation volleyed one way and another. The McLaughlin brothers were good husbands and fathers. George stood out as a remarkable father, too. Watching all four fathers with their children made him think of his own dat. James, Liam, Patrick, and George were different with their children than Vin's dat, although he couldn't quite put words to how they were different. His dat seemed to have no flexibility. None. He saw things how he saw them, end of story. These dads were flexible in their thoughts and opinions while firm in their belief that treating others as they wanted to be treated was essential to the Christian message. Vin hadn't treated Celeste as he wanted to be treated. He'd failed her in that. What else had he failed her in? Would he get a chance to love her as he should? To return to his family and be a truly good husband and father?

Ester brought a cake from the kitchen. "To celebrate that Vin can still hold a fork after all the writing he's done since arriving here."

The group laughed and clapped.

"And . . ." Ester cut into the cake. "To celebrate that George and Tandey made it here and will make it to Pennsylvania safely."

The group clapped again. Ester passed George the first piece of cake and gave Tandey the second one.

She set a piece of cake in front of Vin. "Now that I understand *how* to teach reading, I'll continue working with adults and children, just as thee did."

"I know you will, and you'll do a good job of it, too."

Ester could read and write well. She was the one who'd written the letters to Liam and Patrick. James had dictated them. Her parents and her Quaker foster parents, the Coopers, had taught her. They used the sight word method, and she'd caught on, but that method hadn't worked for her husband or children. Vin taught her how to break down the alphabet by vowels, their long and short sounds, and by the sounds of consonants and diphthongs. The desire to learn to read and write was strong in this family, but no one had a lot of time for schooling on this farm, just two half days each week, plus time in the evenings when work was done, if they weren't too tired to think.

Patrick moved to a seat near Vin. "You ready to begin your travels tomorrow?"

"I think so. It might take us until midmorning to be organized enough to head out. We've got so much to take with us. We're taking four horses, one for each of us plus a packhorse."

"Aye. Ester has you taking several things to the Coopers and her sister."

"That she does." Since pencils weren't available, he'd created his own drawing sticks and paint using nature, and he'd made portraits of Ester, James, and their children to take to Anke. The sisters hadn't seen each other in eight years. To keep the sketches dry during his travels, he'd made a cylinder of leather, sewing the seams tightly. He rolled the papers, slid them into the cylinder, and dipped the cylinder in wax. Then he created a larger leather cylinder and put the first one inside the second one and sealed that one with wax. They also had to pack plenty of food, coins they'd earned while here, dried tobacco as another currency, and everything three people needed to survive sleeping under the stars until they got to Pennsylvania. Once there, they could stay at tavern inns, but not until then just to be safe.

The Coopers' home in Lancaster, Pennsylvania—that was the destination. George and Tandey would figure out their lives and livelihoods in a safe state. Vin's plan was murkier. Until tonight, he'd only known he'd beseech God and try to hear Him about how to get home to his family. But now he knew he needed to approach Anke. She might be able to help him figure out how to get home. It was an unbelievable blessing that Ester had a sister and foster family in Lancaster, and she assured Vin they'd be happy to help in any way they could. He prayed that was true.

"I'm going to miss ye," Patrick said. "Will we see ye again?"

Vin hoped not. If he saw them again, it'd mean he couldn't get back to his time or his family. "I . . . I don't know. If I can find my way home, I might not be able to send a letter or visit, but I'll always carry you and your family right here." Vin tapped the center of his chest, blinking back tears. "Always."

Patrick slapped him on the back. "Ye were a good find out in the wilderness."

Vin laughed. "*You* were indeed."

"Ye got a map to guide ye?"

"Not much of one." Vin took a bite of cake, enjoying its deliciousness. A dessert like this was a rare treat. "The good maps don't cover the route we'll take. But we've got a good compass."

"The easiest route is the National Road. First paved road in America."

"Paved, yes. But taking that road would be the opposite of easy since we'd have go through parts of two slave states, Virginia and Maryland. We're a group of three with runaway slaves. We'd stick out. I could go that route on my own, but since I'd like to arrive to the Cooper place alive, I prefer to travel in a group."

The part of Virginia he'd just mentioned would be called West Virginia one day.

"From what I've seen, each of you have useful skills that will work well during your journey. What's the plan?"

"We'll go north and stay on backwoods paths and Indian trails. We may have to go through a sliver of Virginia to cross over into Pennsylvania, but I'm hoping not. Either way, we'll cross the Ohio River and make our way into a free state with good laws as quickly as possible."

They'd need at least a week to get to Pennsylvania and another three or four weeks to get to Lancaster. They should be at the Coopers' by the end of October, a month before the first winter snow. In his day, getting from here to Lancaster by a hired driver would take less than six hours. Here, they could be on the trail for six weeks.

There were so many unknowns ahead of them.

Patrick took a sip of his water. "William and Margaret Cooper are good people with giving hearts. They each mean what they say, so trust that."

"Thanks for letting me know." But Vin's mind was on Anke. Would she be open to helping him get home? "Um, Patrick." Vin rubbed a napkin across his bearded face. "You know I was separated from my wife and sons when I fell."

"I think thieves stole everything you had and then threw you off a cliff. How else does a man have nothing, not even a knife or a piece of jerky in his pocket?"

"That sounds logical, doesn't it?" Vin shrugged. "But what's on my mind is Ester said Anke is able to connect with God and learn things."

"Like where your wife and sons are and how to get to them?"

"Jah. What's Anke's temperament like? Is she likely to be willing to help me?"

Vin tried to sound merely curious, but his hopes that she'd be able to help him were growing exponentially.

"Hard to say. I know she heals people, but I've never heard of her doing anything outside of that."

"Do you think she'd be willing to try?"

"Maybe. She's a little different. She's polite, but she's also very private. I think the Coopers are her only friends. She's very pretty, but she's not the least bit interested in finding a husband or having a family of her own. I've never seen that before. Have you?"

"On occasion." Then again, he lived in the 1980s. "Ester hasn't seen her in years. Does Anke still pray her way to the Gott Brucke?"

"She does. I've seen people bring their deathly sick children to her, and days later, they leave the Cooper home no longer sick, even when a doctor couldn't do anything. It's exhausting for her, so the Coopers ask Anke and those she helps to be discreet about her abilities."

Discreet . . . Was Anke merely discreet or was she hiding? Did that even matter as far as her helping him?

He'd been *discreet* about his artwork. Maybe there had been absolutely nothing wrong with Vin drawing faces, but there was a lot wrong with hiding who he was from the person he loved most. He'd felt closer to Celeste than his next breath, and yet he'd built a wall of lies between them and didn't even realize it. Because *she* didn't know it was there. If she'd known, he would've felt the gulf between them. He'd believed his own lies . . . believed he had pulled her close, believed he'd been willing to do anything for her. But he'd lied to himself first.

He couldn't walk in selfishness any longer.

George said God led him to escape with Tandey and had guided him from deep inside Virginia through five hundred miles of woods into Ohio. He said God showed him how to get free of the shackles on his ankles and directed him on when, where, and how to snare food so they could stay alive. He'd said it was so difficult—the pain, hunger, exhaustion, and fear . . . the lack of having a moment of comfort for months and months. But they'd made it, and George fully believed God sent him to help Vin stay alive, and then God used Vin to help George and Tandey connect with the McLaughlins. Vin longed to hear God and follow Him the way George had. Would He lead Vin home or had Vin not learned all he needed to yet?

Dear God, whatever I've done that You sent me here, have mercy, teach me my lesson, and please, send me home again. Until then, may I use my time as You desire.

The front door of the cabin opened, and Liam walked in. He looked straight at George.

"Pa!" His daughter hurried to him.

He hugged her and kissed the top of her head. His wife and other children followed suit. He greeted them, then said, "Nora, take all the little ones, cousins included, outside. I need to talk with the adults about the upcoming journey." Liam gestured at Tandey. "You stay inside."

There was quite a clatter as the moms helped the children put their cake on a large wooden plate and go outside.

Before all the children were out the door or the noise dulled, Liam pulled a folded piece of paper out of his pant pocket and passed it to George. "A patroller passed it to me," he said.

George opened the yellowed, stiff paper, studied it a moment, and passed it to Vin. A sketch of George and Tandey stared back at Vin.

"What does it say?" James asked.

Vin rubbed across his mouth, feeling his full beard. He no longer looked Amish, part of his plan to not look like a slave sympathizer to an onlooker. He cleared his throat. "Mark Alexander of Meckelenburg, Virginia, offers a bounty for two runaway slaves. George Alexander, age thirty-five, and his son, twelve-year-old Tandey Alexander. Two-hundred-dollar reward for the return of George, six feet tall, broad shoulders, stout. A hundred and fifty dollars for the return of Tandey, five and a half feet tall, thin but strong. Last seen traveling together in central Ohio."

Two hundred dollars would probably be equal to somewhere around four thousand in Vin's day. That was a huge incentive for the hunters to try to catch George and Tandey.

Liam sat. "There're groups of patrollers gathering, some of them from Ohio, who intend to go house to house, looking. All wanting that reward money."

Vin stood. "You did good, Liam." He clasped his shoulder, knowing how much Liam tried to steer clear of anything that could make him appear to be helping runaway slaves. "Real good."

George stood. "We got to get our stuff and saddle up."

"Jah. Let's try to leave here in twenty minutes."

"It'll be dark soon," Ester said.

"Not ideal," Vin said. "But if we stay the night, we may never get the chance to head for the hills."

She shuddered and opened a cloth napkin. After putting Tandey's piece of cake on it, she tied it up. "May God go with you as full and protective as He did to get all of you here." She hugged Tandey.

The room was quiet for a moment. Too many things to say that no words could express. But Vin couldn't spare a moment waiting for the right words. They had to grab what they'd already packed, leave the rest, saddle up, and go.

Could they get to Pennsylvania without running into any patrollers?

Chapter Twelve

Josiah stood in the nursery, trying to see well enough by the lone kerosene lamp to remove the plastic battery cover on the back of the new Fisher-Price baby monitor. He should've done this while it was still daylight outside. But Steven and Drew were finally asleep.

Celeste walked into the room holding out a nine-volt battery. "It feels sinful."

Josiah glanced up. It'd been two months since Vin disappeared, and her physical wherewithal seemed to be growing worse. She was pale and really thin, with circles under her eyes. Her hands shook at times throughout their workday. Living without her husband was taking its toll.

"Nee." He shook his head. "You got the wrong *-ful* word. It's called useful, not sinful."

"I never needed one before."

"This thing is every ounce practical, and the word *practical* is synonymous with the word *Amish* or so they say. I don't exactly believe it, but what do I know?" he teased.

Celeste's eyes held uncertainty. "I don't know any Amish with a baby monitor."

"My guess is you've never known a young Amish mom who's had to juggle single parenting."

"True."

A cold front had come through a few days ago, and without warning, mid-September felt like mid-November. She'd had to close the windows to the house, making her unable to hear the boys if they woke while she was in the shop.

"It's good use of common sense to use this." He put the battery in the transmitter. "Kumm on, Celeste. This is God's way of giving you peace." He held up the monitor. "A piece of what exactly, only God knows."

He was hoping for a chuckle from her, but she shrugged and turned away. No doubt she was hiding tears. He put a battery in the receiver and turned each one on. The receiver crackled and whined. Celeste grabbed it and left the room, stopping in the hallway. The noise quit.

"How'd you know to do that?" He spoke near the transmitter and his voice came through the receiver that was in her hands.

"It works." She shrugged. "Let's get back outside to Aaron and Lois."

His younger brother wouldn't mind that they'd taken five minutes to set up this monitor. Lois might be annoyed, but he'd invited her to come in the house with them, and she'd declined. He set the transmitter on the table between Steven's and Drew's beds and walked into the hall with her. They went through the dimly lit home with its low-burning kerosene lamps.

"I deeply appreciate all you and Aaron and Lois are doing to help me. I fear I don't sound grateful, but I am."

"I know that."

She sounded like a woman drowning in grief and confusion, but she kept plodding forward. If her family lived closer, she'd probably be faring better. If more people in this community weren't so standoffish toward her, she'd probably be faring better. It appeared to him as if she'd wrapped her life around Vin and their children. Around running the home and the shop. She didn't seem to have any close friends here. Then again, she hadn't grown up here. She'd grown up in Indiana.

They stepped outside, and the cool autumn air and aromas filled the air. A few insects were chirping, but nothing like a month ago. A whippoorwill called. It seemed late in the season for a whippoorwill to still be this far north.

"I . . . I just didn't know how hard it was for Vin to make ends meet."

"It's harder for you. He wasn't a single parent. Your time is divided, but the rent on your home remains the same. Your lifestyle hasn't been about building a business and earning money. It's been about other things that Vin couldn't do, like having babies. Let me tell you now that you're doing a much better job as a carpenter than any man could ever do giving birth."

She chuckled. "I'd gladly take being me and being Steven and Drew's mamm as my first priority. But the rent on this place takes so much of what I make. I just never knew."

"Kitchen cabinets are a big-ticket item, lots of money for the time invested. Vin had a good reputation for his skill and speed at making and installing cabinets."

"True. I helped sand and stain a lot of kitchen cabinets over the years, although I never helped install them."

The sound of Aaron hand sanding echoed through the open

windows and door to the shop. When working hard, it was too warm to close the windows and door, even with this mid-September cold front. They were mere feet from the door of the shop when Lois's voice rose from inside, probably so Aaron could hear her over the block sanding he was doing.

"Apparently looks just weren't enough to make her husband want to stay."

Celeste stopped walking.

Embarrassment flooded Josiah. Lois *had* to know better than to repeat mean things about Celeste, especially when on her property. He drew a breath and tried to speak up, calling out to Lois before she said anything else, but only a squeak left his mouth.

Celeste seemed as frozen in place as he was.

"I'd die of embarrassment," Lois said, "if anybody, let alone that many people, believed I was such a horrible wife and that my Amish husband, taught from birth the value of family, left me anyway. But I can sort of see *that* in her, can't you?"

"I'm going to need a minute." Celeste's voice cracked, and she trudged toward the neighbor's pasture that ran behind her house.

"Well?" Lois asked.

"What?" Aaron stopped sanding. "You know I can't hear you, right?"

Thank God his little brother hadn't added to what Lois said. No wonder Lois was talking so loudly, but the person nearest the noise still hadn't heard her. Josiah took a few quick steps toward the shop's door.

Lois opened the screen door just as he was reaching for the handle. "I thought I saw someone out here."

He peered down at her. "Go to the phone shanty and call for a hired driver."

"Oh, are we going home now?" She sounded excited. "I thought we had two more hours."

"*You're* going home now, jah."

"What? Why?"

"She heard you, Lois."

"But I was just saying . . ." She huffed, but her face flushed red. "Everyone is saying—"

"Nee. We're not talking about this right now. I'm too angry and embarrassed, and you're feeling too defensive."

"I don't know what you thought you heard, but—"

"Go to the phone shanty and call for a hired driver."

"I won't be told what to do because of the likes of her."

Josiah's heart raced. "Okay. No problem. You do whatever you want to do. That and gossiping seem to be your gifts."

"How dare you talk to me like that!"

"How dare you talk about anybody the way you just did Celeste." She stared up at him, looking wounded.

"Look, I told you I was too angry to deal with this right now. You owe her an apology. I think she went into the pasture to walk for a bit."

"No way. She steals our time together every week, and she's never apologized to me."

Josiah blinked, unable to see the woman he loved for this petty person standing in front of him. "That's not even a little bit true, Lois. She's apologized numerous times. Last week she made you a cake, a thank-you-for-your-time cake."

"She was showing off that she can bake better than me. That's all."

"Showing off?"

"Jah, I made a cake a month ago in her kitchen while you and Aaron and she worked in the shop, and it fell in the center."

"She's grieving the loss of her life as she knew it, and you're jealous of her?"

"Good heavens, nee!" She walked off, heading straight for the phone shanty.

He went into the woodshop to grab his backpack. He had something Celeste needed to see.

Aaron still had a block sander in his hand, wide-eyed as he stared at Josiah. "I . . . I . . ."

"Jah, that about sums it up. I'll be back in ten." He went outside and toward the pasture, hoping to find Celeste and offer an apology. He opened the cattle gate, shut it behind him, and searched for her. Although he couldn't see her, he started walking. After a few minutes, he saw her silhouette under the canopy of a white ash tree, leaning against it. A lot of trees were barely changing color yet, but the leaves of the white ash were a beautiful yellow in the daylight. They looked rather brown under the night sky.

He stopped ten feet before he got to her. "You okay?"

"Sure. I just needed a minute. It's not her fault. She's just tired and repeating—"

Her words flew all over him. He was sick of politeness covering her genuine emotions. "Could you stop trying to be strong? Stop holding in that massive pain that's eating you alive?" What was he doing? How was that an apology for what Lois said?

Celeste stood up straight and marched to him. "You want honesty? I can't do this! I can't cope knowing my husband, the love of my life, might have left me. How did I not know what was happening under my own roof? He was in the same room with me, night after night, drawing in his sketch pad when he wasn't reading or we weren't playing board games, and I never knew anything!" She stood on her tiptoes, screaming. "I want my husband back!" Tears fell. "I want the life I thought I had! I hurt all the time so much I can hardly breathe or eat or sleep, and all I can think is: how did I not know? How did he want to be free of me so much he just left, and I thought we were in love? Madly, crazy in love?"

"You believed it because it was true."

She studied him. "What?" Her hoarse whisper bored deep into his soul.

He unzipped the backpack and pulled out Vin's sketch pad that his uncle, the bishop, had taken to his house. Uncle Mark had wanted to remove it from Celeste's home because it was forbidden, but he couldn't make himself destroy it, so he'd stashed it at the back of his closet. Josiah hadn't asked if he could have it. He doubted his uncle would ever notice it was missing, but Josiah knew that one day, when grown, Vin's sons would need to see that piece of their dat's heart. He also knew that Celeste needed to look at it anew. He held it out to her. "He sketched hundreds of pictures of you, Steven, and Drew, but mostly, by far, you. Every detail he drew shows the respect and love he had for you."

She eased it from his hand and flipped through the pages.

"Look at what he saw, Celeste."

She walked out from under the canopy, and the muted light from a crescent moon fell on the pages.

"Don't think about it being forbidden. See the obvious, Celeste."

Her fingers trailed his most recent sketch of her, and she sobbed.

"Look, I don't know what happened, but I believe if the man who sketched those was capable of coming back, he'd have come back even if he'd had to crawl on his belly. He died, Celeste. Something happened, and the man who promised to be home before you fell asleep died before he could return."

She clutched the sketch pad to her chest, turned away from him, and wept hard.

Tears blurred his eyes, too.

She cleared her throat and drew a breath. "I was so mean to him that night, so angry and hurt and disappointed in him. I accused him of wanting to be free of our vows. How can I live with that?"

"You trust that if he didn't understand your hurt and anger in the moment, he would've understood it when tempers cooled, and he completely understands it now." Would Josiah feel differently about Lois when his anger subsided?

She used her apron to wipe her eyes before she faced him. "I . . . was still holding on to hope he'd return to me."

"I know. But he can't." He understood the myriad of thoughts and feelings she had about her missing husband. Each possibility she clung to also ate at her. He wasn't sure how he understood it, but he did.

Her body wavered. "I ache for him to hold me. To feel his warmth embracing me. I miss him so much."

"I know."

A faint smile crossed her lips. "Denki."

"Gern gschehne."

With the sketch pad clutched to her chest, she walked toward the gate. The weight of her doubts seemed to lift from her, leaving a ton of pure, simple grief. Josiah knew she could face that.

Could he and Lois learn to face their future with as much vulnerability and strength as Celeste had?

Chapter Thirteen

A man was sitting on the ground near a campfire. He looked a little familiar, but Vin couldn't see him clearly. He seemed to have on Amish clothes, but Vin wasn't sure about that either. The man opened his mouth to speak. Vin stood on the other side of the fire, heart pounding, waiting for him to answer the question: *How do I get home?*

Vin startled awake. Did the man in his dreams know the answer to his question? Five times since leaving the McLaughlin farm eight days ago, he'd had the same dream and woken longing to have stayed in the dream until the man answered him.

He drew a deep breath and opened his eyes, staring into an overhead canopy of trees against a dark sky. The leaves had the first hints of changing to fall colors. The ground beneath his bedroll was cold, and the aroma of soil and fall hung in the air.

George and Tandey were on their bedrolls a few feet from him, sound asleep.

He pushed off the buffalo skin coat he'd used as a blanket. It must've gotten down to the midfifties last night. He stood, wondering what time it was. Maybe five or five thirty. If he ever came across a pocket watch, he'd buy it. He wouldn't trade his horse for it, but he'd give just about anything else he owned—buffalo coat, leather gloves, blankets, bedroll, food, coins, tobacco leaves. After shaking his coat out, he put it on. He'd slept in his leather gloves.

Could they cover twenty miles today? They averaged twelve to fifteen miles most days. But if they could manage twenty, they might make it to the Ohio River before dark. It'd been a hard eight days of travel. No hot meals, no campfires at night, just backsides in saddles all day long as they took narrow, winding paths. All three of them knew firsthand that the aroma of fire and food traveled too far and drew people.

He put feed into four feed bags and hung one around each horse's neck. They were low on feed since they were avoiding every town, but once they crossed into Pennsylvania, they could stock up. After leading the horses the short distance to the creek to drink, he ate beef jerky while the horses drank.

Dawn arrived, lifting some of the darkness. When back at camp, he saw George and Tandey stirring. "Morning."

George grinned. "Morning, Vin."

Tandey gave a quick wave and went toward the deeper woods.

Vin loaded the packhorse, tying down their few worldly goods nice and tight. The first rays of sunlight filtered through the treetops.

If it be Your will, God, I beg of You to have mercy on George and Tandey and let us get safely to Pennsylvania, and I beg of You to have mercy on me and send me back to Celeste, Steven, and Drew. Until then, may I use my time as You desire.

While saddling his horse, Vin felt the hairs on the back of his neck stand on end. He stepped away from the horse and searched through the forest, trying to see if something looked out of place. He saw nothing unusual.

He moved to the path they'd followed here, staring down the back trail, still seeing nothing out of place. He left the trail and walked toward his horse. If he'd learned any survival skill in the two and a half months since he'd woken in this time, it was to hear when God was whispering about things Vin couldn't see.

"George." Vin spoke barely above a whisper as he fastened the girth to the saddle.

George looked up from the log he was sitting on, a stale biscuit and a piece of jerky in his hands.

"Let's get mounted up."

"You're in a hurry this mornin'." George chuckled. "Tandey ain't back from his call of nature yet."

"I'm aware," Vin whispered. "Use my horse as cover and fetch him. Slow and easy, but as quick as you can."

George's eyes grew large, reflecting that he now understood the weight of what was happening. With the horse beside him, he went into the woods to get his son.

Vin quickly saddled George's and Tandey's horses. He tethered them to a branch on the log and then returned his focus to the thick woods behind them. What he'd give for a telescope. Was that a glimmer, like sunlight bouncing off glass or metal, or was it his imagination? He couldn't be sure, but it seemed as if a lone rider had been coming their way and now wasn't. If that's what Vin had caught glimpses of, it meant the rider was a scout, likely for patrollers, and now he was returning to give a report. Had he seen George?

When Vin turned back toward the camp, he saw empty ground. They'd picked up the bedding, and any hint that there'd been three men sleeping on the ground was gone.

Vin walked his horse to the path. His knee kept him from moving smoothly, but he was managing well enough.

George climbed into his saddle. "Our horses are too tired to outrun Grandma."

"True enough, but we're gonna get moving and hope a plan forms."

"There were rocks and cliffs along the trails yesterday. Maybe there are some ahead of us too. Me and Tandey can hide there while you stay on the path with all the horses and keep on going. They'll catch up to you, but after they go on, maybe for an hour, you can circle back for us."

Vin nodded. His heart had a steady beat as they pushed to make better time than usual. Two miles later, as they rounded a bend on the dirt road, he caught a glimpse of men on horses about five hundred feet back. James had described what patrollers often look like, and the men trailing them looked like patrollers to Vin. He slapped the reins. "Get!"

If they had lingered at the campsite for even five more minutes, the patrollers would've caught them.

George pointed. "I see rocks and jutted areas."

Vin nodded.

"Keep your eyes out for flat ground with a covering of rocks," George said.

Vin understood. It would be best if George and Tandey dismounted on a bed of rock and could follow that up the hill to a cliff or cave to hide in.

"When you come back for us, use the mourning dove call followed by the eastern bluebird call."

"Jah. I will. Just like you taught me."

"There." Tandey pointed.

Vin saw it, a glittering of mica coming from the ground. They continued on, pushing the horses to go as fast as they could until they came to the natural path of rocks leading to the bigger rock cliff. That would hide their footprints.

George and Tandey got off their horses onto the barely visible rock. They dropped the reins and took off.

The horses were too tired to make a run for it . . . or make a walk for it. Vin slid off his horse and grabbed the reins to the others. He quickly removed the saddles and tied them on the horses in a way that made it look as if no one had been riding them. Taking a last look into the woods, he saw George and Tandey disappear. He redistributed some items from the packhorse to George's and Tandey's riding horses, making it look as if Vin was a lone man riding with three horses in tow.

He mounted his horse again and dug his heels in. "Get."

The four horses picked up their pace, but their energy waned. He hadn't gone far before a man's voice boomed.

"You! Stop!"

Vin tugged on the reins.

A man with a pistol in hand brought his horse to a stop near Vin. "I'm Lieutenant Cannon. We're looking for slaves."

Thank You, Gott, for letting me know about these patrollers in time for George and Tandey to get to hiding.

"I'm Ervin, and I haven't seen any slaves." He hadn't. He'd seen free men being hunted. But why had he given his full name? Maybe nervous. Maybe thinking it sounded more 1800s than the name Vin.

"Why you out here with three horses, each carrying less than half a load?"

"These are gifts for a prominent family. They're probably gonna give these fine creatures to their children."

The man clicked his tongue. "Well, it might be stupid of them, but it's not illegal."

Vin smiled and nodded. Would he now need to give these

horses to the Coopers so he wasn't a liar? Or was lying okay with God in these circumstances? Vin had done plenty of lying to his wife over the years. He'd just done it by omission.

"Lookee here," a man called out.

Vin turned in his saddle to see a kid, maybe eighteen, going through the saddlebags. "He's got coffee, beans, biscuits, and bacon, sir!"

Cannon motioned with his gun. "We got more men scouring the nearby hills, and all of us are hungry. We'd be real pleased if you'd make camp and feed us."

Scouring the hills?

Vin nodded, hoping to get a fire started and food cooking quickly. Maybe the aroma would cause the men searching the hills to head for the smell. Vin dismounted and gathered dried leaves and kindling. Also, he could make biscuits, acting like it was for his own supper or tomorrow's breakfast, and take some back to George and Tandey.

Lieutenant Cannon picked up several pieces of dried wood. "For your trouble, we'll escort you through the rest of Indian country."

Vin's skin prickled with angst, but he nodded. He didn't need guides. James said the Indians in these parts were friendly, mostly the Piqua or Makojay, branches of the Shawnee. But the less Vin said to these patrollers, the better. The McLaughlins said it was always best if an enemy thought you were far more stupid and scared of the surroundings than you actually were, but he intended to listen to every word said.

Once the smell of food was wafting through the forest, three more patrollers showed up.

A man got off his horse. "No signs of humans. The only thing we saw was a black bear."

Vin breathed a sigh of relief. George and Tandey knew how to hide. They'd proved that getting from eastern Virginia to Ohio, but had they needed to go farther into the mountains to get away from these patrollers?

The men talked among themselves while they ate. When they were done, Vin packed up, taking the dirty pans, utensils, and plates with him because they weren't at a water source. Soon all of them began going down the narrow, trodden path. It seemed forever had passed by the time the sun hung low in the sky. Still, the men stayed with him, talking. Vin kept riding his horse, leading the other three horses as he went, so weary of their company. Would they stay with him until he fed them breakfast tomorrow? Maybe lunch too? The hours dragged on.

Some of the conversation he'd overheard at the campsite while fixing them food was none too encouraging. Mark Alexander was out for blood. He wanted to find and make an example of several slaves who'd escaped, including George and Tandey. That was the bad news. The good news was one of them said something about a Maud Alexander—George's wife. Apparently she was now on a plantation somewhere in Maryland, and patrollers had been sent there to see if there was any sign of George or Tandey.

"Ervin," Cannon said, "we'll be going now."

Relief flooded Vin. "Yes, sir." He kept the horses walking forward as the patrollers moved on ahead, eventually disappearing. He kept going for a few more miles. When Vin was convinced it was safe, he turned the horses around.

Daylight waned as he got back to the spot where he'd left George and Tandey. He got off his horse and led all four horses off the beaten path and up the side of the rocky hill, his knee complaining but staying strong. He made his birdcalls and kept going uphill.

He heard a birdcall in response and stopped. A minute later, George and Tandey crawled out of a jutted rock.

"You all right?"

"Yeah." George dusted off the front of his shirt. "That took a lot longer than I expected."

"The price of them eating most of our food was them escorting me out of Indian country." Vin reached into his saddlebag and held out two biscuits with bacon to Tandey.

Tandey grabbed them and started eating.

Vin passed two more to George. "We can't use that path again. More patrollers coming behind them. There are patrollers up and down the Ohio River."

"Then we go north and cross on land if we can. We'll stay on Indian trails few whites use."

"Jah, I hear you, but I thought that's what we were trying to do."

"We'll do it better. I thought I saw a possible trail on our way up this mountain. Finding it is our best bet. But it's too late and too dark to search for a path tonight."

Vin unbuckled the girth from the saddle. "This area looks as good as any to stay the night."

"Tomorrow, at daylight, we'll search for signs of a hidden but well-used Indian path."

"You and Tandey will find one," Vin said. "A good one."

How long would it take them to find a path heading north and then east into Pennsylvania?

They removed the loads from their horses and put bedrolls on the ground.

Vin wanted to tell George what he'd heard about a Maud Alexander, but it seemed unwise to mention it in front of Tandey. Maybe it was unwise to mention it before they arrived at the Cooper place. If the Maud Alexander the patrollers spoke of was George's wife, it wouldn't change that George and Tandey needed to get to a safe state before Master Alexander's patrollers caught them. But was he hiding information George had a right to know, just as he had done with Celeste?

Master Alexander must have far more ego, resentment, and money than he had common sense. It had to cost a fortune to search for George and Tandey like this, as well as searching for other slaves that had escaped his plantation. Did the man have a clue how evil he was?

Vin wanted to be a good man, even if it cost him his traveling companions. He turned to George. "We need to talk. Not sure you'll want Tandey to hear what I need to say."

George glanced at his son. "We've faced everything together. If I need to know it, he does too."

Vin drew a breath. "The patrollers said something, and I'm unsure what to do with the information." He sat on a rock. "They said the name Maud Alexander."

George's eyes grew wide. His and Tandey's eyes met before he looked to Vin. "My Maud? She still alive?"

Vin didn't want to get his hopes up. "It's possible it's not the same Maud Alexander."

"Sure it is. Those patrollers were lookin' for me and Tandey, and they were talking about my wife and Tandey's mother."

Vin had been trying to discount the possibility of it being her, probably so they could keep moving toward safety, but George was right. "They sent patrollers to the plantation where she is to see if you and Tandey had gone to get her or hide out near her."

"Patrollers went to Texas? That's where Master Alexander said they sold her."

"I think he probably lied to you or maybe she was sold again, but the patrollers said Maryland."

George turned away from Vin, staring into the woods for more than a minute. Tandey said nothing, but his eyes stayed on his dat.

George turned. "This is good news." He nodded at Tandey. "Your mother is alive, Son. But we can't try to get her now. It won't do nobody any good if the three of us all get strung up or shackled in slavery for the rest of our lives. We'll be wise as serpents and gentle as doves." He grasped Tandey by the shoulders. "This is good news."

Tandey nodded, wiping tears, and the two hugged.

Vin had been afraid George would want to take off to get Maud today, but any man who had made it all these miles and followed his instincts so well this far knew how to sacrifice what he felt and follow a survivable plan.

"We good?" Vin asked.

George chuckled. "You say some odd things, but jah."

Vin chuckled too, but he was ready for some time alone. He climbed a rock and studied the land, seeing mostly trees and mountains. The patrollers knew this land. Vin and George didn't. Could they stay ahead of them until they reached Pennsylvania? Or would they lose so much time getting turned around that the patrollers would catch up to them?

If they arrived at his home county, would it be the bridge to God sending him back to his wife and sons? Would Anke be willing to help him search for the bridge?

If it be Your will, God, I beg of You to have mercy on George and Tandey and let us get safely to Pennsylvania and have mercy on me and send me back to Celeste, Steven, and Drew. Until then, may I use my time as You desire.

Chapter Fourteen

Celeste's nerves squeezed her tight as she closed the back of the wagon that she and Josiah had filled with furniture. She'd made the pieces by herself, but she'd been unable to load them without help.

Josiah studied her. "You have your secret weapon?"

A shudder ran through her. "Jah, under the seat. Denki, Josiah." She climbed onto the wagon bench.

"You sure you don't want company?"

She wasn't sure at all, but she shook her head and took the reins in hand. "I need to do this by myself. Besides, your aunt will need help keeping up with Steven and Drew while I'm gone."

She waved at the bishop's wife, who was standing in the fenced yard. "Denki, Lovina."

Lovina had Drew in her arms, bouncing him as they waved. "Glad to help."

Steven hurried out of the gate and across the driveway. "Siah."
He held up his arms.

Josiah chuckled. "I guess I will be busy." He removed his straw
hat, picked up Steven, and set him on his shoulders.

Steven waved at her. *"Mach's gut, Mamm."*

Tenderness radiated in his little voice as he said *Make it good,*
Mom, which also meant take care, so long, and goodbye. He wasn't
smiling but seemed to be accepting that his dat was gone and that
life still had good moments to offer. It was a lesson she'd yet to fully
embrace, but she was trying.

"Mach's gut, Steven." She waved and clicked her tongue. Sugar
Bear started walking, pulling the wagon full of furniture she'd
made onto the road.

She felt awkward and lonely stepping into this area of life
without Vin. But she lifted her face skyward and drew a deep
breath of fall. She couldn't keep mourning all that she didn't have.
Well, she'd continue mourning it, but she couldn't let that pain
own her.

Her mind meandered as the horse clippety-clopped. She passed
the turnoff to Drumore Mill. She and Vin used to take that turnoff
and ride along the Susquehanna until they got there. That old mill
sat on Fishing Creek, a place where they'd spread a blanket and
had a picnic along its shores many times. Her understanding was
Drumore Mill had been a gristmill, sawmill, fulling mill, hemp
mill, cornmill, and a distillery going back to the mid-1700s. In
the 1800s, the old mill was part of the Underground Railroad and
later a lookout during the Civil War.

How could so much of life have a deep, beautiful history, yet
her history with Vin was years shy of a decade?

The thirty-minute ride went by fast, and soon she was pulling
onto Main Street. It was a quaint-looking town with old shops, a
few built as early as 1754.

She sighed. "Your life is in the here and now, Celeste," she mumbled. "Focus. Be present. Your babies are depending on you."

Rent was due on the first of every month, which was tomorrow. She'd shorted the landlord a hundred dollars a month for August and September. Would she manage to have all of it tomorrow? The garden was still producing, but she hadn't bought groceries more than twice since Vin left. Her boys needed better than she was providing, and *no*, she wasn't taking money from Josiah or even his aunt and uncle.

She pulled in front of an Englischer store that had a sign for lots of things, including Amish-made furniture. It was time to find the gumption to ask if they'd buy her Amish-made goods. Her stomach knotted. Was her plan too brash? It felt like it, but she needed money. No doubt.

She got out of the wagon and looped the reins around a hitching post. Standing next to the horse, she studied the old door to the shop. It stared back at her. Taking a breath, she reached under the seat of the wagon and pulled out the secret weapon . . . as Josiah teasingly called it.

A poster, mounted on a board. It was a way of marketing, a possibility of drawing buyers to her furniture. Her goal was to be bold, but was this move a bit crass? What would her community think of this marketing plan?

She went inside. The shop smelled musty and of a time long past.

"Can I help you?" An older gentleman looked up from the antique cash register.

"Hello." No other words came to her, so she held up the poster board for him to see. The images on it were enlargements from several sketches Vin had drawn of her and their boys. In these drawings, he'd hidden their faces tastefully, with angles and the boys' hats.

"Wow." He moved closer.

It was an endearing set of sketches to be sure, now enlarged and creatively placed on this poster. She'd taken the sketches to a Fast Foto, and they made several posters for her. Maybe it would help sell her pieces. The poster read, *Amish-made furniture by Celeste*.

"It's a pretty sign, but I don't need any more Amish-made furniture. Tourist season is over."

"Tomorrow's October, and people will start looking for Christmas gifts soon."

"Yeah, but not that soon. I've lived in this area my whole life, and I've never heard of a woman woodworker before."

"It's unusual. Can I show you samples that I made myself? I have a wagon outside with farmhouse-style end tables, pie safes, TV stands, coffee tables, consoles, kitchen carts, couch tables, stove covers to go over the top of the oven, and outdoor chairs and tables."

He shrugged. "You can show me." The man gestured toward the front door.

She hurried out. Despite his age, he climbed into the wagon and inspected her work. "You made these?"

"I did. The price is on each one."

He lifted a tag that dangled by a small rope-looking thread and whistled. "That's your price? You know I have to raise the price to make money, right?"

"I'll take 80 percent of the price listed."

He nodded. "Okay, I'll take all of these and put up your posters. When someone buys a piece, you get paid at the end of that week. Deal?"

An Amish buggy slowed as it went by them. The Miller family—a man, wife, and children, craning their necks to see what Celeste was doing. There she was, standing on the side of the road with the poster facing out. Why hadn't she thought to leave it in the store? She didn't need her community thinking she was trying to profit off Vin's absence.

Her heart was trying to beat out of her chest, but she gathered her thoughts. "I . . . I can't pay rent or feed my babies today on what you might pay me next month or next week."

"Babies?" The man's brows knit. "What's your name, honey?"

"Celeste."

"Yeah, the sign says that. What's your last name?"

"Lantz."

He stopped inspecting the inside of a pie safe and stood up straight. "Oh." He scratched his head. "Is your husband the one who came up missing about three months now?"

Celeste's eyes threatened to fill with tears. She blinked, refusing to allow it. "He is."

"Ain't you got no man to help make ends meet or do this kind of business deal for you?"

Ain't you got no woman to help you know a good deal when you see one and know when to be quiet? The sarcasm that rose shocked her. And disappointed her. It was a new thing, as if the unbearable pain was turning to deep-seated anger. Sometimes it caught her so off guard, she didn't recognize herself.

"I appreciate your time." She slid the poster under the wagon bench.

"Hang on a minute." He eased his way out of the wagon. "I ain't done haggling just yet."

"I am. There are other shops. Someone else will be interested in my items—made by the Old Order Amish woman whose husband came up missing—and will take me up on my offer."

"Here's the deal: I'll pay you 85 percent of the price marked up front, but you only sell to me in this town."

"Ninety." Who was she? "And I won't sell to other shops on Main Street, but past that land boundary, I decide."

He shook his head. "Good grief, woman." He held out his hand. "I'm Paul Johnson, and we have a deal."

The money from this would take care of back rent, plus tomorrow's rent and groceries. Could he sell enough of her items that she could make ends meet every month?

The Miller buggy went by again, slower and watching her even closer. How much trouble would she be in with the ministers when they caught wind of what she'd used to make posters? Would the ministers revoke her right to be a woodworker?

Chapter Fifteen

Snow. It was *actually* snowing. Soft white flakes fell as Vin held the reins loosely through his leather gloves, trusting his horse to find its footing along the narrow, slippery path. "Mid-October." He sighed. This was the earliest he'd *ever* seen snow.

But they were in Pennsylvania. Let it snow! They were in Pennsylvania. They could stop in towns, stay in tavern inns, knock on the door at an occasional farm they ran upon, or build a campfire. Relief had never felt this good.

Celeste. The thought of her ate at him constantly—he'd never felt such an intense longing. What a fool he'd been, even in a moment of discontent, to doubt who they were or where his heart belonged. He hadn't doubted it for one second since falling off that cliff. *If it be Your will, Gott, have mercy on me and send me back to Celeste, Steven, and Drew. Until then, may I use my time as You desire.*

His horse started down another mountainside. Getting out of Ohio with bounty hunters dogging their tracks nine ways to Sunday had been no easy feat. They'd had to take different trails and backtrack to throw them off. Every offbeat trail had been harder to navigate and less direct.

About ten hours inside of Ohio before getting to the border of Pennsylvania, a snake had spooked the horse Tandey rode. The horse bucked hard and took off running. The boy hit a tree before landing. He'd been unable to walk or ride for a week. Vin had been afraid if they put him on a horse, any internal bruising or bleeding he had would rip open and he'd die. So they tethered the horses deep in the woods, inside the underbrush as cover. Vin and George made a makeshift camp in a small cave under a nearby cliff, and they'd holed up there, praying patrollers didn't find them. The next morning, the horse that had run off was standing in the same area with the other horses, ready to receive oats for the morning feeding.

Their camp became home for a while. Not comfortable or fun, but temporary living with the knowledge that better living would happen in their future. Hope was sustaining. Patrollers never found them.

When Tandey could walk and ride again, they made it to what Vin believed was the Mahoning River and swam beside their horses until they reached the other side. They didn't go straight across. The current pushed them farther south. It'd been cold and everything they owned was wet, but they mounted their horses and kept heading east . . . in case they were in Virginia instead of Pennsylvania. A day later, when they happened upon a cabin, Vin knocked on the door.

The owner, Wilhelm Kemper from Germany, confirmed they were in Pennsylvania. The hollers from Vin, George, and Tandey had caught the man off guard, but he laughed, saying he felt the same way when he and his wife got off their boat at the New York port.

He offered them a hot meal. His wife, Erna, joined him on the porch. After a minute of chatting, she motioned for them to come eat.

Cooked food had never tasted so good—corn bread, fried squirrel, and home-canned tomatoes and lima beans. Neither George nor Tandey had seen or eaten a tomato. But they all ate plenty that night and took some with them. They hauled and heated water for a hot bath and they washed and hung out their clothes. It felt as if the Kempers had passed Vin a huge, delicious slice of mental health. He didn't know how else to think about it.

That was two days ago.

Outmaneuvering the patrollers and dealing with Tandey's injuries had cost them time, but they were in one piece and still making progress. For that, Vin was eternally grateful. In the four weeks they'd been heading for Lancaster, they'd covered about a hundred and fifty miles, gone over numerous mountains, crossed rivers, waded through endless creeks on foot or on horseback. Best Vin figured, they had about two hundred and fifty miles to go.

"Hold up!" George yelled.

"Whoa, boy." Vin patted the horse as he came to a stop.

It wasn't a good idea to turn his horse around on this slippery slope. Instead, Vin remained in the saddle and turned as best he could, catching a glimpse of George. The cold spell and high winds had all three of them wearing about as many layers as a man could and still ride a horse—fur hats that covered their ears and backs of their necks, buffalo hides with fur, several pairs of wool socks, thick boots, leather gloves, and numerous blankets.

George had his hand up, signaling for Vin to wait. He tilted his head, listening for something. Vin removed his fur hat, uncovering his ears while looking as far as he could in the blowing snow. He heard nothing, but snow was a great silencer of sound.

Once they were closer to Lancaster, maybe before they entered

York, the terrain would be rolling hills with north-south ridges to cross and a lot of flat, open fields and forests. That was the terrain he grew up with. When they reached the Susquehanna, they'd cross by ferry and finally be in Lancaster County. Even if it snowed enough that they'd need to find lodging until it melted, it would melt quickly this time of year, and it'd be unlikely to snow again for a couple of weeks. They could be in Lancaster the first week of November. At that point, he'd be within twenty miles of Peach Bell.

Peach Bell. Maybe once he was there, God would send him back to Celeste. He longed to feel her warm lips welcoming him home. See her holding up the blankets, inviting him to slide in the bed next to her. Sketching faces had nothing to offer compared to being with his family again. Absolutely nothing. Still, it was a loss of part of who he was, just one he accepted with peace.

A tinny sound caught his ears, and his daydreams vanished. He angled his head like a dog trying to understand.

Tandey pointed north. "That's a bell ringing and screams."

Vin heard it too. He dug his heels into the horse, and all three of them left the trodden path. Vin held on tight, urging his horse to hurry. But it was hard to make out which way the sound was coming from while the horses' hooves crunched across snow and dead leaves.

George took the lead. Vin and Tandey followed. They came to a clearing and paused. The bell continued to ring, and they took off toward the sound of it. Soon a cabin came into view. Flames leapt from the roof and windows. A child, maybe seven, stood in the yard, screaming and ringing a dinner bell. A youngster, maybe two, was near a tree, also screaming.

A woman ran outside, carrying two buckets, her blonde hair dangling wildly. She looked up at them. *"Helfen Sie uns! Bitte!"*

Help us! Please! She was German.

"Jah." Vin jumped off his horse.

George grabbed the buckets from the woman and lowered them into the well. Tandey went with his father to help. Vin hurried into the cabin. Smoke churned through the room and fire roared overhead. They couldn't stop this. The burning roof would crash, falling inside and catching all of the cabin on fire.

All they had were a few minutes to salvage what they could.

He grabbed bedding and ran outside, throwing the items on the ground. "Do you have a box or washtub?"

The woman shook her head. "*Nein* English."

"A *Waschwanne*."

"Jah." The woman pointed. A huge washtub sat near the clothesline that had a quilt hanging on it. The washtub had unfrozen water in it; maybe she'd been outside washing laundry earlier or tending to livestock.

He dumped out its contents. "George, forget drawing buckets of water. The roof will crash soon. Grab as many items as possible—clothes, food, utensils."

He hurried inside, and the woman came in behind him, looking wide-eyed and panicked.

George and Tandey ran into the house carrying a quilt. They took armfuls of items from the kitchen and put them onto the blanket—all sorts of dry goods and cooking and eating utensils. They gathered up the blanket, each holding a side of it, and ran outside.

"*Wasser! Eimer mit Wasser!*"

"Nein!" Buckets of water wouldn't do any good.

Vin grabbed stacks of clothes and diapers from a shelf near the sole bed and threw them into the washtub. "*Die Kabine kann nicht gerettet werden. Sparen Sie Kleidung, Decken, Lebensmittel, Utensilien.*" He repeated to her similar to what he'd told George. The cabin couldn't be saved. Save clothes, blankets, food, utensils.

"Nein! Nein!" She grabbed his arm, shaking it. *"Wir werden ohne Obdach sterben!"* She screamed they'd die without shelter.

He pulled free and grabbed coats off of wooden pegs and boots from under the edge of the bed. *"Wenn Sie nicht greifen, was Sie können, verlieren Sie mehr als die Kabine. Du wirst alles verlieren."* *If you don't grab what you can, you'll lose more than the cabin. You'll lose everything.*

He tossed the items into the tub.

"Nein!" she shrieked.

Was she beyond being able to understand words regardless of the language? A man could hunt for food. No one could survive the cold without proper clothing.

There—a tiny closet. He grabbed everything he could from it, including a wedding dress that appeared to be from a much fancier time than life in this cabin. A piece of the roof fell mere feet from him. He pointed at ceiling. *"Wir müssen raus!"* *We have to get out!*

She looked up. Perhaps it was dawning on her since she ran the few feet to the kitchen and jerked a small rug off the floor. She lifted a small door and pulled a leather pouch out.

"Let's go!" he shouted.

She didn't budge.

"Lass uns gehen," he repeated in German.

She stood there, looking frozen as she clutched the leather pouch. Vin threw the tub toward the front door. George and Tandey picked up the tub and its contents and rushed into the yard. Vin grabbed the woman by the arm and pulled her from the cabin.

They moved farther away from the cabin. The children were quiet now. The woman, most likely their mother, was stone-faced as she watched the cabin burn.

Everything surrounding the cabin was wet from the thin layer of snow, and sparks dissolved in midair and wherever they landed.

That was excellent news. If it had been an average dry fall day with brown leaves exposed, this mountainside would be on fire right now.

Vin went to the pile of dishes on the quilt and picked up a tin mug. He went to the well and drew a fresh bucket of cold water. He took it to the woman. *"Trinken Sie."* When she didn't drink, he held it to her lips. "Trinken Sie."

She did as he said. He didn't know the specifics of why, but he knew that drinking water when stressed reduced the negative mental and physical impacts. "Gut."

She didn't take the cup, but he tilted it again, and she drank more.

"When's her husband supposed to be back?" Tandey asked.

Vin repeated Tandey's question in German.

"Er ist tot."

Vin looked her in the eyes, seeing a vacancy she wasn't going to come back from anytime soon.

He looked at Tandey. "He's dead."

"Dead?" George repeated. "Does she have family . . . or anyone that could take her in?"

Vin asked her. She remained stone-faced, staring at the burning cabin as she answered him. She had no one. She and her husband and the children arrived in this country nine months ago without any family or friends. Her husband died in August.

Vin needed a moment alone. "No. She has no one," he said. "I'll be back in a bit." He strode down the path leading from the cabin—it probably went toward town . . . however far away it was. His knee was a bit stiff, but he hurried anyway.

"Gott . . . ," he whispered, unsure of what else to say.

If only he could go back to Celeste and make things right, repent for being selfish, and spend the rest of his life not being that way. But over and over, circumstances slowed him and added to the impossibility of his task to get to Lancaster. His home county was no promise of getting to his home time. Still, he was weary of the fight to get to the Coopers'. And the longest stretch of the journey was ahead of them.

"Love suffers long..." A whisper reached his ears, and he stopped cold. The wind rustled through the trees, branches and leaves stirring in response. Had he heard a voice, or had he imagined it? Did it matter whether it was audible or just so strong inside him it sounded audible? More thoughts based on 1 Corinthians 13 came to him.

It . . . love . . . does not dishonor others. It is not self-seeking . . . It always protects . . .

This was a new revelation. He loved Celeste, no doubt, but he'd also been self-seeking and dishonoring. Did that mean he hadn't learned to love with a God love? Had he expected her to love him with a godly love while he loved her as a man for a woman?

He'd been selfish. He could see that, but how selfish? Ninety percent? Seventy? Twenty? He wasn't sure, but walking off to be alone was his biggest mistake and how he landed here. No, he wouldn't do that again. Vin turned, going back toward the still-burning cabin, its smoke billowing.

He knew what had to be done. The nameless woman and her children had to go with them. There was no other way. She was in a similar predicament as Celeste—no husband around while raising two little ones. He wanted to do more than just drop her off at some stranger's house and hope they did right by her.

It'd be a hard trip with a broken woman and two possibly traumatized children. But love was patient. It didn't dishonor, wasn't self-seeking, and it always protected.

If being selfish without realizing it got him here, would learning how to care for and protect this widow and her children the way he should've loved and protected Celeste and their children help him get home again?

Good grief. He rolled his eyes. Even his question reeked of self-seeking. He hadn't meant it that way, but basically his question was, if he did good by this woman and her children, would it bring him the reward he wanted?

I don't mean to think that way, Gott. Forgive me.

He went to the woman. *"Ich bin Vin."*

"Mama is Johanna," the little boy said. "I'm Gustav. My *Schwester* . . . uh, sister is Gretchen."

"Hallo, Gustav. You speak some English?"

He nodded. "Papa."

"Your papa taught you? Gut." Vin put his hand on his head, then said, "George, can we talk for a minute?"

George and Vin stepped a few feet away.

"If Johanna is willing, I can't leave them behind, even at a local preacher's place in a nearby town. It feels wrong, but I don't want to make decisions for you. If you and Tandey want—"

"We don't. We're a team."

Relief eased across Vin's shoulders. "Denki."

They walked back to Johanna, and Vin explained the situation to her in German and asked what she wanted to do—stay, go to a preacher's home, or travel with them to the town of Lancaster. He didn't know how she and the children would survive if she chose to stay, and he didn't feel good about the preacher's home, but he wouldn't make the decision for her. That'd be too close to kidnapping someone.

The boy nodded. "We go with *Sie*? Jah, we go." The boy said it with authority, as if he was answering for his mama. "Wagon." He pointed to a small barn Vin hadn't noticed until now.

Johanna's eyes never moved from the burning cabin, but he felt sure she'd heard him and was trying to muster the strength to decide and to answer.

Minutes ticked by. Finally she nodded. *"Wir gehen mit Ihnen."*

We go with you. Her eyes met his, and he wondered if she'd even remember this moment in time. She wiped tears. *"Danke."*

"Gern geschehen."

"We go with Sie?" the boy asked again.

"Jah." Vin tousled the boy's hair. "Jah, you go with us."

Relief entered the boy's eyes. "Danke."

Vin offered a faint smile, knowing the journey held a lot of dangers for little ones.

He and George walked to the small barn. There was an odd-shaped wagon with a canvas cover over its bows. It was a small wagon, narrow in width, probably to make it easier to get between trees along the trail. It must've been specially made to traverse the narrow mountain trails and be able to go around and through trees rather than cut the trees as they went. He, George, and Tandey could load up what had survived the fire in the wagon, along with the little ones.

How hard should they push to get to the Coopers' home before the winter snows set in? This crazy, cold fall . . . If this half inch of snow in October was foreshadowing what the following weeks would hold, they could become stranded without shelter and die. It happened even in Vin's days with weather forecasters and rescue teams. Snow and ice stranded people in their cars on highways and back roads and sometimes they died. He had no way of having a hint what the weather would do two days from now, let alone two or three weeks.

George tapped the wagon with the flat of his fist. "Let's get this out and loaded up. We've got miles to make before the sun goes down."

Chapter Sixteen

Celeste picked up a pine board from its storage shelf. She glanced out the window and smiled, her heart warmed by the sight. Steven and Drew were bundled up to ward off the mid-November air while playing in the fenced yard beside the shop. She took the wood to the table with the reciprocating saw. She'd given her boys lunch just a few minutes ago, and they were snacking on pretzels while playing, so maybe she'd get twenty minutes of uninterrupted time before one of them needed something.

The sound of a buggy on her gravel driveway caused her to go to the front window. The bishop and his wife? Why were Mark and Lovina here? A moment later, another buggy pulled into her driveway. She removed her leather apron, put on a black sweater, and went outside. The second buggy held the deacon and preacher.

She closed her eyes, steeling herself for what this meant. The deacon and her father-in-law, Eli, had been best friends since they were little boys. The deacon was bound to have heard an earful of strife against Celeste. Was that why they were here?

"Hi." Lovina got out of the rig, looking sympathetic and kind. "The ministers need to speak to you, so I'll play with the boys. Okay?"

Celeste nodded. "Denki."

It'd been nearly eight weeks since she'd taken furniture into town with the enlarged sketch of her and the boys on a poster. She'd hoped the length of time without a visit meant the ministers had accepted what she'd done, and she wouldn't be questioned about it. Maybe the Millers hadn't mentioned what they'd seen in town. Had the ministers just now caught wind of it, or had they been discussing what to do about it all this time?

Mark's face was solemn. He gestured toward the house. "Could we sit at your dining room table and talk?"

She once again nodded. Her heart pounded and she clenched her sweaty palms. The four of them walked across the driveway and yard and went into the house.

Her kitchen was a mess—dishes overflowing from the sink, various food items across the counters, and their lunch plates and cups still on the table. How a woman kept a home was a sign of her value, something taught to each girl from early on. She quickly removed the items from the table, got a wet cloth, and wiped off jelly and peanut butter. Drew's high chair looked like a health hazard all by itself. One of his great joys was seeing how much of a mess he could make out of food before he ate it. Unfortunately, she no longer had time to clean it properly after every meal . . . or a week of meals. Her face had to be red. She knew the judgments they were thinking right now, despite how silent they were. Then it dawned on her. Not one of them had ever had to raise small children while trying to make ends meet. If they'd been caught in a situation like that, they'd have moved back home for their mamms to give them relief or they would've remarried by now.

"Celeste, it's fine," Mark said. "Kumm sit."

Alvin, the deacon, was the most terrifying of the ministers. The bishop was often a mediator between a member and their conduct, but the deacon had the real power. Her dat once said that when the deacon spoke, God Himself better pay heed.

Leonard, the preacher, was a rather calm soul, but he preferred everyone just do as he thought they should and let him get on with his day. He was nearing seventy-five now.

"Let's open with prayer," Mark said. Each one bowed their head, but no one said a word.

She shut her eyes tight, begging God to give her the right words. The men shifted, and when she opened her eyes, they were watching her.

The deacon put his Bible on the table. "It has come to our attention that you've made a board of some kind with photos of you and your boys on it."

"Jah, a poster board to advertise who created the furniture."

"What you've done with those images, does it feel right to you?"

Celeste had never had to answer to a minister like this. She'd always been a good girl. *Gott, I need gut and godly answers.* "Nothing feels right about what I'm going through. I need ways of making more money so my bills are paid, and what I did feels different and unusual but not wrong."

"We can take up a collection for you," Leonard said.

"Nee, but denki. Our people have enough bills of their own. Besides, if anyone had wanted to give me money, they would have done so without the ministers pressuring them through a collection."

Alvin touched his Bible. "'Pride goeth before destruction.'"

Celeste stared at the Bible. Was her attitude prideful? "Is it pride to not want people to give what they don't wish to give? Am I mistaken that God's Word says to be a joyful giver? If I want what others have and they don't want to give it away, it seems I'd be closer to envy than godliness."

"She makes a reasonable point about that, I think," the bishop said.

"But . . ." The deacon held up his index finger. "It's still a matter of taking sketches to a photo shop and enlarging them and making a board with your image and that of your sons in order to sell things. You also put your name on it, as if you're proud of yourself."

Celeste nodded. "I thought the same thing, but while praying about what to do, I remembered seeing a billboard on the highway a few years back, showing Amish men from our community at work building play sets. Their faces were hidden, but their names and phone numbers were listed. Did I do something they didn't?"

"It's wrong!" Alvin said. "Why are you questioning us like this? Losing your husband does not give you the right to talk to us ministers in this way!"

Celeste blinked, unable to comprehend that he thought her questions were disrespectful. "I . . . I don't understand."

"You are in a woodshop working like a man. It's wrong," Alvin said. "You promote yourself, using your husband's absence as a way to profit from it."

Celeste turned to the bishop. She knew the three men were to present a united front, even if one of the others disagreed, but she was hoping for some sign that he saw this man's outburst for what it was—unfair. But the bishop gave no indication of what he thought.

"I know my situation is different, and I'm asking everyone to be accepting of this odd circumstance. We Amish live by the Old Ways and the accepted practice of what women do and don't do, but I need the woodshop. It's my only way of making a living, and my sons need to learn a trade, just like all the other Amish boys are learning a trade."

"Women have been in your place before, and they baked goods to sell or sewed clothing or cleaned houses," Mark said.

"Have they been in my position?" Celeste asked. "You know of single young women with children who can't remarry but must provide for their little ones? Women whose community is so unsure of how and why their husbands disappeared that they can barely talk to them at church meetings, let alone support them with an open heart?" She reached across the table and touched the Bible. "Please don't use this as a weapon against me because my actions fit my circumstances. I understand that I don't appear Amish enough for onlookers. But if you correct me over that, aren't you allowing fear of what the Englisch think to rule how you treat your own?"

"That's *not* what we're doing," the deacon said. "The Old Ways do not allow for a woman to do as you're doing."

"I've always helped Vin in the woodshop, and that was allowed. Other women do the same, keeping the books on their husbands' businesses or ordering supplies or going into the fields to plant and harvest or into the milking parlor to milk cows. I don't have a man to stand beside as we toil together, so I must bake or sew or clean, even though my sons need me to hold on to this woodshop? Even though those jobs would not come close to helping me make ends meet? Am I a sinner now because I continue in a vocation I worked at when Vin was here?"

"It's not right," the deacon repeated.

"I agree," Celeste said. "This place where I find myself is *not* right. None of it is right. Will you make it even more wrong for me and my sons than it already is?"

The deacon stood, and the bishop and preacher followed suit. She rose.

"We will discuss this privately before we make our decision." Alvin tucked his Bible under his arm and walked out the door. Leonard followed right behind him.

The bishop hesitated. "I know this is hard, Celeste. I'm sorry for that. But if the vote does not go in your favor, perhaps it's time to rethink moving back to Indiana with your parents." He left.

Celeste crumpled in her seat. Was this what Vin felt—as if he was doing no wrong, but the ministers decided it was sin where there was none? It was such a hard place to be, feeling unheard yet judged.

She couldn't imagine moving back to live with her parents. After the wedding in Indiana, this was where she and Vin came to live as husband and wife, where they had their babies. This was where she began to truly connect with God as an adult . . . as a wife and mother. It was hard living here, but she felt connected to herself, to God.

She didn't want to be in sin, and she didn't want to be made to believe something was a sin simply because it was outside the Amish norms. Her life was outside the Amish norm. She was having to get used to it. Were they capable of adjusting too?

Chapter Seventeen

Snow flurries swirled as Vin steered the wagon through Lancaster. He'd been bone weary for weeks, but right now, all he felt was a surge of gratefulness and energy. His breath made puffs in the air, and like those traveling with him, he had on many layers of winter clothes. What strange storybook character must he look like in his full, shaggy beard and his buffalo fur coat and matching hat?

Men on horseback as well as men and women driving horse-drawn carriages filled the dirt road, and people bustled along the wooden sidewalks.

He looked at Johanna, who sat on the far side of the wagon seat with her son between them. She reminded him of Celeste in many ways. They were each in their midtwenties with blonde hair, blue eyes, and two little ones. They were each as vulnerable as they were strong, and they were willing and able to pitch in and be serious help. No matter what else was going on in their minds and hearts, they were always nurturing and protective of their children.

Every time Vin reached out to offer Johanna a hand throughout the long days and nights of hard travel, he prayed someone was helping Celeste in the same way. Life was not designed to be lived on one's own, especially with little ones to fend for.

"Biz-eee." Johanna peered around Gustav from her place on the wagon seat. Gretchen was asleep in the bed of the wagon.

"Busy, jah."

She'd hardly spoken a word the first two weeks of traveling. She and her children had been with them for six weeks now, and she was trying to learn English. Her eyes held grief, but she was putting effort into coping and into being strong for her children. Was Celeste struggling like this? He'd been gone four months. Was someone helping her as the McLaughlins had helped him? As he was helping Johanna?

The wind picked up, and a shiver ran through him. He was used to driving a rig in winter, but he'd mostly gone short distances, maybe thirty minutes one way, before getting out somewhere warm for hours. Riding in the cold from sunup until sundown, with no enclosed carriage as a windbreak, was hard in ways he could never explain.

He'd lost track of the date but knew it was late November. Maybe the first week in December.

"'Let it snow, let it snow, let it snow.'" He sang the old song he used to hear in Englischer stores, knowing it'd yet to be written or recorded. The song burst out of him, his heart so relieved to have made it here—and that they'd arrived before winter snows truly set in.

This town looked so different in 1822. Dirt roads. A few cobblestone streets. Horses. Wagons. Four miles ago, he'd entered the city of Lancaster and marveled at all he saw. He'd already seen the steeple of the Holy Trinity Lutheran Church and the double steeples of the German Reformed church. Those were landmarks he'd seen his whole life, and he had no words to describe what this felt like. In his day, life seemed to be taken for granted, and it was never quite enough while also being too much. In this day, people seemed to think about God more than their own agenda. Those churches still stood in his time, but he'd never thought much about them. He'd spent his time thinking about his next job or the money he'd make or how he'd use his leisure time, but—from his first encounters with George and Tandey, Bridget and Patrick, James and Ester—people in this time seemed deeply connected to God, asking Him daily what He wanted to accomplish in and through them that day.

He drove on past a blacksmith shop. A leather shop. Woodcraft shop. Dress shops. Shoemakers, drapers, milliners, haberdashers, bakers, butchers, grocers, and gunsmiths. The unfamiliar noises of town in the 1800s rang in his ears like memorable songs from church Sundays, and his soul rejoiced.

George and Tandey were on horseback behind him, following him to the Coopers' place. He'd like to see the looks on their faces as they took in the town that would become home for them, at least for a while. It was the best built and busiest city in Pennsylvania at this time. Philly would pass it soon, maybe in five years.

He felt closer to Celeste already, as if riding down some of the same roads they used to travel together using horse and buggy built a bridge between them.

He was home. Wrong century, but no doubt this was home. He hoped Anke, the Gott Brucke believer, would be able to help him.

They'd made it. He breathed another sigh of relief. They were safe after seventy-three days of traveling. Ten weeks of crossing rivers and creeks and mountains. Surviving on determination and the grace of God. They were here—smellier, stronger, with more scars than when they left Ohio, but mostly in one piece.

"Haw fur?" Johanna asked.

Gustav grinned. "Just o'er a hundred more mountains."

"Nein!" she shrieked, laughing before she kissed the top of his head.

Gustav laughed. "Through a dozen more wooden bridges?"

"True?" She looked around her son to Vin.

"Nee. One, possibly two more wooden bridges. No mountains."

She smiled at him. "Gut."

"I think we're about eight miles and a couple of turns away from the Coopers'." He based that on directions Ester had given him, as well as his personal knowledge of where the redbrick mansion was on Harvest Road. But roads were laid out a little different during this time, and everything looked so altered that even when he knew where he was, he wasn't sure he was where he thought.

"I work hard." Her voice wavered.

"We all will, jah."

"I work hard."

He nodded. She was nervous about needing a place to stay. Whatever she had in the leather pouch that she'd grabbed from under the kitchen floorboards must not have monetary value. She kept it close to her, and it seemed to mean a lot to her, but she intended to be worthy of the trip here as well as worthy of help from the Coopers. All a person really had was what they could offer to another, and for poor folks, that meant hard work.

If it be Your will, God, I beg of You to have mercy on me and send me back to Celeste, Steven, and Drew. Until then, may I use my time as You desire.

The sights and sounds of town faded behind them as they entered southeast Lancaster. The roads were smooth, especially compared to all they'd come through crossing the mountains. Memories and thoughts flooded him in this familiar place. The brick mansion came into view, looking picturesque as snow flurries swirled. Out of nowhere, nerves rattled him, too. The place was huge. Beautiful glass windows, a large wraparound porch. He stopped the wagon at the end of a long brick walkway that led to the house. He couldn't take his eyes off this place.

The mansion looked much like it had when he and Celeste toured it, but the surrounding acreage looked better tended to and didn't have signs or a parking lot.

"Hello." A woman's voice interrupted his thoughts. A radiant woman, with silver hair peeking out from under her bonnet and a basket of kale and beets in hand, walked up the red cobblestone sidewalk from the garden. Her clothing was simple—not what Vin would picture the matriarch of a mansion wearing—but he had a feeling he was looking at Margaret Cooper.

She paused. "Is thee in need of food?"

Shame at his haggard appearance prickled at him. He hadn't shaved or cut his hair since arriving in this time, and the last proper bath he had was more than a month ago at the Kemper place, although he'd washed up in rivers, creeks, and streams. "My name is Vin Lantz." He gestured at George and Tandey. "We've traveled from Ohio, where we became friends with James and Ester McLaughlin."

"Friends?" Excitement filled her voice. "Oh, what a surprise! Are they well?"

"Jah. All of them are—James, Ester and their children, as well as Patrick, Bridget, Brendan, Liam, Delia, and their four children."

She smiled. "Thee has brought us good news on the eve of Thanksgiving."

"Tomorrow is Thanksgiving?"

She nodded. "For our household it is. Decades ago, we chose to honor President Washington's 1789 proclamation and use Thursday of this last week in November, as he stated Thursday as the day to be grateful and pray. And now we have even more to be grateful for."

Once, he'd read a book about the history of Thanksgiving. This region of Pennsylvania had especially strong ties to recognizing Thanksgiving as an important day of prayer, although others used a date in December and some October. It'd be four decades from now before the event would get a fixed date and become a national holiday.

"Today's date?" He'd never get used to not knowing the exact time or date.

"November 27. Will thee come in? My husband will be home soon, and supper is in an hour. We can talk about the McLaughlins and thee's journey."

That sounded like a slice of heaven, but he and the others were grungy and in need of baths. More than that, they weren't there for a meal with the Coopers. "We've traveled for months, hoping you'd provide us a place to stay for a while."

"That is even better news than sharing one meal." She gestured down the road. "Turn right at the corner and follow the road to the barn. Put thine creatures away and we will heat water for baths and find clean clothes."

Without a moment of warning, his eyes welled with tears. "Denki." His voice cracked.

Her brows furrowed slightly.

"It means thank you."

"Thee is most welcome." She gave a slow nod of her head that looked more like a slight bow to begin a prayer. "We have nothing that is not on loan to us from God, and thee is welcome to enjoy it with us."

He clicked his tongue, and the horse did his bidding. He and his fellow travelers were in the barn at least half an hour, tending to the horses' hooves, brushing thick dirt and mud off them, and making sure they felt safe and secure in these new surroundings. They fed and watered them, so grateful for their hard work. This group couldn't have made that trek without these amazing animals, and for the first time in forever, these creatures would sleep under a roof and not have to work tomorrow.

Before they were halfway up the stone path that led to the back door, Margaret came outside. "Did thee find everything thee needed?"

"Jah. This is Johanna Bohmer and her son, Gustav. The little one in her arms is her daughter, Gretchen."

Johanna curtsied. "I work hard."

Margaret nodded. "We always need help, dear, but for the next few days at the least, thee and each one are our guests."

Johanna looked to Vin and he repeated what Margaret said in German. Johanna had probably caught most of the words but not enough to be sure she'd understood.

"*Danke,*" Johanna said.

Vin gestured. "And this is George Alexander and his son, Tandey."

"Welcome. I'm Margaret Cooper, and since we're all God's children and all equal in His eyes, we will call each other by our first names."

That was the Amish way too. Whether a student speaking to a schoolteacher or an adult talking to the bishop, they typically used first names without titles.

A young woman came to the door of the house. She favored Ester in every way, and Vin knew he was looking at Anke. His heart turned a flip. Hope soared that she could help him find the Gott Brucke, so God would give him the knowledge he needed to return to his beloved Celeste and sons.

Anke stopped in the middle of the stone path a few feet from him. Her green eyes locked on his; not a hint of a smile or welcome crossed her face.

"Anke," Margaret said. "These dear ones have traveled from very far and—"

"Have we met?" Anke's eyes stayed glued to his. The question was innocent enough, but her tone hinted at a potential accusation.

Vin smiled. "We haven't, but I've been looking forward to meeting you since—"

"But you're from around here," Anke stated, sounding confident in her assessment. Had she bristled?

"I . . ." What could he say? There was no telling what someone might sense when they connected with the Gott Brucke as she did. And he certainly was hiding a lot from everyone . . . for their sakes. "I . . ."

"My darling girl," Margaret said. "Vin is from Ohio, and they have all traveled from a long distance. How could thee have met?"

Her eyes searched his for a long moment, and if he was reading her right, she didn't trust him.

"Anke?" Margaret called.

"Oh." Anke broke eye contact. "Of course." She took a breath before looking to the others. "Welcome."

Margaret put her arm around Anke's shoulders. "They know Ester and James and their children."

Anke's eyes lit up. "You know my sister?" Her expression warmed as she glanced at George, Tandey, and Johanna, but she didn't look Vin's way. "Oh, that is *wunderbar*."

Margaret chuckled. "Wunderbar means *wonderful*."

George removed his hat. "Ma'am, just the menfolk know your family."

Margaret nodded.

"Wunderbar?" A rare smile crossed Johanna's lips. *"Anke, sprechen Sie Deutsch?"*

"Jah." Anke nodded, assuring Johanna she spoke German.

A young woman came out of the house, walking down the stone path. "The baths are ready, although they are a little too hot at this moment."

How had they boiled that much water for four baths so quickly?

"Very good, Elizabeth. Thank thee," Margaret said. "Anke, would thee share enough about the home so our guests understand how to have their needs met before leading them to their rooms? Our guests have had forced closeness sharing a wagon or campfire for a very long time. Johanna and the children will stay in the blue room. Vin will sleep in the oak room. George, we have enough rooms ready for thee and Tandey to each have one. Unless . . ."

George glanced at his son, who nodded. "Tandey would appreciate a separate room. Thank you."

Margaret nodded. "Anke, lead our guests, please."

"Yes." Anke led the way into the home and paused inside the first room. "This is the back storage room. If you run out of firewood for your room or are in need of a tool, a crate, a fresh bucket of water, or a place to dry clothes or muddy boots, this is the room for it." She then repeated the words in German before she motioned to a bench that had boots and shoes under it. Vin sat on it and began removing his boots. The others followed suit.

From the bench, he caught Anke's eye and smiled, trying to be warm and friendly, but she looked away, took a step back, and seemed to shudder. Once Vin and the other guests had taken their boots off, Anke walked through the kitchen, pointing out a few things as she made her way to the foyer. They followed in their stocking feet. She paused occasionally, giving the names of various rooms in English and German—the parlor, the library, the breakfast room, and the dining room. Her eyes and smile went to each person . . . except Vin.

He watched her, smiling and nodding. Maybe he was trying too hard. Was he reading more into her behavior than he should because so many of his hopes were riding on her acceptance of him?

A loud thud echoed through the room. She startled, glancing at Vin and instantly moving farther away from him.

Nope, her wariness of him wasn't his imagination.

Margaret spotted the source of the noise and laughed. "Benjamin, thee must hold the armful of firewood more securely when stocking rooms for the night."

Benjamin appeared to be about twelve. "Yes, Margaret. I will."

Anke pressed the palms of her hands down the front of her apron. "This way." She took a wide berth, avoiding getting near Vin.

Even if Anke were willing to help him, could she hear from God on his behalf when she was this leery of him?

Vin's hopes that Anke might be willing to help him find the Gott Brucke faded like sunlight slipping below the horizon.

Chapter Eighteen

The bouquet of delicious aromas from the Thanksgiving meal filled the air as Anke carried a tray upstairs. Agnes, the cook, had been up early preparing the special dishes, and there were still hours to go before time for the feast. Light streamed through the windows at the end of the hall. Anke stopped outside Johanna's room, listening to be sure she and the children were still awake. Agnes said they'd come down for breakfast, but it was possible they'd needed a nap after their arduous journey. Anke heard Johanna talking to one of her children, and she knocked.

Johanna opened the door.

"A midmorning bite." Anke held up the tray, feeling confident Johanna understood without the need for her to speak German.

"Danke." She opened the door wider. *"Komm herein."*

Anke entered. The little ones were sprawled on the floor playing, and it made her smile. It must feel heavenly to be out of that wagon and inside where everything was stationary and warm. *"Darf ich?"* Anke gestured, making it clear she wanted to set the tray on the floor and using the simple words *May I.*

Johanna nodded, and they both sat on the floor. The Coopers often had guests stay or visit for a few days or weeks, but there was something unusually pleasant about this woman, unlike the man Vin that Johanna had been traveling with. Was he her husband?

Margaret stopped at the doorway. "Anke, there thee is."

Anke had asked Elizabeth to bring her dinner and breakfast to her bedroom just to avoid Vin. She couldn't keep avoiding him, especially not on Thanksgiving Day, but he wasn't who he pretended to be, and she was unsure what to do about that yet. She didn't fear that he meant physical harm to anyone. Her sense of it said he wasn't a thief either. But she hoped to avoid him until her hunch was sorted out.

"Thee missed dinner and breakfast. Our new guests have stories of thine sister, dear."

"I look forward to you sharing them with me."

Margaret sat in a nearby rocker.

When a shadow moved in the hallway, Anke shifted her attention to it. Vin stopped directly in front of Johanna's bedroom door, but a few feet away, staying more in the middle of the hallway. Was he being polite or just pretending to be?

"Vin." Johanna grinned. *"Guten Morgen."*

Johanna didn't seem to hold any reservations about the man.

He returned her smile. "Good morning, Johanna."

Johanna said several things in German, asking how he'd slept. Apparently their paths hadn't crossed thus far this morning. Vin moved to the doorway and responded to Johanna.

He shifted. "Margaret, Anke, I have something for you." His voice was soft, and he held up an odd-shaped object covered with what looked like candle wax. "Some of the contents are maps and information for William, but the rest is from Ester for you and Anke."

"Letters, what a blessing from God." Margaret got up from the rocker and took the cylinder.

"I came close to losing this a few times during the journey when crossing rivers, so I wanted to give it to you before anything else can happen to it."

"That's kind of thee, Vin," Margaret said. "Isn't it, Anke?"

Her heart pounded. "It is." She wanted the letters that must be inside it, but more than anything else right now, she longed to question this man. Still, he was William and Margaret's guest, and neither would put up with any hint of inhospitality. It dawned on her that rather than doing what felt comfortable and avoiding him while praying, she should have gone to dinner and breakfast and peppered him with gentle, polite questions.

"I feel it was the least I could do," Vin said.

Margaret turned to Anke. "He says Patrick and Bridget saved his life and that Ester helped him heal from an injury. He has many stories to share with thee."

"I do," Vin agreed. "Your sister and all the McLaughlins have told me good things about you, Anke."

Anke imagined they told him a lot while in return he'd said very little to them about himself. She could feel it. Secrets and dishonesty went hand in hand. Sometimes when people heard about her, they tried to take advantage of her connection to the Gott Brucke and use it for personal gain.

But she had secrets too, she supposed. Not dishonest ones, but private ones. Was she wrong to distrust him? "Did you sleep well?" Anke asked.

"I'm very grateful to be here, to sleep in a warm bed, but nee."

"What language is *nee*?"

"A version of German. It's a habit that I should've overcome by now. It's slang for nein, no."

"Who are your people?" If she asked enough questions, would she understand her reluctance to be near this man?

⚜

Vin should've worded his answers more carefully, but he had no choice about answering her. Others were aware he was Amish, and it wasn't an issue, but he felt sure she would scrutinize it. Not a helpful thing since his roots were in his time, not hers. "Amish."

She studied him. "With a full beard?"

He shrugged. "Many Amish are abolitionists, and it seems to me it's best not to look like one. I could've shaved last night, but while I'm here, I hope to be useful."

"But being useful is not why you're here, is it?"

"Anke," Margaret whispered.

Anke rose from the floor, picking up the tray as she did. "What have you heard about me, Vin?"

She was guarded and had no fear letting her concerns be known. If, as Patrick had said, she didn't have any friends outside the Cooper family, Vin was probably looking at why. She set the tray on a small table.

He wasn't ready to speak of the Gott Brucke. "Everyone I spoke to loves you very much."

"I never doubted that."

The way her eyes took him in left little doubt that she knew he was evading her questions. If Margaret wasn't here, he felt sure Anke would question him more directly.

She patted her cheek. "The beard . . . you're married . . . to Johanna?"

At the mention of her name, Johanna looked up from her spot

on the floor, where she was playing with her children. George and Tandey had walked into town, enjoying what it meant to be truly free and have the law on their side.

Margaret studied Anke, seeming confused that she thought Johanna and Vin were married. But Anke hadn't been present when he introduced himself and the group to Margaret. He definitely needed to clarify his marital status, but he knew some of this conversation was moving too fast for Johanna to follow. He smiled at her and slowed his words. "Nee . . . uh . . . no. Johanna is a widow. We came across her and the children on our way here, but I am married and have two young sons."

"Suh-lest, Steven, and Drew," Johanna said.

"Jah, gut, Johanna." Vin gave a nod.

Anke turned to where she'd set the tray and poured tea in a small, delicate cup. "But it seems that if you're Amish, you would shave your mustache to honor your wife and the Amish ways."

If he was Amish?

She offered the cup to him, but he shook his head. He'd had more delicious foods and beverages since arriving last night than he had in the ten weeks of traveling after leaving the McLaughlin farm. She then offered it to Margaret, who took it.

"Like I said, I'm trying to not look like an abolitionist."

Margaret took a sip of the tea. "Some Quaker men shave their mustaches like the Amish. Most don't. Quaker men wear distinctive clothes—low-brimmed hats, dark-colored suits, and shirts with no collars—but what we've learned is runaways in need of help will trust approaching men dressed Plain, knowing they are sympathizers."

"That's good to know," Vin said. "My position was one of hiding runaways while traveling and trying not to look like a sympathizer when patrollers questioned me. I . . . I might be in that position again."

Margaret rested the dainty cup in the palm of her hand. "I suppose there is a time and place for each appearance."

Anke poured another cup of tea and handed it to Johanna. "You're not fond of questions."

If he gave full answers, they would reveal that he'd traveled in time, a truth that would likely terrify her, make her believe he was insane, and she'd be unwilling to even try to help him. Besides, he wasn't great at answering questions. Celeste's questions the night he disappeared haunted him. "It's easy to give the wrong answer, one we can't take back. All of us get caught in that on occasion, Anke. Sometimes I feel I happen to live there."

Margaret stared at him. "You live there?"

Of course, that wasn't a saying in the 1800s. "An expression, meaning I stay in a place of regret over words I've said." Mostly to his wife, but he didn't wish to offend his hostess. Perhaps Margaret had never spoken out of turn and couldn't imagine anyone's struggle with it. That aside, he wanted to change the subject from Anke's inquiries.

"I arrived at your sister's place physically weak and limping. I about fell into Ester's arms, begging her to carry me and save me from the pain."

Anke finally smiled. "You're teasing."

"I am, but that's how it felt. She made me go to bed, used her limited supply of ice in July for my knee, and dared me to disobey her order to rest."

Anke chuckled. "As her little sister, I can tell you, she is not one to disobey, but a kinder, gentler heart she could not possibly have, and I miss her so very much."

"I understand." Celeste, Steven, and Drew were a constant source of longing.

She tilted her head, and the wall of ice separating them seemed to melt just a little. "You truly do, don't you?"

Vin needed to give her space for now. There was much he wanted to talk to Anke about, but he'd rather keep their encounters sparse and paced until she warmed to him. A person's inner feelings altered what they heard another person saying.

"I should go."

"You should stay," Anke said.

"Anke," Margaret whispered. "That's very bold, dear."

Anke gently took the waxed cylinder from Margaret. "I have questions." She tapped the cylinder against her palm as if its contents might be the source of her questions. He knew better.

"Well." Margaret set the teacup on the tray. "I will read the letters later. It looks as if thee two are fine without me, and there is a Thanksgiving feast to help the cooks prepare for."

It made sense that Margaret wasn't antsy to read the letters. She knew all was well with the family. Vin had stated that upon arrival. He, George, and Tandey had talked about how all the McLaughlins were doing over dinner and breakfast. Margaret was allowing Anke time to read the letters from her sister first.

"Prayer and giving of thanks begin around the dining table at one," Margaret continued. "The meal follows. Then all will retire to the library. The library is William's favorite room. Does thee enjoy reading, Vin?"

"Very much."

"Good. Thee will not be disappointed in William's collection. But for now, there is cooking I need to tend to."

"I help?" Johanna asked Margaret.

"Yes, dear. The children can play in the storage room or bundle up and play in the backyard."

Vin repeated what Margaret had said in German. Johanna looked pleased as she gathered the children's coats and hats and motioned for them. Soon the room was quiet.

Anke turned to him. "You've been in this house before."

Vin hesitated.

"I was in prayer before you arrived, and sometimes afterward, I am sensitive to things about others." She set the cylinder on a chair and put a metal cover over the jar of jam on the tray. "You're asking yourself how much to tell me. Just answer me. You've been in this home before you arrived yesterday."

He had no choice. "I have."

"If you were a guest, I would've met you, so you were a builder, I suppose. Why have you returned? What is it you're after?"

His heart thudded. "Your help."

She poured a cup of tea. "*That* I believe." She took a sip. "You seek my help because of what my beloved sister and her family told you about me."

"An accident separated me from my wife and sons, and I need help getting back to them."

Her eyes bored into his. "You're frightened."

He was. Afraid Anke wouldn't help him. Afraid he couldn't find his way back. Afraid of what Celeste was going through without him and at the same time of what she'd feel once he was home. And his sons—how well did children fare after a parent disappeared?

"Jah." He held her gaze, hoping that despite the secrets she sensed about him, she'd see he was trustworthy.

"Where did you last see your wife and children?"

"In our home."

"Which is where?"

What answer could he give? "It was in south Lancaster."

"Was?"

Did she intend to pick apart every word?

"Was," he said.

She set the teacup on the tray. "Was this your plan, to come here, say little, and get the help you needed? Did you ask yourself what I could possibly do if your few words made no sense?"

"I . . . I prayed God would make a way."

"Even God uses words that make sense so we have a chance of understanding what He wants of us."

"All I'm asking is that you seek the Gott Brucke, asking God to show me what I need to know, what I need to do, what steps I should take to repent fully and be able to get back to my family. Just ask Him. Surely you can try."

"I do not *try* to extract knowledge from the Almighty that He may not wish me or anyone to know. That is a simple matter of respect. Your request feels dark. That is a line I will not cross. And how is it that you do not know what steps to take to repent for wrongs?"

Could he tell her the full truth? Or would it only confuse her and make her put up more walls between them?

He touched the cylinder. "Let's end this conversation for today. It's Thanksgiving, and Ester would be pleased if you enjoyed what she worked to get to you." He'd told her what he needed. It wasn't within his power to convince her of his motives.

"You accept that I will not approach God on dark or selfish matters?"

"I respect how you feel, Anke. I pray God will change your mind, but for now, please accept this gift from your sister."

Anke's shoulders and face were taut as she took the cylinder from him and broke open the first seal, dried wax falling onto the floor. She got scissors from a nearby dresser and cut the leather strip he'd used as thread to sew the cylinder shut. "There's another one of these inside the first, also covered in wax."

"Jah, we crossed many rivers getting wet up to our necks. I'm hoping all the papers stayed dry." The cylinder had floated downriver twice while they were crossing over, and he'd had to swim after it.

She broke the next seal, cut the leather thread, and opened it.

Unrolling dozens of papers, she went to the bed and pulled out the maps and laid them on the quilt. She looked at the first sketch. "Oh. Portraits of my dear sister and her children." She clutched the stack to her chest without having looked past the first one. "They are dry. They are." She studied each one, going through the stack.

Finally she looked up. "These are remarkable. Who drew them?"

"I did, but the gift is from God, and they are good subjects for drawing."

It felt natural and freeing to be able to say without guilt or shame that his gift was from God. It used to feel like a reason to bear shame, a thing that everyone barely tolerated. His dat never approved of Vin drawing. He'd scowl and scold from Vin's earliest pictures he drew at four and five. Then Vin did the unthinkable and dared to draw faces.

"You?" She studied him again, seeming to see him in a little different light. "I've never seen anything like this. How did you do it?"

"I crushed charred wood, mixed it with wax, and shaped it like a quill pen. When charcoal is available, I use the same process. The paint is from various plants and berries, crushed and mixed with water. I used feathers and animal hair to make paintbrushes."

"It is quite a gift God gave you. These are beautiful."

Was more of the ice wall melting? It felt as if it was.

She returned her attention to the sketches. "Subjects?"

"Whatever it is that I'm drawing is the subject."

"Oh, jah." She traced her finger across the images. "I miss her. I've only ever seen her oldest child, and they have three now. She and James left here seven years ago. That is such a long time to be gone." She looked through all of the portraits again before lowering them. "Vin, you commune with God, and that is clear. His creativity is a part of you. But what you ask of me . . . I've never sought to know where someone is. With much prayer and fasting, I can hear God's whisper concerning how to make certain medicines using herbs and fruits He gave the earth. I'm very grateful for what God does in meeting me on the Gott Brucke to show me how to mix His blessings for healing, but that is the limit to my ability."

"Have you tried to hear more from God than about what to do when someone is dangerously sick?"

"Nein."

"You knew I'd been in this home before yesterday. You said that happened because you'd been praying about other things right before you saw me. Maybe you can hear God about this with my wife and sons. Please, at least agree to try. I'll pray and fast with you."

Anke lowered her eyes, knelt, and began picking up pieces of wax off the rug and floor. It was clear that she needed a bit of time to think.

Vin gave her proper space, but he knelt and began picking up pieces of wax too.

With her apron carrying pieces of wax, she dumped it onto the tray. She sat on the edge of the bed, staring at the floor for a long time. "I'm sorry. Your request feels shrouded in darkness and secrecy. I cannot—"

"Vin," William called. "Could thee join me in the parlor?"

He went into the hallway and looked down the stairs. "I'll be right there." He returned to the bedroom and gathered up the maps from the bed, fighting disappointment. "I told William I'd show him the maps before the Thanksgiving feast."

Vin left the room, his heart racing. This couldn't be a dead end. Maybe God had another plan or maybe He would change her mind.

If it be Your will, God, I beg of You to have mercy on me and send me back to Celeste, Steven, and Drew.

If it be Your will . . . His own words rang in his ears. What if Vin's returning home wasn't God's will? The idea threatened to undo him, and he shifted his thoughts elsewhere.

He walked down the steps carrying maps of what would eventually be known as the Underground Railroad. Many men had contributed to the information on these maps, including abolitionist friends of James and Ester's, and vital information had also come from George and Tandey. It'd taken Vin a long time and tedious conversations to draw some of these maps.

He walked into the parlor and stopped cold. William had a guest. Was the man sympathetic to the abolitionist movement? He quickly rolled up the maps.

The man looked up from a paper of some sort in his hands. He looked familiar. Had Vin possibly met him? No, that wasn't it.

"Vin." William glanced at the rolls of paper in his hand. He then gestured at the man. "This is James Buchanan, a lawyer who lives right here in Lancaster."

James Buchanan. That's why he looked familiar. Vin had seen photos of him in various books his whole life. The resemblance to the photos was uncanny.

"Good to meet you, Mr. Buchanan." Vin dipped his head.

The man barely nodded before he returned his eyes to the lone sheet of paper in his hand.

Vin remembered very little about most politicians, but Buchanan had lived in Lancaster during part of his life. He was a lawyer and politician. He became president of the United States in 1857, one term ahead of Lincoln. The man was known for believing slavery was morally wrong, but then he used his skills as a lawyer and his power as a president to ensure slavery was upheld as law. What did this man believe?

Suddenly he remembered what he had in his hands. Should he ease them behind his back? Wouldn't holding his arms behind him stick out just as much as the rolled-up papers? *Please, don't notice the maps . . .*

Mr. Buchanan lowered the paper. "William, your argument that increasing trade within slave states is good for the commonwealth of Pennsylvania as well as those other states is well-thought-out." He folded the paper and put it inside his vest. "I'll share this at the next meeting."

"The sooner the better, James. We don't need any more talk of laws constricting business with slave states." William motioned toward Vin. "This is the man I was telling thee about who arrived from Ohio yesterday with a widow and her children as well as a Black man and his son."

William had mentioned George and Tandey. Did that mean Buchanan was a safe man? Vin couldn't risk asking. *Please, don't see the maps . . .*

"Yes, I remember." Mr. Buchanan looked at the rolled-up papers in Vin's hands. "What do you have there?"

Great. Vin wasn't sure what to say. Any intelligent person who looked at the maps would realize that the marked trails weren't roads free people would use. The paths led from one farm to another many miles away, skipping all sorts of towns or homes along the way. The maps gave an escape route for runaway slaves, and the paths went to specific homes in Pennsylvania.

Anke entered the room, holding a couple of rolled-up papers herself.

William walked to her, smiling. "I missed thee last night at dinner and again at breakfast. Thee doesn't look as if thee has been feeling poorly, my dear." He bent as if to kiss her cheek, but he whispered something. They parted.

"I needed time to pray." She glanced at the papers in Vin's hand. "You have more for me." She took them. "Vin drew portraits of my sister and her family who live in Ohio."

"I'd like to see them," Mr. Buchanan said.

"You are more than welcome to after Margaret and I have seen them. I fear my sister would be upset if I showed these to you now." She held out the papers she'd entered the room with. "But you are welcome to see these."

He took them, and Anke made a quick exit.

Mr. Buchanan unrolled the papers. "Look at that. I haven't seen Ester since her wedding day when she married the wrong James." He laughed, sounding like a good friend who was teasing someone's daughter.

That's right—Buchanan never married.

The man held up a portrait. "And look at those beautiful children."

Vin breathed a sigh of relief. Anke had saved him from his naive entry into this room, and she'd done so without a stutter of nervousness.

He'd learned from Ester that people knowing who a slave sympathizer was didn't pose a problem in Pennsylvania, but word getting out of who specifically helped the movement could be dangerous, giving possible undercover enemies too much information. No one knew what side James Buchannan was truly on, and that often included the history books in retrospect. But Vin knew the man caused a huge divide in this country while trying to soothe each side to be reasonable. How could owning people and treating them as prisoners with no rights possibly be considered reasonable?

If he could get back home, he would continue to stand up for the rights of the underprivileged. He'd spent entirely too much time restless and wanting more when he should've been using his energy to help fight for social justice. Amish believed in fighting for those things . . . joining peaceful protests, marching with those who needed a louder voice, giving time and money. But first and foremost, he would put time into healing the harm he'd done to Celeste.

I beg of You to have mercy on me and send me back to Celeste, Steven, and Drew. Show me what else I need to learn, what else I need to repent of. Please, show me, and I'll do all I can to make my life right before You.

There were no words to describe how much he longed to return to Celeste, to hold her, to love her, to help raise his sons.

Could he find the Gott Brucke without Anke's help? Could he connect with God and learn what he needed to do to get home?

Chapter Nineteen

Celeste picked up the letter off the kitchen counter, where it had sat since arriving yesterday. She read it one more time and then ripped it in half and tossed it into the trash can. She wouldn't let it ruin today.

The house smelled of Thanksgiving. She opened the oven and pulled corn bread dressing out. The steam rose, carrying the scent of sage. She slid a pumpkin pie into the oven. After setting the timer, she went to the boys' room to check on them. Steven was on his bed, playing with a wood horse his dat had made him. Drew was asleep. She padded down the hallway to her room. Soon they'd go to the bishop's house to join him and his family for Thanksgiving.

A holiday without Vin. The ache in her chest was unbearable. If only he were here, he'd put his arms around her from behind, kiss her cheek, and tell her how much he loved her. They could steal a moment together.

The cardboard box in the top of her closet called to her. It held a few things that had belonged to Vin. After removing the lid, she lifted a shirt out of its plastic bag. It hadn't been washed since he'd last worn it, and it carried his smell. She removed it from the bag, buried her face in it, and breathed deep. "I miss you."

She put the shirt on and got out his sketchbook, flipping through it.

"You had such talent, Vin. I'm sorry we argued over it." Tears threatened. If he'd died in a way where he could be buried somewhere close, she'd go there to talk to him, even knowing his soul wasn't there. A few clothes, his old boots, and a sketch pad were the most of his earthly body she had now.

It still peeled her skin off to know he hadn't told her about his art, but it made more sense now. He hadn't felt safe telling her. He'd known she wouldn't understand and that she'd side with the Ordnung. She was, above all else, a rule keeper . . . or that's who she'd been before he disappeared.

She set the sketch pad aside and pulled out his suspenders. It was odd how important unimportant things became once someone was gone. "I . . . I have to tell you . . . I'm going to lose the lease on this place. I'm not sure where we'll go. Maybe to my folks' place in Indiana, but that doesn't have any feel of you, and I wanted to hold on to some sense of you for our boys. It's hard enough that they lost you. I wanted them to be raised in the community where you were raised. I wanted them to be surrounded by your tools. I wanted them to play in the barn where you used to harness Sugar Bear. But I've struggled to pay full rent since you left, and now the landlords are increasing the rent. There's nothing affordable for us in Lancaster County."

Someone knocked on the front door. She put the sketch pad

back in the box, put the lid on it, and returned it to its hallowed place in the top of the closet. She hurried to the front door and opened it.

Josiah? He stood there, a slight smile on his lips.

"Hello. Was I expecting you?"

"Nee. Uncle Mark sent us to pick you up, helping with the boys and the baked goods."

"He's a kind man, but *us*?"

"Aaron." Josiah turned to look behind him and chuckled. "He must be checking on something in the shop."

"Kumm." She stepped back. "Drew is still asleep, and I have a pie in the oven that's not ready yet."

"No problem," Josiah said. He scanned her. "Do you need us to come back in a bit?"

She looked down and realized she was still wearing Vin's shirt. "No need for that. Have a seat at the island." She removed Vin's shirt and folded it. "It smells of him." She gently set it on the counter, but she'd need to put it away in a few minutes for safe-keeping.

Josiah nodded. "If I come across things that smell of Lois, am I supposed to wear them instead of burn them?" His grin was contagious.

He and Lois had broken up in September, not long after Celeste overheard her mean statements in the woodshop. Celeste felt bad that she was part of the incident that led to the breakup, but Josiah assured her they hadn't broken up over that.

"If you come across something, you have the option of returning it to her. How are you bearing up?"

"It's not fun. It's not comparable to yours, but grief is hard."

"Yours has similarities to my grief. You'd envisioned your life with her, and this broke all of those hopes and dreams. The breakup came with a lot of embarrassment and judgment you have no control over. And she disappeared after what you thought was a simple argument to work through; the immediate move to Ohio to live with an aunt gave you no time for closure."

"You're right. Odd as it sounds, I feel better about feeling bad now."

She chuckled. "Gut."

"Truth is, on a good day when I can see straight, I know this whole mess is less painful than being married to someone who has no respect for others, including me. How did I not see that about her?"

"You're asking the wrong person, ol' Siah. I sat in the same room with my husband and never knew what he was thinking or feeling. I guess we humans do a lot of assuming and natural trusting that things are what we think they are." She touched the shirt sitting on the counter. "I go from missing Vin so much I can hardly breathe to being so angry I can't stand to think of him. But I do think of him, almost every minute of the day and night, so sorry for the argument and how I couldn't hear him for my fear of the Ordnung and what others would think. Then when I'm angry, I wish we'd never met."

"Exactly. Then the next hour comes along."

"Yep." She picked up Vin's shirt. Time to put it away.

"Ach, I forgot. There's some good news. The ministers met last night, and they've decided that you can continue working in the woodshop and you can advertise as you're doing now."

"It was a battle for nothing."

"Why?"

"The landlords are raising the rent."

"Let me give you the difference."

"Nee. You give your time to me as it is, and we both know it's part of what cost you Lois."

He clutched his hands together. "Denki!"

"Do all men deal with grief through sarcasm?"

"Wouldn't know, but no girlfriend. No fiancée. No wife. No children. Plenty of money. It's not a bad trade-off if you think about it."

She chuckled. "Look, I appreciate your friendship and all you've done for us, but it would be asking too much, and I won't do it."

He nodded. "I sort of get it. So what's the plan?"

"I don't know. For now I continue praying that God provides a place in the area for me and the boys."

"If Vin knew how much strife his own dat has stirred against you, he'd haunt the man. I've considered haunting him a few times myself."

"He's a frustrating person, but we'll weather the storm. People will come around."

"You've been saying that for four months."

"Siah!" Steven ran into the room and climbed on Josiah.

Celeste walked to her room with Vin's shirt. She pulled the box down from the top of the closet and opened it, then buried her face in the shirt again. "Vin, I need a place to live, an affordable place that isn't with my parents in Indiana," she whispered. "I've lost you. Our boys have lost you. And now I'm a few months from losing this place too. What am I going to do?"

Chapter Twenty

The grandfather clock in the foyer ticked along as it marked the seconds that passed. Vin remained in the parlor, unsure if his host would consider it rude if he left. William and Mr. Buchanan were enthralled in a conversation.

Without warning, an odd sensation engulfed Vin. He could smell his wife's scent, the Dove soap she used, the lilac shampoo, the hint of fresh air mixing with baked goods and sawdust from the shop. Ach, how he missed her. His chest felt warm, like it used to when she laid her head against him. Her whisper tickled his ears; he couldn't hear clearly enough to know what the words were, but he could sense her desperation.

Gott, I beg of You to have mercy on me and send me back to Celeste, Steven, and Drew.

Anke walked back into the parlor with more rolled-up papers.

She'd gone upstairs and traded in the maps for more sketches. She held them out for Mr. Buchanan. "More for you."

"Thank you, Anke." He took them.

Anke turned. "Vin, do you know the history of our grandfather clock?"

"It's a gorgeous clock. I was admiring it earlier this morning." She gave a nod toward the foyer and walked in that direction. He followed her as she talked.

"The raw materials for the inner workings came from England in the early 1770s, before the Revolutionary War. But there were no clockmakers who could build the clock until after the war . . ." She stopped in front of the clock. "History lesson over. I just wanted a moment to talk to you out of earshot."

"How did you know someone needed to intervene in the parlor earlier so I didn't have to hand over the maps to Buchanan or offend him by refusing to?"

"I was in my room when I heard his voice, and a moment later, it dawned on me you had maps in your hand, so I grabbed rolls of paper he could view and hurried downstairs. William confirmed it when he whispered to me."

"Your timing is much appreciated."

"Vin." She drew a deep breath, watching the grandfather clock. "I keep a prayer journal, and after you came downstairs, I went to my room to look through it. Answer me this: when did you get separated from your wife and children?"

"Late evening on July 11. Possibly, if it was past midnight, it was on July 12."

Her eyes remained focused on the clock. "Did an event of note happen in September?"

"Jah. September 24. Patrollers would've caught us for sure if God hadn't warned me of their presence in time for George and Tandey to go into hiding."

She slowly shifted her gaze to him. "It's you."

His heart pounded. "Is that good?" Did this mean she would help him?

"Based on my journal entries, I startled awake before daylight on July 12, urged to pray for a man I didn't know, and I couldn't stop praying for days. That very strong sense hit me again before daylight on September 24, and I had to stop all else to pray for the same man's safety and his companions."

God had her praying for him starting the day he woke in Ohio and again the day the patrollers almost caught him, George, and Tandey?

"Where are your wife and sons?"

He couldn't tell her of time travel. It could turn her against being willing to help. "Anke, they're not in a place where I can get to them without a miracle, so ask nothing else and pray as you feel led."

"Did they die?"

"No."

"Gut. I will pray fervently, and perhaps God will see it as befitting to reunite you with your wife and sons."

A stream of thoughts passed in front of him like a speeding train, and in the swoosh, he heard Celeste's whisper—she was losing their home. "A home. She needs a home."

"Johanna?"

Had he said those words out loud? "Celeste."

"I . . . I don't understand."

"I left one evening, thinking I'd return in a few hours. But I fell. When I woke, I was in another state. Now she's on her own with our two little ones."

Anke's eyes got large and she bolted out the front door. He went after her. Outside, with a dusting of snow on the ground, she gasped for air. "It was not a dream." The words squeaked out, and her face drained of color.

What? "Breathe, Anke. Look at the red brick under your boots, focus on the cobblestone," he spoke softly and slowly. "Good. Now smell the aroma of winter in the air. Feel your toes in your boots. Take slow, easy breaths."

He gave her time, and her breathing slowed. He went inside, got their coats, and returned. Her face had regained some color.

He held her coat out. "Put this on. It's below freezing out here."

She slid into her coat. "I was praying one night while in my bed, half-asleep, when I saw an Amish man fall through time, screaming his love for his wife and sons. Later, I thought it was a dream, the kind a person has when they're a little awake and a little asleep. But it was not a dream, was it?"

Should he tell her? How could he not tell her?

He put his coat on. "It wasn't a dream, Anke."

As the words left his mouth, a huge weight lifted off him. His sense of isolation and abandonment eased greatly. Someone knew the truth about him. God had told her.

Anke's brows knit. "When is your time?"

"One hundred and sixty-three years from now."

She shook her head, unable to speak for nearly a minute. "H-how is that possible?"

"I don't know. Like I said, I thought God sent me here as a punishment or to teach me lessons. What were your immediate thoughts when you saw me fall?"

"I wanted to stop you from falling. I felt . . . *Nein, nein!* In every prayer, although I did not know you, I knew God was on your side in your struggles."

God was fighting with him and for him? Was he not here as a punishment for his selfishness? Could it be that God hadn't dropped Vin in this time as much as it had just happened, and God wanted to help him get back? That changed so much. He'd felt like a pauper begging a king, but he was a warrior fighting with his King.

Fresh thoughts of Celeste washed over him. "I long to know how to get back to Celeste, but right now I believe she needs a home or maybe a way to afford the home she's in. The rent is high because it's a farm, but we don't farm the land."

"We will commit the problem to prayer. It is all we can do right now. We don't know how to get you home and we do not know how to help your family from this time. So we pray."

"For months I've had the same dream. A man, maybe an Amish man, is sitting in front of a fire, and I ask him a question about how to get home. Each time he opens his mouth to answer me, but I wake before he says anything."

"Perhaps we need to know what he is trying to tell you. We'll pray about that too."

After months of solitude about falling through time, it felt wonderful to have someone in his corner.

Thank You, Gott, for Your mercy. You've kept me safe. You've guided me here. Show me how to get back to Celeste, Steven, and Drew. Show me how to help them until then. And while I'm here, help me use my time as You desire.

Today truly was a day for thanksgiving.

Chapter Twenty-One

Celeste pulled her thick black sweater tighter around her. It was chilly, for sure, but for the first week in December, it could be worse. The sun warmed the dark material, and she was comfortable. The young people around her seemed even less bothered by the nip in the air as they played on or cheered for the two teams playing volleyball on the makeshift court in her yard.

The sounds of laughter and smells of baked apple pies . . . if she closed her eyes, it felt almost like she was attending a youth gathering again herself. She and her friends loved to play games, tell jokes, and she could lock eyes with Vin as he—

No. That chapter in her life was closed, and she needed to be okay with that. God was showing her that she still had much to give, even though Vin would never return. She was still worthy and still had years of laughter and fun left.

The woman who was supposed to host today had ended up going into labor two weeks early yesterday evening, and the community scrambled to find a new place for the gathering. The bishop had volunteered Celeste.

Now Bishop Mark walked to her at the snack table sitting on the grass. She'd moved the picnic table closer to where the games were. She'd just refilled the bowl of chips and set out another carafe of hot apple cider. Please, let no one else notice how nervous she was.

She smiled at Mark. "Hallo."

"So good to see you, Celeste."

Lovina was inside playing with Celeste's children and a few other small ones who belonged to some of the chaperones. Where would Celeste be without the support of her bishop and his wife? But God had provided. He *always* would. Even after one of the worst things that could happen to a person.

"Denki for letting me host," she said.

"You're thanking me for what must've been a ton of work thus far today?" He grinned.

"I'm thanking you for pushing people to move past the gossip they've heard, move past their assumptions about my guilt as a less-than-perfect wife, and see me—a human in need of a warm, forgiving community."

"Ain't that the truth?" He blew a stream of air from between his lips. "I can't imagine how tough this time has been for you, and I respect the patience you've expressed. But it's way past time this community warms up to you again. A situation like this can easily break an entire community, just dissolve it into ongoing anger and mistrust. I've witnessed that happen many times in many Amish communities. So I've given them time to think, feel, and say whatever they needed. I hope I've handled this the right way. All I know for sure is the Old Ways can't grow charity in a soul, and when people feel forced to be kind and forgiving, the community becomes toxic, being polite to someone's face and backbiting when they leave. Grievances, whether based in real wrongs or imagined ones, have to be allowed to air out. But it's been five months since Vin disappeared, and it's time our people began to warm up to you again."

"Even if no one warms up, staying busy helps, ya know?"

He nodded. "'In all toil there is profit.' Like in all the Proverbs, there's a truth to be found there."

Josiah jogged up to the table. "Nice. Snacks."

It seemed the volleyball game he'd been a part of had just wrapped up, and new teams were forming. A few of his friends joined him getting food from the table: finger sandwiches, home-made bread, cubes of cheese on toothpicks, and Christmas cookies.

Two late-teen girls at the other end of the table whispered something to each other; then both smiled at Josiah. Did he look a little red? That was funny. Maybe he was thinking about dating again. It'd be good for him.

As the two girls walked off, Celeste used the serving tongs to nudge him from across the table. "Becca's new in town, staying with her cousin Abigail. Did you talk with her yet?"

Josiah laughed. "She's too shy! I tried to talk to both her and Abi, recruiting them for my volleyball team. They refused but watched us play the whole time."

His uncle nodded. "She's an obedient and kind young woman. Even though she hasn't lived in this district, I know her parents well. Perhaps a date would free her tongue a bit?"

Josiah coughed on his cider.

"Oh, give our Josiah a break." Lovina carried a fresh bowl of rolls to the table, winking at her husband. Little Steven and Drew followed behind her, each carrying a stack of cloth napkins—which had probably been folded before the kids carried them.

Josiah knelt next to Drew and Steven. "Oh, just in time!" He took a napkin and wiped his mouth. "I just tried to inhale my cider. Thanks, boys!" He repeated his words in Pennsylvania Dutch.

Her boys beamed—how they loved being able to contribute—and Josiah helped them place the rest of the cloths on the side of the table, in various states of disarray.

Celeste smiled, moving over to fold them. Yes, God had blessed her by putting this family in her life. She and the boys would be okay. But it was also okay to hurt over Vin's absence.

Bishop Mark held his hands in the air. "I'm trying to give him a break! A man needs a good woman in his life to get breaks. And bread." He lifted a roll from the basket, then smiled at his wife.

Josiah took a longer drink from his cider mug, then set it where a few other dirty ones were gathered in a basket. "Hey, Steven, want me to show you how to shoot some hoops with the big guys?"

"Jah!" Steven jumped up and down. He hadn't misunderstood Josiah's English words. Steven would begin school this fall, and Josiah had been talking to him in English of late. All Amish children learned English once in school. She supposed there was no harm in Steven getting a head start.

Josiah took his hand and led him about twenty feet away, where volunteers had set up a little basketball court on the driveway. Drew pulled at Celeste's skirts, and she hoisted him onto her hip and kissed his cheek.

Mark shrugged. "Well, I scared him off."

Celeste smoothed the now-folded napkins with her free hand. "How's he been doing?"

Lovina gave a slight shrug. "He's coping. You know how rare an engagement break is. Lois was his first love, and he's got lots of concerns as to why he'd fall in love with someone who didn't think much of him. He'll sort it out and be better off for it, but it'll be some time before he's ready to date again. God will mend his heart and teach him why he fell for her."

Celeste hadn't even dated anyone besides Vin. She hadn't needed to—he'd been "the one." Now where did that leave her? But she wasn't a young person, not like Josiah was. She was a mother to little ones. She'd never date again or remarry. Marriage required trust. Trusting herself. Trusting her husband. She had no trust of either, not after Vin casually sat in their home, most often in the same room, in defiance of his vows, and she never had a clue. But even if she wanted to consider becoming a part of a couple, which she definitely didn't, the fact that Vin was a missing person meant she'd have to wait seven years before the law counted him as deceased. It'd probably be another year after that before the Amish would allow her to date.

A few other youth members came to the table, and Celeste helped serve them food, chatting for several minutes with them, Mark, and Lovina. It was nice to be here. Maybe, with just a little more time, she'd feel like a true part of the community again.

Car tires crunched gravel on her driveway as an Englisch car with darkened windows pulled up, coming to a stop down the hill from the basketball game on the hardened dirt.

"Who on earth . . . ?" Celeste wondered aloud.

Mark rubbed his beard. "Kumm. Let's go check it out together."

"I'll mind the little one." Lovina held her arms out for Drew. He clung an extra second to Celeste but allowed her to pass him to Lovina.

"Maybe it's about a client." Celeste touched her prayer Kapp, making sure it was in place.

On second thought . . . her heart sank. She'd seen this car in her driveway once before. It was an unmarked police car.

As Celeste and Mark walked toward the car, a man stepped out of the driver's side, wearing a white collared shirt with a matching gray jacket and pants and black sunglasses. He pulled off his glasses and tucked them into his shirt pocket. She recognized him then:

Detective Jasper Powell. He'd spoken with her personally here at her home and at the police station each of the times she went there to beg for more information.

He nodded at Celeste. "Mrs. Lantz. I'm not sure you remember me, but—"

"I remember," Celeste interrupted his spiel. Had they found Vin? Was he alive somewhere?

"I called your phone and left a message, trying to give you a heads-up that I was coming to see you this afternoon."

She'd been scrambling so hard to finish everything for today, she didn't even think of checking the messages on the answering machine. What if she'd missed something important about Vin? But her hope that he might be alive didn't resonate in her heart. No, she was about to hear bad news, judging by the expression on the man's face.

"Do you have somewhere private we can speak?" Detective Powell asked.

"Jah. This is my bishop, Mark. I'd like him and his wife to stay with me throughout whatever you're about share."

"Of course." The detective pressed his lips together and nodded. This *was* bad news. He looked around, seeming to take in the massive amount of Amish gathered for the youth event.

Where did she want to receive this news? What place would be seared into her brain as the place where her world crumbled . . . again? "Let's speak in the shop." It was the place with the most of Vin left. Maybe it was befitting. "There are many teens and young adults in the house."

"Sure."

The three of them walked across the property toward the woodshop. When they neared Lovina, Mark whispered something in her ear. She nodded, then asked three teen girls with little siblings, and therefore experience, to mind Drew. Steven was still safe with Josiah. Celeste had felt Josiah's eyes on her as she passed him, Steven, and a few other young people playing basketball. Did he have a guess like Celeste as to why this Englischer was here?

The detective, Mark, Lovina, and Celeste entered the shop, and Celeste gestured to the best stool for the detective to take. She pulled out three more for herself and the couple.

Detective Powell sat, never taking his eyes off Celeste. He leaned toward her. "I'm going to start by saying that I've been praying all the way over to your house on how best to deliver this news. It's . . . not easy to say. But perhaps it'll bring you some peace and closure."

Closure. He was dead. Of course he was dead. He'd be here if he wasn't. He loved her. Despite the stupid fight, despite his desire to draw faces, despite everything, he was hers and she was his, ever since they were the ages of the youth at her house today. And now, proof he was gone forever. She nodded slowly.

The detective took a deep breath and sighed it out. "Okay. We found an Amish buggy at the bottom of Ash Rocks, the place which the local Amish call Kissin' Mountain." He pulled a sheet of paper out of his pocket and unfolded it. It was printed with a type-writer. "Inside the buggy, we found these items." He passed her the paper, and she held it up so Mark and Lovina could also see.

It listed all the items Celeste had described to the police as being in Vin's buggy, which mostly were two boxes of gently used clothing that were to be taken to a charity box.

She lowered the paper and met Detective Powell's eyes. He swallowed, looking uncomfortable.

"We also found a body. Did your husband rappel, Mrs. Lantz?"

"Rappel?" Mark asked.

"Basically, it's a way to descend from a rock face using ropes. It's a sport for rock climbing."

Celeste shook her head. "Not that I know of . . ." Was that something else he'd kept from her?

"I needed to ask, but I don't think it's important." He drew a breath. "It appears the carriage went over the edge, and then your husband, probably using rock climbing gear that was already there, rappelled down to take a look. Something went wrong, and he fell."

Celeste could feel the panic he must've gone through during the fall.

The detective smoothed his tie. "Due to degradation and Vin's lack of dental records, our local team was unable to definitively say that the body matched Vin Lantz. However, the age, height, and hair color do match. He was mere feet from the carriage. Our forensic team has more information, and we can pursue further methods of identification if you wish."

"What does that mean?" Her voice shook. Despite that, it was as if she were floating outside her body, watching this scene play out, no emotion hitting her yet. Was this shock?

"There is a new thing to just hit the US forensics called DNA testing," the detective continued, "but it's extremely expensive and no one in my department is confident in how accurate it'd be for something like this. I've seen an out-of-state case where they found a match to hair, but the person was alive." He sighed. "You don't need all these details. Let me just get to it. The remains of this man were next to the buggy. He had on Amish clothes. And like I said before, his bones match those of a male Vin's age and stature. It is my professional and personal opinion that we've recovered the body of Ervin Lantz, and the cause of death was a fall from the cliffs at Ash Rocks . . . Kissin' Mountain."

Her eyes traced the ceiling of the shop, taking in the details created by Vin. He was truly an artist in all aspects of his life. His smile flashed in her mind, a snapshot from when they'd played horseshoes at a youth meeting. She'd never need a drawing or a photograph to remember that moment in the grass the first summer they met, when her eyes and heart first connected to his, and the feeling of rightness washed through her body. Vin. She could still remember the smell of him when they were newlyweds, coming in from working this shop, and they'd joke they both smelled like they'd been exploring the innards of a tree like termites. Then he laced his fingers into her messy hair and kissed her. Her entire body zeroed in on the sensation, as if he was all there was in the whole of life. He was her world, and now he was gone. She'd never, ever see him again as long as she lived.

"Detective, do you mind if we say a prayer?" Mark asked.

Celeste couldn't even hear the words. Couldn't make herself truly pray to God. If He was the just God that everyone said He was, how could something so awful like this happen?

"Patience, my love," she remembered Vin saying to her one day when she was frustrated at the number of orders piling up. *"Everything is made right with time. We do the tasks one by one, and the work gets done."*

With time. Weren't all human lives here on earth but a blink in the eyes of God? Was not their true home in heaven? The Word had been teaching her this all her life—was this what she needed to believe? She'd never see Vin again in this life, yes. But after wrestling with all the doubt, all the pain, she'd come to know that if he could've returned home, then he would've. Josiah was the first to get that across to her, and once she heard his reasoning, her doubts faded, and she knew the truth.

Vin was gone, and now she had proof. Closure, as the detective had said. She'd move through her days, continuing to do each task and the best work she could for her boys, for the community, and for her God. And then when the work was done, she'd see Vin.

That peace was balm to her shattered heart.

Mark finished praying.

Celeste turned to him and Lovina. "He didn't leave us. Not me, nor our sons. He didn't leave. It was an accident."

Lovina pulled her into a tight embrace, rubbing her back, and Celeste sobbed. The relief was a full-fledged wave now, rolling through her. She held Lovina like she was a raft in the storm.

When Celeste had composed herself enough, the detective pulled out a small pocket pack of tissues, opened it, and passed her one.

"I'm so sorry, Mrs. Lantz. I truly hoped we'd one day get to bring you better news. There's a process now that has to happen before the forensics team can return his remains to you. First, we have to perform a nationwide check with authorities to verify that there's no other man missing during this time who might've been in the vicinity of Kissin' Mountain. This is what you'd call a formality. But it takes time since many of our police stations still don't have computers, and those that do have them don't have all the information loaded on them yet. Once that box is checked off, we'll set a court date for you, myself, and a few experts from my team where we'll meet with a judge. You don't need to worry about this part—we just need your presence. My department will present the evidence. The judge may ask you a question or two to verify what we've said, and then the judge will declare Vin dead. At that point, the county will release his death certificate and send it in the mail to you."

The words seemed to bounce off Celeste's brain, without comprehension taking root. "Months?"

"Yes, ma'am. I'd advise patience, and for you to accept that these things will take time, and know it'll probably be around March or April before the police department and the county can complete the whole process. I wish it were faster. I'll walk you through each step. When the legal parts are complete, Vin's remains will be sent wherever you instruct for them to go—a funeral home or an Amish undertaker."

"And we'll support you," Lovina said, squeezing her hand.

And Josiah. He'd known from the start and supported her as a widow. He'd shared with her his belief about Vin—that Vin had loved Celeste beyond what she knew, and something happened to him. He'd never once wavered in that belief. She'd pull him aside and tell him he'd been right as soon as she could.

The detective passed her a card with a phone number on it. "You already have my number, but just in case you lost it or need another copy. Is the phone shanty number my department has still the correct one?"

"Jah. I just was busy today and didn't check it."

"There's no emergency, and from here on, leaving a message is just fine. If I can help you in any way, don't hesitate to give me a call." The detective stood, shook her hand, the bishop's, and his wife's, then left the shop.

Celeste couldn't make herself get up and move. As the shop door opened and closed, she could hear the happy sounds from the gathering still going on. Life would go on. Her sons would grow into the good men they'd become, and she'd age. There'd be many happy gatherings like this, as well as funerals. What about Vin's funeral?

She wiped her tears again and turned to Mark. "Will the community allow me to bury Vin in the Amish cemetery?"

Mark adjusted his black felt hat. "I wish I could give you an answer. The community will need to have their say, and then it'll take a unanimous decision by the deacon, preacher, and myself."

"But he didn't leave me. He meant to return and make things right."

"I know. But our rules are what they are. He was in disobedience of the Old Ways, and those who perish while in disobedience aren't buried beside the faithful. I'm so sorry." Mark sighed. "It'll take time for a decision to be made, but this news needs to be shared as soon as possible. First with his parents, who I'll go see in a few minutes. Then with the community. I'll use your phone shanty and make some calls. Like you, people have been waiting for months for this news, so I'll arrange for a district meeting within two hours at the Lapps' home. It's best for this news to be shared and discussed before tomorrow's church gathering so our attention on the Lord's Day can be as focused on Him as possible."

Celeste nodded, unsure she'd caught all of what he'd just said.

"Celeste, it'll be a very emotional meeting with some hard things said." Lovina put her hand over Celeste's. "Perhaps you should spare yourself, and we'll both stay here with your sweet boys."

Celeste didn't have it in her to hear unkind things spoken about Vin or herself, and she nodded again.

With so many in this community blinded by their bias against her, how could they be fair in deciding where Vin should be buried? The unfairness of being separated again stung. Celeste couldn't be with Vin in life—couldn't they at least be buried beside each other in death, giving their sons a sense of unity and peace between them, their dat, and the Amish faith? Wasn't this loss hard enough all on its own without their sons' father being buried somewhere other than the local Amish cemetery for the faithful?

Chapter Twenty-Two

Josiah listened, his blood boiling. He sat on a hard bench inside the Lapp home—not that he knew the family very well, but they were part of Celeste's district, and their bishop was his uncle. The house was already set up for church services tomorrow with living room furniture moved out and rows of benches on two sides with an aisle between them. Men were on one side and women on the other. Celeste wasn't here, but Eli, Vin's dat, was.

The bishop nodded as another naysayer finished his speech. "Denki, Brother Matthew."

Matthew sat. He'd spent nearly five minutes sharing his thoughts on why Vin shouldn't be buried in an Amish cemetery.

Where was their mercy and grace for Celeste?

Josiah tapped his fist against his lips, trying to keep his mouth shut. This was not his district. He had no say, even though he'd joined the Amish faith last summer in preparation to marry Lois. A brief thought of Lois grabbed his heart and squeezed it. But he understood now that he was grieving who he'd thought they were together. In reality, he'd let go of a figment of his imagination wrapped in the body of a beautiful woman. He hoped the best for her, but her leaving him was the best for him.

His attention returned to the meeting. His beliefs were different from many who were here tonight voicing their overwrought concerns. He didn't believe that joining the church equaled being faithful to God. Only by faith was he saved. If he'd died before he joined the Amish church, he wouldn't have cared where his body was buried. His soul would be with God. But it mattered to Celeste where Vin was buried because of Steven and Drew. Those little boys would become black sheep in their school. Steven would begin this fall, and he would be ridiculed by his peers, as would Drew in a few years, if they had a deceased parent who'd been buried with the Englisch.

But Josiah had to remain quiet. His uncle allowed him to sit in and listen, and he'd been a kind, giving bishop to Celeste and her sons. Still, his uncle had yet to speak up today. Where did Mark stand on this subject? Surely someone would bring forth mercy and some common sense to this meeting.

The bishop looked out at his flock. "We're almost done for tonight. We appreciate knowing your thoughts before we make the final decision. We aren't in a rush, so after tonight, we may take weeks or months to decide."

"Won't he need a resting place fairly soon?" a man asked.

"The detective explained that there's a bit of a lengthy process. Just routine procedures."

Eli stood. "My son deserves to be buried in the cemetery of our ancestors, the resting place of our parents and grandparents. His body has lain in the elements for five months!" His voice cracked as he fought tears. "I don't have much good to say about Celeste. Maybe she helped him over that cliff but—"

"Wait." Marvin Yoder rose with a soft voice. "Eli, enough strife against Celeste. I know losing your son has been severe, but many of us are weary of hearing Celeste being cast as an evil person when there is not one bit of proof. She's an innocent widow."

Eli pointed at Marvin. "Sometimes the facts stand for themselves."

Josiah knew his uncle wasn't like most bishops. He allowed people to air their grievances, but it seemed as if sometimes he should use his authority to make people like Eli be quiet. Wasn't that biblical? Josiah would like to make Eli see all he was blind to, but he didn't possess the gift of making the blind see. He couldn't make a headache go away. How could he open anyone's eyes?

"What facts, Eli?" Marvin asked, his voice calm. "What do you think happened? Your stout son was pushed over an edge by a petite woman? Where were their babies? At home by themselves, but no one heard them crying? Or Celeste had them with her, and she toted those babies a few miles home? Do you think she could walk for an hour or more along that road, carrying nearly half her weight in wiggly children, and no one saw her? Because facts say the horse walked home a day later, so no one rode her back. Please, stop. I don't know where Vin should be buried, but I know my ears ache from all I've heard over the months about your son's widow."

Eli's face resembled a storm cloud, and when he sat down, he wiped his eyes. Finally, after all this time, people were beginning to speak up for Celeste. It should make Josiah feel better, but it just stirred anger. Those against her or neutral toward her should've opened their eyes and ears long ago.

The deacon stood. He was an exacting man if one ever existed, and Josiah knew some of the reason why Celeste had received a cold shoulder was because this man believed Vin and Celeste were reaping what they'd sown. The deacon read numerous Scriptures about idolatry and keeping one's word and the importance of obedience. Every reference was aimed at reasons why Vin's remains shouldn't be buried in the Amish cemetery. Josiah's blood ran hot as the man used the Word to also cast hints of doubt on Celeste's innocence.

The deacon raised his Bible in the air. "If Vin Lantz hadn't disappeared, he would've been shunned for idolatry. Would he have repented? We can't know that. What we do know is he broke his vow, argued with his wife, and left."

"Where is the mercy and grace for us as imperfect humans?" Josiah heard his own voice ask. His face burned. When had he jumped to his feet? *Sit down!* But he couldn't. "Many have been lukewarm toward Celeste since Vin disappeared, confused by the accounts, afraid of coddling a sinner, unsure what to believe because of gossip." He moved to the front of the room and turned, needing to see people eye to eye. "She's asked nothing of her own people since Vin disappeared, but now she's asking you to let her deceased husband be among the faithful. If you can't agree to it because of her, please be merciful for her children's sake." He picked up his uncle's Bible. "Part of the problem is that everyone knows personal details of a private argument. When you argue with your spouse, would you sound worthy of being buried with the faithful?" He tapped the Bible. "The Word says not to commit idolatry. But are we sure what he did was idolatry? There was a time when any artwork was forbidden. Drawing a bird or a cow or a home or a garden used to be considered idolatry, but we grew to understand that it wasn't. It was enjoying the beauty of God's creation. What if one day the Ordnung allows artists to draw faces? Some of you have dolls with faces in your home, but two decades ago, that was called idolatry. Will we condemn a man to be buried elsewhere, heaping shame on his children forever, for something that your grandchildren may do out in the open?"

Josiah looked at the Bible and back to the crowd. "Let us stand with mercy and grace, and if we're wrong, God will forgive us. But how will God look at us if we choose to cast the first stone?"

Uncle Mark eased the Bible from his hand. "Denki, Josiah."

Josiah was shaking, head to toe. He nodded as he returned to his seat. His head roared. What had he said? He wasn't sure. Words kept firing in his brain, and the minutes passed in a blur as his thoughts circled wildly. What had possessed him to not only speak up, but to do so as if he were a preacher?

Was he in love with Celeste? He knew he liked her. A lot. She was truly kind, very talented, and an amazing mom to her sons. But love?

"Look." A man's voice came from behind Josiah, and he didn't recognize it. "Maybe the Amish will accept drawing faces one day, but Vin made a vow to obey the Old Ways, and then he disobeyed them. I can appreciate how this young man feels, but he's not a part of this community. What message are we giving our young people if we allow Vin to be buried among the obedient?"

Several people spoke at once, agreeing with the man. Others spoke up on Vin's behalf. Eli looked at Josiah, tears in his eyes as he barely smiled.

Mark glanced at Josiah, frowning. "Let's end tonight with prayer, and when the ministers have made a decision, we will let you know."

This wasn't good. Josiah never considered that speaking up might cause some of these men to be less merciful toward Celeste and the boys.

Chapter Twenty-Three

DECEMBER 1822

Snowy winds howled through the cracks in the barn wall. Vin's makeshift woodshop in a corner of the Coopers' barn was chilly, but the walls kept most of the snow out, and this space was far warmer and more comfortable than driving an open wagon.

It'd been two weeks since Anke realized Vin had fallen through time. Someone else knowing the truth, believing him, had made the weight of this situation lighter, easier to tolerate. Still, he was antsy. He knew no more today about how to get home than he did two weeks ago. His recurring dream still haunted him. Was the man in the dream him? Did some part of Vin know the answer? It was irksome. It added to his restlessness, but there was nothing he could do about it.

He wavered between being grateful to be here and safe and

being vexed, with no answers of how to get back to his wife and children. Did God judge him for feeling torn?

The barn door opened. Anke and Johanna entered, each carrying a stack of wool blankets, Johanna with a basket on her stack. Was the snowstorm so bad they'd needed to use the rope that George had strung between the barn and the house a few days ago? Last he checked, visibility and the force of the wind weren't that bad.

"Food." Johanna set the basket on the ground. *"Essen, Vin."* She set the stack of blankets on Vin's workbench.

"Denki." He'd eat later.

"It needs to be warmer in here." Anke repeated what she'd said in German to Johanna.

"I appreciate it. But it's warmer in here during this winter storm than it is in a wagon on a normal winter's day." He repeated his sentence in German too. Johanna was grasping English well, but she'd said it helped her most when someone spoke English and then repeated it in German.

Johanna nodded. "True. He not lie."

He chuckled. "Danke."

Anke got the ladder to the loft and moved it to Vin's corner space. "There's four feet of snow on the ground," she said. "And that doesn't count how deep some of the snowdrifts are."

"Mid-December in Pennsylvania can be like that."

The weather wasn't keeping Vin from doing the most important thing—constantly praying.

Anke and Johanna talked as they hammered the blankets into place against the barn wall, forming an insulation barrier. He scrubbed homemade sandpaper over a three-foot-long piece of walnut. As the dresser he was working on formed in more detail in his mind, memories of seeing this piece somewhere grew clearer and then faded. At times the piece seemed familiar, but it was something he'd thought of only last night, a Christmas gift for the Coopers. The base with the drawers would be Shaker plain, but the feet and the frame for a small mirror would be Victorian style. It would be practical and look plain but also have bits of lavish woodwork. That felt like who the Coopers were—practical with some ornate qualities all throughout their lives. He also intended to make a chest for the foot of their bed to hold quilts, and he would build a false bottom in it for safekeeping of maps. But at the moment, building the dresser had his full attention.

"Vin, you need Essen," Johanna repeated her earlier statement, trying to take care of him.

"I'll eat soon." Right now he was focused on the work in his hands.

Why did this piece of furniture look so familiar? Wasn't this dresser one of a kind, a piece he'd created in his mind? If he'd seen it before now, when and where?

The wind rattled the barn doors, shuttered windows, and the loft above them, but Vin's workspace corner was now much more protected. He held a small wood chisel and hammer as he created dovetails to hold the sides of the drawers together.

His mind meandered as he prayed and worked. George and Tandey were going over information with William to see if they might have overheard specific details while on Master Alexander's plantation that would help William know where in Maryland Maud had been sold.

It would likely be spring before anyone could travel to Maryland to search for her, but William intended to use all his resources to try to uncover where Maud was sold and to whom. It wasn't at all how the abolitionist movement usually worked, for someone in the movement to search for a specific slave to help her escape. It was an undertaking, to be sure. William said their best chance of finding her was to gather information from George and Tandey and from sales records and sympathizers in Maryland.

Information was vital to life. Vin realized that more with each passing day. If he knew what the man in his dream wanted to tell him . . . If he knew how to help Celeste, even from this time . . . If . . .

An odd sensation pricked his skin, and he saw Celeste and him inside the Cooper home in 1979, standing in front of a roped-off room, peering into it. Was that where he'd seen this piece of furniture he was working on? It'd been in that room, a room he now knew was William and Margaret's bedroom. His wife's voice washed over him, remarking how beautifully the old finish had held up on the dresser. He responded to her, saying he didn't recognize what style of furniture it was.

Of course he hadn't recognized it as a specific style because it was two styles being combined into one piece.

His legs felt a bit wobbly as it dawned on him. "I . . . I saw this in the Cooper home."

Anke and Johanna stopped hammering nails down the sides of the blanket.

"What?" Anke studied him.

He motioned at the dresser. "I saw this in the Cooper home." But which came first? Did he see it in 1979 because it was there to see? Or did his building it now cause the memory to form?

Did it matter which happened first? He was here. Celeste was there. Could he do something now that would impact her life? Could he find a way to get a letter to her? Or money? Or . . . ? His heart jolted. "A house. I could build her a house."

Johanna studied him, looking concerned. *"Das verstehe ich nicht."*

She didn't understand. He was talking way too fast for her to catch his words. Anke turned to Johanna and asked her in German to give them a minute.

Johanna paused, tilting her head. Like Celeste, she could read him to a degree, and he was hiding things from her. "Vin?"

"I'm gut." He smiled and nodded. "I'm good."

She nodded and walked to the far end of the barn.

"Vin, what are you trying to tell me?" Anke asked.

"The Cooper home is still standing in Celeste's time. It belongs to the preservation society, which means those within the society are very careful about keeping and taking good care of everything they can from this time period. Maybe the Coopers will put the estate in a trust to go to the county or state when they die."

"Jah. They had a lawyer arrange for the house and farmland to remain in use by family, including myself, for as long as we need it. The same is true for their children and grandchildren as well as Ester's and my children and grandchildren. When no relative or ward wants to live in the home, it will be given to Lancaster County to use as they see fit. Many can live here, but no one can sell it. I don't know why they chose to give it to the county, but that is the decision."

"If I could build a home on this property for Celeste, and we write a will or a trust that can be found and followed, the house should get to her."

"How?"

"I . . . I don't know exactly. We get a lawyer involved. The Coopers did it. They pledged this home to go to the county, and it did. I saw it in my time."

"Hallo?" Johanna called. "I come back now?"

"Sure." Vin motioned for her. He ran his hand across the top of the dusty dresser. "It can be done. I'm sure of it. But she needs help now, and it's winter. I can't start building a home in winter. If I start this spring, it won't be done until fall, which means she can't inherit it for nine or ten months from now."

"Unless . . ." Anke rubbed her forehead. "You gave her my house. It's old. It needs an overabundance of work, but it's already built."

"You have a house?"

"Kumm." She grabbed the ladder and moved it to the loft. "Go."

He needed to go first because the women were in skirts, and the polite way was to not be at the bottom as they went up, so he scurried up the ladder. Johanna followed him. Then Anke.

Anke went to the loft window and unlatched it. The wind pushed the wooden door open. He caught it and tethered it open.

"It's hard to see it from here with the snow but look to the horizon." Anke pointed. "About five hundred feet that way."

His heart pounded. He saw it. Moreover, he and Celeste had been inside it. The small home wasn't part of the tour, but when he asked a groundskeeper if they could go inside, the man used a skeleton key and unlocked it for them.

Anke shivered and buttoned her coat. "It belonged to my parents."

"Ah. So that's how you and Ester are connected to the Coopers. Your parents were neighbors."

"Margaret and Ma were good friends. Margaret was twenty years older than Ma, and her own children, those who'd survived childhood, were grown and gone before Ma and Pa passed." She wiped a tear. "My parents were gut people, and they'd be pleased for you to have their house." She shrugged. "It's still standing. That's all I know."

As exciting as the prospect was, Vin couldn't accept the gift of her home. Patrick had said she wasn't interested in getting married or having children, but she was young, probably twenty, and she had a lot of time in which she could change her mind. She might want to raise her own children in that home.

"Anke, that's very generous. But—"

"Accept the gift, Vin. Just trust my instinct and accept it."

"The gift is you letting me fix it up. I don't need the home, at least not for a hundred and sixty-three years from now. It's yours for your lifetime, and even for your children and children's children, to use as you desire. When your use of it is done, with the help of a good lawyer and God's providence, it'll be bundled with the Cooper place to go to the county and eventually pass down to Celeste." Excitement at the prospect pumped through him. "I would begin making repairs today, but I don't have supplies or the money to pay for them."

"Geld?" Johanna asked.

"Jah, money," Anke said.

He smiled. God had provided an answer to his question of how he could help Celeste, and then He'd provided a home, all within the same few minutes. With God's guidance, Vin would figure out a way to earn money, even in this season. "I'll work hard."

Johanna moved to stand in front of Vin. "Geld for you?"

"Jah."

"Ich have for you."

Vin blinked. She had what? "You have money?"

Johanna nodded. "You have it."

He didn't understand. Why would she plan to work hard for their hosts if she had money?

"In leather *Beutel*," she said. *"Geld, Gold, und Juwelen."*
Money, gold, and jewels.

"In the leather pouch?" he asked. The one she'd grabbed from under the floorboards of her burning cabin and kept close? "I can't, Johanna."

"Jah. You have it." She nodded. "It gut amount. My *Ehemann* tell me."

Her husband told her it was a good amount.

"You want to give some to me? Nee." Vin couldn't take any of her possessions. She needed them for herself and her children.

"Wait." Anke raised her index finger. "Johanna, can we have a minute?"

"Jah. Talk." Johanna poked Vin's shoulder. "I give. You take this time." She studied him. "Jah?"

Taking care of her and her two little ones had felt as if he was somehow bartering with God that He would provide someone to take care of Celeste in similar fashion, but he hadn't considered that Celeste gave as good as she received. Johanna did too. From out of nowhere, Celeste blessed him time and again. Now Johanna was doing the same.

She went to the ladder, humming while giving Anke and Vin time to talk.

"Listen to me, Vin," Anke said. "Use her money. That allows you to get started on the house right away for Celeste. When you're done, we will give the house to Johanna and her children."

Vin's heart turned a flip. "You're set on giving your parents' house away?"

"I am. The house has been empty for far too long. I guess for Ester, me, and the Coopers, it's sort of been a memorial to my parents, left frozen in time because it hurt too much to use it or sell it, but it's time that old home met someone's needs."

Eagerness raced through him. Johanna's staying with the Coopers was fine for now, but eventually she would need a home of her own, just like George, Tandey, and he would, so the Coopers would have available rooms the next time people were in need.

He turned toward Johanna and motioned for her, ready to ask her if she liked his and Anke's ideas. His heart pounded. He'd woken knowing nothing he could do to help Celeste, and now he had a solid chance of getting a home to her.

And he had a definite way of providing a permanent home for Johanna and her children.

"You gut?" Johanna asked.

"Anke and I have an idea we want you to consider."

Chapter Twenty-Four

MARCH 1986

People and food filled Celeste's home. *Pay attention. You're going to want to remember Vin's wake. Your children might ask one day.* Even now, those words didn't go together: *Vin's wake.*

She shifted Drew to her other knee at the kitchen table, grateful for the warmth and feel of his small body. He had a wooden horse in his hand—a hand-carved gift from Josiah. Where would she be without her community today—the day she put her husband in the ground?

But there was a disconnect inside her. After so many months of waiting, it didn't feel right. Something about today felt as real as Drew's toy felt like an actual horse. Even the almost-springlike weather of mid-March hadn't helped her feel connected to herself or to the burial.

Celeste had been to burials before, but not for someone close to her. Today, when the men used ropes to lower Vin's pine box casket into the ground, she'd felt the same as she had during burials for near strangers. She just watched respectfully. She was a bad widow. But she didn't feel like a widow—that box *didn't* feel like Vin.

Lovina put a comforting hand on Celeste's shoulder, then slid a mug of tea in front of her, a tiny whiff of steam rising from the top. "I put in a cube of ice to cool it enough that even if the little one grabs the mug, it shouldn't hurt him."

"Denki." She hugged Drew close again and kissed his soft, round cheek. She couldn't start beating herself up for what she did or didn't feel. She had to keep moving on, for Drew and Steven's sake. They were her future, and their father was firmly in her past. In the ground.

"Celeste?" Lovina pulled one of the many chairs over to sit next to her. "How are you holding up?"

Celeste looked up. Had Lovina been standing there since she passed Celeste this cup of tea? She took a sip. It was good—fruit flavored. Should she be honest? "Lovina, will you pray for me that God will give me more closure?"

"More closure?"

Celeste shook her head. It wouldn't make any sense to Lovina, or anyone else, probably. "I . . . feel closer to Vin when I touch his old shirt. I can smell him and almost feel the echoes of him through the items he used before he disappeared. Sorry. I'm sure it's my imagination and I'm reaching hard."

Lovina smiled and put a hand on Celeste's shoulder, rubbing it with her thumb. "Oh, of course you want to reach out for Vin. When we have to carry on without our loved ones who are in heaven, we look for them everywhere. You've shown an incredible amount of strength through this. I think today is a new start for you in many ways."

It didn't feel like one. It still felt like she was stuck waiting for Vin. He'd *never* come home. So why was she still waiting?

"Look around you. It took time, but God softened their hearts. Our people showed up, and they want your forgiveness. They want to love you as they now know they should have all along."

The house was busy, albeit more subdued and quieter than the usual community gatherings. Vin was at rest now in the cemetery among the faithful in good standing. It *should* be a relief.

"Jah, I know." Celeste took another drink of the tea. "Even Eli," she whispered. "He's . . . been nicer toward me. The first time was back in December, after the community met about where Vin should be buried. The next day was a church Sunday, and he spoke to me with kindness."

"God can put a new spirit within all of us, if we give Him the chance."

Could He put a new spirit in Celeste? One that could move on and accept that Vin couldn't return?

"Later that week, some within the community anonymously mailed gifts of money, and it felt as if they were doing so because it's what they wanted to do, not a mandatory giving because a minister asked or told them to, so I accepted the cash, and it has covered the higher rent of this place since January."

Lovina touched the edge of the wooden horse that Drew still held. "Did you know that Josiah is the one who took up for Vin, insisting he be allowed to be buried among the faithful? Sometimes all it takes is a little push, and God can take over the rest of the way. Now look at everyone. Time can change and soften people's hearts. I think in time your heart will feel that relief and closure you seek."

Josiah had been the one to make this happen? It made sense. He'd been in her corner from the start—a man who looked so young, when she first met him, that she'd thought he was still a boy, but he had more courage and empathy than experienced men with their thick beards. She scanned the room, trying to find him. There—he was talking to Eli and Naomi. "Denki, Lovina. For everything. Would you hold Drew while I speak with Vin's parents?"

"Come here, Bobbeli. Show me your horsey." Lovina held her arms out to Drew. He looked to Celeste, but when she smiled to reassure him, he went to Lovina without fussing.

Celeste left the mug on the table—she'd come back and finish it. She wove around people as she made her way to Eli, Naomi, and Josiah. Lovina was right—a gathering like this would've been impossible without lots of prayer and effort to soften hearts. But God had done it. He could help her move on, too.

As she approached, Eli's eyes met hers. They didn't glare with hate upon seeing her anymore, but they held sadness and probably regret. It was difficult to not let bitterness and self-righteousness poison her heart after how he'd treated her. But he was trying now, and resentment served no one but itself. Besides, no one in this mess had been perfect, her included.

Eli stroked his beard while talking to Josiah. "Jah, that could be a good thing for people."

Naomi touched her elbow. "Josiah was telling us about his idea for a charity. In Vin's memory."

"Hmm?" Celeste looked at Josiah.

He scratched the back of his neck. "I was gonna tell you next, Celeste. I started thinking about it a few weeks back, and the rest of the idea came together at the burial. Uncle Mark told me that you and Vin gave freely to your neighbors, and sometimes Vin didn't quite have enough to take care of your own stuff—like updating that broken buggy wheel. I was thinking we could take up a donation in Vin's name each year around this time or have an annual woodcraft sale. Then, with the proceeds, we could buy a new rig that we'd donate to either a newlywed couple in need or a family that's struggling."

"So it'd be a charity in our son's name, and the proceeds go to help other Amish," Naomi said.

Celeste nodded. "That sounds thoughtful and kind, Josiah. I know Steven and Drew will appreciate being a part of that each year."

Did her words come out as she'd intended? Her mind was so foggy today . . . this week . . . most of this past year.

The broken rig. She thought of it often. She hadn't known it had issues. But she realized later that's what Vin was telling her the night she'd found the sketch pad. He'd come into the room, saying something about the wheel on the rig not being right. Vin hadn't wanted her to use it.

His art . . . he hid it, also wanting to protect her, not realizing that lies never protect, not in the long run.

"Mamm!" Steven came running up, a pile of letters in his arms. He started explaining how he broke the little box next to the front door, the one Celeste used to store mail from the mailbox until she had time to deal with the stack.

Josiah ruffled Steven's hair. "I got this, Celeste. I'm sure it's nothing some fresh pegs or a little wood glue won't fix."

"Jah, it's okay." She kissed Steven's cheek, taking the letters he held out to her. She hadn't gone through the mail in a few days, too distracted about the upcoming burial and wake.

"What's that one?" Eli asked, pointing to an official-looking letter on top of the pile.

Huh. If she'd seen this, she would've opened it rather than shoving it into the box. She tucked the rest of the mail under her arm and opened the envelope.

Preservation Society.

Notice of Inheritance.

Renewed land survey in 1985.

What was this? Her eyes scanned over the page once, twice, three times. She'd . . . inherited a home? How? The home was on a piece of property adjoining a historical property nearby in Lancaster known as Freedman Estate and Museum, but this *inherited* house hadn't been deeded to the county, and all these years they'd thought it was part of the Freedman Estate.

She skipped words, unable to process all of it. But she caught enough. The home should have descended to Moses Lantz of Lancaster County at the death of Anke Mast Cooper, an Old Order Amish woman.

For unknown reasons, the home and three acres of land had been annexed into the Freedman Estate and Museum. Based on the legal documents recently discovered and a fresh survey made, the home and land legally belonged to the firstborn son of many generations of firstborn sons in the lineage of Moses Lantz of Lancaster County, circa 1885. The home originally belonged to Anke Mast Cooper, circa 1822, and she set in motion through attorneys whom the home would pass to, and she paid the taxes accordingly. Based on the legal documents, the home could not descend to a Lantz firstborn son who was older than forty, which would exclude Eli inheriting it. The lawyers had followed the ancestry, and the home's rightful owner in 1986 would be Ervin Lantz. In the case of Ervin Lantz's death prior to the home descending to him, the home was to go to his wife. If she was not alive, it would descend to Ervin Lantz's firstborn son.

"This is crazy," Celeste murmured.

But clearly she was the next in line to inherit it—a place that'd been unknown and basically invisible to the Lantz family for over a century.

Hadn't she and Vin gone to the Freedman Estate and Museum one day years ago? The name sounded familiar, but she couldn't recall.

"What is it?" Eli asked. "If it's legal trouble, we're here for you. We . . . I . . . haven't been treating you like a widow the way the

Word directs. I'm very sorry for that, Celeste. But I assure you, I am—all of us are—on your side, the way Vin would've wanted us to be."

His words were amazing to hear but yet another thing she couldn't process right now. Still, she looked in his eyes and smiled as tears brimmed. "Denki, Eli."

She refocused her attention to the paper in her shaking hands. "Um." She blinked. "According to this, someone from over a hundred and fifty years ago gave me a house."

"What?" Eli took the paper and read it. His face went pale. "It's God's judgment."

Celeste took him by the arm and led him to a seat in the living room.

He looked up at her. "God has moved mountains to support you because I stood in the way."

Celeste sat next to him. "'There is therefore now no condemnation to them which are in Christ Jesus, who walk not after the flesh, but after the Spirit.'"

"But I did walk after the flesh. I didn't know it, but I know now that I've been so very wrong that God has moved mountains for you."

"You've been wrong, and it's been hard on me." She nodded. "Vin was wrong. I was wrong. Others have been wrong. I wish we'd seen what we needed to at the right moment instead of seeing through the eyes of anger, hurt, and grief, but we didn't." If she had seen that night differently, responded differently, Vin wouldn't have left the house, and he'd still be here. "In privacy between us and God, we've each asked for His forgiveness, jah?"

He nodded.

"Then we don't need to fear God because we acted like humans in pain. He knows us. He died for us so we could be forgiven. Let's live for each other and do better."

Eli wiped tears from his eyes. "My son could not have chosen a better wife. Why couldn't I see that before now?"

She didn't know what to say. She read the paper one more time and decided to go to the phone shanty and call the number at the bottom of the page. To her surprise, she was put through to the lawyer without a moment's delay. The lawyer filled her in on her rights.

"You could sell the home back to the county if you wish. They would pay a very handsome figure of forty thousand dollars."

The idea of having that much cash sounded wonderful, but she couldn't turn around and buy a home for that amount. She'd need double that or more to get a place sitting on three acres. If she used that money to help cover rent, it'd be used up within a few years.

"Is it livable?"

"Yes, Mrs. Lantz. It's old, but the county kept it up nicely over the years. They made improvements to it a few years back, thinking they would turn it into more offices, but after some of the work was done, the county voted against allowing it to be used as offices."

"If it's livable, I won't sell it back. I need to see it first to know what I think."

"I can send a car for you today and the driver will have a key so you can get into the house. We've done our homework on this, but I'll still need to see your husband's birth and death certificates and your marriage certificate. Then you'll need to sign some papers."

Celeste wanted the bishop, Lovina, Josiah, and her boys to go too. "I need room for four adults and two children. I . . . could call an Amish driver, one who has a van."

He chuckled. "No need. We have a vehicle on standby for you."

"For me? Why?"

"It's a huge deal for the county that they annexed a home into the Freedman Estate and Museum without due diligence. It would cause much backlash in the county that this was done to an Amish family. Whether you choose to live in the home or sell it back, we want to make this transition as easy for you as possible."

"Thank you for the offer of driving us. I can't leave for hours yet. We buried my husband today. I . . . He's been gone a while. It's just . . ."

"Yes, Mrs. Lantz. We're aware of your situation. My condolences. I know it's been a hard journey. I'm glad you called. If we hadn't heard from you within the next two days, we would've made a visit to your home. What time would you like for the car to arrive?"

"Would four o'clock be okay?"

"It would, Mrs. Lantz. I'll see you then."

He would see her. The lawyer would drive them? Why was he being so nice? Was he concerned she might sue the county for their lack of due diligence that had apparently been going on since long before she was born?

She hung up the phone. The afternoon passed in a blur. The wake had a different feel now, one of unity within the Lantz family and the community, but also one of awe and hope. They sang worship songs as they cleaned up and washed dishes. Celeste left the other women still working in the kitchen and went to the living room, sat down, and read the letter at least ten more times.

How?

She wanted some part of Vin with her this afternoon, so she slipped into her bedroom and layered his shirt under her Amish clothing, then put on a sweater, buttoning it and tucking the collar of the shirt under the sweater, trying to hide it. But if someone still managed to notice, they wouldn't mind. Not today.

Soon the wall clock chimed four times. She left her room. There were still a few stragglers there when a large van arrived, but no one was offended with her about anything, not today, not since Eli's heart had softened, not since she'd miraculously inherited a home.

Her boys were tired, and they wanted to go home with Eli and Naomi, so she let them. Maybe Celeste should sit in the front seat and be cordial to the lawyer, but she moved to the back of the van. Mark, Lovina, and Josiah each got in. The others chatted, but she couldn't manage to hear them.

She played with the cuff of Vin's shirt, hidden under her dress and sweater. Eli was right. It seemed God had moved mountains to help her. How did she own a home outright, no mortgage, no rent? She couldn't figure it out. The Lord working in mysterious ways, indeed. Surely He'd show her how to make space in the home or build a new woodshop so she could continue her business.

They went down a narrow road, the van slowing. A rock home came into view. She remembered this place! A clear memory danced before her—one of her and Vin looking in an old home on the Freedman Estate property.

"The architectural style is called Federal, a very popular style in the US starting in 1780. We believe the Mast family built this home in 1795. The house was originally a simple square box that was two stories high and two rooms deep. At some point in the early 1800s, someone added a wing to the home, and we think that's when the tile roof was added. The mostly blue-gray rock exterior is fieldstone from Pennsylvania. Some of the stones are red and purple, which is rare for fieldstones from other states."

He sounded very invested in the history of this house. Was she an intruder to something that belonged to all of Lancaster County? *Vin.*

She recalled so clearly them enjoying the day they toured the property.

The driver stopped the van near the home. He hopped out, jangling keys in one hand and with a briefcase in the other. He unlocked the door and opened it.

The air inside the home whooshed. *Vin.* The house smelled

of him—of sweat and sawdust and love. An eerie feeling surrounded Celeste.

The lawyer went inside and gestured for her to enter. She stepped inside.

"The walls are original. They're called coquina, but coquina was simply the product that glued all the tiny shells and ground rocks together to create a wall. Usually floors in a home from the early 1800s were made of similar material to the walls and painted to add beauty, but these floors are solid oak, a real extravagance for the time, and we think the original floors were replaced at the same time a wing and the new clay tile roof were added."

Celeste couldn't budge. *You're home.*

Vin's name kept coming to her. Was it because she'd buried him today?

No, that wasn't it. She ran her hands across the old cabinets.

"Yes, we believe these cabinets, which are quite unique for the time period, were also put in around the same time as the wing, roof, and oak floors."

You're home.

It sounded like Vin's voice whispering to her.

That made no sense.

Josiah walked into the room from an adjoining room. "Wow, look at this place, Celeste. It's amazing!"

She couldn't manage to answer him. What was wrong with her?

"Are you okay?" Lovina asked.

All Celeste could do was nod. It made no sense. It couldn't feel like Vin, and yet his smell, his *presence*, was everywhere here.

She played with the cuffs of his treasured shirt again, not caring if someone saw it peeking out from under the sleeve of her sweater. She and Vin never were able to build a home together, like they dreamed, but *this* old house was every bit like she'd imagined. All the details they'd spoken of while lying on their backs in bed.

This wasn't closure—no, the opposite. Vin was *alive* here, like he was standing at her side.

"What do you think, Celeste?" Josiah asked, turning from a window he was looking out to see her.

How could she move on from Vin when every part of her soul ached to be with him?

Chapter Twenty-Five

With a basket of food and water in hand, Anke went out the front door of the Cooper home and to the waiting wagon. Vin stood near the wagon, talking to Johanna. George was leading a saddled horse from the barn.

Anke put the basket under the bench seat and took in the day. A bit brisk for the last day of March. But birds sang. Some of the trees had buds. Flowers were blooming, yet there were still mounds of snow dotting the ground.

She pressed her hands down her wool coat. The trip was a mix of joy and apprehension, and her insides quaked. They—Vin, George, and Anke—were going to a town near the border between Maryland and Pennsylvania on the Susquehanna River. There was no set reason for her going, but when she asked if she could, the Coopers, Vin, and George had been agreeable to it. She hadn't been out of the city of Lancaster since she was a child, and for more than a month, her inner man kept niggling for her to go along. It would take them all day to get there. Anke and George would stay with friends of the Coopers while Vin crossed the river into the slave state of Maryland in hopes of extracting George's wife, Maud, from a plantation. They might be in south Lancaster for a month, so Tandey would stay in Lancaster township. He was apprenticing for a local blacksmith, a man who'd also once been enslaved.

The trip had months of planning and a lot of money behind it. Included in the planning was the unique design of the wagon George and Vin had made. It had a false bottom, but the wagon was made to look like any other wagon with goods to sell—wooden crates filled with valuable pieces of pottery and ceramics packed in straw. The cargo was part of Vin's cover, and he had an order in hand to sell these items at a store in Ellicott City, Maryland, giving him a reason to be in the area. William Cooper's connections with the business world made it easy to create believable decoys. But no amount of planning or financial support could make crossing into Maryland to free a slave safe for Vin.

Johanna was struggling with that fact. He stood near the wagon, apparently trying to assure her he'd return safe. No one knew if that was true.

Anke climbed onto the wagon bench. Everyone had spent last night and this morning saying their goodbyes in one way or another. Vin had spent extra time with Gustav and Gretchen, hugging and kissing them. The children were now out back with Margaret, playing. But clearly Johanna's emotions had the best of her.

Vin was face-to-face with Johanna. "I'm a bit unsure of the timing, but I will be back."

Johanna's eyes held tears. "Maybe no."

Anke understood how Johanna felt. The woman had been

a recent widow when Vin entered her life, and the two hadn't been apart since the day her cabin burned down. Men left. They didn't always return. No one knew that in more painful ways than Johanna . . . and Celeste.

Vin spoke to her in German, softly assuring her that he intended to return, but if this was a forever goodbye, she was safe here. She had a home and safety with the Coopers and Tandey.

Johanna wrapped her arms around him, and Vin held her.

He stepped back, holding her shoulders at arm's length. "No matter what happens from here, you will be fine."

She nodded, wiping tears.

Vin lowered his arms. "While I'm away, maybe give Kurth Miller a chance. He's a good man."

Johanna shrugged, but she moved away from the wagon. George mounted his horse. Vin climbed onto the wagon bench, saying nothing. Johanna waved as they drove off. George rode ahead of them. Another horse was tethered behind the wagon. The rig jostled along, and Anke held her tongue, giving Vin some time to think and maybe let go of Johanna's fears.

Johanna and her children now lived in Anke's former home, a place Vin had toiled endlessly for months to make solid and gorgeous. Months ago, Johanna started sewing dresses by hand, making women's clothes for local stores. Well, one particular store, a dry goods store belonging to Kurth Miller, a single man of German descent who was about four years older than Johanna. He'd cleared out an area of the store exclusively for dresses Johanna made, and he had one hanging in the window. They sold as fast as Johanna could sew them. Kurth lived in his dry goods store and had never been married. It seemed to Vin and Anke that the man was clearly smitten. Johanna didn't dislike him, so that was good. She probably just needed time.

But being a seamstress was perfect for Johanna. Maybe one day she'd want to own a dress shop, but not now. Despite the difficulties of saying goodbye to Vin, Johanna had survived the harshest season of being a widow and she was beginning to thrive.

A wagon wheel hit a pit in the road, and Anke bounced up. Vin grabbed her arm, steadying her until she was firmly seated again.

She laughed. "I may take flight like a bird." Talking while riding on a noisy wagon took effort, raising her voice so he could hear her.

Vin drew a breath. "And then thud against the hard earth like a felled tree. Try holding on to the bench seat. The false bottom seems to make the wagon a little less stable when it hits holes, even though the back is loaded with wooden boxes filled with pottery. But my guess is that kind of bounce doesn't happen when the weight of a human is between the real bottom and the false bottom."

His voice sounded heavy. Was it because of what lay ahead of him? Or was it because Johanna feared he might not return? Was it because if he failed to get Maud out, George and Tandey would grieve for the rest of their lives? More than anything else, she felt he was weary because he still didn't know how to get home.

Anke couldn't help but smile on such a wonderful day as this one. "We are finally free to travel. It was such a brutal winter. I haven't seen that much snow during one winter in my lifetime."

"It was brutal." Vin nodded. "No matter how much I wanted to get to the Wright's Ferry area since arriving in Lancaster township the day before Thanksgiving, there was no going there before the snows stopped for the winter."

"Wright's Ferry," she repeated. "It's where Kissin' Mountain is?"

"I think so."

Months ago, as soon as Vin had realized that he'd be near Kissin' Mountain when going to the river town the Gibsons lived in, he'd plotted out on a map where the mountain would be and showed it to her. He'd said he wanted to see it again, maybe climb it and sit and think, like he used to.

He loosened the reins, allowing the horse to find its own pace. "Apparently there are two Wright's Ferry towns and the towns' borders as well as the state lines are different now, but I think one of them is what is known as Peach Bell in my time. It's also possible Peach Bell is there, only its district lines are very small and not yet marked on maps I've seen. But a town by any other name would smell as sweet."

She laughed. "A play of words on Shakespeare."

He nodded. He'd spent the last three months not only working on her former home but working with lawyers on how to get the house to Celeste. There were no guarantees his plan would work, but whenever they talked about it, he seemed to have complete faith it would.

"Do you think someone in your time has uncovered the legal papers yet?"

"Maybe." Vin fidgeted with the reins. "The lawyer had the paperwork in order four weeks ago. It's now part of the documentation for Lancaster County, for the Cooper home, and in ledgers for the public."

Anke watched the Conestoga River drift along beside them. It wasn't very deep, and she remembered her dat saying it should be called a creek, not a river. Patches of skunk cabbage, with its mottled maroon and bright yellow-green spiked leaves, were all along the riverbanks. Her mind returned to Celeste time and again, and she prayed that after Vin returned from Maryland safe, God would show him how to get home to his wife and sons.

She thought about his wording. "The house will be . . . descended. Is that the right word?"

"Jah. It'll pass through the generations until it reaches Celeste, but since I have no memories of any Lantz owning your former home, I'm guessing no one found the paperwork down through the generations. At least the information about your will stating the homestead goes to the Lantz family is legal and binding and listed in as many places as I can fathom to list it. We can trust we've done all we can and pray God will draw it to the right people's attention."

He'd explained to her how he'd figured out the generations down the line and specified the wording so the house went to the Ervin Lantz family—not that the documents could specify his name, but he'd done the paperwork through the lawyer in such a way that no other branch of his family or his father became the inheritor. When the lawyer asked why he was being so specific, Vin said he'd had a dream about who should get the house. That was true. Vin definitely had a dream of getting a home to Celeste and his boys.

Vin slowed the wagon as they crossed a long hole on the right side of the dirt road. "The land survey that should've renewed in 1985 should cause the preservation society to take a closer look at the property and who owns what. It might look and feel a little odd to whomever finds the legal paperwork, but I've covered reasonable explanations, based on your Amish family once owning the home, as to why it was descending to another Amish family in Lancaster County." Vin moved the reins to one hand and scratched his thick, full beard. "You looking forward to time with Jacob and Rebecca Gibson?"

The plan was for Anke to stay with the Gibsons while Vin went to Ellicott City, Maryland, and found Maud. George would stay there tonight, maybe tomorrow night, but he intended to find work loading and unloading ferries as they crossed the Susquehanna. If he got a job doing that, he'd find room and board nearby. George intended to stay as close to the border river as possible so that he was there when Vin returned.

"Jah, I'm looking forward to time with the Gibsons. Even

though they're Quakers and friends with the Coopers, they were also friends with my parents. They came to the Coopers' to visit about three years ago, and I've not seen them since. It should be an enjoyable, interesting place to be while you're in Maryland. You think we'll get there before dark today?"

"I think so. I sort of know the way, so that helps. Based on William's maps and instructions, they live about seven miles west of Kissin' Mountain. I'm hoping to find it first."

Every time of late, whenever Vin said *Kissin' Mountain*, Anke felt odd—like her insides were one of Johanna's pincushions.

"And if you find it?"

"I'll have you and George take the wagon and go on to the Gibsons', and I'll ride horseback up the mountain, spend an hour or so of time alone there." He shrugged. "I'm not sure why it's so important to go to my old thinking spot, but I'd sure enjoy it. I'll meet you and George at the Gibson place by bedtime."

Pinpricks jabbed her again. Hadn't he told her one time that returning home before bedtime was sort of what he said to Celeste the night he fell from the mountain? A bridge formed in her mind, but an Amish man was on it, facing her. Was that Vin, an older Vin?

"You heading to Ellicott City first thing tomorrow?"

"Jah, because of stops I need to make along the way to make contact and share information with others in the abolition movement, it'll take a week or more to arrive at the plantation where we believe Maud was last sold. But coming back, we won't waste a minute getting out of Maryland."

The older man on the bridge in her mind's eye opened his mouth to tell her something, but then he and the beautiful see-through yellow bridge disappeared.

She focused, trying to hear what the man wanted to tell her, but she wanted to keep talking because it seemed to help Vin.

"I heard William say where you're going is a ten-thousand-acre plantation owned by a Charles Carroll III. I cannot imagine such a huge piece of land. The Coopers own about two hundred acres, and the care of that land feels overwhelming. Do you have an exact plan for Maud's escape or just a general idea?"

"We have three exact plans based on various possibilities. If none of those work, I'll do my best to figure out a better plan."

One evening last week, she'd accidentally seen scars on George's back. She'd tapped on his door to give him fresh water for his basin, and she thought he'd said come in, but based on the look on his face when he turned toward her, that's not what he said. He'd been putting on his shirt, and his back was to her.

"Vin, I would be terrified to try to escape if I was Maud."

"Jah, that's a strong possibility. If she's too afraid to try, all of us have to respect that." He tapped his foot against the false bottom under his feet. "But with maps to routes and homes that help with safe passage of runaways to give out, the trip will be an important one either way."

"William says if you're caught helping a slave escape, you will get six to fifteen years in jail."

"I'm aware."

"That is all you have to say on the matter? I know you have been quiet about it thus far, but I thought once we were traveling, you would say more."

"Maybe falling through time has given me a different perspective—"

Anke grabbed his arm, and he stopped midsentence. A vision of Vin falling from the cliff hit her hard, and for a brief moment she saw the older man trying to tell them what they needed to know.

"What's going on, Anke?"

"I'm not sure. Keep talking. You said, maybe falling through time has given you a different perspective . . ."

"I . . . I don't remember the rest."

"Try."

"I . . . uh . . . I know I've made a lot of foolish mistakes in life, and I have regrets I have to deal with and answer for. But slavery makes a person carry the burden of another man's stupid, selfish choices while making that man rich and comfortable. There aren't enough words in any language to explain how unjust that is."

"I agree, and that is an incredible insight." But his talk of slavery and doing what's right did nothing to make the vision reappear. Why had he been on the mountain to begin with? Did that matter? "What is your biggest fear about being stuck in this time?"

"Being unable to get back."

A faint yellow bridge reappeared in her mind's eye and the man was closer. It *was* Vin. The older Vin was trying to tell her more. She tried to relax and focus. Older Vin radiated love and acceptance, but he also carried with him an overwhelming desire for his young self to return home sooner. He longed to get Maud out safely, and he'd give his all, but if something went wrong, he might never get the chance to return to his beloved Celeste.

She shook those thoughts away. "What would an older you tell a younger you about getting home?"

"I have no idea, but that's part of my fear—that the answer I'm looking for is right in front of me, within easy view, and I can't see it."

The faded image of the bridge grew stronger.

The older Vin on the bridge opened his mouth and chills covered her. "Say it," she said.

"What?" Vin on the wagon bench beside her asked.

She ignored him and stayed focused on the vision of the older Vin, hoping he didn't disappear. "Say it."

"Anke?" Vin slowed the wagon. "I have no idea what you're talking about."

"Say it," she whispered. "Say it!"

The older Vin drew closer, walking on that golden bridge, whispering. But she couldn't make out the words. She tried to read his lips. He seemed to be repeating two words, one started with an *M*. She walked across the bridge, closing more of the gap. The man's eyes were earnest, tears filling them as he whispered, seeming to talk as loud as he could, and she read his lips. *M . . . M . . . Mountain.*

She grabbed Vin's arm. "Mountain."

He glanced at her. "Kissin' Mountain? We're not in that area yet."

"Vin . . . ," she whispered, squeezing his arm as she heard the man in her vision whisper. She spoke what she heard. "Search where you lost them, and you'll find your way home. The mountain. A solitary rock. Many boulders. Find the crag."

The rig jolted to a stop.

Anke's heart pounded. Had she crossed the Gott Brucke and brought back answers or had her imagination just run wild?

Chapter Twenty-Six

Vin dropped the reins and jumped from the wagon, his heart threatening to beat out of his chest. "The mountain!" Emotions rolled through him so hard he couldn't sit still. "I never once considered . . ." He removed his black winter hat, searching the land. "Kissin' Mountain!" he screamed, stretching his arms out wide as he laughed. How had he never pondered even once that the crag itself had something to do with his traveling through time?

"More than the mountain being the answer, how did I get to this time?"

"God," Anke said.

"Maybe not God." Vin grabbed a stick off the ground and snapped it. "I mean, clearly yes, God allowed it." He paced, trying to settle his emotions enough to think. "Maybe the crag I was holding on to when I fell was like a portal, like getting on a train or plane. God allows the invention and the travel, but people go from one place to another by boarding it."

In truth, Vin had no interest in the theology of it. He just wanted to go home.

Would the crag return him to his time? If so, how could he go to Maryland tomorrow and spend weeks, likely more than that, in a time he didn't belong in when finding Kissin' Mountain could return him to Celeste?

From a few hundred feet ahead, George was riding toward them. He'd clearly noticed they weren't following and was coming to check on them. Vin made his decision: he had a mission to accomplish for his friend, and he wouldn't shirk it.

"Hallo, George. Sorry. We're not stopping here to rest. Up ahead, maybe a mile or so, we'll drive off the main road. There is a mountain in that area that I used to climb as a kid. I'd like to put my eyes on it. I won't climb it, but we'll stop at the foot of it for a spell. Spread a blanket. Eat."

"Then let's keep moving. You lead. I'll follow." George gestured to Vin to head out.

Vin climbed back into the wagon. "The mountain." He chuckled, shaking his head. "All this time, the answer was that simple." He drove, humming praises to God.

"Vin." Anke sounded apprehensive.

"Jah?"

"The old man in your dreams *is* you. He is dressed Amish and at peace with that way of life and all its rules, but more than any religious ways, you're fully at peace with yourself and the ways of God that are higher and deeper than any religion can fully see or embrace. That man is you."

"That makes sense to me. In other words, old me has finally matured and separated some of the less-than-perfect church ways from the honesty of God's ways, and I have peace with both."

"Jah."

He hoped mature thinking was a deep part of him by the time he returned to his wife and sons. Anke's words still rang in his ears: *"Search where you lost them, and you'll find your way home. The mountain. A solitary rock. Many boulders. Find the crag."*

He was still pondering when he pulled off the beaten path, looking for Kissin' Mountain. George followed. They traveled another fifteen minutes across bumpy terrain.

Where is it?

The Coopers had pretty good maps of this area, and everything else lined up reasonably well with what he'd expected. There were no homes or familiar roads to use as landmarks, but he'd expected that. Still, he should've come across the rock cliff by now.

His heart pounded. Everything felt surreal, making him question once again what was really going on. He stopped the wagon. "George, we're looking for signs of a lone mountain with a cliff face and crags." He pulled a sketch pad and piece of compressed charcoal from the hidden compartment under the wagon seat and quickly drew Kissin' Mountain and all its crags. "There are numerous overlooks and cliffs in this area, but Kissin' Mountain looks like this. The formation of the crags at the foot of it is the most telling feature."

George took the drawing. "Let's spread out."

"I'll ride the other horse bareback and look. We don't have much time to search for it today, but maybe George or I can locate it within the next thirty minutes."

"Go." Anke shooed him. "I am fine here."

Riding bareback, Vin followed the lay of the land, but he couldn't locate the mountain. Unfortunately, thirty minutes wasn't much time, and he had to head back to the wagon. Soon he spotted Anke, walking, probably stretching her legs. Maybe mumbling prayers as she searched for the Gott Brucke to let them in on why they couldn't find Kissin' Mountain.

Vin rode to her. "Any thoughts?"

"Nee. Any signs of the mountain?"

"Nee."

George rode to them and stopped.

"Any luck?" Vin asked.

He shook his head. "I searched like you said, but I only saw a few jutted-out rocks and cliffs. None that looked like the drawing you gave me. If we went toward the Susquehanna, we'd find a lot more than is in this area."

"It has to be here. The cliff wasn't any closer to the river than in this area we're searching." Vin dismounted. "How are we missing it? If it existed in the late 1900s, it has to exist now, doesn't it?"

George tilted his head, squirming in his saddle. "I don't think I heard you right."

"It was within a few miles of here." Vin gestured at a grassy hill covered with trees. "I used to go to the top of it as a little boy. It's where I was when I fell through time."

George's eyes narrowed. He got off his horse. "We'll keep looking. If we ain't found it by dark, we'll start again in the morning. But it's been too long since we ate. Let's eat and rest a bit."

Vin looked at his friend. George was worried about him, maybe thinking Vin was losing it. Should he tell George the truth? "We can't keep looking. It'll be dark in an hour, ending our ability to travel or search. If I'm going to be at the ferry soon after sunup, I need to get Anke to the Gibsons' now."

"All right," George said. "I'll take the sketch with me, and I'll come here every day while you're gone, spanning out my search each time until I find it."

George had other plans, but he'd do that for Vin without it making a lick of sense as to why.

Anke reached under the bench of the wagon and got out the basket. "George is right. You need to eat."

George grabbed a wool blanket from the wagon. "Let's put this on the ground and rest for a bit."

George spread the blanket. Anke set the basket on it and began removing tin plates and cups. She put slices of cheese and homemade bread on the plates. It was simple, but it'd sustain them.

Vin wanted to tell both of them he was fine, but he sat on the blanket, stretching his legs. Anke passed out the plates. She poured water from a flask into tin cups. Vin ate some while thinking, and he decided his friend deserved to know the truth.

"George." Vin took a sip of the warm water. "Anke knows. You should too. I'm from another time. I was on Kissin' Mountain, angry and confused after an argument with my wife, and I fell through time."

George blinked. "You feeling all right? Your head hurt or something?"

"It's how I landed in the middle of Ohio with no survival skills or tools or money or a horse. I had nothing. Days later, you and Tandey stumbled across me after I passed out. You kept me alive. The next day, I saw Patrick and Bridget's wagon, and when I passed out in front of Bridget, they took me with them. The next morning, I came across you and Tandey again."

Anke removed her sunbonnet. Despite her hair being in a bun, she brushed wisps from her face. "The reason I know about this is the day after you arrived, I realized it was Vin that I had seen in my prayers as the man who fell through time."

Vin poured George more water.

"Fell?" George asked.

Anke and Vin took turns explaining various things.

George studied them, looking from one to the other. "It's hard to believe, and if anybody else said it to me, I'd doubt them. But you're telling me, Vin, and I believe you."

Another surge of relief went through Vin. He had two friends who knew the truth about him and accepted it. Honest connection to others was incredibly powerful, so much better for the soul and for mental health than hiding parts of himself from his wife.

"I still have times of struggling to believe," Vin said. "Today is one of those times. Kissin' Mountain should be in this area." He stood. "I've worked for months on a house for Celeste, believing it could be passed down to her, but she's a hundred and sixty-three years in the future. That's crazy talk!"

"Tell me about your time, Vin," George said. "Are all men like you there, ones who don't believe in slavery?"

"There's no slavery in my time. A war is coming. It's a ways off yet, right at thirty-eight years in the future. It'll rip this country apart. Many cities will burn. People will suffer great loss. Some will go hungry. But when it's done, slavery will be over for the entire nation." Vin took a bite of bread. "The president who will set all this in motion and fight hard for the win is only in his teens. Harriet Tubman, a person you've never heard of, was born a year or two ago." Vin chuckled. "She was born a slave in Maryland, but in less than thirty years, she'll escape to Pennsylvania. Then she makes her mark on history." Vin didn't want to say too much about Harriett's heroic efforts to free other slaves. George wanted to go with Vin into Maryland to rescue his wife, but Vin had pleaded with him until George agreed to stay safe. "The war will last four years, but decent laws and good treatment of Blacks will take much longer. It continues to be a work in progress in my time, and after slavery is abolished, the next big push to right wrongs happens in my lifetime—the Civil Rights Movement. Still, you and yours will be free, and that's worth a lot."

"It is. Praise God, it is! My people get free in all states?"

"They do."

"Do you know if you find Maud?"

"Nee. I only know what I've read in history books."

"Why is the mountain you're looking for so important?"

"We realized today that the crag I was holding on to when I fell through time may be my way of getting back to my wife and sons."

George ate the last bite of the homemade bread in his hand. "But if that's how you got here, why is it missing?"

"That's the question, for sure." Vin couldn't understand it. But he knew this much: life held out to him the opportunity to give George his wife back. Worse for the wear, he was sure—more traumatized than the last time George saw her. But she'd be free with her husband and son. On the other hand, Vin could stay here, trying to find his way to his own wife.

Vin stood. "It'll be dark soon. Let's go on to the Gibsons'."

Anke gathered up the mostly uneaten food and the jar of water. "Maybe they will know something about a rock cliff in this area, and we can use that information to search again tomorrow."

He picked up the basket of food and examined the lay of the land one more time. "We'll ask, but I need to stick to the plan. If Maud is at the Carroll plantation, her best time to escape unnoticed will be early to mid-April, during fresh plowing and planting time. I might have to hide out in the woods on the planation for weeks before there's an opportunity to get her out of there. Tomorrow is April 1. It's a three-day trip to get there, and I have numerous stops to make along the way to deliver maps to friends of William's and Margaret's. I can't afford to give more time to Kissin' Mountain right now."

"I will ask around about it," Anke said. "Someone will know something. I'll also try to get old diaries and read about this area, and when George or I have time, we will continue to search."

"We will," George said.

"Denki. I appreciate it."

When Vin returned, he would go over every inch of this area until he found Kissin' Mountain.

Chapter Twenty-Seven

The Gibson home smelled of fresh baked goods as Anke went out the front door carrying a basket of still-warm cookies. Vin called them biscuits. Either way they would keep him from going hungry for the next several days.

Birds sang. Pink clouds hung low in the early morning sky. Some of the wooden crates from inside the wagon were on the ground. Vin was inside the covered wagon, hammering, probably repairing or making a last-minute adjustment.

She set the basket on the wagon bench. "More food."

"Denki." Vin climbed out the back of the wagon. He picked up the crates from the ground and put them back in.

Jacob Gibson came out of the house carrying a roll of paper. He stepped off the porch looking very similar to William with his typical Quaker clothes, including his neckcloth and clean-shaven

237

face. "I added the other safe homes that William was unaware of to the map."

"Denki." Vin took it. "When I'm done traveling each day, I'll log that information onto the other maps."

"We will pray for thee's safety night and day, Ervin Lantz." Rebecca Gibson tightened her shawl.

The modest house behind her hosts was nothing like the Cooper place, but Anke felt very at ease here. There had been no way to notify Jacob and Rebecca that Anke, Vin, and George would show up on their doorstep last night. But the couple welcomed all of them, making them feel as if their visit and need for a place to stay was a high honor. Rebecca got up hours before daylight, stoked the fires in the hearth, and helped Anke bake cookies in the brick oven that was part of the hearth.

George approached, leading a horse pulling a surrey. Anke found it much easier to steer a surrey. Its lack of a roof and sides and only one bench seat made it lightweight and easy to maneuver, and she and George were returning this morning to search for Kissin' Mountain. None of them could go to the Pennsylvania side of the running ferries with Vin. Rumors spread easily, especially as ferries with talkers crossed from Pennsylvania to Maryland all day long, day after day. If George and Vin were seen together, Vin would appear sympathetic to abolitionists, which would show Vin's hand as he went into Maryland to try to blend in as a man on business. Anke didn't feel capable of driving back to the Gibson place or to the Kissin' Mountain area on her own. She could lose her way.

"This wagon has a false bottom?" Rebecca asked.

"It does." Vin pointed to the front of the wagon. "It's made to look as if those crates are sitting low, but the crates are short, same as the ones in the back."

Jacob peered into the wagon. "Even knowing it and looking

at them, one can't tell with the way thee has placed the straw for packing the crates so carefully. Thee is a very clever man."

"I can't take credit. But denki."

Anke knew the whole story. In Vin's time, he'd read about a false bottom wagon for hiding precious cargo. The creator lived in a Quaker community in North Carolina, and he used the same system of a false bottom and stacks of hay to protect valuable pottery in order to help runaway slaves escape.

Anke and Vin came toe-to-toe. She looked into his dark-brown eyes. "You will be safe. You will be successful, and while you are gone, we will continue to look for Kissin' Mountain."

"Ach, nein." Rebecca reached into her apron pocket and pulled out a small book. "I almost forgot. When Anke asked me about Kissin' Mountain last night, I knew I'd never heard that name, but during the night, I remembered seeing a similar name in one of my father's old diaries. In his day, it was called Missing Mountain."

"Missing Mountain?" Vin asked.

"Jah, his diary said that sometimes men would go there and never return." She held the book out to him, her index finger holding a spot. "Maybe sixty years ago, after another disappearance, the community decided to cover the rocks and crags with dirt and plant trees and shrubs."

Missing Mountain.

"What?" Vin took the book and read. He passed it to Anke. "I showed you and George where it should be on the map. Use that map to see if you can locate the cliff and its crags."

"Why do you want to locate that cliff?" Jacob Gibson asked.

Anke studied the open diary. "Something important to Vin's family came up missing there before the locals buried the cliff."

"Ah." Jacob nodded. "Then whatever is missing was probably buried there."

Anke read the passage again, her heart going crazy. "We will use the maps, Vin." She closed the book. "You do your part. We'll do ours." She hugged him. "We'll see you in a month, maybe less."

He took a step back from her and hugged George. "When I see you next, I pray Maud will be with me."

"I know you do, but all any of us can do is our best, and that's good enough." George's voice broke.

Vin climbed in the wagon, waved, and clicked his tongue, causing the horse to begin walking.

Anke passed the book back to Rebecca, and Rebecca gave Anke a small basket of food to hold them throughout the day.

George climbed into the surrey beside her. "Let's stop by the barn and get some tools—a pickax, shovel, and sickle."

After the tools were in the surrey, they rode in silence until they came to the area where they should find Missing Mountain.

"The mountain's name seems befitting." Anke brought the rig to a halt.

"It's missing for sure." George got out of the surrey and tethered the horse to a nearby tree. "Do you think Rebecca's father was right, that only men go missing?"

"I don't know." Anke grabbed the map of this area and stepped out of the rig too. "Have only men climbed it? Or did Rebecca's father mean *people* go there and then come up missing, but he wrote the word *men*?" She opened the scroll. "What do you think, George?"

"I think Missing Mountain should be around here somewhere, and we got to start looking for holes in the ground where dirt that was packed onto rock may have washed away over the years, and we need to keep an eye out for the tops of rocks showing in the field."

"Jah." She rolled up the map. "All of which could be a part of nature and not something to do with mankind covering Missing Mountain."

"We got time to find it before Vin returns." George grabbed a shovel. "Let's spread out a bit."

Anke began walking the slope. Was Missing Mountain under her feet? She topped a knoll and kept going, searching for any signs of the mountain. At noon she returned to the buggy and got a cookie and some water. Although she didn't see George, she knew he'd returned to the rig at some point because there were cookies and water missing. She started looking again, spanning out farther. Soon it was dusk, and an odd sound tickled her ears, as if it wasn't really a noise, but a sound nonetheless.

What was happening?

🍂

APRIL 1986

Panic owned Celeste, and it was all she could do to stay on her feet. "Steven!" She cupped her hands around her mouth and yelled with all she had. "Steven!"

Lovina walked down the ramp of the U-Haul, eyes wide, skin pale. "I looked carefully, and he's not in there."

They'd been loading the U-Haul all day. She'd seen the boys in the fenced yard just . . . a few minutes ago? Fifteen minutes ago? Half an hour ago?

What kind of a mother didn't know the answer to that?

The bishop came out of the barn. "No sign of him."

Sugar Bear meandered into the yard—saddled, bridled, and no rider.

Celeste's legs threatened to buckle. Sugar Bear had returned without his rider once before, and the panic of the memory stole her ability to breathe. *Not my son too, please, God!*

She shook herself free of the silent screams and turned to the bishop. "This can't be happening! This is exactly what happened the night Vin disappeared!" She wanted to pull her hair out by the roots and scream at the top of her lungs.

"Steven's not big enough to saddle a horse," Lovina said.

"I . . . I saddled her," Mark said. "Hours ago, Steven asked if I'd saddle her and lead her around while he rode her. After doing so, I left her saddled at the hitching post, and I forgot about her."

Lovina rubbed her forehead. "At that age, my boys led the horse next to the split-rail fence and climbed it to mount."

Steven knew that trick too. What Amish boy didn't? Celeste's head spun. Steven was comfortable going long distances on a horse too. Vin used to let Steven ride horseback with him, and they'd go into town or to the river to fish. Would her little boy go that distance on his own?

Maybe Sugar Bear had pulled free of the hitching post on her own, and Steven hadn't ridden her somewhere. She ran to the phone shanty and dialed the number to her new phone. "Pick up. Pick up."

Steven could've slipped into the hired car Josiah used to return to her new home less than an hour ago. It was possible. Josiah had loaded up the car with boxes of kitchen items, and then he rode in the front seat, so maybe Steven had crawled into a hiding place in the back or the trunk.

"Hallo?" Josiah's familiar voice washed over her.

"Steven's missing. Please tell me he's with you."

He didn't answer.

"Josiah!"

"I . . . I'm sorry. I haven't seen him, but he can't be far. Breathe, Celeste. Just take in a few deep breaths."

"Don't tell me what to do like you're my husband! You don't understand—it happened just like Vin! Sugar Bear returned saddled, but no rider! Do you hear me?" She might have broken his eardrum screaming into the phone, and that was her question?

"Celeste." His voice was calm, and she wanted to slap him. "Breathe. Or he'll return to a passed-out mamm. Breathe in." He waited.

She hated herself for it, but she did as he said.

"Breathe out nice and slow."

She did so. He repeated himself a few times, and she could think with a little more clarity.

"My baby is missing just like my husband, Josiah." She barely got the words out before she sobbed.

"He'll return. I promise you that. Do you hear me?"

Somehow, despite everything, she believed him. "Jah."

"I'm going to hang up and call for a driver. I'll be there as quick as I can. He'll probably be in your arms by the time I arrive. He's hiding somewhere, thinking it's funny. Or he rode the horse up the road, got off, and the horse broke free and came home. Now Steven is walking home."

"He's barely five!"

"But he's a smart, adventurous five-year-old."

That was true. "Call a driver. I need to see you."

"I'll call right now."

"And, Josiah . . ."

"Jah?"

"I'm sorry for screaming at you. I . . . I'm sorry for my words. That husband comment was unnecessary."

"You're forgiven. I knew you couldn't be completely perfect because the earth can only have one of those at a time, and I'm it."

She laughed. Hard, while fresh tears fell. "Hang up and get here. You can find him. I know you can."

"We'll find him, safe and sound and feeling proud of himself for the adventure. And, Celeste?"

"Jah?"

"Go easy on the boy, okay?"

"I will." She hung up and cried. *Dear God, please, please, don't let me lose my son.*

Chapter Twenty-Eight

Anke remained still, trying to hear the sound clearer.

George topped a knoll in the surrey, and a moment later he was near her. "It's about time to go back to the Gibsons'."

"Do you hear that?"

He stopped the rig and tilted his head. "I don't hear anything, Anke."

She listened again. "Is that a child crying?"

George stood in the rig, turning his head one way and another. "I got good hearing, and I don't hear nothin'."

"Sit, please." She got in the rig and took the reins, trying to follow a sound that couldn't be heard.

"We're so far from where you said you heard a child crying, there's no way you could've heard one."

She kept going.

Stop, child.

She brought the rig to a halt and got out. She followed the sound up an incline, and George went with her.

"I hear something now," George said.

They continued walking until she saw a small child sitting on the ground covered in dirt, his knees pulled to his chest as he sobbed.

"Hello," she said softly. "Are you lost?"

He looked up. His clothes looked odd to her. His braces, what Vin called suspenders, had stripes to them. His shirt had the strangest collar she'd ever seen. What were on his feet? It looked like a cross between men's shoes and moccasins.

"Ich will mei dat."

His German was a bit unusual, but he'd said he wanted his dat. Would he understand her German?

"Wo ist dein dat?"

He shrugged in response to her question: *Where is your dat?* He wiped his eyes. She knelt and put her hand on his shoulder.

He flung his arms around her neck, sobbing as he told a disjointed story. Anke's whole body was covered in chills. He spoke Vin's kind of German, and the story . . .

"What'd he say?" George asked.

"He says he has overheard the adults talking for months about how his father went missing. They buried him a few days ago, but he rode a horse up Kissin' Mountain, found a rope attached to bolts in the ground, and used it to go down the cliff. On his way down, he reached out to grab a crag and he landed here."

"Ask him his name."

She told him her name and George's, and then she asked his.

"Steven Lantz."

Anke shifted from kneeling to sitting on the ground, the boy still in her lap. Steven *Lantz*? It seemed impossible, and yet here he was. Once sitting, she saw a small hole of fresh dirt. She pointed. "There? *Dort?*"

Steven looked at the hole and told her he'd had to dig his way out.

Anke looked up at George. "I think we've found Missing Mountain—and Vin's son!"

"Ich will mei dat."

Anke hugged him tight.

"Vin's son? What's he saying?" George asked again.

"He wants his dat."

George knelt. "I understand he wants to see Vin. We all do, but Vin won't be back for weeks or longer, and we got to try to get this boy back home now. Vin will go through the crag as soon as he can, but this boy's mom has lost a husband. She don't need to think she lost a child too."

Anke nodded. George was right. Vin was going to be thrilled when she and George told him. He could go home! *"Heemet. Mutter braucht Sie."* She looked at George. "I told him his mother needs him."

Steven nodded. *"Dat kumm heemet alleweil?"*

He wanted his dat to come home now. She explained as best she could that his dat wanted that too, but Steven would need to be patient. Was she telling the boy too much? What if Vin didn't return from his dangerous trip? What if he returned, but traveling through the mountain didn't work by then? The understanding was beyond her.

Steven wiped tears from his face. *"Heemet geh.* How?"

"And?" George asked.

"He has agreed to go home, but he doesn't know how."

The hole . . . she'd have to go into it with him. The dark sight of it sent a chill up her spine. She knew nothing about how this worked—for all the facts she had, it could take them somewhere else in time and not back to Celeste. Her head swam and she drew a deep breath. "George, can you dig out that entry a little better, so I can fit through it?"

"I can." George strode to the surrey and came back with the shovel, a lantern with candle, and a char kit. He set the lantern on the ground and passed the kit to Anke. He jammed the shovel into the entryway and scooped up dirt. "I should go with Steven."

"Nein. He and I speak the same language . . . mostly . . . good enough. Wherever we land, if we can travel at all, we have that one thing going for us. I can comfort him. You tell Vin where this place is and what's going on."

"You thinkin' you'll be gone that long?"

"I don't know. If I am not back quickly, you tell Rebecca and Jacob that I decided to return to the Coopers. It is the only thing that will keep them from being frantic. The Coopers will think I am with the Gibsons, and the Gibsons will think I am with the Coopers. Tell the Gibsons I saw a stagecoach, and since they've only been in operation a few years, I wanted to see what it was like, and that I hope to return later in the spring."

She opened the small leather kit and got out the char cloth, flint, and steel. After tearing a piece of char cloth off, she laid it on the flint and struck the flint with the steel. Soon she had an ember on the char cloth. She blew on it gently, and when it ignited, she opened the lantern, lit the candle, and closed it, grateful to have a light to go into the hole with.

She looked Steven in the eyes and asked him if he wanted to go ahead of her or behind her, because the hole was too small for her to carry him on her back. He chose to go ahead of her. She lay on the ground, inching along after him, holding the lantern on the ground ahead of her, foot by foot. Moving along like a worm in a dress was slow, especially as she had to set the lantern ahead of her a bit and then inch to it, moving dirt with her body as she did.

"There." Steven yelled. *"Seller."*

"That one." She repeated his German, barely able to make out a part of a crag. *"Berühre es nicht!"* She didn't mean to yell *do not touch it,* but her nerves got the best of her.

The tunnel had a bit more space here than anywhere else. Holding the lantern outstretched, she wiggled until Steven's back was pressing against her chest. Was that how time travel worked: if she was holding him, they'd go to the same place? She had no idea. She set the lantern on the ground.

When Vin fell from the cliff, he must've grabbed on to the top of this crag. When Steven used a rope to descend, he must've touched the top of the crag on his way down. They were at the bottom of the crag. Would the base of it work like the top had? Because in this time, the top was buried in mounds of dirt under a layer of grass and trees.

With one of her arms holding Steven around his waist, she splayed her fingers on her other hand. Steven seemed to instinctively put the back of his hand in her palm and slip his little fingers between hers. "We touch the rock together."

"Jah."

She'd forgotten to speak German. The boy seemed much better at understanding English than speaking it. She held him tight as she reached out, taking his little hand with hers. They touched the crag. Everything went dark. Suddenly she was standing somewhere, still holding the boy.

Denki, Gott. She turned him toward her and hugged him tight. Then she blinked. Where was she?

"Siah." He pointed.

What did *Siah* mean? She turned. She was in front of the Cooper home. Why? The yard looked so different since she'd left yesterday.

Oh—she was in a different time. Her brain seemed unable to catch up with her body and surroundings.

"Siah," the boy said again.

She looked where he was pointing. A man stood near her old homestead. She couldn't imagine how the boy knew who it was from this distance, but she began walking the five hundred feet. Dusk had settled in by the time she reached the yard of her old homestead. The man was pacing the length of the yard as if thinking or waiting for someone.

"Siah!"

He turned. "Steven!"

The little boy wriggled down. Something large pulled onto the driveway. A horseless carriage? But it didn't look anything like a carriage. It made an awful noise. Twice. Reminding her of the sound a bugle made in the hands of a child. Anke ran into the woods and covered her ears, trying to tune out the onslaught of emotions hitting her. Was she losing her mind? What was that loud, smelly thing? She realized how little Vin had told her about what life was like in his time.

She hid behind a tree and peered around it.

The man seemed to pay no attention to the noisy, horseless carriage. He picked the boy up. "Where were you? How are you here and not at your mamm's house?"

"An angel." Steven pointed to where Anke had been, but she was hiding now.

"Jah. I saw her." The man bounced the boy in his arm. "She looked like an angel to me, too." The man searched the yard as if hoping to spot her.

He was beautiful. No, that wasn't the right word. But whatever word best described him, he wasn't at all pioneer rugged like so many men she knew. Rather than brute force of survival being etched on his face, she saw kindness and intellect there.

The man and boy embraced, and the man told him in Vin's form of German that he had a driver to take them to his mamm, but the man was going to call her first. Then while carrying Steven, the man stepped into a strange-looking building not as big as an outhouse.

Anke's mind raced, trying to take her emotions with it. She closed her eyes and breathed just as Vin had taught her. She focused on what she did know. The little boy was safe and well loved. The man would take Steven to his mamm. All was well.

Except she had no idea how to get back to Missing Mountain from here. Would it take her home again? It was late. Darkness was falling, and the temperature was too. She didn't have her coat.

Why had they traveled to the Coopers' old home?

She could hear Vin's voice telling her to focus on what she did know. She knew this land and the Cooper home, although little about it felt like home.

Would anyone mind if she slipped into the house and found a place to rest?

Chapter Twenty-Nine

With the footers to the new woodshop dug out, Josiah hammered forms in place, adding rebar as he went. The concrete truck should arrive within the hour. But as fast as he was moving to get the woodshop built, it would still be a month before it was finished. Concrete needed three to four weeks to cure.

Bent toward the ground, Josiah swung the hammer, jamming planks into place in the footer. Yesterday evening had been so weird. The stories Steven returned home with were wilder than any dream Josiah recalled having. He and Celeste chose to hear him and not dispute anything he said, but Josiah couldn't deny all of it within himself. He'd seen the angel.

"Anke." He stood upright, realizing he'd heard that unusual name recently. Had it been in the letter Celeste received about the woman who'd once owned this property? He seemed to recall it had, but he needed to double-check that. He hammered a few more nails into the forms and went toward the house.

Once the poured cement cured, the community would pitch in building Celeste a woodshop as if they were raising a barn. It was a nice gesture from this new-to-her Amish community, especially since some were unsure a woman should be doing woodwork as a job. Josiah had grown up in this community, and he wasn't surprised by their grace. People from her former community would come to the shop raising too, including the ministers. The preacher, deacon, and his uncle Mark would shake hands with her new ministers in this district, assuring everyone present that her former ministers had sanctioned her move to the new place, and they were placing her under the care of the ministers in this district.

With the U-Haul fully packed at Celeste's former home, they were waiting on the hired driver to get it and bring it here, which should happen this afternoon. Celeste and the boys were here, unpacking kitchen items he'd brought over the night Steven went missing. She had a moving schedule, and she hoped that by day after tomorrow, she could get into Engle Cabinetry and get some woodwork done. Until her shop on this property was in working order, Josiah's dat had offered to split a working schedule in his woodshop.

He walked inside. Celeste had Steven sitting on a counter, passing items to him as she unpacked a box. She'd not yet let him out of her sight. Celeste and both boys slept in the same bed last night, although she'd said she hadn't slept much for needing to cuddle Steven and keep thanking God her boy was safe.

"Hey, Celeste. Any chance you can put your hands on the letter the lawyer sent?"

"I think so." She kissed the top of Steven's head before she spun in a slow circle, searching the area. "Oh, jah." She opened a cabinet drawer and pulled the envelope out. "I kept it close in case some Englischer stops by here and asks what we're doing moving in. I just keep thinking the lawyer or county is going to backtrack on giving us this house."

He flipped open the envelope and pulled out the letter. "I understand the feeling, but it won't happen. You signed the papers. It's yours."

Steven hopped down off the cabinet. "Drew, *guck*." He pointed at toys sticking out of the top of a box. The two boys were soon rolling a wooden train car to each other.

"Why are you rereading the letter?"

"Here, look." He put his finger on the page.

Celeste moved in close, smelling of lilac and kindness. "The woman's name who once owned this home?"

"Jah. Anke Mast Cooper."

"Oh." Celeste's blue eyes grew large. "Steven said his angel was named Anke." She shivered. "That's eerie."

"The glimpse I caught of her, she had on old clothes."

"Old or vintage?"

"That's womanspeak, right there," he teased. "Like knowing the difference between sky blue and baby blue."

"Old clothes mean well-worn or ragged. Vintage means from an earlier time period."

"Oh, so there is a difference between sky blue and baby blue." She chuckled. "Of course."

He enjoyed making her laugh. "She wore vintage clothes. I only caught a glimpse at dusk, but her dress looked pale gold, floor-length. She had on a scarf around her shoulders, maybe one tucked in the neckline of her dress, and her head covering was something between a prayer Kapp and a smashed sunbonnet with only a small brim. Everything she had on was covered in dirt, just like Steven's clothes were."

"I've seen clothes like that in Vin's history books. It sounds like something from the sixteen, seventeen, or eighteen hundreds."

"Jah, that's how it looked."

"You think the Anke he spoke of and the Anke in this letter are the same, and maybe she acted as a guardian angel over Steven?"

He shrugged. "It's a really nice thought, and I can see where we'd both like to believe it. But I'm sure the names being the same is just a coincidence." Even though it was an obscure German name, and he'd never met or heard of a modern Amish person with it.

Celeste looked up at him. "If I think about it too long, it all boggles my mind. How this home came to me and the boys. How Steven rode Sugar Bear up Kissin' Mountain but ended up here in the arms of some stranger who disappeared once Steven hopped down. Steven's vivid memories of digging out of the dirt like a mole, and both he and the woman being covered in dirt."

Josiah didn't like the shakiness in Celeste's voice as she talked about this. He put the letter away. "It's just a coincidence."

Celeste touched his face, and he stopped cold. "Denki. For everything. All the time."

This was a moment he'd been hoping for, and he wanted to enjoy it, to see whether it took them to a romantic place of warm kisses or to a place of backpedaling, realizing it wasn't who they were. But a blur of pale gold seemed to pass by the wavy glass windows that ran along the back of the house.

He gently took Celeste's hand into his. He didn't want to lose this moment, but . . . "You hold that thought, okay?"

She nodded. Josiah dared to kiss her forehead, and lucky for him, she didn't pull away. Gut, he hadn't misread the moment. He hurried out the back door. The blur of pale gold moved into the woods, and he strode after it. She couldn't be an angel, not if she was trying to hide in the woods.

"Hallo?" Josiah called. "Hallo? *Brauchst du Hilfe?*" Steven had said his angel spoke German like the preachers often did during church meetings. Josiah couldn't think of a less frightening, more inviting thing to ask than if she needed help. But he saw no one, heard no movement. It couldn't have been his imagination. He saw her last night, and Steven confirmed it with his stories. "Danke . . ." In his best High German, Josiah thanked her for bringing Steven home and told her if she needed help, all of them were here for her.

He waited several minutes, hearing no shuffling of leaves. He walked back toward the house, but an odd warmth covered him, and he turned.

A woman in a pale-gold dress stood a few feet away from the patch of woods, sunlight surrounding her. Her head covering was removed, and her hair shone like a new copper penny.

Josiah couldn't budge. She absolutely looked like an angel.

He took a few slow steps toward her. *"Brauchst du Hilfe?"* He repeated his question, asking if she needed help.

"I . . . I don't know how to get back to Missing Mountain. I mean . . . I think you call it Kissin' Mountain."

She had the most unique accent he'd ever heard. It sounded a bit British with hints of German being her first language.

"I know where it is. Are you from around here?"

She shook her head, looking frightened. "I . . . I . . ."

"It's okay. I don't need to know."

"What is *okay?*"

He didn't understand. "Everything is okay. You being here is okay. You bringing Steven home was better than okay. It's all okay. No problems."

Her brows scrunched. Had he not assured her everything was fine? She'd brought Steven home. He wanted to reward her some-how, not scare her off.

"Where are you from?"

"My people are Quaker."

"That's interesting. There aren't many Quakers anymore, and I didn't know Quakers still dressed Plain."

"There aren't many of us left?" Her green eyes held shock. "What happened to us? There were so many, and we made a difference to the United States. What took us? Sickness? War? Indians?"

War? Indians? He couldn't find his voice. What was she talking about? He hadn't meant to upset her. He thought his words were a simple observation that she'd agree with. Maybe she'd been raised more like the Swartzentruber Amish—completely out of touch with modern life, even modern life that was part of the Old Ways.

She closed her eyes and inhaled and exhaled slowly. "Can you help me find Kissin' Mountain?"

"Sure." He held out his hand. "I'm Josiah Engle."

She stared at his hand for a long moment before shaking it. "Anke Mast—"

A loud engine roared and even louder backup beeps came from the cement truck. She pulled her hand from his. Did she say *Mast*? The first and middle names matching the name of the woman who'd owned this home over a century and a half ago?

She backed away from him and covered her ears. "What is that?"

"It's just a loud truck. It carries cement."

"What is *truck*? What is *cement*?"

The young woman knew nothing of modern life. How was that possible? Even the Swartzentruber Amish knew *of* these things, didn't they?

The driver laid on the horn.

Josiah turned to face the truck. He motioned. "Be right there." He turned back to speak to the woman, but she was gone. "Hallo? Anke?" He waited several long seconds, but he saw no one. "Anke, you there?"

The truck horn blasted again.

Seriously? Josiah had waited hours for this truck to arrive, and the driver couldn't give him one minute?

"I'm coming!" Josiah ran toward the truck. As angelic as she looked, she wasn't an angel . . . unless angels got lost and needed mortal men to show them how to get to Kissin' Mountain. Why that mountain? The very one where Vin died. The one where Steven said he fell into a tunnel, dug out of it, and met Anke the angel who brought him home. Why did this woman need to go there? Nothing existed there except a dangerous precipice, overgrown grass, and bramble.

Once this cement truck was gone in a couple of hours, would she approach him again?

Chapter Thirty

Sweat dripped down Celeste's back as she carried another box up the steps. Her heart palpitated when she peered into the boys' room and saw them on the floor, playing with toys. *Denki, Gott. Denki for bringing my son home safe.*

Her heart overflowed with those words a gazillion times an hour . . . or so it felt. She'd hardly let Steven out of sight since then, and she wondered if he'd soon grow weary of her constant hugs and kisses. But his telling of what took place didn't make any sense. He kept saying he'd traveled to a dirt cave. At his age, he didn't have the words or ability to explain what had really taken place. The only thing that truly mattered was that he was back with her and safe.

A dozen Amish men were here today, and the U-Haul would be emptied soon. Hopefully all the helping hands would then go home. There was much to do, but she could manage it on her own . . . with enough time. The men had already put the bed frames together and added the box springs and mattresses. She could do the rest. Hang shades and curtains. Find towels so the boys could bathe. Locate sheets and blankets so beds could be made. Whip up scrambled eggs or pancakes for supper. It was almost dinnertime, and she was desperate for some time by herself. Well, time with her and Steven and Drew.

Josiah.

They'd barely spoken since the moment between them yesterday. She set the box on the floor and opened it. The box was marked *bedding* and that's what she found inside it. She pulled out a set of sheets and moved to her bed.

"Hey," Josiah said.

She turned. He held two boxes. The air between them was awkward now, and it was her fault.

"Each box says BBBB," he said. "I think that's womanspeak for give me candles, a bubble bath, and get out."

She laughed. "How would you know about such things?"

"Sisters. Too many of them. But one learns if he smert."

She chuckled again. "I take it you're smert?"

"Very smert. But, uh, where do these go?"

"Steven was practicing making his Bs on those boxes. They both go in the bathroom."

"See, I knew what those Bs meant. Beside that claw-foot tub you love?"

The antique claw-foot tub was part of the old house, but the toilets and plumbing were from a time when the county had planned to use this home as offices.

"Sounds good."

He went down the hall.

What had she been thinking in that moment yesterday? She'd

reached for him, touched his face like they were a couple. He'd kissed her forehead. Neither should have happened. He was twenty-one! Four years younger than her. She was a widow with two children. Josiah was barely old enough to date when she and Vin had Steven. Physical age aside, as a widow and with all she'd been through, she was a lifetime older than Josiah and always would be. They were both lonely . . . or they would be if they didn't have each other. She had to talk to him about this. How awkward would that be?

In part Josiah and Lois had broken up because of the time he spent helping Celeste and because of how much Lois despised her. Did Celeste feel she owed Josiah a relationship?

No. That wasn't it.

He was truly a kind and generous man. Slow to judgment. Quick with humor. He was great with Steven and Drew.

She fluffed out the bottom sheet, letting the air slowly move aside as gravity won out.

"Anke . . . I mean, Celeste."

She turned. Had he just called her Anke? "Jah?"

"You live within a few miles of numerous restaurants now. How about if we go to one of them and grab a bite of dinner after everyone leaves?"

She studied him. Blue eyes. Blond hair. Tall. Broad shoulders. Gentle kindness quietly radiated from his soul. Maybe it was the hardships he'd gone through over the last nine months, losing Lois and the double job between working for his dat at Engle Cabinetry and helping her, but something had scrubbed away his teenage look.

"Mamm! Siah! Look!" Steven ran into the room, pointing at a window.

They moved to the window. A woman in a long pale-gold dress stood in the woods behind their house. Celeste doubted they'd be able to see the woman that deep in the woods if they weren't on the second floor, looking down through barely budding treetops. "Is that Anke?"

When Josiah didn't answer, she turned to look at him, but all she saw was his back as he hurried out of the room.

"Sell iss Anke!" Steven grabbed her hand. *"Kumm."*

But she didn't budge. Soon Josiah strode across the yard. That was Steven's angel? Had Josiah talked to her before now? He seemed comfortable approaching her. The whole of it was eerie. Steven's stories of what happened. Anke's help and disappearance. Her name on the letter.

"Kumm." Steven tugged at her hand.

"Jah." Celeste wanted to thank her. Invite her inside for coffee or tea. But she had to get Drew first.

A thud rumbled, and she heard Drew break into a loud cry. She recognized the wail—he was hurt. Maybe it would just need a kiss or maybe he'd need a bit of ice on a boo-boo. She hurried down the hall.

Anke pulled her skirt from a briar and hurried deeper into the woods. This was a miserable place to be. No one had any hospitality. They had ropes cordoning off so much of the Cooper home, thick, velvety ropes across doorway after doorway. There were signs everywhere stating Do Not Touch. Do Not Enter. Stay Off Grass.

Yesterday she'd had to wait in the woods until all the people left the Cooper home. Thankfully they left around five. Unfortunately, they locked the doors behind them. Once they were gone, she'd snuck out of the woods and around the back of the house, climbed up a downspout, and eased onto the small balcony that used to lead to Ester's bedroom. She and Ester had done this as children. The downspouts were different now but still sturdy. She had that to be grateful for. It hadn't been easy, but she'd managed to get the French doors on the balcony to open. And there were no signs about using the tub, so she'd played with those knobs until warm water ran. Who could imagine such a thing? She'd soaked in a bath, washed her hair, and then worn her undergarments while she washed her dress. She'd hung the dress up, and this morning when she woke from where she'd curled up on the floor to sleep, it was dry.

During the day, she couldn't find a safe, comfortable place to be on this property, and yet her familiarity did give her a bit of an advantage over leaving this farm . . . estate.

A few days ago, Anke had known this land and home like the back of her hand. Today, little of it made sense. Most of the woods were gone, but they had houses on them. The same was true of the plow fields. Houses were everywhere.

Anke's name rode on the wind, and she turned.

Josiah stood there, concern in his blue eyes. "You're still here."

"I need to get to Missing Mountain."

"There's nothing there. It's a small cliff with rocks."

"It is the only thing I need of you. I beg of you."

"Sure. I'll make sure to get you there if that's what you need, but why there?"

Her world spun. "I . . . I have not eaten."

"There's no food on the mountain."

What did the mountain have to do with food? "Am I not speaking English? Can you not understand my words?"

"I understand the words. They just aren't making a lot of sense."

"If we wait for this to make sense, we might be here for another hundred and sixty-three years."

"Um, jah, that is a very specific amount of time."

"Josiah?"

"Jah."

"I have not had anything to eat in days, and I feel faint."

"Oh. Come. Celeste will feed you."

She studied her former home and saw a lot of people there. People meant questions. She'd learned that by being seen inside the Cooper home yesterday morning when a crowd unlocked the doors and walked in. They threatened to call the police . . . which she could only guess meant patrollers or a watchman. Why? Had they felt threatened by her? When she tried to pay a fee to stay in the museum side of the home, the one who took her money accused her of stealing it from a display. Then he picked up some odd-looking thing and vowed he was calling the police right then.

Josiah looked behind him, apparently trying to see what she saw. "They will be gone soon."

"Same is true of those inside the Cooper home."

"The Cooper home?"

"I . . . I think the sign out front calls it the Freedman Estate and Museum. All of them arrive in fast, horseless rigs. The Amish men at my . . . your place arrived in horse and carriage."

"Jah. Old Order Amish use horse and buggy. The *rigs* are cars or trucks, and Englischers drive those."

"So many people and homes on what used to be Cooper land."

"Jah, Lancaster is a thriving city."

"Horse-drawn carriages and cars parked beside each other."

He nodded. "You won't see that in every state, but where there are Old Order Amish and Old Order Mennonite, you'll see it."

The word *state* caused a question she'd wondered about a few times, and now it came to her anew. "Is it true that slavery is over?"

"Come again?"

"Slavery? In all states?" She knew the conversation probably sounded like lunacy to him, but she'd had no one to talk to and there was so very much going on inside her head.

264 || UNTIL THEN

"Uh, jah, for a hundred and twenty-five years."

"Civil rights over too?"

"Well . . . uh, that's still going on, but the movement that goes by that name is over, yes."

"My people may be few now, but we accomplished much."

"I'm sure they're good people and that they are missing you." He removed his straw hat and scratched his head. "Can I help you get back to them?"

"Are you and Celeste together?"

He shook his head. "She's in mourning."

"Jah, I forgot her time of mourning will be at least two years."

"One, but jah."

"One? Then she only has a few months of that left."

"You know when Vin died?"

She wanted to tell him Vin was very much alive, but he'd never believe her. She steadied her heart. "Listen to me, Josiah Engle. You should not take her heart or give yours. It does not matter if my words make sense. I speak truth."

He glanced at the house. "You're serious, aren't you?"

"I speak truth."

He seemed confused.

"What is this look on your face, Josiah Engle?"

"Maybe torn between believing you and tempted to be angry. You rescued Steven, for which Celeste and I are eternally grateful, but . . ." He shrugged. "Look, since you're reluctant to come inside, could I bring food to you?"

She nodded.

"I'll call for a driver. If you and Celeste speak—I know she hopes to say hello and thank you—please don't mention Kissin' or Missing Mountain. She lost her husband there. And that's where Steven had ridden his horse and then was missing for a while."

"You're right. I should not speak of it to her. Her husband

would not like that." Vin wouldn't want to get Celeste's hopes up in case he couldn't get back to her.

"Uh, jah."

She knew that voice. Josiah didn't believe her.

He put his hat on again. "If you go through these woods, you'll come to a paved road. Wait there. If some of the Amish workers here today see me getting you into a car, it'll cause more questions than I'll know how to answer. But we'll be out of sight there. I'll call for a hired driver, and I'll meet you out by the road." He pointed. "We'll make sure you get to Kissin' Mountain."

"Very kind. I have some coins." She opened her purse and pulled out several silver pieces, holding them out toward him.

He took one from her hand and studied it. He looked from her to the coin several times before returning it to her. "You can hold on to your coins. I'll pay for your ride to the mountain."

A door slammed, and Josiah glanced at the house.

Josiah's face said he wanted distance between her and his family. Except it wasn't his family. Still, she'd get to the mountain and go back home.

"Anke!" Steven called.

The little boy and a woman carrying a toddler came toward her. Oh, how much Vin would love knowing Celeste and his sons were well and whole, and they'd inherited the home he'd worked so hard to repair for them.

"Hallo." Anke knelt and opened her arms. Steven ran into them, and she hugged him tight. "Oh, you're home and safe."

He nodded. "Mamm. Drew." He pointed.

She rose to her feet. "You're Vin's Celeste." She held out her hand.

Celeste glanced at Josiah, and in that moment, Anke realized what she'd said. Celeste shook her hand. "Denki for helping Steven get home."

"Gern geschehen. You're little Drew."

"Jah. He fell a few minutes ago and gave himself a bloody lip."

"He is precious." Anke couldn't soak this in enough. Vin would be so pleased.

"Would you like to come in?" Celeste asked. "I can fix you a cup of tea or coffee. Maybe you could stay for dinner, although it won't be much since I recently moved in and haven't been grocery shopping. But I'd love to hear how you and Steven connected and how you knew to bring him here."

Anke glanced at Josiah. "I . . . I cannot. I need to get back home. I just need a little help finding my way"

"Oh, okay. Denki." Celeste clutched Anke's hand. "I can't thank you enough."

"You're very welcome."

Josiah held out his hands for Steven. "Bath time."

Steven jumped into his arms. Josiah removed his hat and put the boy on his shoulders. "Celeste."

Josiah left, heading for Anke's former home as he walked beside Vin's wife. He seemed closer to Celeste than he wanted to admit to, probably didn't want to disclose his feelings because she was in her time of mourning.

Anke knew women like her. She'd seen them in her own time. They drew good men to them like a creek draws thirsty deer in summertime. Vin was one of the kindest men Anke knew, and now Josiah seemed to be from the same mold. Were Vin and Josiah related?

Truth was, it didn't matter. All that truly mattered was getting back to her own time. Was this how Vin felt—vexed, uneasy, desperate to get home? If Vin wanted his wife still unmarried when he returned, he best get back fast.

Chapter Thirty-One

Josiah slathered peanut butter on a slice of bread. He did the same with strawberry jelly. A driver was on his way and would meet Josiah on the other street as instructed.

"I wish she would've come inside. She's not an angel." Celeste shoved chips into a sandwich baggie. "But who is she? I wonder where she lives—her clothes and accent are so odd."

"I don't know." He put the sandwich inside another baggie. "Lots of good questions, but she wants to go home, and I've called for a driver to get her there."

"Will you ride with her?"

"Jah. She made sure Steven got here safely, and I want to make sure she gets home safely."

"Where's her home?"

"Southern part of Pennsylvania."

"That's a rather broad answer."

"I don't know any more than that right now." He steadied his breathing. Anke seemed to know a lot about Celeste's family. How? And why? "I'm unsure where we'll need to drive in order to get her home, but we'll figure it out."

"Any idea how she came across Steven?"

"I think she's from that area or was visiting that area."

"Why is she dressed in vintage clothes?"

"Maybe someplace nearby was having historic days or something."

"True." Celeste pulled a can of Coke from the fridge and set it near him. "You seem upset by her presence. Am I reading that right?"

Was it that obvious? "You are. I'm concerned by how confused she seems to be. She called vehicles a horseless carriage, but maybe that's how her people refer to them." He shrugged. "Whatever is going on, I'll feel better once I get her home and with people who know her." He shoved the sandwich and chips into a brown bag. "I need to go."

Without waiting on a response, he went out the back door and through the woods. Anke was waiting near the road, and he'd arrived just as the driver pulled up.

He opened the door for Anke.

She stared into the car but didn't budge.

"It's safe."

She continued staring into the car.

"It's much safer than traveling by horse and carriage." He was sure she'd done plenty of that in her life.

"I'm going with you." He got in and slid across the back seat. "Come on."

She got in.

He reached across her, closed the door, and the car started moving. Her eyes were wide—she'd really never ridden in a car.

"Here." He flopped the brown bag into her lap.

She opened it, took out the sandwich, and fingered the thin plastic wrap.

He opened the flap for her.

She sniffed the sandwich. "This is bread?"

"Jah."

She ran her fingers across it. "Smooth and light."

"I hope you don't mind peanut butter and jelly."

"I like jelly. I don't know what peanut butter is." She took a bite and covered her mouth. "It is delicious," she mumbled.

Where was she from that she'd never had peanut butter? He popped open the Coke and passed it to her.

She shook her head. "It's very cold."

"The cans get very cold in the fridge. Thus the name *cold drink*."

She looked at it. "I do not understand."

He put an imaginary can in his hand, lifted it to his lips, and tilted his hand.

She mimicked his actions, spilling some down her chin and onto her dress. She giggled. "It tickles."

"It's a carbonated drink."

"Very, very sweet."

Had she never tasted a soft drink? "Sweet sells."

They rode in silence while she ate her sandwich and chips and drank the Coke.

The car came to a stop. "Here?"

"Close. Go another half mile up the road."

The driver did as Josiah said and came to another stop. "There are no houses around here," the driver said.

Yeah. Tell him something he didn't already know. "Thank you." Josiah paid the driver. "I'll pay double that amount if you wait here."

The man nodded. "I'll wait an hour."

Josiah gave the man the money—he could only hope he was good to his word.

Anke climbed out. "Where are we?"

"Peach Bell. At the foot of the path that leads to Kissin' Mountain." He pointed.

She gathered her skirts and tromped through overgrown grass. They walked for what seemed like forever. She had endurance. He'd give her that. She had no issues climbing this hill in a long dress with flat-heeled lace-up boots.

They finally arrived at the top.

"Now what?"

"I . . . I do not know." She looked around. "There." She went to where a rope ran through something attached to the rock itself.

"What are you doing?" Josiah asked.

"I feel sure this is what Steven used." She wrapped the rope around her.

"You can't rappel to the bottom, especially not in that outfit."

"Rappel?"

"You can't use the rope to go down the side of this cliff. Period. But especially not in that dress."

"What exactly did you think I came up here to do?"

"I don't know, but this wasn't it."

"I will be fine."

"Nee. It's not safe. Vin died falling off this cliff."

She bit her bottom lip. "This is the only way I can go home, and we both want me to get home."

"There are no houses down there. Look."

She smiled at him. "Let's sit."

They sat on the rock, their feet dangling over the edge. "Josiah, my only chance of getting back is to rappel, as you say, down this cliff, and touch a specific crag. If I am still at the end of the rope, you can pull me back up. But I must try. If you cannot let me try, I'll return here on my own and do it by myself."

"Nee, like I've already said, it's not safe, and it—"

She swung out on the rope, lowering herself quickly.

He jumped to his feet. "Anke, hold on tight." He scrambled to the rope and grabbed it. He wasn't sure what he was hoping to do, but he peered over the ledge, seeing Anke hold the rope with one hand and reach out with the other. She grabbed a rock.

And disappeared!

"Anke!" The rope was slack now and he pulled it up. "Anke!" Had he just witnessed her disappearing into a rock? How?

"Anke!" He clung to the rope and lowered himself so he could get a better look. She was nowhere to be seen. "Anke!"

He leaned his forehead against the rope, then pulled himself back up to the cliff. She was good at disappearing. He'd seen her do it, but this time he'd had his eyes on her and there were no trees to hide among and no rocks large enough to hide behind.

He sat on the top of the cliff, trying to wrap his head around what just happened. A car horn tooted, and he realized time had slipped by as he'd aimed to understand. If he wanted a ride back to Lancaster rather than walking, he best get back down the mountain.

What had he just witnessed? His mind was a jumble of thoughts and his emotions kept screaming at him. How was this possible?

Wait. She traveled through the rocks, and she spoke of Vin like she knew him . . .

Nee. That couldn't be. Vin's body had been found at the foot of the cliff.

Was it possible?

He got into the car. "Thank you for waiting."

"That's what you paid me for."

Josiah sank back into his thoughts, his mind traveling faster than the vehicle he was in, peppering him with questions as he tried to believe what he'd seen. She disappeared into a rock. Disbelief was still crying out when he realized they'd arrived back to the city of Lancaster.

The car slowed as it approached Celeste's home. The parking spaces for the Freedman Estate were empty. It was past closing time for the offices and museum.

He blinked. A woman in a long dress stood on the lawn to the estate. "Keep going!"

The driver did as he said, and Josiah could not believe his eyes. "Stop. Here. Thanks." He got out.

The dress was the same. The woman turned, a dusting of dark soil on her head covering and clothes and face, just like the first time he'd seen her.

"Anke?"

Her green eyes held confusion. "Why am I back here?"

⚜

Celeste tugged on the left rein, pulling onto the Engle driveway. She drove her rig past the house and toward Engle Cabinetry Shop, passing a gaggle of young women on Josiah's front porch.

"Mamm." Steven laughed while pointing at the women surrounding Josiah, talking as he made his way to the porch steps. Drew laughed because his big brother was laughing.

She didn't know what was going on, but she wasn't surprised to see a flock of young women trying to get his attention. Maybe the girls had nothing better to do on a Saturday before noon. Earlier in the week, when the community was helping her move in, she'd heard from a few of the mamms that their daughters were over the moon for Josiah.

Knowing him as she did, right now Josiah was unamused as he descended the porch steps. Still, he was being cordial to the young women. Embarrassment flooded her. She'd made the first move a few days ago—she, a widow dressed in black with two little ones, had made the first romantic move on a desirable young catch.

Her face flushed hot. They had to talk about this. Maybe not today since she was here to get woodwork done and orders filled, plus she had the boys with her, but soon. It'd taken her time to sort out what was going on inside her, but she was clear on what she wanted now.

His feelings about that moment, despite kissing her on the forehead, probably explained why she'd hardly seen him since he'd stood in her kitchen making a sandwich for Anke three days ago.

She stopped the rig in front of the hitching post.

Josiah strode toward her. Hands in pockets, no smile. "Hallo."

"Hey."

"We ready to get furniture made?"

"I can do the work on my own . . . unless your dat would rather I not use his tools without supervision." She got down before removing Drew from the rig.

Steven jumped into Josiah's arms. Her little boy missed his dat all the time, especially at night, but Josiah filled a little of that longing. That was part of the reason she felt a connection to Josiah too.

Josiah's mamm came to the back door.

"Mamm," Josiah said. "You remember Celeste?"

"Jah, she might not remember me. I'm Beth, and I sure could use some help making cookies . . ."

Steven's face lit up. "Jah, Mamm?"

She nodded. "Denki, Beth."

Beth waved. Steven jumped down and hurried toward her. Celeste walked Drew to her.

Josiah waited at the shop door, and he held it open for her. "How's the unpacking going?"

"It's pretty close to done."

"Close to done?" He followed her inside and got several pieces of pine planks off a shelf. "I've never moved, but that seems fast."

"Several full days of unpacking." Plus, she hadn't been able to sleep since moving. Her embarrassment with Josiah bothered her a lot at night, but more than that, there was something disorienting about that house. The ache for Vin seemed to be all new again. Fresh. Deep. Miserable. "You've been unusually busy the last few days."

"I have. A totally unexpected, life-changing thing happened."

"Jah? Gut one?"

He stayed focused on the wood in front of him, brushing sawdust off it. "Can I ask you something a bit odd?"

"Anytime, Josiah. Shoot." She went to a box with her name on it and opened it. Josiah had moved it here days ago. It had all sorts of knobs, clasps, and pegs for making small pieces of furniture. She sifted through the items, looking for copper hinges.

"A bit of a creative question. Let's say, for an unexplainable reason, there was a chance Vin could return and an equal or perhaps greater chance he couldn't. Would you want to know?"

Whatever she'd expected him to ask, this wasn't it. She threw the hinges on the workbench. "No."

"Well, that was a fast answer."

It wasn't. She'd struggled with all the hypothetical questions before. And she was tired of them. "I've been in that unknown place too much since Vin disappeared. Did he leave me? Did he die? Was he somewhere injured and couldn't get back?" She sighed. "It's torment not knowing what to believe. I would never volunteer to be in another *maybe this is true* or *maybe that is true* place again."

"I . . . I guess I can understand that."

"Why would you ask that?"

"Something Anke said." He shrugged.

"Ah, okay. Did she get home all right?"

"Not exactly, but she's working on it."

What sort of answer was that? Celeste went to the stack of one-by-two-by-eight and picked out two. She cut each board in half lengthwise. Then she cut each of those in half widthwise and glued sets of two width-wide pieces together to create the legs.

Josiah fell in step with her, but the air crackled with unease.

She turned the air pressure saw off. It was time she addressed the elephant standing between them. "I . . . I'm sorry."

His blue eyes bore into hers, and it felt like the room would explode in awkwardness. All of this discomfort over her barely touching his face and him kissing her forehead? But it wasn't about the physical touch. It had felt . . . odd. She was older than him and not even a widow for a year. She still longed for Vin every single day, and those desires were worse at night. Josiah had so many young women interested. He could choose any single woman he wanted.

"Celeste." He removed his straw hat, revealing a mess of blond hair. "I'm the one who should apologize. I'd been waiting for a moment between us, hoping for it. I kissed your forehead and then got interrupted, and that interruption seemed to almost erase what had taken place between us. But that made no sense. The next day, I asked you and the boys out to eat, and then I got interrupted again, and that time it changed me to my soul. It was a wake-up call that I can't explain to you right now. I hope to one day soon. I really care about you. You're willing to be vulnerable and real, and you're also the strongest, kindest woman I've ever known, but . . . we're not meant for each other."

What a relief. He was voicing exactly how she felt. "I agree."

"You do?"

She nodded. "Jah. We seemed easy in some ways. Convenient. We filled the lonely gaps for each other."

"We did. I had much to learn about myself and what I wanted in a wife, and I learned everything I know from you. You set the bar high for me."

She smiled. "That's kind." It was doubtful anyone else in the community felt this way.

"You did. I look at the young women at church meetings or singings, and it's like they've become transparent. I see selfish motives and egos and weakness. I see good things too but know none of them are the one. All the things I couldn't see until I started spending time with you, and I'm very grateful for that."

"Can I ask you something?"

"Anything."

"Despite what you've said, I get the feeling you've met someone. Am I right?"

He shook his head. "Not really. My story doesn't end with two people building a life together, but I believe with every ounce of faith I have that yours will." He clasped his hands around her biceps and leaned in, kissing her on the forehead—this time it felt like a gesture from a younger brother. "Trust, Celeste. Don't let loneliness or how life looks or anything else discourage you or add to your grief. Just trust." He took a step back and grinned. "We gonna talk about girlie-gushy stuff all day? Or we gonna act like men and build something?"

She made a muscle arm. "Act like men," she growled.

He put his hat on. "I'm glad one of us is up to that task. Personally, I'm gonna keep talking about gushy stuff. Pink ponies. Valentine cards. Sparkles. Glitter." He frowned. "I think I've run out of intelligent things to say on the gushy topic."

"Oh, buddy, I think that happened before you realized it."

He laughed. "Did not. Prove it."

"Pink ponies. Valentine cards. Sparkles. Glitter. Half or more of which are not Amish items."

Despite her teasing, Celeste needed a moment to gather herself and went to one of the few closed windows to raise it. It hurt a little to know he'd keep pulling away more and more as the weeks marched on. She'd hardly see him once the woodshop was built and the equipment, shelves, and raw wood were in place a couple weeks from today.

She moved closer to the window. Was that a woman just inside the hayloft window of the Engle barn?

Was it Anke?

Chapter Thirty-Two

APRIL 1823

Vin dragged the branches of cut underbrush across the wagon tracks. He'd pulled off the main dirt road that led to the Doororegan Manor and driven into the woods before retracing his path and doing his best to cover the tracks. The wagon sat about half a mile ahead of him, out of sight of anyone passing on this road, but he was definitely on Charles Carroll's ten-thousand-acre property. Still, he had to hide until he had a set plan. He'd rather not be seen by the owners or overseer in the same wagon he intended to use as a getaway vehicle.

Faint noises made him stop cold. He remained in place but relaxed when he only heard the normal rustling of nature in the woods.

It'd been a productive fifteen days since he'd left Pennsylvania. He'd attended eight meetings of abolitionists and gone into five businesses and nine homes of men and women who vehemently disagreed with slavery. He'd passed out maps and talked to groups, giving them the most updated information available. Some planned on selling their homes and moving elsewhere, disagreeing with slavery but afraid to get caught helping. The stakes were high for free folk. Higher by far for runaway slaves.

Vin closed his eyes, praying, and when he opened them, looking skyward, he saw a Black child in a tree among the new green leaves. The child hugged the tree tight, and it was nothing short of a miracle that Vin even saw the child amid all the foliage.

Vin lowered his eyes as if he hadn't seen a terrified human. He continued walking toward the wagon. It bothered him that he couldn't rescue everyone—not that the child in the tree would trust Vin enough to let him help. Vin looked like any other unshaven, wealthy businessman who might be a slave owner. He pretended to be someone he wasn't in order to try to rescue someone who was living a life God never intended. So many slaves. So much injustice.

If Vin had to guess at the root of all of it, he'd say it was lies. Lies about what God's Word meant in its references to slavery. Lies people told themselves to justify their cruel, controlling actions. But most of all, lies that the love of money wasn't the root cause of all these injustices.

"Master . . ." The whisper was faint.

Vin turned back, looking in the tree.

"Whatcha believe?"

Vin walked closer, knowing his whisper had to carry. "In 'all things whatsoever ye would that men should do to you, do ye even so to them.'"

"You good?"

Vin wanted to answer no. That would be truthful. "What do you seek?" Because Vin didn't have much to offer. He couldn't reunite this child with any family that might've been sold. But Vin had stale biscuits, and if he and the child were brave enough, he had a stale wood box to hide in.

The child climbed down wearing what looked like an old night-shirt or nightgown that was several sizes too big. "You got food?"

Vin guessed he was looking at a girl, maybe ten years old. He looked around the woods. It still appeared safe. "Kumm." Once at the wagon, Vin reached into the basket and pulled out two biscuits a Quaker family had given him the day before yesterday.

The child chomped into the bread.

He opened a ceramic jar that held fresh water. "I'm Vin. You?"

"Charlotte." She tore another piece of biscuit with her teeth.

"Where you from, Charlotte?"

She turned, pointing south. That was the direction of the Doororegan Manor. With her back to Vin, he saw bloodstains dotted across her nightgown. He was so weary, so sick to his stomach day and night at how blind mankind was. Him included. Was he still as blind as he'd been before?

"I'm looking for Maud Alexander."

"Don't know her," she mumbled around a mouthful of food. "Master got hundreds of us. How old?"

"Between thirty and thirty-five."

"She not a house slave or I'd know her." She chugged the water. "If she a field slave, she be on the lower forty about now, south of the river. If she cook for the field hands, she be near one of the kettles. If she sittin', she be near the east grove."

"Sitting?"

"Watchin' the babies during spring planting. But to do that, she either got to be near birthin' a baby or too injured to work the field."

Vin hadn't considered that Maud could be pregnant. Could a pregnant woman survive days in a wooden box, bouncing hard like riding a bull at the rodeo?

Vin scraped a spot on the ground, clearing it of old leaves and other vegetative decomposition. "Can you draw me a picture in the dirt of what's where?"

She put the last bite of biscuit in her mouth. "You take me too?"

"It'll be dangerous and a hard way to travel."

The girl studied him. "Being a slave is dangerous and a hard way to travel this fallen place."

Those words sank deep inside him. "Can you do as you're told, whether the need is for complete silence or staying put or running?"

"I'll obey faster than a rabbit can disappear."

Looking in her eyes, he believed her. "I'll do what I can."

"I can curl up small."

He was sure of that. She was a little thing and the way she got down from that tree, he knew she was flexible. "I'm sure you've got people, and I'm sorry, but there's no room for anybody else. You understand?"

She nodded.

"I got information I can leave for them." He didn't know when, where, or how he could safely leave his maps, but an opportunity would come up. He held out a stick to her. "Start with the mansion."

She picked up a nearby rock and put it on the ground. "That's the manor. It faces east."

Maybe Charlotte being in that tree today was an answer to many fervent prayers—his and hers. But prayers were an unpredictable thing. This part could be miraculous, but the actual rescue of Maud or getting Charlotte to safety still might not work out.

APRIL 1986

Josiah laughed hard, causing the reins in his hands to shake, and the horse picked up speed. He loved his time with Anke. Right now he had remarks he wanted to make, but he couldn't stop laughing long enough to talk. It wasn't so much what she'd said as how she'd said it.

She grinned as she eased the reins from his hands. "Easy." She spoke deep and measured to the horse and he slowed. Her clothes were a cross between Amish, Mennonite, and modern. She'd made them. She batted her eyes at Josiah, a thing he'd jokingly told her about during the outings over the last two weeks. "I did not think you'd find the story from my time that funny. But the man who challenged the preacher wasn't wrong, Josiah. Every word the preacher spoke in his sermon, the man had read them before listening to the preacher."

"Jah." Josiah choked back laughter. "But I expected the man to prove his point by bringing the preacher a Bible, not a dictionary."

She chuckled. "You have the best laugh, Siah."

His heart raced. They were good together, a perfect fit in lots of ways, except their lives existed more than a century apart. They could talk endlessly without holding back in self-restraint for any reason. He could be completely vulnerable with her, perhaps because she was so vulnerable with him first, telling him of her God-given ability to cross the Gott Brucke. He'd heard of the Gott Brucke all his life, but he'd never known anyone who'd crossed it. He could be himself with Anke, but she was still trying to go through the crag several times each week, so they knew their time was very limited, which made every moment more treasured. He understood her need to get back. She'd explained several reasons, but one worried her the most: People would eventually realize she was missing, and she'd been with George right before she traveled in time. It weighed heavy on her that if she didn't get back soon, George could be blamed for her disappearance.

But while she was here, they put each day to good use. She'd stayed in his hayloft for a few nights, but then she searched for a room to rent in someone's home. She found one with people who owned an old home that once belonged to friends of hers. To have enough cash to rent it, she and Josiah made a trade. She gave him her old coins, and Josiah gave her cash based on today's value of each coin. He'd have given her any amount of money she needed, but that wasn't her way, and he had to respect that.

She'd cleaned the house where she was staying as an odd job and cooked for them. But she'd finally settled into a part-time job that brought in steady money by being a maid at a local hotel. They didn't require her to have ID or a birth certificate. They paid cash for the hours she worked.

A roar shook the air, and Anke pinned herself against the back of the open carriage, staring as a plane flew low overhead.

Josiah eased the reins from her. "That's an airplane, Anke." He'd explained them to her, but at the moment they were riding quite close to the Harrisburg airport, and she was seeing them up close.

Her breathing was labored. "*That's* lunacy!" She sat upright and turned to look behind her, watching as the plane ascended higher into the skies. "It's huge. How can it fly?"

"Aerodynamics."

"Whatever aerodynamics are, they work better for that huge plane than the featherweight paper planes we made last night."

"Jah, no one wants to pay for a ticket to fly on a paper airplane. Maybe there's a museum with planes nearby."

"Like the train museum we went to yesterday?"

"Nee, this would have airplanes."

She frowned and pulled her eyes from staring into the sky to look at him.

He chuckled. "Jah, like the train museum, except with planes."

She gently elbowed him for teasing her. "Modern life is interesting, but it stinks." She reached into her purse.

The strong smells of fuels and engines were especially pungent to her. He reached into his pant pocket and pulled out her handkerchief.

"How is it you have my handkerchief?" She held it to her nose.

"I believe the words you were looking for were *denki, I'm so glad you had a handkerchief for me.*"

She'd left it on the seat of the buggy when he dropped her off at her rental place last night.

"My sincere apologies." Her tone was gentle. "But no, I was not looking for those words," she mocked, barking the second part of the sentence.

"Listen to how you talk. I believe you've moved from the early 1800s to the late 1900s in more ways than just your physical body."

"It's so much to take in, I can hardly rest at night, but it helps for us to tease and laugh as I soak in new information."

They'd spent most of their off time in libraries and museums. Anke was trying to absorb as much information as she could about herbs and healing. She only worked part-time, and he'd taken off a lot of days since she arrived. Museums were her favorite, a place where she could study the changes in the lives of mankind from early days until more recent. She said it gave her ideas she could put to good use when she returned to her time. At least three times each week, she hired a driver and went through the crag, but she landed back on the lawn of the Cooper home every time. They didn't know why, but they'd agreed to use their time wisely as long as she was here.

He pulled into a parking space that put them as close to the door of the Harrisburg Museum as he could get. "This is it, Anke." He held out his hand, and she took it to climb down.

They went inside and paid for tickets. While still at the desk, he had an idea. She'd yet to see a vending machine. That just might be the most interesting part of today for her. Packaged food one could buy with coins and a push of a button. The man at the desk told him how to get to the break room. They meandered a bit before they stumbled on it. The room was small. Two tables with four chairs each and two machines. No one was here.

Anke stared at one of the machines. "Water in bottles?"

"And sugary cold drinks too. And candy and Hostess treats all kept fresh in sealed plastic bags."

"That's plastic? It's not the same as the sandwich baggie."

"It's not. I agree." He put coins in the machine. "What would you like?"

She pointed.

"That's D5." He pressed the letter and number, and a Hostess cake fell to the bottom. "And voilà. Food." He grabbed it out and passed it to her.

"Are you sure it's food?"

He laughed and opened it. "See?"

She leaned in and sniffed the open bag. "It smells good, but food stored in a machine?"

"There is a first time for everything."

She gazed up at him. "I've had a lot of firsts since the day I saw you, Siah."

He liked her calling him that. "You have. If there's something you want to experience before you return to Missing Mountain, just say the word."

She mumbled something, her cheeks turning pink. Had she just asked for a kiss?

He tilted her chin upward. "Could you repeat that?"

"I've not had one. Ever. I doubt I ever will in my time."

He didn't doubt that she would, but now wasn't the time for that conversation.

It was an odd place to kiss, but then again, everything about them was different. He lowered his lips to hers, and sparks in him ignited into a bonfire. Never had he imagined feeling such a connection to someone.

She didn't break from him until a noise caused her to jump. A door had slammed somewhere nearby.

She was breathless. "Better than all my dreams of it, Siah. Danke."

"My pleasure."

It was so important to her to get back to her time, and he wanted that for her. But for himself, he was also glad to see her when she showed up on the Cooper lawn again and again.

Would the outcome be different if he tried to go with her?

Chapter Thirty-Three

It was nearly dark as Anke wiggled into the leather harness Josiah had made for her to rappel down the face of the cliff. The hired driver had a flat tire on the way here, and it'd taken him quite a while to change it. She'd been in this time for a month: The first time she'd gone through the crag and landed back right here was April 2. Now it was May 2. It was way past time to get home. Why hadn't Vin made it here yet?

She tried to focus on today, on the here and now. Rather than Josiah coming with her to Missing Mountain each time, he waited on the lawn of the Cooper home. She found it disorienting when she landed back there but having him on the lawn waiting for her helped a lot. It was so late—he probably thought she'd made it to her own time by this point. If going through the crag didn't work again, would he still be waiting for her on the Coopers' lawn?

She held on to the rope and eased her way down the cliff. With the help of a few classes on how to rappel, she'd gotten better at this. Her mouth was dry as her shoes touched the earth at the foot of the cliff. Nerves. She wanted to get home. Didn't she?

Slipping out of the harness, she decided it was best to not ask herself any more questions about what she wanted and to focus on her goal. She left the harness dangling. If she landed back on the Coopers' front lawn again, she'd use that harness next time. Why could she go through the crag but kept landing back in the same spot?

She stood in front of the crag, almost touching it. Memories of Josiah and her over the last month tugged at her, and soon she was smiling.

"I need to go home now, Gott. Please, help me return to the time I was born in. I desperately need to get back. Margaret and William will grieve hard when they realize I'm not at the Gibsons' place nor have I been there in a month. They won't understand why George lied to them about where I am. Please, I need to get to my time."

Since she longed to know why Vin hadn't gone through the crag, maybe cross the river to go in search of him, and she was desperate to verify to the Gibsons that she was alive and well for George's sake, the best place to land would be the Gibson place.

She closed her eyes, visualizing being in the Gibson kitchen.

Josiah checked his watch again.

It'd never taken Anke nearly this long to appear. She'd probably returned to her time this go-round, but he wasn't leaving yet, probably not for another hour, so he sat on the grass and propped his arms on his bent knees. Memories played out, and he let all of them roll through him, entertaining him and tormenting him equally.

He checked his pocket watch again. She should've been here an hour ago or more. He was happy for her. Sad-happy, he supposed. Very glad for her. But he already missed her.

For the past two weeks, in the evenings, off days, and on the weekends, Anke and Josiah had continued hanging out. They'd taken historic tours of places in Lancaster County, and she knew who had it right and who was mistaken. She knew lots of day-to-day life details of her time that fascinated him. Learning history through her eyes had been so much fun. So much sharing. So much laughter.

They'd done other things—gone fishing, had a picnic, visited a Quaker meeting. But the most rebellious things they'd done were sneak into the Cooper home several times after hours and sit in the parlor to talk. She'd given him the tour of the old place, her mind afire with vivid memories. Those were the best times. During one visit she went through a wooden chest at the foot of a bed, removing quilts made by people she knew personally or knew of. She told him Vin had made the chest and the dresser as gifts for Margaret and William and that the chest had a false bottom. Once the quilts were removed, she tilted the chest on its back, poked the eraser end of a pencil into what appeared to be two natural knotholes in the wood, and released the false bottom from the chest, revealing several maps from the abolitionist movement, a prayer journal of Anke's, and a book by a Dr. Brendan McLaughlin, written in 1848. She didn't open her prayer journal and made him promise he wouldn't either, vowing that she wouldn't read of future hardships, losses, or blessings. That was for God to unfold in His timing, and it felt disrespectful and dangerous to dabble in knowledge that God might not will for her to know yet. But she'd been deeply moved to find the autobiography by Brendan McLaughlin, allowing herself to barely open it and skim one page. She didn't intend to read it for the same reasons as her prayer journal. Within minutes, she returned the maps and her journal to the chest, but she held on to the autobiography, promising she'd return it in due time. They put the false bottom back in place, righted the chest, and returned the quilts, agreeing that eventually the curator of the museum needed to learn about the false bottom and remove those items to put in the museum. But they'd figure that out later . . . after Anke was back in her own time.

During each visit, they sat in the parlor or the library and opened up, talking for hours, and it felt like mere minutes.

He should go, but he couldn't make himself leave yet. When he slept tonight, he'd dream of her. When he woke, she'd be his first thought.

A flash of pale gold caught his peripheral vision. His heart leapt, and he jumped to his feet, relief she'd returned outweighing his disappointment that she'd been unsuccessful.

Her eyes met his. Confusion. Frustration. Disappointment. But she said nothing. She sat, and he joined her.

"You're later than you've ever been before today."

"The driver had a flat tire several miles before we got to the mountain."

He was glad he'd waited.

"Siah, why can I disappear into the crag only to land back here?"

"I'm sorry." He was very sorry for her sake. But they both knew he didn't know why she kept landing back here.

She leaned her head against his arm. "Maybe I haven't mastered the use of modern technology yet. Maybe I'm here because you need more belly laughs."

He grinned. "The funniest was your jumping on a chair when I turned a knob on the propane stove to light a burner."

"My first week here, and blue flames do not appear from thin air . . . or at the turn of a knob . . . where I come from."

Her reactions to the propane-powered stove and her disbelief over the refrigerator were so hilarious he might always find them smile worthy. She'd been seriously excited to learn how to cook with a propane stove, but the execution had made both of them laugh until their sides hurt. How could one have mastered cooking on an open hearth and baking in a brick oven yet be so inept on a propane stove? Not that she was inept anymore, but it had been funny.

"Whatever you do this time, don't play with the wringer washer." He chuckled. She'd been so fascinated with it she'd washed every piece of dirty laundry in his house while he worked in the cabinetry shop.

"That will be my first order of business—to do laundry and let your mamm think you did it. She was so taken aback at the laundry being done, she wasn't sure whether to be proud of you or call the doctor."

"So very true. Poor woman. I think she considered calling the ministers to pray over me. Seriously."

Anke chuckled. But she was disappointed to be here. He heard it in her voice.

"I guess I return to my boardinghouse again tonight."

"Do they call them boardinghouses anymore?"

She shrugged. "I do."

"That's good enough for me."

"I guess this means I keep working at the hotel and learning at the library, and between those things, I keep trying to get home." She sighed. "I . . . I'm trying to trust God and relax about what's going on, but I don't understand why I can't go through the crag and land in my own time."

With her head still leaning against his arm, he caressed her face.

He'd rather kiss her and beg her to stay, but he lowered his hand. "We'll figure it out, Anke." He stood and held out his hands. She took them, and he pulled her up. "Let's try something different. Let's go over everything we know from Vin's passage through the crag and from the first time you came through and landed on this lawn in 1986. Where did Vin land?"

"In the middle of nowhere in Ohio. No houses. No towns. Just days of walking until he couldn't go one step farther." She told him of Vin's encounter with George and Tandey and how he'd later met up with two of the McLaughlin brothers on their way to her sister's home. "But he doesn't know why he landed there. At first, he thought God sent him there to punish him for wanting to draw portraits and forgetting to love his wife and children as he should. But later he realized that wasn't the hows or whys of it."

"He went to the mountain that night to clear his mind, right?"

"Jah."

"He was a bit vexed, maybe wanting time alone, time away from being Amish, time to explore and figure out who he was."

"Jah, that's my understanding. But you knew that. We've talked about it."

Josiah nodded. "We're trying to piece together the whys of the crag. Vin traveled. You traveled. But you didn't land in the same place. Why?" He paced. "Celeste has a book she bought him earlier that day at a yard sale. It's about the history of Ohio, and she said he loved it. Were his mind and heart on historical Ohio when he fell? Why did Steven land at the foot of the mountain, going to a new time but staying in the same place—the bottom of Missing Mountain?"

"Steven wanted to find his dat, and in his mind, his dat was at the bottom of Kissin' Mountain because that's where Vin fell, and that's where someone's body was discovered."

"In his mind . . ." Josiah stopped pacing. "Vin wanted to do right before God, but he also wanted space and time, and his personal interest had been on the early history of Ohio for several months, and that's where he landed."

"I came through the crag, wanting to get Steven back to his mamm. Did I come here instead of her old home because Steven considered this home, even though they hadn't moved in yet? Or did we land here because he wanted to be near his dat, and his dat had poured his heart into remodeling that home for Celeste and the boys?"

"Or did you land here because this place is familiar to you, and it was home for you, yet also met Steven's desire to return to his mamm?"

She shivered. "Traveling feels much scarier now."

"Jah, but it seems to me we just have to think for a bit. Vin wanted space and freedom when he fell, and he landed in a place with an abundance of space and freedom. Steven wanted his dat back, and he was trying to find Vin near where he went missing. Then Steven wanted to come home, and he landed here. When you go through the crag, do you feel a desire to have more time on Cooper land in today's time? Or are you wishing you could go into the home your parents left for you, the one Vin fixed up?"

He waited. She closed her eyes, her beautiful face holding peace.

A few minutes later, her brows flinched, and her face grew taut. She opened her eyes, and they seemed glued to his. She started to say something but took a step back and shook her head, lowering her eyes. She knew something now that she hadn't earlier. Would it be enough to help her get home?

"Anke?"

"I'll sort it out." She lifted her eyes from the ground, once again staring into his. "I'm not staying, Siah. I'm not."

"I know that."

She took another step back. "Do you? Do I?"

"I'm confused."

"It's you. I landed here, and I saw you, and I was drawn to you. I think you felt something too."

His heart turned a flip. "I thought you were an angel, and I wanted a moment with you. Then I discovered you weren't an angel, and I wanted more than a moment."

"I can't stay."

"And I've thought about it, been tempted by the idea, but I can't go even if I could use the crag—and we have no way of knowing if I could."

"You'll be working tomorrow with the Amish community to do the barn raising for Celeste's woodshop."

"Jah."

"Use that time to bond with your people, to get your head and heart straight. There's a woman for you in this time and from inside the Amish community. I'll use the weekend to get my head and heart straight too."

He'd never known anyone as forthright as Anke. She said her piece exactly as it was without fanfare or embarrassment. Still, until now, even when they kissed, they'd not said a word about their hidden feelings. How could they not feel drawn to each other? The warmth he experienced at first sighting had been strong, enough to make anyone want more. They'd had a month together since then. She could be an angel and there would be less electric energy radiating from her and drawing him. Clearly some part of her had also felt it when she first saw him, and it'd grown for her too.

"I'll get my head and heart straight," he said. "You ever been to an Amish barn raising?"

"I've been to a German house raising but never a barn raising and certainly not a woodshop raising."

"You could put on Englischer clothes and stay at the edge of the woods to watch."

She studied him. "No. Listen to me, Josiah. We have to choose the life God put us in. I have family who love me and important events in the US to be a part of ushering in."

He walked toward the Cooper home and stared at it. He needed a few minutes to sort and process.

Being here with Anke, trying to help her, was different from trying to be there for Lois, wherever *there* was. He'd ignored his internal checks in order to support Lois. He'd rationalized her unkind, gossiping ways as just a matter of immaturity. Maybe it was, but Lois was tiring. He'd never felt confident in how she truly felt about him, but she had no hesitation in assuring him how unfavorably she felt about Celeste and many others. All relationships had times of one sacrificing for the other, one holding up the other during hardship, but he now understood that each person needed to be able to be their best selves on their own, without draining someone else on a regular basis.

Being here for Anke was also different from being there for Celeste. At first with Celeste, he'd simply wanted to do right by a widow who needed help. Then they became friends as he mourned his relationship with Lois. His need to heal and grow over most of the last year was a little similar to Celeste's need to heal and grow, and they bonded during that time. But without Anke in the picture, he and Celeste would've come to their own conclusion that they weren't right for each other. It would've taken a few more weeks or maybe even a month, but they would've known that they made excellent friends who saw and understood each other, who respected each other, who needed each other, but they'd never be great life partners.

Still, whatever they felt, Anke needed to return to her time. They both knew that. In this time, she was innovative and capable of making good in a difficult situation and could easily fit into his life. But in her life on this same land in 1823, she was an integral part of people finding the Gott Brucke. Vin had helped her understand herself, and now, as she grew in strength and understanding of who she was, she longed to return home and step into all she was meant to be.

She moved to his side. "We can do this, right?"

He longed to hold her hand, to kiss her lips. But more of those things would only help anchor her here.

"Absolutely, Anke." He'd do his part in letting go. Pray his way through it. Resolve his way through it.

"I'm not the same person I was when I first met Vin or from when I found Steven in my time. Knowing them and seeing love and faith through their eyes changed me. But you changed me even more. The way you see people with such kindness and generosity . . . the way you think about life and embrace it with laughter. I'll always be grateful for your view and sense of humor that I'll carry with me." She slid her hand into his. "But I've got to go back, Siah."

He held her hand as they looked at the home she'd return to, maybe get married in one day, raise children, and fight to make a positive difference through her connection to the Gott Brucke. But today they held hands while choosing to let each other go.

"Monday, then," he said.

"Monday," she whispered.

Chapter Thirty-Four

Vin steadied his breath as he waited in line to board a flat-bottom ferry to cross the Susquehanna. The ferry heading toward him from the Pennsylvania side of the river—probably fifty feet long and ten feet wide—could only hold one wagon at a time, pulled by one or two horses. The front and back ends of the wooden ferry raised and lowered, much like the back end of a station wagon, making each end a ramp as needed, whether the ferrymen were banking on the Pennsylvania or Maryland side.

The ferry coming toward him carrying a horse and wagon couldn't arrive fast enough in Vin's estimation. Patrollers were checking wagons diligently. Violently. The border along the Susquehanna was Maryland's last opportunity to catch runaways before they made it to freedom, and patrollers took their job seriously.

The ferry coming toward Vin was halfway across the river. George was going to be thrilled when Vin saw him again. He'd found Maud—and her and George's four-year-old daughter, Hope. When Maud was sold almost five years ago, George hadn't known she was pregnant.

The journey had been harrowing. What should've been a three-day trip to get to this crossing had been an eighteen-day nightmare. Charlotte was with them too. Vin couldn't imagine riding the ferry like those three were about to, locked in a box while crossing a river. If anything went wrong and the ferry sank, they'd be stuck inside and drown.

But freedom in Pennsylvania was on the other side of this river, less than a mile away. And the waters were calm. That was good.

Three men approached Vin. Two were on foot with pitchforks. The other, on a horse, holding a rifle, said, "Hold up."

Vin wasn't going anywhere to need to *hold up*. He was sitting in line, next to board the ferry when the wagon on the ferry debarked, with numerous wagons in line behind him.

The man on a horse stopped near him. "State your business?"

"Returning home to Lancaster with fine wares." He'd sold the shipment he'd gone to Maryland with and purchased new items. Very delicate and impressive items meant to intimidate men like this. The cargo had done its job along the way. Would the newly purchased fine wares do their job again? Freedom was so close he could smell it.

One of the men with a pitchfork jammed it hard into the bales of hay. "Somethin' ain't right. He needs to wait while we unload and search better."

The man on the horse turned to Vin. "You'll need to do as he says."

"Fine by me. Just be careful with the cargo. There's porcelain items, some from Bavaria, and most of the shipment is for US

House Representative James Buchanan of Pennsylvania." There was a hint of truth in all he said, but lying came easier than it ever had, and he knew it was the right thing to do. Lying for personal gain or to cover his tracks to do as he wanted was sin. No doubt. Lying to save God's own was a gift to undo the lies men told themselves in order to hurt the powerless.

The man on the horse held his hand out toward the man with the pitchfork. "You sure about this?"

"I hear movement."

Vin laughed but sweat dripped down his face. "Well, I sure hope so. Otherwise, my horse is dead, and all the trappings running from the horse to the wagon will stop moving."

The man on the horse gestured to the pitchfork guy with his gun. "Check the wagon, but don't be clumsy with the cargo or I'll shoot you myself."

"Yes, sir." The man removed a crate of goods. It'd be a matter of minutes before they removed enough bales of hay to realize the inside of the wagon wasn't nearly as deep as it'd been made to look.

Flashes of the exhausting fight it'd been to get here crossed Vin's mind. Maud, Hope, and Charlotte were sandwiched between wooden boards and had been for days on end. If it hadn't been for the sympathizers he came across along the way, ones who gave them safety, food, and a reprieve, they'd never have made it this far.

A ferryman lowered the ramp of the ferry boat, and it smacked against the thick planks covering the muddy ground on the banks of the river. The wooden path creaked under the wagon's wheels as it began driving off the ferry.

Vin was so close. If his wagon wasn't being checked, all he would need to do was wait another minute, maybe two, and he could drive across the thick wooden planks and onto the ferry.

Voices rose in the distance. Screams of anger. Of terror. A

wagon was in the water on its own. Men on horses were shouting orders. The wagon turned over, spilling contents. The form of a human floated from the wagon.

Tears gathered in Vin's eyes. He was sure what was happening. Someone else trying to cross a slave to freedom.

"Let's go!" The man on the horse went around the wagon and toward the commotion happening fifty yards away. The other men took off running.

Out of nowhere, a young woman screamed for help, flailing about in a now-see-through white dress. She had all of the men's attention, which was probably her intention. But Vin kept his eyes on that someone who had slipped unaware from the overturned wagon. He or she floated downstream, no head, feet, or arms visible, but Vin was sure the person was alive. Why else would the woman be so desperate to distract the patrollers? Vin watched as the almost-invisible body appeared to drift along with the current, but their arms and legs were probably moving frantically just underneath the murky water, desperately propelling them toward the freedom on the other side of the river.

Vin had no power to make a difference, and his mind moved back to his own responsibilities. He wasn't getting out of the wagon to retrieve the crate of goods. He'd leave it behind, hoping no one noticed in the fray of whatever was going on downriver. The wagon coming to the Maryland side was off the ferry now and out of the way. The ferry was empty, waiting for Vin to get on it.

One of the two ferrymen came to the side of Vin's wagon. Vin held out more than enough silver coins. The ferryman didn't pause to look or take the money.

"Get on!" The man looked downstream, to the same almost-invisible human Vin had been watching. "Now!"

Vin didn't need to be yelled at twice. He clicked his tongue and slapped the reins. The man grabbed the horse by the bridle and ran onto the ferry. Once it was fully on, the man brought the rig to a stop. Vin got down, ready to offer assistance in shoving off.

The second ferryman, whom Vin hadn't seen get off the ferry, was hurrying back on the boat, carrying the crate of goods the man with the pitchfork had removed from the wagon. The quiet ferryman set the crate in the back of Vin's wagon, grabbed a setting pole, and shoved the end of it against the wood planks on the bank. The first ferryman plunged a pole into the murky waters, using it to propel and steer the flatboat toward Pennsylvania. The boat barely moved a foot. There—an extra setting pole. Vin grabbed the pole and shoved the shoe end of it into the muddy river bottom. He pushed with all his might. If they could get away from the bank even thirty or forty feet toward the middle of the river, their chances of getting to Pennsylvania without being stopped would increase.

The commotion around the overturned wagon quieted, and the man who'd been on the horse rode fast along the shore toward Vin's ferry. Vin plunged the setting pole into the river again.

With the ferry now moving away from shore, the first ferryman, the one who'd yelled at Vin, dropped his setting pole and grabbed a rope. He caught Vin's eyes and nodded toward the Pennsylvania side. "Get behind me. Cover my actions, but don't look any direction but at the Pennsylvania shoreline. You see and hear nothing behind us."

Cover his actions? Vin got behind him, faced the Pennsylvania shoreline, and used that pole as if lives depended on it, which they did. The first ferryman was in front of him, also facing the Pennsylvania shoreline.

The man got near the edge of the ferry, swinging the rope around and around, as if trying to gain momentum. Then Vin understood what the man was trying to do—discreetly rescue the person who'd slipped from the overturned wagon. The person in the water was choking. How many times had they taken in water? The ferryman hurled the rope. Hands reached out of the water, grabbing for the rope. But the person went under and the rope floated loosely on the surface. The ferryman reeled it in, looking as if he could not possibly move any faster. He swung it around and around and flung it into the water again, this time closer to the person. The person grabbed it, remaining as quiet as a fish on a hook.

"Eyes ahead!" the first ferryman yelled.

Vin returned his focus to the Pennsylvania shoreline, as did the other ferryman. The man on the Maryland shore, the one on the horse, yelled for them to stop, and from the sounds of water and people yelling on the shore near the man, it sounded as if the horse was in the river, helping his rider swim toward them. The second ferryman and Vin plunged the setting poles into the river over and over, pushing hard.

Finally the man on the horse stopped screaming for them to return. A faint smile crossed the first ferryman's face. He tied the rope and grabbed his setting pole. All three of them continued to push. Vin had a feeling this wasn't the first time these ferrymen had been in a similar situation.

The first ferryman blew a shrilling whistle three times and made some sort of arm gesture as if giving a signal. Soon two men were swimming out to the person clutching the rope.

As the ferry came to the bank and stopped, Vin kept an eye out for George.

The first ferryman took Vin's pole. "I'll take your money now."

Vin gave him the fare plus extra.

"Get on your wagon. You're on free soil, but that won't stop thieves from kidnapping your cargo."

"How did you know I have cargo?"

"Desperate to cross. Willing to pay without haggling. No care for whether your crated goods went with you or not. I been doing this a long time and don't intend to stop until I'm dead. *You* don't stop until you're sure you're out of sight of onlookers. That patroller done brought attention your way. Free state or not, there's lots of men near this border who'd capture slaves and return them for a profit."

"I'm looking for a friend. He works helping to load and unload ferries."

The ferryman raised his hand and whistled loud, but with his mouth, not with that shrill whistle he kept in his pocket.

A boy, maybe thirteen, lifted both arms and waved them while hurrying toward the docked ferry.

"Tell the attendant what you need and then keep moving." The man looked him dead in the eyes. "Keep moving."

"Thank you." Vin climbed onto the wagon and took the reins. He drove the wagon across the ramp and boarded planks on the bank until he was on dry land, stopping once out of the way. The boy ran to him.

Vin reached under the wagon seat to a hidden compartment. He got out a sketch he'd made. "This man. His name's George."

"I've seen him. He's a mile or so up the river at another ferry."

"Tell him his friend he met in Ohio is back from his travels." Vin put a silver coin in the boy's palm. The boy nodded and took off running.

All Vin could do now was keep going, heading for the Gibson place. Once he was away from prying eyes, he could stop and let Maud, Hope, and Charlotte get out. He drove the rig past places to eat, and his stomach growled. One thing he was used to in this time was being hungry and tired. He kept going until the noise and busyness around the ferries began to fade.

"It's a beautiful day," he sang loudly, knowing his cargo could hear him. "We're in Pennsylvania on this beautiful day. Just need some time. Just a little time on this beautiful day."

He hated that they were finally in a free state and still cooped up under the false bottom in the wagon, but better safe than sorry. He sang "It Is Well with My Soul" in order to assure them they were safe. All three of his passengers loved that song. It calmed their anxieties as they lived in a wooden box in hopes of not getting caught. But the writer of the song hadn't even been born yet or undergone the tragedy that caused the song to rise within his soul.

Vin drew a deep breath, hoping and praying Anke and George had found Missing Mountain while he was away.

Celeste. That's where he belonged. He didn't have to wrangle with himself about whether he should stay in this time and continue doing what he could for the abolitionist movement. He'd chased after Celeste hard, wooed her, taken a vow before God to always be by her side as long as he had breath. He'd helped bring new life to this planet that wouldn't be here otherwise, two sons, and Vin's first earthly love, his first vows before God, his first duty was to the three of them.

Life was too big, too complicated to wrap one's mind around. Love, faith, and hope interspersed with the simplicity and complications of life. He couldn't save everyone . . . or even a fraction of any group. He couldn't undo any of his selfishness from the past. All he could do was his best in the moment God gave him, regardless of the time he lived in, regardless of the comforts or lack thereof. Each minute of a day, he could live to the fullness of the Golden Rule.

He continued singing, and about thirty minutes later, he came to a patch of woods. He pulled off the road and into the woods and kept going until there was no path between any trees for the wagon to fit through. It had to be safe here to let them get out and ride in the wagon or walk.

He went to the back of the wagon, removed bolts, and lowered the gate. "We're several miles into Pennsylvania. You're safe."

Charlotte uncurled her body and scooted her way to the opening, much like an inchworm. She looked around without a trace of excitement or relief on her face.

Four-year-old Hope did much the same. "Ma, come."

Maud's thin, muscular body moved toward the edge of the wooden box like a woman getting out of bed after giving birth. Once her legs and waist were out of the box, Vin reached for her hand. She took his hand and pulled herself the rest of the way out.

She looked at the woods, and he was sure what she was thinking—were they safe to get out of the wagon?

"A patroller singled us out, and I didn't want anyone helping run the ferries to see you get out of the hiding place. It might cause trouble. But you're safe now."

She drew a deep breath and slowly a smile lifted her lips. "We made it to freedom," she whispered.

Vin laughed. "Your husband said much the same thing when I told him he'd made it to Ohio."

Hope grinned and danced a bit. Charlotte took Hope by the hands and they both danced, but all of them kept quiet. He understood. An abundance of quiet had saved their lives numerous times on this journey.

"When will we see my husband?" Maud asked.

"Shortly, I expect. Today for sure."

Maud knelt in front of her daughter. "You're gonna meet your pa today." She reached for Charlotte's hand. "We're free, and we're gonna be a family. All of us."

"Me too?" Charlotte studied Maud.

"You too. You and Hope gonna learn to read and write. You're free, child. We're free."

Charlotte broke into tears. She moved from Maud to Vin and wrapped her arms around his waist. "God bless you."

He held her. "God blessed me when I saw you in that tree. I

couldn't have gotten Maud or Hope without you. You're a smart girl, Charlotte. Let that serve you well."

She didn't let go for a long moment.

Their tattered, dirty clothes were a giveaway that they were runaway slaves, although his clothes were almost in as bad of shape by this point. But even poor folk kept their clothes a lot cleaner than what the three females had on. Still . . . "Anyone care to ride on the wagon bench or in the wagon?"

"Would you mind if I walk?" Maud asked.

"You're a free woman. You tell me what you're going to do."

"Vin—" she grinned—"I'm gonna walk for a spell."

"Good for you."

Charlotte took Hope's hand. "Let's ride where we can see where we're goin'!"

The girls got on the wagon bench. Vin walked to the front of the horse and took it by the reins. He made the horse move forward and backward until he turned the wagon around. They walked through the woods and back toward the main road, Maud and Vin beside the horse and the girls on the bench.

The girls sat wide-eyed. Hope giggled a lot. Maud shook her head, smiling big. Once on the road, Vin climbed up on the bench with the girls and took the reins. They moved steadily along the way, and Vin wondered if they'd see another soul before reaching the Gibson place. Maud walked next to the horse, looking back at the girls every few minutes.

Birds sang. Clouds floated through a light-blue sky. The May air was breezy with a fragrance of spring. Freedom. It was amazing, just like it'd been when he'd crossed into Pennsylvania from Ohio with George and Tandey.

Hoofbeats came at them, fast.

"Maud!" George yelled. "Is that you?"

Maud turned, her face as bright as this spring day. "George!"

She sprinted in bare feet. Vin stopped the rig. He climbed down and helped Hope and Charlotte off the bench.

While dismounting, George pushed himself away from the saddle, leaping from his horse. He ran to Maud. The collision of their bodies and the joy in their shouts moved Vin's soul as much as going through time had moved his body. He longed for that with Celeste. But in his wife's mind, he was dead, or he'd abandoned her. What would their reunion be like?

Hope slid her hand into Vin's. "Is that my pa?"

"It is."

Vin couldn't hear much from where they stood, but he heard George say Tandey's name, and Maud hugged his neck, screaming with joy. Her son was safe. Vin had told her that, but the reality of it must feel new and clear with George saying it.

After Maud and George's warm reunion, George returned to his horse and grabbed the reins. He and Maud started in their direction but stopped cold at one point, George staring at his wife. He then hugged her tight, and they started walking again. They walked hand in hand when they approached the girls. Vin could feel the tension in Hope's body.

"George," Maud said, "this here's Hope. Your daughter. And this here is Charlotte. She's gonna be our daughter too. We wouldn't be here without her."

George knelt before the girls and grinned. "I've never been so honored or happy to meet anyone in my whole life. I'm grateful to you, both of you, and you're safe here. Welcome to the land of the free."

Hope studied him for a bit before putting her arms around his neck and crying. Charlotte was reserved, but she smiled.

George held his daughter on one arm and hugged Vin. "You did it."

Vin nodded. Words wouldn't form. He and George both knew

only God could bring something like this to fruition, but they also knew as marvelous as this victory was, God wanted all of His children set free.

George held Hope toward her ma. "I got to talk to Vin in private. Will you drive the wagon with the girls while we walk and talk?"

Maud kissed his cheek and headed for the wagon.

George turned to Vin. "We found the crag. It was buried under dirt and trees and shrubs. I've cleared all that out for you."

"Excellent!" Vin raised his arms in victory. "Excellent!" He fisted his hands. "Yes! I'm going home!"

Why wasn't George at least smiling?

"But . . . ," George said.

Vin's celebration halted. "But?"

"Your boy showed up a month ago."

Vin's heart moved to his throat. "Steven?" His voice cracked. No . . . he was so small. Had his boy suffered being lost and confused and hungry? Was he still in this time?

"Yeah," George said. "Anke found him sitting near the crag that was buried in the soil, right after he arrived. She heard him without her ears. That's how she learned where the crag was. She held him tight and went back through with him to get him to his mama without delay."

"That's fantastic." Relief flowed through Vin, and he put a hand over his heart. "That's exactly what she needed to do."

"We thought so too, but that happened a month ago, and she ain't returned yet."

"What?" Fresh panic rose. This meant they had no proof that Steven was safe—and what of Anke?

George repeated the last part. "Thing is, while shoveling dirt away from the crag, I thought I saw a streak of her dress arrive and disappear in a flash. That happened a few times as I spent a couple of weeks digging out that area. I tried going through the crag to see if I could find her or help her. At first, I thought I went nowhere, but when I settled my mind and tried again, I realized I was going through and landing back where I was, only with the shovel in my hand."

Vin had to go through the crag *today*. He had to make sure Steven had gotten back to Celeste. This new information complicated everything. There was no guarantee he could get home . . . no way of knowing where the crag would take a person. His heart and head pounded.

Vin had planned on going to the Gibson place with the others and having a night of celebration—songs, laughter, praise. He wanted to share memories between him and the others, a way to find peace with the ordeal they'd been through. And he'd pictured himself in clean Amish clothes and properly shaved before he returned to Celeste. But there was no time. He closed his eyes, steeling himself against the dream that she would run to him and embrace him as Maud had George.

"I can't spend any more time here. You go on to the Gibson place. Make some sort of excuse to the Gibsons—they'll treat your family well. How do I find the mountain from here?"

"I don't think you can miss it now that it's no longer buried, but I marked the trail with pieces of cloth tied around trees."

George was resourceful—a good friend. He'd miss him. "Thank you. I'll take your horse and tether her to a tree." Vin mounted the horse. "You come get her later tonight or tomorrow." He cupped his hand to shout to Maud. "Hold up."

The wagon came to a stop. Vin rode George's horse to the front of the wagon and dismounted. "Maud, Charlotte, Hope, I'm going to need to head in a different direction."

"Now?" Maud eased from the wagon and held out her hands for Hope. The little girl went to her ma.

"Jah. Your husband relayed events that took place with my family while I was gone, and I need to go to them. I don't know if our paths will cross again, but it's been an honor knowing you."

She hugged him tight, and Hope put her arms around his neck. "God be with you."

Charlotte hugged him, too. Vin mounted the horse as George caught up to them on foot.

George reached up, holding out his hand. "Thank you for everything. I'll be prayin'."

Vin shook his hand, feeling the power of their connection. "Same to you, George."

In that moment, Vin could sense all that George and his family and the future generations would become, and it was beyond powerful and beautiful.

He squeezed the horse with his boots and the horse took off.

Chapter Thirty-Five

The sound of dozens of hammers pounding nails into a frame echoed across the lawn, making Celeste smile. She had a carafe of coffee in one hand and a plate of homemade doughnuts in the other. Drew rode in a baby carrier on her back as she carried the refreshments, other women helping in similar ways nearby. It wouldn't be appropriate for her to help the men build her new workshop. But she didn't mind. Life had all sorts of boundaries, and being allowed to have a woodshop and build furniture was enough for her. She set the items on the table while trying to put her eye on Steven. She spotted him with a hammer, pounding a nail into a practice board one of the men had set up for the children.

"Mamm." Drew's little voice sang various words. "Tewen, Mama. Tewen. *Gaul*, Mama. Gaul."

311

He had a habit of saying her name and then saying a singular word of something he saw or thought. He'd said his brother's name and the word *horse* this time.

"Jah. I see." Well, she didn't see Steven right this second, but she had just a few seconds ago.

The men had arrived not long after sunup, and they'd soon be ready for a midmorning boost of energy. Some of the wives came with them; others arrived here and there all morning, depending on what they'd needed to accomplish before coming here to help feed the men.

An odd sensation washed over her, one she'd had since first laying eyes on this place, as if Vin surrounded her. The feeling usually came from the home, seeing it, being in it, but this time . . .

She turned toward the edge of the property, where Englischers stood watching the Amish work together—men building the frame of the shop and women tending to children and keeping the men fed.

Lovina carried a tray with a dozen plastic cups of icy lemonade. "We have a lot of Englischer onlookers today." She set the tray on the table.

"Jah." Celeste continued to study the group. What was this feeling?

Of the four dozen Englischers standing about at the edge of the wood, one man standing behind others caught her eye. She couldn't really see his face. It was hidden under a brimmed black hat and behind a long, shaggy beard, yet he appeared to be staring at something. She tried to follow the direction of his attention, and soon she saw Steven. Was he watching her son? She looked back to the man. Was he smiling? He seemed to notice her looking at him, and he lowered his head. Something about him drew her.

"Would you lift Drew out and keep him for a bit?"

"Sure." Lovina took Drew from his baby carrier.

"Denki." Celeste took off the baby carrier and set it on the table. "Excuse me." She picked up the tray with plastic cups of lemonade and walked toward the Englischers. She saw a flash of coppery hair, the shade familiar.

Anke was here? Celeste blinked, trying to see clearly despite the sunny morning contrasting with the shade of the wooded area. It was Anke. She had on a tea-length tan dress and her strawberry-blonde hair was in a single braid that fell over one shoulder and went to her waist. Was she talking with the man? He turned away and walked deeper into the woods.

Celeste hurried as best she could with a tray of drinks in her hands. Once at the crowd, she passed the tray to a stranger. "Welcome. Help yourselves." She pushed through the onlookers.

Once Celeste was past the crowd, Anke was suddenly there, standing in her way. "Good morning, Celeste."

Celeste peered around her, seeing the man in filthy, torn clothes hurrying away. Was he frightened? If so, why? He hadn't been scurrying away until she spotted him. Was he afraid of *her*? She didn't recognize his build—thin with broad shoulders. Then the man stumbled, and his hands grabbed a nearby tree. A series of memories flashed in her mind. She knew those hands. They'd held her, caressed her face and body. They'd held her babies, rocking them for hours during the nights.

Vin?

Celeste sidestepped Anke and hurried toward the man. "Vin?" She cupped her hands around her mouth. "Vin!" she screamed with all that was in her.

The man stopped, remaining with his back to her.

Was she crazy? Her husband was buried in the cemetery of the faithful.

The hammering and sawing had ceased, although she wasn't sure when. A few seconds ago? A minute or two ago? She didn't know, but she needed to turn away, return to the shop raising, and apologize for thinking she saw her husband. Hopefully people would understand that grief and desire played with people's minds. If they accepted that, they wouldn't call for someone to take her to a psychiatric hospital. But she couldn't make herself go back and behave as if she'd merely had an overwhelming moment of thinking she saw Vin.

People spoke in her native language, murmuring among themselves, and she knew her actions had everyone's attention on herself and this man. Clicking sounds seemed to go with bright flashes of light. Was an Englischer taking pictures?

Demanding her feet move, she walked toward the man. "Vin?"

He turned, and when his eyes met hers, her legs threatened to buckle.

Tears were flowing down his face, dark with dirt and sun, and into his shaggy beard. "I . . . I didn't mean for us to meet like this, catching you this off guard and everyone watching."

"Vin?" She tried to move, and it felt like she was stepping through molasses. "You . . . you left me?"

Josiah had been so sure Vin would've returned if he could. She'd believed him. Comforted herself with that belief time and again. Had she and Josiah been duped?

"Nee." He stepped forward and brushed his fingertips down her cheeks. "I'd *never* leave you, Celeste. I . . . I fell off the cliff, and I . . . I've been trying to get back to you since."

What? Was that true? She gazed into his eyes, trying desperately to understand.

"You're alive!" Bishop Mark yelled. "You've been deceiving all of us! You're a liar!"

Vin's eyes stayed on her, as if he didn't hear or didn't care what the bishop had to say. He seemed to only be invested in what Celeste thought or said. Her eyes filled with tears. This man in front of her, she saw the truth in his eyes. Whatever else had gone on—physical injury, brain injury, maybe mental health issues—he was telling her the truth. He'd fallen and couldn't find his way back until now.

Her vision blurred with tears. How many nights had she longed for him to be here, in any condition God returned him in? She'd longed for her husband to come back to her, and here he stood.

"You're home," she whispered.

He nodded. "I'm home."

He looked frail, but she eased her arms around his waist and rested her head on his chest. His body felt like solid muscle. He wrapped his arms around her, trembling.

Vin buried his face in her shoulder and sobbed. "I'm home."

She held him tight as he shook and knew that whatever else had gone on, he was beyond himself with relief to be home.

"Mamm?" Steven called as he burst past the crowd.

Celeste took a step back. *"Guck, Steven. Dat iss heemet."*

"Dad is home," Vin whispered. "What beautiful words I've prayed to hear for so very long." He caressed her face.

A thousand questions pelted her, and she knew they had to be answered in time, but right now her husband was home. Her children's father was home.

"Dat!" Steven ran to Vin. "Dat!"

Vin lifted him. "Steven." He embraced his son. "You're safe. You traveled, but you're safe."

Traveled? That was the same odd word Steven used over and over again.

"Anke gebracht mich heemet," Steven said.

"Jah, I know Anke brought you home. George told me."

Steven sat up in Vin's arms, looking his dat in the eye. *"Ich verpasst du."*

"I missed you too." Vin gazed into Celeste's eyes. *"Denki."*

She didn't know all that he was thanking her for—maybe for

this moment of welcome, maybe for fighting to keep his children fed and safe in his absence, maybe for loving him or for not denying him access to his sons today—but she knew they had much to talk about. So very much.

There was a commotion among the Amish. Clearly the bishop or deacon had been talking to the crowd while Celeste and Vin and Steven were lost in their own world.

The deacon approached them. "You are not welcome here, Ervin Lantz. You lied to us. Tricked us."

"Vin?" Eli stared at his son, and soon Vin's mamm came to her husband's side, her eyes glued to her son as well.

Celeste backed against Vin, facing the crowd interspersed among the trees and into her backyard. "He is welcome here. This is my home and my property, and he *is* welcome."

"He must repent first." The deacon shook his fist. "You have moved districts and have new ministers, but they too will agree with us. The Amish will do nothing to support him, a sinner in rebellion of his vows. The work on the woodshop stops now. We will not welcome a wolf into the fold."

"Vin?" Eli repeated. "Son, is that you?"

"It's me, Dat."

Eli and Naomi moved in close and hugged their son, crying.

The deacon talked to the Amish in Pennsylvania Dutch, issuing an immediate shunning, which meant the gathering was over, the work was over, and for everyone except Celeste and Vin's children, the open displays of affection were over.

Eli and Naomi eased from Vin and joined the crowd. It didn't mean they were against him. It meant they would submit to the deacon's words.

When the deacon turned to face Celeste and Vin, Josiah stepped between them. "You've said your piece without asking any questions. Even God asks and listens before He decides."

The deacon motioned for the people to disperse. He then turned to Josiah. "Your standing is in question too, Josiah."

"As is yours before God, I think."

The anger drained from the deacon's face and he turned to leave, gesturing for Vin's parents and any other Amish still there to follow.

Lovina walked to Celeste and passed her Drew, hugging Celeste's neck. "God is with you, now and always."

"Denki." She hugged her friend, a woman who'd been like a mother to her since Vin disappeared.

Lovina walked away.

Josiah didn't leave. He turned to the Englischers. "That's all the excitement for today. We'd appreciate it if you'd make your way off the property now."

People did as he asked.

With Drew on her hip, Celeste took Vin by the hand. "Kumm. Let's get you home and fed."

Vin lifted her hand to his lips. "I dreamed and hoped you'd welcome me home, but I didn't expect your warmth to be like this, and I'll never forget this day."

His kiss warmed her hand and her heart. Whatever mountains they would have to climb, they had each other and their children. She was grateful for what they had right here and now, knowing many on this planet would give anything to have the blessing of a loved one returned to them . . . however broken that person was.

She looked at the woodshop with its skeletal framing of walls still on the ground and no roof. Did that represent what their relationship to the community would be like moving forward— needs unmet and works in progress abandoned? What would it take to work their way back into good standing?

Chapter Thirty-Six

Anke watched as Vin and Celeste walked into their home with their sons in tow. Celeste had accepted Vin's presence without questioning him. When the ministers were unkind, she'd stood her ground on his behalf. It was everything Anke had been praying over for months, and after the reunion, she felt the possibility of home open again. Something she couldn't explain—she just knew if she touched the stone, she'd be back in her time. Why, then, did she still feel such pain in her heart?

Josiah walked to her. "You came to the woodshop raising." His eyes met hers. "You okay?"

"Jah. I . . . I think I can go home now. It's time." Time was her friend and enemy. She couldn't have known that in coming forward like this, she'd meet the man she'd never want to say good-bye to.

Hurt entered his beautiful blue eyes and maybe a hint of anger.

"Okay." He took a deep breath. "You want to go back to your place and change clothes, and I'll call a driver to pick you up there?"

"You're hurt." She stared into his eyes. "I was going to try on Monday. Why is it a problem that I'm trying two days earlier?"

"It's not a problem. I didn't say it was, Anke."

"You didn't say it, but I can see it. You mind my plan to try now."

"Your inability to leave was about Vin returning to Celeste. That's obvious to me now. But yesterday we came to the conclusion that the real reason you couldn't return is us—how you feel toward me and I toward you."

Anke closed her eyes. Of course it wasn't about Vin. Did Josiah not understand what he meant to her? "Siah . . . I wish things were different." Why couldn't he have been born in her time? Flashes of what could've been between them kept running through her mind. But she couldn't tell him—she couldn't keep him.

"Maybe you kept coming back to make sure Celeste and I held our distance until Vin returned, but she and I would've come to the same decision regardless."

Anke bit her tongue. Anything she said now would only clear the air, binding her and Josiah tighter. "If I don't get home, George could pay the price. The Coopers think I'm staying with the Gibsons, and the Gibsons think I returned home to the Coopers. There's no phone or mail to let them know otherwise, so news is slow in my time. But a month has passed. If the fact that I'm missing isn't known to either family yet, it soon will be."

"I understand . . . there are a lot of reasons for you to return home. I'd feel the same way in your shoes. I just . . . don't know what to do with these feelings. What's the truth of the bond between us?"

She wanted to tell him that she loved him and always would, but she had to hold on to the clarity, the magnetic pull to return home. "I'll go to my rented room and change. Please call the driver for me."

He nodded, but he didn't move. It took all the physical strength she had to make her legs move. She needed to walk past him and keep going. Once beside him, her fingers reached for his.

What was she doing?

They said nothing. Neither looked at the other, as if they were trying to keep their actions a secret from parts of themselves in hopes of getting her home. "You know the truth between us, Siah." Tears welled. "Now tell me goodbye."

He gently squeezed her fingers, a sigh seeming to run through his entire body. Did he know the truth? "Bye, Anke."

She made herself pull free and hurry away.

With the boys down for a nap, Vin lingered under the hot water in the shower, rinsing off another lathering of soap. He hadn't bathed in weeks while playing a game of hide-and-seek with patrollers in Maryland. But getting Maud, Hope, and Charlotte to George had been more than worth all the anxiety and hardship of the journey.

George had Maud, and even though Celeste didn't know what had happened to Vin, she'd welcomed him back. But in the hours since he'd arrived here, he could almost hear more and more questions spinning in her head. They'd yet to have time to talk. Individually, one after another, dozens of Amish women had come to their home, checking on Celeste, making sure she felt safe, and asking where Vin had been all this time.

Celeste had assured them she was perfectly safe and she didn't know where he'd been. She said she was giving him time to adjust, and then they'd talk.

After the second person in less than a minute interrupted them trying to talk, Vin had taken the boys upstairs to their rooms. He'd spent the hours since then on the floor, playing and talking with his children. Drew was still leery of him and asking for Siah, who-ever that was. But Steven had hardly left his dat's lap, despite that Vin stank and wanted to shower. What Steven needed came first.

Now the water pouring down him felt amazing. Relief at being back in his time washed over him as fully as the hot water, rinsing away all his fears of never returning. *Denki, Gott. Denki.*

But questions pummeled him. Would Celeste believe him about time travel? Who was this Siah person that Steven and Drew talked about? Did Celeste already have another man in her heart? Her loyalty to Vin was apparent, but did he need to win back her love?

When the hot water began to run lukewarm, he turned off the shower. He stepped out, and the aroma of roast and potatoes filled his nostrils. With a towel around his waist, he wiped condensation from the mirror. He stood at the sink with a pair of scissors, cutting his hair and beard. The doorbell continued to ring every ten minutes or so. The little ones would be up in a bit. Would it be late tonight before he and Celeste got time to begin a very long conversation?

He shaved half of each cheek and all of his mustache, then brushed his teeth over and over again. When he was in the past, baths were always a welcome thing, and putting salt on a piece of wet cloth and rubbing that over one's teeth felt much better than doing nothing for them. But the simple pleasure of how people cleaned up in this time—hot showers, toothbrushes, and toothpaste—felt like pieces of heaven.

"Vin?" Celeste tapped on the door. "I'm setting you some clean clothes on the table outside the bathroom. I need to step out—"

He rinsed the minty toothpaste from his mouth with cool water. "Kumm rei, Celeste." He wiped his mouth on a nearby hand towel.

She opened the door, still holding clean clothes for him. Her eyes moved down him slowly and back to his eyes. "I . . . uh . . ." The pause was long, but she finally laughed. "I forgot what I came to say."

Vin chuckled. "I think that was my second *welcome home*." He winked.

She gazed into his eyes. "You don't look, uh . . . I mean, you appear, um . . . never mind."

"Shaven and clean, I don't look as mentally unstable as when you first saw me. I'm aware, Celeste. I know how I looked."

"I didn't mean it as judgment."

"I know. It was a possibility that didn't cause you to turn me away. I will hold that in my heart forever."

She studied him, seeming unsure of what to say. He knew it'd take them time to adjust and work through the awkwardness. So far, he thought they were doing great.

"And look, you have clean clothes for me." He lifted them from her hands. "You started out saying you needed to step out."

"Ach, jah." She gestured toward the far window of the bathroom. "Josiah's been on the lawn of the Freedman Estate and Museum for at least an hour. I'm thinking maybe I should go check on him."

"A man you know is standing in the Coopers' yard? Why?" Vin went to the window and peered around the drawn shade. "I remember him. He's the one who spoke back to the deacon, letting the deacon know he'll answer to God too."

"Jah. His uncle is Bishop Mark."

"Mark screamed at me earlier without asking any questions. The deacon too."

"Mark has been like a father to me since you disappeared, and he's angry, feeling you betrayed his daughter. I think he'll calm and return to his usual supportive, patient self. But whether you're here and hiding drawings, disappearing without warning, or reappearing in the same manner, you do seem to have a gift when it comes to stirring up anger among the ministers."

"I agree. I couldn't help how I disappeared, and I didn't realize that returning when I did would stir up such a hornet's nest, but I should've handled my artwork more directly, petitioning for changes rather than hiding what I was doing. I'm sorry for the trouble I've brought to you, and you've barely settled into a new district."

"I'm glad you feel that way about your artwork, to be open and direct with them and push for change. Together, we'll deal with this current stirred hornet's nest of your returning to the best of our ability."

"Denki, Celeste. You're the best wife a man could dream of. But who is Josiah to you?"

"A friend."

Josiah. Vin pieced something together. "Is that who Steven and Drew call Siah?"

"It is."

Vin slid into a clean white shirt. "I mean no disrespect or even a hint of an accusation, Celeste, but why is another man as close to our children as Steven expressed, and why is he on the lawn near our home, waiting for at least an hour?"

"Other than Mark and Lovina, the community turned on me when you disappeared, thinking it was somehow my fault. I needed help to make an income. Josiah's dat volunteered him to be that help. He came to our home to help me learn woodwork that I could do and sell on my own. One of his brothers or his fiancée came with him each time."

Relief eased the tension across Vin's shoulders. "He has a fiancée?"

"He had one."

"Great." This moment begged for sarcasm. "But that aside, I'm very proud of you needing a woodshop."

"I can't do what you do, but what I can do, I'm very good at."

"And Josiah helped you become good at it?"

"He did. I knew a decent amount from you and me working

together." She peered around the blind and out the window. "I think I should check on him, ask if something is wrong."

Vin slid into his pants. "Maybe his problem is that your husband is home."

"Nee." She released the blind and smiled. "We're not that kind of close friends." She moved in and buttoned Vin's shirt. "I can't believe you're home. We keep having to behave like life is normal, act as if my mind isn't screaming with disbelief, excitement, and confusion. I want time to stare at you for hours while we talk. I want to understand."

"I know, and I will explain every bit of it." He wasn't sure she would believe it, but he'd tell her. Her aroma—Dove soap and lilac shampoo—stirred his soul. He pulled her close and engulfed her lips with his. "I'm home," he mumbled around the kiss.

She returned his movements, seeming as unwilling to pause as he was. Soon he tasted saltiness and realized she was crying.

He stopped kissing her and wrapped his arms around her.

Her body trembled. "I can't get my head around it. You're home." She cupped his face with her hands. "You're home. In my arms. But I need you to forgive me. See—"

"Me need to forgive you? That's just nonsense. You didn't do anything wrong."

"I did." She stepped back. "When we argued before you disappeared, I didn't hear you. I heard the rules. I didn't see you when you desperately needed me to see you, to trust you. I saw disobedience of doctrine you didn't believe in but not you. When we married, I promised I'd always believe in you, but then I chose to ignore you and believe in the Old Ways more."

He drew her hands to his lips and kissed the palm of one and then the other. "You're forgiven. I'm the one who needs to apologize to you. I—"

"And we need to talk about that—I know we do—but the doorbell has stopped ringing and the boys are asleep." She smiled up at him. "We could stop talking and have uninterrupted time now."

His wife didn't know why he'd disappeared or why he'd stayed gone for so long, but she trusted him this much? He wasn't sure he deserved her, but his lips met hers again.

There was a tap at the bathroom door. "Dat?" Steven called.

Vin laughed. "Some things never change."

Celeste grinned. "Apparently not." She returned to the window to peek out the drawn shade again.

Vin opened the bathroom door. "Hallo. Kumm rei." He picked up his son. "I thank Gott some things never change."

Steven ran his palms down Vin's shaved cheeks and smiled at him.

"Celeste, go. I got the boys, and I'm here if you or what's-his-face needs me."

"What's-his-face." She chuckled. "You make sure that you are here when I return."

"I promise."

She left in a flash. With Steven in his arms, Vin hustled downstairs, bouncing his son hard, knowing he would enjoy it.

Steven belly laughed. His laughter filled Vin's heart. A dozen little things each hour welcomed him home. He was home!

Was that a tap at the back door? He hoped it wasn't the ministers here to grill him and judge him. Despite being grateful the bishop had been good to Celeste in his absence, he wasn't in the right frame of mind for their nitpicking at him for things he wouldn't and couldn't explain.

Chapter Thirty-Seven

Anke waited at the back door, hoping Vin was awake. He had to be exhausted. She didn't know much, but she knew he'd barely crossed from Maryland to Pennsylvania before he went to the crag and traveled here. If he was awake, she hoped Celeste wouldn't mind if they spoke.

Gratefulness washed over her when Vin opened the door. A moment later, he smiled. His countenance looked better than she'd ever seen before.

She returned the smile. "You're shaved and have a fresh haircut. You're the man I first saw in my dream-prayer."

"I am." He took a step back and motioned. "Kumm into your former home."

She walked inside carrying the book she'd brought to share with him.

"Anke!" Steven ran to her.

She swooped him up and propped him on her hip.

Vin ruffled his son's hair, smiling at him. "How are you faring, Anke?"

"Not well, and I needed to see you before I leave. We only caught a few fleeting minutes earlier."

"You're going to the crag now?"

"I said I was leaving for Missing Mountain hours ago, but then I realized it might be dangerous to travel while upset." She'd rather not say who she'd told that to.

"Jah, I think that's true about the crag, but I was plenty upset when I came through earlier today, and I landed here, smack-dab in the middle of this room with Amish women preparing food."

She laughed. "What did they say?"

"I can hardly believe it, but none of them saw me. They all had their backs turned in various directions, focusing on talking to each other and food prep. I ducked into the closest closet. When the moment was right, I snuck out a window and made my way to the woods."

"I guess it served you well in that moment that you knew this house with such detail."

"Definitely."

A noise came from upstairs. "Drew," Steven said. He wriggled down and ran up the stairs.

"What's on your mind, Anke?"

"I want to go home. Getting Steven here felt straightforward and easy, but the more I go to the crag and the more I don't know of how it seems to work, I'm scared to time travel. But I *need* to get home. As far as you know, does anyone realize I'm missing yet?"

"Nee. I feel certain George would've mentioned that part, and he didn't."

"Gut. I was with George and people saw me with him the day I disappeared. When they realize I'm missing, it'll go bad for him.

That's the reason I keep trying a few times each week to get home. I've got to get back."

"Jah, you're right about that part. I hadn't thought of it, but George could hang for your disappearance."

Bumps from upstairs thudded through the house and giggles rang out, assuring them the boys were playing contently.

"Tell me good things, Vin. Things that will help me focus on getting back home."

"I found Maud. She is now with George. They have a daughter, Hope. Maud was pregnant with Hope when she was sold, and George had no idea they had another child. I met a ten-year-old runaway named Charlotte, and she's now George and Maud's ward."

"You did well."

"I did what I could. God did what I couldn't. Together it worked for the good of George and his family. You'll enjoy getting to know them, right here on this property in your time."

"I've been reading about the history of my own time and learning what are good businesses to begin. George and Maud could use what I know to start a thriving business that could still be in existence today."

"It's not something someone else is intended to invent later, is it?"

"Nein. That would be wrong. One idea is candy."

"Candy?"

"It's already invented, although only the wealthy serve it, mostly at parties in other countries. But even in the colonial period, most cooks knew how to make it in their kitchens when honey or sugar is available. It's seldom made even in my pioneer era because it's time-consuming and an impractical use of a hard-to-come-by commodity—sugar. But people love sweets, and if they were easily available, maybe put near the cash register at Kurth Miller's dry goods store and other shops . . ."

"Interesting."

"If that idea doesn't work, I have others. None of which involve creating something that hasn't been invented yet."

"That's something only you can do in your time—help George and Maud establish a viable business. You'll love watching George and his family thrive over the years, and you can soak it in for me, because this is my time." He turned on a faucet and filled a kettle with water. "What has you so upset you're afraid where the crag might take you?" He set the kettle on the stovetop and turned on the burner.

"I didn't know why I kept returning here. Then I was sure it was because of how I felt about him. Today, when you returned and Celeste welcomed you home, I felt as if I could go back, but I . . . I . . ."

"Him?"

"Josiah."

"Ah, him." He got two mugs down from a cabinet and put a tea bag into each one. "Celeste went to see him. She says he'd been standing on the front lawn for quite a while."

Anke went to the side window and peered out. "No one's on the lawn now. Where did they go?"

"I have no idea. Not far, I'm sure."

Anke turned from the window. "When I went through the crag and ended up back in this time, that's where I landed—on the Coopers' front lawn. Josiah was always there for me. Each time, a hired driver lets me off at the foot of the incline. I go up by myself and rappel down the face of the cliff using a rope."

"Josiah knows you time travel?"

"Jah. The first time I tried to return home, he saw me disappear into the crag . . . and then reappear on the Cooper lawn."

"Maybe he told Celeste. She's completely blown my mind in how accepting she's been of my reappearance in her life."

Plunking sounds came from the steps, as if the boys were rolling wooden balls of some sort down the stairs. Whatever they were doing, their laughter said it was a lot of fun. Vin glanced that way, grinning.

"Nein." Anke spoke above the noise. "Josiah said nothing to her about time travel. He didn't want to keep that kind of important secret from her, but he did ask her a hypothetical question about you."

He poured boiling water into each mug. "And?"

"Her answer was clear and without hesitation. She had no desire to know if you *might* be alive or *might* be able to return. He said that when you first disappeared, she didn't know if you'd left her or were too injured to return or dead. The not knowing about drove her to her breaking point."

"That makes sense, but she's been so kind and understanding since I returned today that it also makes me feel like a lifetime won't be enough to love her through."

"Jah, but you're here to give it your best every single day."

He set a steaming mug on the kitchen table. "True."

Anke sat in a chair at the table. "Why can't I go back to my time, Vin?"

"I don't know. Do you want to live in this time or in the time you were born in?" He set a jar of honey and two spoons on the table.

"Both, maybe. I need to go home, but I don't want to leave Josiah. After I saw you were home today and saw Celeste welcome you, I thought I could return to my time, but then Josiah and I had a small argument. I did what I could to make it better, but my emotions say that's not enough. If I make it too much better between Josiah and me, I fear I'll never get home."

He sat across from her. "Being unable to get home is a fear I can relate to, but I don't have an answer for you."

"Did you waver, maybe feeling you should stay in my time?

You're so very skilled at helping in the abolition movement. It comes natural for you."

The pitter-patter of feet and giggles from above them caused Vin to look at the ceiling and smile. He drew a contented breath. "Before I traveled, when in my own time, I wavered on where I wanted to be, unsure the Amish way was as right as it thinks it is when it comes to artwork and what is or isn't idolatry. I wavered in my honesty to Celeste. But as I was hanging on to a part of the cliff, before I fell through time, I saw my life clearly, saw the importance of my love for Celeste and our family. I never wavered after that." He stirred his tea without adding honey. "But—and this is a very important distinction between you and me—I had a wife and children. I took a vow before God to take care of them for as long as I lived. It wasn't a matter of keeping my vow out of duty. I made the vow as a promise of love before God that as long as I was alive, I would honor my marriage, and He would help me to keep that vow. Whatever else I can accomplish in whatever time in history, this is the one I belong in. I know that without any doubts. I'm here to spend a lifetime loving as I should have before I fell. But you have to decide for yourself where you belong."

"Maybe that's my problem." Anke added a bit of honey to her tea and stirred it. "I'm unsure where I want to be."

"I have no doubts about that, Anke. As much as wanting two opposing things at the same time is part of our human experience, the crag seems to take us to where we want to be the most in the moment when we touch it. Earlier today, I wanted to go home, wanted to live with Celeste and our sons, and when I touched the crag, I landed in the center of this house." He laughed. "At the most inconvenient time for others . . . because that, too, is life."

"I keep returning to the spot where I first saw Siah."

He lifted the mug to his lips and blew on the steamy liquid. "I think if I had been honest with Celeste all along . . . if I'd cleared the air between us and let her in on the secrets, when I fell, the crag would have sent me home. But I didn't tell her because I didn't want her disappointed in me. I didn't want us to be hurt through arguments. I didn't want her privy to a secret that our church was against. So for those reasons and more, I kept it all pent up inside, and its power grew, making me want it more and more as time went by. I made the secrets inside me remain quiet and hidden, and yet all of it was heard in the long run anyway . . . in the most hurtful, challenging ways possible. Go talk to Josiah. Tell him your anger over your unwanted feelings toward him. Tell him your greatest fears. Tell him he's completely worth it and yet not worth it. Pray. Talk. Argue. Cry. Pray more. But get those emotions out in the open between the two of you, and then, with emotions aired, you'll go where your soul needs you to."

"He's been engaged once."

Vin chuckled. "Sometimes it seems as if the average woman's mind can cover more territory in ten minutes than mine can in a week." He rubbed the back of his neck. "Why is his past relationship part of the conversation about removing obstacles as a way of getting you home?"

"I . . . don't actually know." She took a sip of her tea. "Maybe because I'm in love for the first time in my life, and he's . . . been here before."

"When you cross the Gott Brucke and feel confident you've received an answer on what to do, is your perception always right?"

"Nein."

"So you return to God, asking for better insight, more clarity, right?"

"Jah."

"Josiah was engaged, thinking she was the right answer. Somehow they figured out they were wrong and had the courage to stop the wedding rather than save face and go through with it."

"True."

"Talk to him about how he feels about you. Pray. Always pray. Then listen to your instincts, not his answers. Trust yourself."

"They were close."

"He and his fiancée?"

"Josiah and Celeste."

"Ah." Vin fidgeted with the mug. "Jah, I figured that one out already, but you and I are close, Anke."

"That's different."

"It is." He took a sip of his tea. "But does our cousin-like friendship stay inside its boundary because we knew from the start that I was married? We'll never know. But Celeste and Josiah thought she was a widow. She grieved my loss with a mindset to rebuild her life. Apparently Josiah was there all along the way. But they still didn't fall in love. Trust that."

"You never cease to surprise and amaze me."

"It's easy for me to say that now. I looked in my wife's eyes. She likes Josiah a lot. She respects him, which bodes well for you in vouching for the type of man he is." He grinned, looking truly happy and completely unable to hide how he felt. "But she loves me. She *loves* me." He chuckled. "Stop doubting. If you're afraid loving him will hurt, don't worry. It will. If you marry, he will anger you and let you down, and you will anger him and let him down. There seems to be no way around that part because we're humans with far more biased emotions and self-favoring thinking than we have wisdom and understanding. Nonetheless, go look in Josiah's eyes and trust God to show you the truth."

Vin was right. She had to look in Josiah's eyes and trust herself to see what she needed to, not what Josiah wanted her to see.

Was she up to that task? She had no experience with young

men other than Vin and Josiah, and both had cared deeply for Celeste . . . a strong woman Anke didn't feel she could hold a candle to in this modern age.

She held out the book. "After you and Celeste read this, you need to return it to the Cooper place. I found it with my prayer journal in the bottom of the quilt chest you made."

"That's interesting."

"I didn't open my prayer journal or let Josiah do so, afraid it might tell me things I shouldn't yet know. The fact that book was in the chest you made is interesting, but the book itself is incredibly special, not that the museum people realize that."

The gold print on the hard cloth cover was too faded to read. He opened it. "Written by Dr. Brendan McLaughlin?"

"The boy you saved and taught to read and write dedicated this book to you. He also had some of your drawings printed in the book."

Vin turned to the dedication page. His eyes went wide.

"Jah." Anke took a sip of tea. "I felt the same way when I read it. I think it will help Celeste understand and heal."

"I agree. You know what else this means? When you return to your time, you can write in your prayer journal, and he's likely to be able to read your new entries."

Steven came down the steps on his bottom. Drew came down on his belly, feetfirst. Both laughed while prattling to each other.

"I should go." She stood. "I'll write to you too. If you want to see me off, I'm going to the mountain tomorrow morning around nine."

Vin rose and walked to her. "Of course I want to see you off. I'll see you then, Anke."

Anke hugged him. "Take care of yourself and your family." She went to the back door and opened it.

Celeste came up the few steps, almost bumping into Anke. Her brows furrowed. "Anke, you're here."

Anke looked past Celeste, seeing Josiah. He had a backpack hanging from his shoulders.

"Gut! You're here." Josiah sounded so relieved. "I was worried you went through the crag."

"You two need to talk." Celeste slid past Anke and went inside.

When Anke went down the steps, Celeste gently closed the back door.

Josiah studied her. "Celeste and I went separate ways to get important items. I gave her a list, and she went to the library to grab your favorite books on herbology. She'll buy new ones for the library. I went to a general store and grabbed soaps, matches, canteens, a Swiss Army knife and such. If I had more time, I'd have gone to various relatives' homes and raided medicine cabinets for bottles of antibiotics. We could go by the local pharmacy and get all we can carry in the way of bottles of peroxide, rubbing alcohol, sterile bandages, antibiotic creams, acetaminophen, and—"

"That's very thoughtful, Josiah." How had she not made plans to do something similar? But if he'd thought she was already through the crag, how did he intend to get the items to her? "I'll take what I can with me when I go, but we need to talk first."

"I'm going with you, Anke."

She couldn't respond, but chills ran over her.

He removed the backpack from his shoulders and dropped it on the ground. "I've been thinking about this for weeks. Why should you have to leave your time to be with me? I'll go to your time."

A smile tugged at her lips. She wanted to believe this could work, but she knew he might have too many ties to his time to be able to travel. Still, it meant everything that he was willing to go with her rather than stay in this safer, easier time of history. "But . . ."

"I know it sounds a bit nuts, but why should you make all the sacrifices for us to be together?" He tilted his head, studying her. "I'd be a fool not to go with you, Anke. If you'll have me."

She stared into his eyes, feeling the power of being loved by a good man.

Her heart pounded.

But wait . . . could Josiah go with her even if he wanted to? She was struggling to get back to her own time. Then again, maybe she didn't know everything about how this worked. Maybe his love for her would be enough for him to travel with her.

Hope over fear.

"Before I try again to go through the crag, I need to tell you all of how I feel. We need the air cleared between us . . . as Vin says."

"Okay." He motioned toward a lawn chair.

They each sat, and Anke began talking. Soon the conversation ran deep and wide, and she could imagine them talking for the rest of their lives and always wanting more time.

"Siah." She stood and reached out for his hand. "Take tonight to pray over your decision. If you feel the same way tomorrow, give your family a proper goodbye and meet me at the top of Missing Mountain at nine."

From the lawn chair, he kissed her hand and squeezed it. "I'll be there."

She was sure he'd be on the mountain. But would tomorrow mean goodbye or a new beginning?

Chapter Thirty-Eight

The kerosene lantern glowed softly, dispelling the darkness of night as Celeste talked with her husband while eating dinner. Such a normal thing—she'd never thought they'd get to do this again. Their boys were in bed. Vin had tucked them in an hour ago, staying with them until they were sound asleep.

Vin and Celeste had made small talk throughout most of dinner, mentioning ideas to help win over the ministers and ways to finish building the shop on their own. But they were dancing around what really mattered. What would she find out when she pried a little deeper? There were so many things that didn't make sense. It was like everyone knew something that she didn't.

Celeste ate a bite of roast. "Josiah intends to leave with Anke tomorrow. I don't know where she's from originally. We didn't have time to talk about it, but apparently, wherever she lives, it has no modern supplies nearby. I thought maybe she lived way out in the boondocks somewhere with no doctor or health facility. When I asked him about it, he said he didn't have time to make it make sense and that you'd explain. Where is Anke from? How do you know her?"

Vin reached across the table, touching her hand. "There's no easy way to say this."

Celeste closed her eyes. She tried to hold on to this pleasant moment before—before Vin told her something that would rock her world again.

Vin rubbed his thumb across the back of her hand. "The reason why I've had such a hard time starting this conversation, Celeste, and why Josiah didn't want to say anything, is Anke's from another time. I know time travel sounds crazy. But when I disappeared, I fell into her time. After months of trying to get back to Lancaster . . . I met her family, the Coopers, and then I met her."

Time travel? That was his explanation? The thought of food turned her stomach, so Celeste pushed her plate to the side. What was the next step from here? This was beyond what she could do. "We'll find a suitable doctor who can help you." She wrapped her hand around his. "I'm here for you, to support you, okay?"

"I appreciate your heart in the matter more than you'll ever know, but I'm not crazy. I just sound it."

"Okay." She nodded and smiled but nausea still rolled. "We'll get through this. I promise."

He put his other hand over hers. "Listen to me, please. Hear me without judgment until I finish telling you everything. The night we argued, I went to Kissin' Mountain. I was sitting alone, praying about what to do next. The ground under my feet broke and shifted, and I fell off the face of the cliff. When I woke, I thought I was still in my time, and I started walking, thinking I could get home. Days went by, two or three, and I saw no one. Had no food or water. I passed out. When I woke, I was disoriented and hardly able to open my eyes for even a few seconds, but it was night, and someone was giving me water. It was a man and his son, escaped slaves. They were gone the next morning, and I began walking again. Finally I saw a covered wagon. I've spent the last ten months in another time. It was 1822 when I arrived. After the first of the year, it was 1823."

Celeste could hardly breathe. Was he mentally ill or was he devising a crazy story to cover what he'd really been up to over the last ten months?

"I know how it sounds but bear with me. There is a crag among the cliffs that's like boarding a train. Except once you're on it, it takes you through time."

She gazed into his eyes. This was no made-up story. He believed it. Every single word of it. It seemed the kindest thing she could do was to hear him out.

"Anke is from that time, Celeste. Like I said, I met her several months after I landed in her time. She arrived here a month ago because Steven traveled through time looking for me, and she brought him home. Josiah knows the truth, and he wants to go back to her time with her. He saw her go through the crag, and you can ask him about it before he leaves with her tomorrow morning. But for now—" Vin pushed a small, thick book across the table—"read the dedication."

Was Anke mentally ill too? It was the only thing that added up, because Steven believed the story about traveling through time. A child could believe a story like this, but she couldn't. Could it really be possible that Josiah did?

Vin opened the book to a specific page and slid it toward her again. "I think this will help, Celeste."

She couldn't budge. Couldn't breathe.

"Please, Celeste. Try to hear me. I think this book is a gift from God to help you."

She finally managed to drag air into her lungs. She took the book and read the opened page.

What? She couldn't be looking at what she thought she was.

She flipped to the copyright page. It'd been printed in 1845.

She turned back to the dedication page and read it again. She cleared her throat. "'Dedicated to Ervin Lantz, known to us as Vin, in hopes that he was able to find his way back to his beloved family. We learned much from you, Vin, and may you someday read the account of all of our lives that continued on better for having known you.'"

This was . . . impossible. Vin's story was true?

She stood and rushed to an open window, needing to breathe in fresh air.

Vin stayed at the table. "It would be quite a coincidence for my name and my goal to get back to my family to be in a book written in 1845. Later in the book, he writes about George, Tandey, and me leaving Ohio for Lancaster, Pennsylvania, going to the Cooper home."

"Steven spoke of a George."

"Same person. They met. He saved my life, and we became good friends."

Celeste rubbed her temples. Her heart wasn't the only thing pounding.

"Don't fret about any of it, Celeste. But when you see Anke disappear through the crag tomorrow, you'll find all of this much easier to believe."

"*Through* the crag? She'll disappear through a stone?"

"Jah. It sounds as if Josiah intends to go too. He's seen her disappear, but he's never gone with her."

Celeste tried to wrap her head around this, remembering all Steven had said. Thinking about Anke showing up on their property in a vintage dress. Vin had been unable to return to Celeste, and yet he was alive.

Despite how crazy it sounded, it made a bit of sense. Her husband had fallen and been caught in another time. His name and goal to get home were documented in a book.

Celeste fidgeted with the string to her prayer Kapp. "After Anke arrived here, Josiah realized you were alive. It's why he asked me if there was a chance you could return for an unexplainable reason, would I want to know. I'd said no, so he dropped it."

Vin walked to her, his dark eyes soaking her in.

"Jah, I believe you," she whispered. "You fell through time."

"Do you really?" Vin asked.

It wasn't an easy thing to have faith in, but what in life was easy to have faith in? Vin was worth her trust. "I don't doubt you or the book or what Steven has said. I don't doubt it. I just can't wrap my head around it."

His arms moved around her, as gentle as if she were made of fragile glass. "I understand that thinking."

She looked in his eyes. "I want to know everything."

"Right now the most important thing is Anke intends to go home tomorrow, and I think Josiah is going with her."

"They're leaving . . . through a crag?"

"You can see it with your own eyes."

"I want to see that, but I disagree that it's the most important thing. Tell me of your travels."

"I've learned so many things while gone. I have stories to share for years to come. You have them too, and I want to hear about your time of survival and thriving. I know I was struggling over what I wanted the night I left to go to the mountain, chafing over the rules of the Amish, but while in Anke's time, I helped with the abolitionist movement, and I saw the good that can come from unity within the Plain churches—Amish, Quakers, and Mennonites. I don't want to leave the Old Ways. I prayed constantly for God to send me back to you and the boys, and

part of the prayer was *Until then, may I use my time as You desire.*"
He brushed the back of his finger across her cheek. "I believe my
time there became more useful because I was open to being used
rather than focused on creating the life I wanted. We're on this
planet for a season, and I want to live as if I'm biding my time in a
strange land. I don't know what that means right now, but maybe
it'll mean finding ways to make positive differences for society as a
whole, for those inside and outside our community who don't have
the power to make a difference in their lives on their own. If you
agree with my thinking, then we'll aim to live like that together."

She'd seen this man many times throughout the years. He was
more resolved now, more centered on what to do with his time
and restless energy.

"I agree with you." She caressed his face and kissed his lips.
They were together, and their union was stronger than she'd ever
known was possible. "Your artwork matters too, and we need to
stand for what we believe is right and fair concerning it."

"It's not the most important thing I care about by a long shot,
but I like the way you think."

She wanted to hear of his journey, and she wanted to read the
book that was on the table. But his warm lips covered hers.

They'd talked and read enough for now.

Anke trudged up the earthy slope of Missing Mountain. It could
be the last time she had to do this. In her time, the crag was difficult to find, but at least they didn't have to make this climb to get
to it. In this time, thick briars and hedges filled the land leading
up to the crags below.

Vin and Celeste walked behind her, each holding a child.
They'd decided it would do Steven some good to see Anke go, for

his mamm to see it with him and acknowledge all Steven had been trying to tell her for a month.

When the top of Missing Mountain came into view, Anke's heart made a giant leap. "Josiah." She made herself sound as normal as possible, and she refused to rush to him. If he'd come to tell her goodbye, she wouldn't make it hard for him.

His legs were dangling off the side of the cliff. "Hallo." He stood. She gazed into his eyes, no idea what she should say.

"We ready?" He dusted off his pants, as if men's clothes in her time stayed clean for more than a few minutes. He held out the rope with the seated harness that she used to rappel.

"You're coming with me?"

"Absolutely. My parents think I'm headed to the mission field in a country far, far away. I've penned letters to them that Celeste will pass along."

"You're sure."

"I'm sure."

Her heart soared. "I'll always be grateful, but don't be too disappointed or upset with yourself if you can't go through the crag with me. I know all too well that you could have something unknown to you that will anchor you here."

"I know." He took her hand into his. "But let's do this."

She hugged him tight. "Danke."

He held her as if this could be their last moment together.

She released him and hugged Vin and Celeste and Steven one last time. "I hope we have a chance to return here, but if we never do, check the bottom of the chest for my prayer journal. We'll write in it as soon as we can."

Josiah did the same, squeezing Vin extra tight. She knew Vin was grateful for all Josiah had done for his wife and sons. An answer to Vin's prayers as he took care of Johanna, and in her own way, Johanna took care of him.

It was time to try. Josiah rappelled first, carrying two heavy backpacks. Vin pulled the rope with the seat harness back to the top, and Anke put it on, her heart racing with excitement as Vin lowered her. Her flat boots had barely touched the dusty soil when Josiah steadied her.

"Denki."

"Anytime." Josiah lifted her hand to his lips and kissed it. "Our adventure awaits."

She nodded and took one of the backpacks, resting its shoulder strap in the crook of her arm. "Hold on to me."

From behind her, he put his arm around her waist. She clasped her arm over his, holding on. With her other hand, she splayed her fingers, palms toward the crag. He did the same, and they touched the stone at the same time. A whoosh filled her ears, and she closed her eyes. The world shifted, as if a loss of some sort had gone through her.

Anke opened her eyes. She was alone. The crag was in front of her, but where was Josiah?

She stood up, looking around. The landscape matched her time. She shielded her eyes from the sun and peered to the top of the mountain. No one was there.

"Josiah!"

He hadn't traveled with her. She'd been afraid of this. Had he gone to a different time or was he still in his own time with Vin and Celeste?

"Josiah!" she screamed while spinning around. He wasn't here. She closed her eyes, reaching for her intuition. Was he lost?

Only his heart. He'd stayed behind. She could feel that truth.

She shifted, realizing the backpack she'd had in the crook of her arm hadn't made it through either.

A horse whinnied, and she saw a surrey nearby. George must still be in the area and leaving a horse and rig for her in case she returned. She climbed into the surrey and headed for the Gibson place. If George and his family were there, they all could return to the Coopers together.

She had to get to the Cooper home, write to Josiah in her prayer journal, and leave it in the chest Vin had made. She knew that journal existed in his time, so it was her best chance of letting him know she was here and safe. But did it already have her entry in Josiah's time?

This hurt. She didn't want to stay in this time without him—or any time without him. She couldn't know how Vin felt, being separated from his wife. But this hurt in a different way. She and Josiah never had a chance to begin.

She slowed the rig and closed her eyes, trusting the horse to follow the dirt road. "Gott, lead me. I needed to return for George's sake. Is that all I need to do while here?"

A path formed in her mind, a golden one, looking like an illuminated dirt road. She knew it was her path, and it was in this time. There were people along the sides of that glowing road, and she longed to stop and help them.

She had things to do in the here and now. Maybe she would get to the end of this road in a few years. Maybe not. But she sensed peace mixed in with the hard work.

Patience. She could have faith that she and Josiah would see each other again, when the time was right.

After all, God had never let her down.

Epilogue

Celeste sat on the faded quilt she'd spread out on the parlor floor of the Cooper house, Drew on her lap. Steven leaned his elbows on his knees as he sat next to them, enraptured by his dat's words. About sixteen other children and their families, both Amish and Englisch, sat on their own blankets or folding chairs listening to Vin. Josiah was Vin's assistant, standing off to the side.

Drew was more interested in the wooden horse Celeste was using to make silent clops across his legs. It was hard to believe he was four years old now. He let out a giggle, louder than Celeste intended him to.

"Shh, shh," she shushed him, kissing the side of his head.

Vin, seated on an antique chair at the front of the room facing everyone, paused for a moment in his storytelling and lifted his eyes to hers, a grin playing across his lips.

Ah, her husband. She'd never tire of taking in his face—never forget how it felt when she thought she'd never see him again. Back when she'd worn his old shirts when at home alone, desperate to touch what he'd once touched.

Now she enjoyed his touch every single day and would never take their time together for granted. Neither of them would. She ran her hand across her still-flat stomach. They were expecting again, and they were so excited about it.

Vin dropped his storytelling voice to a near whisper. "The driver of the wagon waited at the edge of the muddy Susquehanna, hoping to cross into Pennsylvania, praying the patrollers didn't discover the false bottom with the three runaway slaves." Vin held his breath, eyes wide, and most in the room—adults and children—held their breath too. "Downriver, another wagon was trying to cross the Susquehanna, but it didn't wait for a ferry because slave patrollers were after them. Once deep in the water, the wagon tipped over, spilling its contents. And the form of a human floated from the wagon," he whispered, "being as quiet as a fish swimming."

Most of the children in the audience leaned forward as Vin quieted his voice.

Although this story came from Vin's experience, many of the stories he told were from history books, and he made each one come alive for listeners.

"Then . . ." Vin raised his index finger before he paused.

Celeste smiled. Vin often used simple facial expressions and changing tones to pull in the listeners' wandering attention spans. This was the final storytelling session of the last six weeks, held once a week here in the Cooper house—also known as the Freedman Estate and Museum. Over the past two years, in this very room, Vin had told various sets of historical stories, but the takeaway was always the same—live an honest life before God, yourself, and all others; live a life of bravery that fights the good fight, and stay connected to God in order to fully understand what that good fight looks like for each of you; live with a heart and mind that values people from all walks of life. Listeners couldn't get enough. Vin stirred people to want to know history on a deeper level and to want to live a life worthy of the gift of existing in this time.

Not long after Vin returned, he had volunteered to tell free historical fiction stories to grade school–age children. He was tested on his knowledge surrounding the time the Cooper home was built, his knowledge of the early 1800s, and his willingness to tell stories to children. The managers listened to Vin give a sample session, and they were sold. Vin stepped into the voluntary position. Everyone involved benefited. His storytelling sessions had upped the historical center's profits while at the same time giving Vin an outlet for his creativity and an opportunity to talk about his adventures, which were now a part of who he was.

He still couldn't draw faces when he did his art. The ministers hadn't budged. But Vin and Celeste were in good standing within their old and new districts. Celeste trusting her husband's story that he'd fallen and couldn't find his way home had smoothed the path for the ministers to accept it. They'd talked to Vin numerous times on the topic, and they slowly grew to trust that he'd survived as best he could and found his way home. That and his obedience to the boundaries set on his drawing were enough for the ministers and the flock to know and accept. Vin said he was fine with not being allowed to draw faces, and Celeste knew he truly was. No more sneaking around and no more secrets between them, ever. And both of them had faith that one day the ministers would realize drawing God's creation wasn't idolatry, but Vin's form of worshiping God's infinite glory.

Josiah passed Vin a setting pole, and Vin continued telling the story. "The driver of the wagon with the false bottom steered his rig onto a ferry. Soon, while two men used setting poles to move the ferry away from the Maryland shoreline, one ferryman slung a rope out toward the shadowy human form that had slipped from the overturned wagon." Vin used the setting pole as if he were digging into the murky waters of the Susquehanna. "Were the ferrymen also determined to be on the God side of history, not the greedy side?" Vin took a moment to look in the children's eyes. He slowly nodded. "Jah, they were."

Vin had told Celeste all these stories, of course, and she'd heard them during these sessions too. She and the boys couldn't come to every session, but hearing them each time made her heart swell.

These history lessons Vin shared also gave Josiah an easy opportunity to slip upstairs and check Anke's prayer journal in the chest. Josiah, Vin, and Celeste continually held out hope for a fresh entry from Anke. The day she went back in time two years ago, Josiah had rushed back to the Cooper home, slipped inside, and gone to the chest to remove the false bottom.

The prayer journal had twenty entries past the date when Anke returned to her time. In the first entry, she wrote about arriving safe from her travels and going to the Gibson place, where she saw George again and met Maud, Hope, and Charlotte. She wrote about how all of them—George, Maud, Hope, Charlotte, and Anke— returned to the Cooper home. That entry was numerous pages long, with many supplications on behalf of each person mentioned.

Her next entry was dated two weeks later, and she'd written about the new life and business ventures in the city of Lancaster for George and his family. Every entry was packed full of encouragement about what was going on and full of the prayers that filled her soul.

Her last journal entry was dated four months after she returned to her time. She wrote of seeing the Gott Brucke, and the bridge was leading her to leave the Cooper home and follow where her prayers guided her. She wrote that she felt sure God was asking her to accomplish a specific set of tasks for the abolitionist movement. She was willing to follow wherever God led her, and if her friend Josiah fell in love, he should follow his heart.

Unfortunately for Josiah, there hadn't been a fresh entry in the prayer journal since the day Anke went back in time.

"When George saw Maud for the first time in five years . . ." Vin continued to tell the piece of history he'd experienced. He looked at Celeste again, like he was looking straight into her soul. She couldn't help but grin. The love between them continued to grow.

Vin gestured to the children. "No matter what times we live in, we can choose the God side and fight against the greedy, self-ish side. How do we know which side is which?" He paused. "The Golden Rule. If we don't want someone treating us a certain way, then we know how we need to treat others. There's a lot in life we can't control. We have very little control over how people feel toward others of a different background. But through faith and living by the Golden Rule, we can find ways to make a difference."

Josiah tossed him one end of a rope.

Vin tugged on it. "The ferryman who threw the rope to save the life of a runaway slave couldn't stop slavery, but he could do what he could do, and that day, it was ignoring the slave patrollers and throwing one end of a rope to a drowning man. The end."

The audience clapped.

"Now, who has questions about this house or what life was like in our beloved city of Lancaster during the early 1800s?" Vin asked.

While people asked questions, Celeste's mind continued to process all they'd experienced and witnessed.

Since Vin's return, the police had asked the public if they had a missing family member, friend, or former coworker who possibly had an Amish background. They asked if, in the spring or summer of 1985, they knew a man who had plans to rappel off Ash Rocks, known as Kissin' Mountain to locals, and had never returned home.

An Englisch man contacted the police, saying he'd had a room-mate who seemed to fit that description. He thought the man had decided to go home to his Amish family. The police soon uncov-ered that the man who'd been found deceased at the bottom of the mountain had been raised Amish and left as a young adult. While living and working among the Englisch in Philadelphia, he heard stories about a crag on Kissin' Mountain that could transport a person through time. The Englisch had no idea where Kissin' Mountain was, but using a map of the area, the former Amish man figured out that Ash Rocks was Kissin' Mountain. He took hiking and rappelling lessons. A few weeks later, he quit work, purchased rappelling equipment, put on his old Amish clothes so his room-mate thought he was returning to his roots, and told his roommate he wasn't coming back. The police felt certain he was the one who had secured bolts and pitons to establish the rappel anchors, and the rope running through the anchors was his too. But he fell from the cliff, and because of the way he left the Amish, his job, and his roommate, no one realized he was missing. His body remained buried in the cemetery. The Amish ministers decided that a lot of odd circumstances had caused that man to be buried in the ceme-tery of the faithful and that perhaps God wanted him there. The ministers and the people wanted no part of removing him.

Question time ended, and Celeste stood, shaking out her dress and apron. She set Drew on his feet.

"Dat!" he squealed, pattering over to Vin. Steven hurried to see his dat too.

Celeste picked up the quilt they'd been sitting on and folded it. She walked to where Josiah stood while visitors chatted with Vin.

"So how's your week been?"

"Gut." Josiah jotted something down in the notebook he held. "Vin did a nice job with tonight's story." He lowered the notebook and shoved the pen in his pant pocket. "Whenever I hear him talk of history, I see Anke making a difference in those times in ways only she could."

Celeste nodded. "I fully agree. Few can find the Gott Brucke like she can, and she has work to accomplish."

Josiah smiled, and she saw contentment in his eyes. "True."

"I know it's been a long, hard two years for you. I still have times of being sorry you couldn't travel back with her on that day. I mean, we're all glad you're here, and that happiness includes how your family and friends feel, but being separated from the one you love . . ." She'd lived it and wouldn't wish it on anyone, even though at least Josiah and Anke knew the other was alive. Still, one hundred and sixty-three years apart . . . it was a vast ocean of time.

"Jah, I went back and forth between being sad and angry about it for a long time, but I'm not either of those things anymore. I've come to accept that we both are where we need to be. And I know that I needed to learn and heal from my past *girlfriend* issues. To be completely okay with just being me. No girlfriend, fiancée, or wife required."

"And now?"

Josiah smiled. "I'm okay with this. Really." He touched his fingers to his heart. "If Anke were on another planet, I could love her across the stars and my love wouldn't diminish. I'm going to keep doing good where I'm planted, and I know from her prayer journal entries that she's doing the same." He smiled and reached out to ruffle Drew's hair. "I learned that kind of acceptance from you. And since his return, from Vin too."

Celeste's heart swelled. *She'd* been a good role model? It felt like she'd been in survival mode in those awful months Vin was gone last year. His time home after his return had been the usual whirlwind of small children, chores, and work.

But then those priceless moments would come, sometimes when she least expected it . . . Vin's playing with their precious boys, stealing kisses in the kitchen over a sink of dirty dishes, listening to all his tales of the nineteenth century while she lay in his arms, enraptured by his skills at storytelling. Those moments *were* their lives together. What was their time on earth but a breath, a collection of precious memories and stories and learning to help others?

Vin and Josiah had slowly become good friends. They both needed that friendship, and now they worked together on certain cabinetry projects. They also had started a nonprofit business, one that fed the poor and made imperative repairs to their homes so indigent families in the area had food to eat and a home with roofs that didn't leak and walls that protected them from the elements.

Vin said goodbye to the last of the guests. He closed the front door of the Cooper home and locked it.

"It's finally time to check the chest again." Josiah went to the stairs. While climbing them, he tore several pages from the notepad.

Celeste and the boys followed him. Vin came up behind them. They knew the routine. Once all of them were in the former Cooper bedroom, Josiah went to the chest Vin had made when living with the Coopers. Josiah folded the letters he'd written and put them in the back of Anke's prayer journal.

His letters never disappeared and always appeared to be in the exact place Josiah put them. When too many collected in the journal, he stacked them up and set them beside it. He was faithful to write to her—sharing prayers and encouragement and words of faith and love. It was Josiah's chance to share his heart and trust that maybe Anke could feel some of what he wrote, perhaps similar to when Vin felt Celeste cry out to him that she needed a home.

Celeste watched Josiah's face fall as he opened the prayer journal to Anke's last entry—the same final entry he'd read the day Anke went back to her time.

He whispered a prayer and gently put the journal back in its place. He replaced the false bottom, set the chest upright, and closed the lid.

The adults said nothing as they turned off most of the lights and locked up as they left the house. Celeste carried the folded quilt. Vin carried Drew and held Steven's hand.

They walked across the Cooper lawn, Vin and Josiah talking about this week's joint cabinetry install project.

"Josiah."

The voice was like a breath, and Celeste turned. Did she really hear that? It sounded like . . .

Josiah froze. "You guys go on without me. I need a minute. I heard her. Sometimes I can feel Anke again. It makes no sense, and I can't explain it. It's like an echo of her. God letting us know each other through His bridge."

Vin turned to Celeste, giving a little smile. Anke and Josiah felt each other—of course they did. Just like how this place had connected Celeste and Vin when he was in the past.

But wait—this was different.

"Josiah—" Celeste glanced across the lawn, seeing only late-summer grass and trees moving with the breeze—"unless I'm also connected to Anke through time, I heard her too."

"What?" Josiah made a circle, searching.

Then . . . right in front of them, where before the Cooper yard had been empty, a young woman in an old-fashioned blue dress suddenly appeared, landing on her feet.

Anke gasped. "The modern Cooper house! Is this real?" She sounded as if she were talking to herself.

Josiah didn't hesitate. He ran for her. "Anke!"

Her face lit up. He picked her up, crushing into her as he held her in a tight embrace. "Thank You, God."

Celeste's eyes watered. Her friend had been so patient over the last two years, not knowing if God would send her back. How many times he must've wondered if he'd live the rest of his life without her, as a single man. His heart was resolute for only Anke. Now she was here!

"Anke . . ." Josiah cupped her face and kissed her.

Although public displays of affection were unheard of for the Amish—even for married people—the sight of her dear friends' reunion made Celeste's heart soar. "Even with all that time separating them, God brought them back together," she whispered.

Vin took Celeste's hand into his and squeezed it. "He's the Alpha and Omega; this is nothing."

"Anke!" Steven rushed her, hugging her legs. Drew wriggled down from his dat's arms and ran after his brother.

Anke released Josiah to kneel down and hug the boys. "You remember me, Steven?"

"You mean so much to all of us," Josiah said, helping her stand. "You're always on our minds."

"As you've been on mine. God has led me to where I belong." She straightened, looking resolute, nodding at Vin. "I have much to tell you. George and Maud are doing well. They own a home with land and two businesses in Lancaster, and they are a haven for recently escaped slaves, helping others learn to thrive in freedom. Johanna married Kurth Miller—the dry goods store owner. They help George and Maud too."

"Gut. That warms my heart."

"You're staying?" Josiah asked, studying her.

"Jah. I'm here to spend the rest of my lifetime."

"She's staying!" Josiah picked her up and spun her.

Anke laughed.

He set her down.

She straightened her dress. "I studied about the Amish church when I was here two years ago—though I'm sure there are aspects I didn't catch. I want to join."

Josiah laughed. "Will you marry me?"

"In any time. In any place. In any type of dress."

Josiah lifted his hands heavenward, laughing. "This is amazing. Thank You, Gott!" He lowered his hands. "I've been working on a refurbished clock to give you, one from your time . . . if God ever did the impossible, listened to my nightly prayers, and dropped you in my life again. Now you're here, and how am I out of time to complete it?"

Anke sighed playfully, grinning. "Well, I guess you missed your chance. You'll have to court me like any other man would need to do with the new girl in town."

"Court you?" Josiah chuckled. "Do people court once they're engaged? Because you just agreed to marry me."

She laughed. "How do I know? You're not outside of your time. I am," she teased, grabbing both his hands in hers.

Vin kissed Celeste's forehead. "I think we're all exactly in the time we need to be."

There was so much Celeste would never understand—like how the crag worked at all or the implications and impossibilities of time. But standing here with her family and beloved friends, she trusted her husband's words—they were all in the right time.

Chapter One

Sweat rolled down Eliza Bontrager's neck as she carried her youngest sibling on one hip and a plate of sliced bread in her hand. Stale bread, and the last of it. The mountain air hung thick with the familiar July aromas. But was there a hint of stench in the air from the feed mill where *Dat* worked? Surely not. Despite how foul that odor was, it stayed in downtown Calico Creek, rarely meandering this far into the rural part.

"*Kumm,*" Eliza called. "*Es iss Zeit esse.*"

The moment she said it was time to eat, excited voices filled their little nook of the Appalachian Mountains. Four children, not looking at all as if she'd hauled water and bathed them last night, scurried to the picnic table. The old wooden benches and marred table wobbled as the little ones clamored to a spot. Despite grubby hands snatching up bread, she couldn't help but chuckle. They were just too cute.

The little one on her hip squawked, reaching for a piece of bread. She passed him a slice, and he bounced up and down.

Four-year-old John shoved a big bite into his mouth. *"Denki,"* he mumbled. Even as he ate, his brown eyes were glued to the remaining three slices of bread, the ones meant for Ruth, Moses, and her, but John stayed so hungry of late, and one slice wasn't likely to fill his stomach.

Eliza did what she could to bring money into their home. Her skill was textiles, mostly weaving fabrics on a small loom from cotton and wool she purchased when she could. She also made quilts and blankets from scraps. But she hadn't been able to purchase threads for the loom in a while, and thick blankets were a hard sell during the dog days of summer. The good news was Dat would be home in a few hours, and today was payday. But without a working flue for the cookstove, they couldn't bake bread, and buying store-bought was out of the question. There was nothing quite as difficult as baking bread using a wood-burning cookstove during the hottest summer months, but it had to be done at least once a week.

She shooed flies away from the bread in the little ones' hands. Most days keeping food on the table was hard work but rarely this difficult. Between the broken flue and Dat's last paycheck being short due to missing more work than he had paid days off, the last week of feeding the family had been more challenging than most.

Cicadas buzzed loudly, a constant song during the hottest months each year. A summer breeze kicked up, and she lifted her head to enjoy it. A familiar screeching sound let her know someone had opened the screen door. She turned to see her sister Ruth coming outside. Ruth was the smart one, and she currently held the spot of a teacher's assistant at the local Amish school. Unfortunately, it only earned about four thousand per year, which was only three hundred a month. Ruth wouldn't look for anything else because her dream was to become a full-time teacher when she turned eighteen, and her best chance of that was to faithfully stay working as a teacher's assistant. She walked to the picnic table, carrying a pitcher of water and three cups. The little ones always had to share . . . plates, cups, beds, clothes, bathwater, and the few toys they possessed.

"*Gut!*" John clapped. "*Jah?*"

He knew the water would help fill his aching belly. Eliza bent and kissed the top of his head. He was always grateful for every kindness that came his way.

Ruth poured water and passed it out before grabbing a slice of bread. "Where's Moses?"

"He's trying to fix the flue, but something broke, and he said he knew what to do, so he put a bridle on Tank and rode off bareback toward Ebersol land."

"Think he can fix it?"

Moses had a good heart, but he was only thirteen. He needed someone older to help him. Most of the menfolk in these parts were at the plant working or sleeping because they'd worked third shift. It wasn't a very Amish way to make a living—or an uplifting way—but it's what was available.

Eliza shrugged. "I'm equal parts hopeful and doubtful. *Mamm* said we should plan on cooking over a campfire again tonight."

Ruth glanced around. "Where is Mamm?"

"She's in the henhouse, prayerfully looking for enough eggs to make a decent meal with." It was always tough growing a vegetable garden on the ridge, but this summer was the worst. "She got a few ears of corn, some cucumbers, and several tomatoes for tonight's supper."

They might not have their fill, but no one would go to bed fully hungry.

The little ones, all except John, had left the table and were beneath a shade tree, scratching sticks across the soft dirt. Eliza's stomach growled as she handed him her piece of bread.

His brown eyes grew large as he threw his arms around her waist. *"Ich lieb du."*

"I love you too." She patted his back before he released her.

Three horses with riders topped a nearby hill. One was Moses. She squinted, trying to make out the others.

Jesse.

Her heart crashed against her rib cage, threatening to leap out of her chest.

How had he slipped back into Calico Creek without her knowing? Oftentimes of late he only made it home every three to four months. It took three hours by car to get here to visit. At apprentice pay and with the cost of living elsewhere, he didn't have money to hire a driver to go that distance and back, so he had to wait until someone he knew was coming this way. Her heart raced, and it was hard to breathe.

Moses rode toward the old barn. She recognized Ben, Jesse's cousin, and he followed Moses.

Jesse. He rode tall and powerful in his saddle these days, three years since he'd moved to Hillsdale to work for Frank Mulligan, a home builder. Jesse was full grown now, twenty-one years old, and dating women in his new Amish community who were fascinating, she was sure. Women who weren't dirt-poor.

Would he forget in a few years that they'd ever been close friends while growing up? Had he even noticed on his visits home that she'd grown up too? She trailed behind him three years, but still, she was grown now.

He rode to the picnic table before stopping. "Ruth." He nodded at her.

Ruth? Why was he addressing her little sister? Eliza's chest burned.

He got off the horse, his eyes meeting Eliza's. "Hi."

Speak, Eliza! You're friends for goodness' sake! But she couldn't find her voice.

He pulled a burlap bag off the side of the horse. "It's two pounds off a smoked ham, a bag of green beans, and half a loaf of Italian bread."

Had his dat been paid in groceries again? Unlike most of the men around here, his dad didn't work at the feed mill. He was a handyman, able to fix almost anything. But it was just as likely that Jesse brought food home to his family and was sharing it with Eliza's family. She wouldn't ask.

He turned to Ruth again and held out the sack. "You need to take it to your mamm to put up."

"Denki." Ruth took the sack and clutched it tight. "I got to say it twice: denki." She smiled at him. "When did you get back?"

That was what Eliza wanted to know. Staying quiet wasn't like her. What was going on?

Jesse's eyes moved back to Eliza. "About twenty minutes ago." He patted his horse. "Levi," he called.

Eliza's eleven-year-old brother hurried to them. Jesse held out the reins. "You know what to do, right?"

Levi frowned, looking as if he'd rather go play. Ruth held up the food. "A tasty, filling dinner. Jesse brought it."

Levi's face lit up. "Uh, jah, I knew about tending to a horse before I's born." Chuckling, Levi took the reins and walked off with the horse.

Jesse had nine younger siblings, including a set of four-year-old twin brothers, and he was comfortable putting any of the older ones to work helping.

"You here for the whole weekend?" Ruth asked.

"I am. Until Monday morning when my boss will pick me up, and I'll return to Hillsdale."

Ruth sent a knowing but wary look Eliza's way. Her sister understood how Eliza felt about Jesse. But Mamm and Dat forbade any romantic notions with the likes of Jesse Ebersol. "Well, gut," Ruth said.

But it seemed to Eliza that when Jesse did come home and they got time to talk, he was most interested in telling Eliza what she needed to do about attending singings and dating. He insisted she do both, and then he'd leave again.

Moses and Ben strode out of the barn.

Moses was carrying a slightly rusty piece of an old flue. "Jesse had this in his smokehouse. Said we could have it."

Eliza nodded, finally finding her tongue. "That's very kind, Jesse. Denki."

"Nee." Jesse shook his head. "It's nothing."

He probably felt that way because he was a giver, but it wasn't nothing. Every piece of scrap mattered in these parts, whether it was metal, rope, boards, or food. All the Amish around here struggled. No wonder Jesse stayed away. How much more time would pass before he stopped coming to visit like this? The only things the Amish of Calico Creek weren't in short supply of were love and respect for each other, work ethics, and children.

When their Amish ancestors settled in these parts hundreds of years ago, they'd thought the mountains would be good farmland. They were wrong. The valley was some of the best farmland, but the ridges were mostly crop-resistant shale and sandstone.

Hard living aside, Eliza was sure God felt like she did about all the children—that nothing was more important than the joy and hope each child brought to this fallen planet.

"Whew." Ben made a face as he sniffed the air. "Country fresh air, but you would not believe what it smells like in downtown Calico Creek. Today's a particularly stale one."

"I thought I smelled the plant a bit ago."

"I guess it's possible," Ben said. "Maybe Andrew is right that someone should investigate if this stench is safe to breathe."

Ruth held the burlap bag against her as if concerned she might lose it. "Since Andrew is the first person I've heard of who seems to think it's a problem, he should be the one to check into it. Who's Andrew?"

Ben removed his straw hat. "You have to know Andrew. He's my best friend. Surely you two have met."

"Maybe. I don't recall it," Ruth said.

"He lives in the next district over, like me. I guess maybe it makes sense that you Calico Creek Ridge Amish don't know all the Calico Creek Glen Amish. Same bishop, but different Amish school, different preachers. Still, how do you not know him? He's our age."

"Ah." Ruth grinned. "So at sixteen years old, he's got lofty, suspicious ideas and nothing he can do with them. It most likely stinks because feed for pigs, poultry, goats, and numerous other animals is being processed and cooked twenty-four hours a day, seven days a week at the mill."

Ben shrugged. "Probably so."

Moses held up the old flue segment. "Kumm, let's get this done for Mamm."

Ruth, Moses, and Ben headed for the run-down house. Eliza paused, hoping for a moment with Jesse, hoping he'd tell her something interesting or funny that happened in his world recently. But when she looked into his beautiful greenish-blue eyes, she saw that something was troubling him.

"You're home for a reason," she offered.

He nodded. "Jah." He cleared his throat. "We need to talk, Eliza. Can you find time later today or tonight?"

Her excitement at his being home fled and nausea churned. He'd found someone. She was sure of it, and she didn't want to hear about it. "Just say it, Jesse."

He pulled a flat, round rock from his pant pocket. "Maybe we could walk to the creek after we get the cookstove fixed."

She didn't want to skip rocks as if time with her mattered. Then again . . . why would she refuse them having some fun? Why not make the most of their time? If he'd found someone, this was likely their last romp in the woods. Could she change his mind? Would she dare even try when he was a fine catch and she was . . . well, nobody?

Besides all of that, they were forbidden. "Tonight, at our old spot by the creek, after my chores are done."

Jesse shifted, lowering his hand a bit. "Sounds gut."

Eliza's heart pounded. She snatched the stone from his palm. "I'll win." She tossed it slightly into the air, ready for it to land in her hand.

Jesse reached in and grabbed it before it hit her palm. "Jah?" Smiling, he slid the rock into his pocket.

"Definitely." Could she win what really mattered? Would she even be able to make herself try?

A Note from the Authors

Hello, again, dear readers! Erin and I deeply appreciate that you're trusting us with your valuable time. We hope you enjoyed this story. When we were very early on in the writing process, Erin and I talked and took notes about this story, feeling unusually foggy about it. I wanted to take the lead in the writing of it, but I wasn't in a creative place. Looking back, I was in the middle of a long journey with physical and emotional pain.

Erin could've taken the lead, but I felt it was important that I do so, hoping my creative side would hear my call and wake up. We brainstormed the specifics of the opening chapter, and I wrote it. That took a couple of painstaking weeks.

But when it was done, where to next? I pondered the question of *what happens next* for several weeks. One morning I woke, knowing the answer—I would have to go back in time with Vin. I was resistant to the idea of writing historical fiction, and that resistance was shutting down creative ideas. But Vin couldn't disappear at the beginning and then reappear in the last few chapters. I'd read plenty of historical fiction, but write it?

The saying is to *write what you know*.

Feeling rather nervous, I plunged into research. I bought numerous books about that region of the US in the early 1800s.

My husband, a registered land surveyor, brought home oversize sheets of topographical maps and road maps that dated way back. I used those and the books to map out my character's road travels, discovering the names of the roads, how they were created, and what raw materials were used. For the first time in months, my creativity stirred.

Erin read each chapter I wrote, feeling they had intrigue and power. A few months later, a worry struck me when I woke. I realized most of what I'd written wasn't supposed to be part of Celeste and Vin's story.

I was crushed and frustrated. Still, I saved all those chapters to a different folder, knowing I was unlikely to ever use them, and I began writing again.

This time my mind and heart were clearer. Creativity was awake and calling to me. Perhaps a bit groggy and foggy but awake.

I think the creative process—whether in a novel, a song, a poem, a painting, or through any other labor of love—is similar to life. We hit hard places, dry places. We may need to give ourselves some time to stay there, but at some point, we must strive to get unstuck. To wake, to walk out of the fog, to dig through the rock in front of us, to chisel our way through a mountain if we can't go over it or around it.

When we have God's light, love, forgiveness, and encouragement, beautiful creativity can awaken and work in our minds and hearts. As always, Erin and I appreciate you all and would love hearing from you at cindy@cindywoodsmall.com about any part of your creative or faith journeys.

Let's fight the good fight of faith. Thank you for walking with me during these challenging, wonderful years. Let's hold on to the light, both for ourselves and for others.

Behatz Sei Hoffning (Embrace His hope),
Cindy and Erin

Discussion Questions

1. When Celeste learns that Vin has been drawing portraits, against the rules of their Amish community, she is horrified, arguing that they must honor the Old Ways whether they agree with them or not. Vin, on the other hand, argues that his art is not idolatry and that the community rules are likely to change with time, so what he's doing is not wrong. Which character did you find yourself agreeing with? Why?

2. Vin begins to doubt his and Celeste's path in life, wondering whether joining the Amish faith reflected what they truly believed or only what others wanted for them. Was there a time in your own life when you faced similar questions about your choices? What did you conclude?

3. Once she learns Vin has been hiding his artwork, Celeste questions how well she knows her husband, feeling that "all she thought she knew of who they were seemed to have crumbled under her feet." How does Celeste rebuild her perspective on Vin and on their marriage? How do you imagine that might have played out if Vin hadn't disappeared?

4. While wrestling with his doubts, Vin wishes for freedom—and suddenly has that desire granted when he falls through time to 1822 Ohio, surrounded by space and freedom but separated from his beloved family. What have you found yourself wishing for in moments of frustration or dissatisfaction? What do you imagine would happen if those wishes were unexpectedly granted?

5. Anke is a woman of unusual spiritual sensitivity, often given knowledge from God that allows her to help others. How does she apply these gifts throughout the story? Have you ever known someone who seemed to exhibit gifts of healing or unique spiritual wisdom?

6. When he arrives in the past, Vin believes God has put him in this time to teach him a lesson or to punish him for his doubts. How does that belief change?

7. Both Vin and Celeste wrestle at times with the boundaries placed around them by the rules of their Amish community. What conclusions do each of them reach? Do you believe all of our gifts are meant to be expressed, or is there ever a time to put them aside for the sake of others? How do you discern which boundaries to accept and which to push through?

8. Vin frequently has to decide whether to lie or tell the truth, both about himself and as part of his work with the abolitionist movement. What conclusion does he reach about when lies are justified in God's eyes? Do you believe lying is ever permissible, or even the right thing to do? If so, where do you draw that line?

9. As the Amish community wrestles with a difficult decision, Josiah pleads, "Let us stand with mercy and grace, and if

we're wrong, God will forgive us. But how will God look at us if we choose to cast the first stone?" Do you agree with Josiah's perspective that it is better to err on the side of grace? Why or why not?

10. Vin prays fervently to return to his wife and sons but concludes his prayers with the refrain *"Until then, may I use my time as You desire."* How is that prayer answered throughout his time in the past? During times of waiting or when your life isn't where you hoped it might be, how might you adopt an "until then" perspective?

Acknowledgments

To my readers—young and old, avid readers to only-Woodsmall readers—time and again you have shown me grace, love, support, and understanding; you have been willing to go on new journeys with me, even a journey or two through time. Thank you.

To our own power duo, Tyndale's own Jan Stob and Sarah Rische—your thoughtful insights, encouragement, and prayerful support mean so very much to Erin and me. Thank you. We are thrilled to publish stories with you, thrilled to dive into your edits, and excited about future books!

To our families—from husbands to children to grandchildren—writing isn't a solo endeavor, and we notice and appreciate all your love and support with your time, expertise, delicious food, and more.

To Amanda Woods, Andrea Garcia, Elizabeth Jackson, and the Tyndale family as a whole—thank you!

And a very special thank-you to Karen Watson for all you do.

About the Authors

CINDY WOODSMALL is a *New York Times* and CBA bestselling author of twenty-six works of fiction and one nonfiction book. Coverage of Cindy's writing has been featured on ABC's *Nightline* and the front page of the *Wall Street Journal*. She lives in the foothills of the north Georgia mountains with her husband, just a short distance from two of her three sons and her six grandchildren.

ERIN WOODSMALL is a writer, musician, wife, and mom of four. She has edited, brainstormed, and researched books with Cindy for almost a decade. More recently she and Cindy have coauthored six books, one of which was a winner of the prestigious Christy Award.

TYNDALE HOUSE PUBLISHERS IS CRAZY4FICTION!

Fiction that entertains and inspires

Get to know us! Become a member of the Crazy4Fiction community. Whether you read our blog, like us on Facebook, follow us on Twitter, or receive our e-newsletter, you're sure to get the latest news on the best in Christian fiction. You might even win something along the way!

JOIN IN THE FUN TODAY.

 crazy4fiction.com

 Crazy4Fiction

 crazy4fiction

 @Crazy4Fiction

By purchasing this book from Tyndale, you have
helped us meet the spiritual and physical needs of
people all around the world.